Verbivoracious Press

Festschrift Volume Six

THE

OULIPO

VP Festschrift Series:

Volume 1: Christine Brooke-Rose
Volume 2: Gilbert Adair
Volume 3: The Syllabus
Volume 4: Rikki Ducornet
Volume 5: Raymond Federman
(Edited by G.N. Forester and M.J. Nicholls)

Reprint Titles:

The Languages of Love
The Sycamore Tree
The Dear Deceit
The Middlemen
Go When You See the Green Man Walking
Next
Xorandor/Verbivore
by Christine Brooke-Rose

Three Novels — Rosalyn Drexler
Knut — Tom Mallin
Erowina — Tom Mallin
The Greater Infortune/The Connecting Door — Rayner Heppenstall
The Penelope Shuttle Omnibus — Penelope Shuttle
Conversations with Critics — Nicolas Tredell
The Utopian — Michael Westlake
Image for Investigation: About my Father — Christoph Meckel
Meritocrats — Stuart Evans
Bartleby — Chris Scott
How to Outthink a Wall: An Anthology — Marvin Cohen
An Aesthetic of Obscenity: Five Novels — Jeff Nuttall
Imaginary Women — Michael Westlake
A Day at the Office — Robert Alan Jamieson
Caliban's Filibuster — Paul West
The Exagggerations of Peter Prince — Steve Katz
The Alan Burns Omnibus: Volume One — Alan Burns

New fiction:

Mirrors on which dust has fallen — Jeff Bursey
Balzac's Coffee, DaVinci's Ristorante — Mark Axelrod

other Verbivoracious titles @
www.verbivoraciouspress.org

Verbivoracious Press

Festschrift Volume Six

edited by G. N. Forester and M. J. Nicholls

THE

OULIPO

This issue is dedicated to Harry Mathews (1930-2017)

Verbivoracious Press

Glentrees, 13 Mt Sinai Lane, Singapore

First published in Great Britain and Singapore

by Verbivoracious Press

www.verbivoraciouspress.org

ISBN: 978-981-11-3866-9

Printed and bound in Great Britain and Singapore

CONTENTS

Introduction

EDITORS

Our sixth issue is a brobdingnagian spectacular fêting the famous workshop of potential literature, The Oulipo, now entering its 57th year. Our contributors were invited to write a piece of fiction, an essay, a poem, or any other hybrid, and (excepting the essays), choose their own constraints. The results have yielded a marvellous sprawl of oulipian homage, from petite poetic tributes to Queneau, to long lipogrammatic bows to Perec. Opening with Irish writer Philip Terry's take on Perec's *Je me souviens* (complete with index), the issue swiftly encompasses an eclectic rondeau of ruminations: among the essays, Warren Motte's 'Abecedaries' is a personal take on the influence of the Oulipo on his reading; Michael Leong's 'The Gendered Politics of Literary Constraints' is a brilliant discussion on the Oulipo's inclusivity and its creative tentacles; David Bellos traces the influence of Victor Hugo on Georges Perec in 'Hugo oulipien?'; Marc Lapprand muses on the Oulipo's prehistoric beginnings; and Christiana Hills celebrates the newly translated novels of Michele Audin. And among the fiction, two excerpts from Jeff Bursey's ambitious lipogram novel *Ennead* showcase a constraint that continues to charm; Andriana Minou's typographically inventive novella *Hypnotic Labyrinth* offers a lyrical and challenging read; Katja Waschneck's choose your own adventure story set in an well-stocked bookstore beguiles; two provocative N+7 pieces: Jenelle D'Alessandro's Trump-inspired take on N+7, and Tom Jenks's reworking of the Book of Genesis serve up satire; and Lance Olsen's grammatically flippant erotic short causes hilarity. A special mention to Pablo M. Ruiz, who has contributed a sequence of terrifically inspired pieces from a forthcoming collection, scattered plentifully across this issue, including obscurely autobiographical lists, Perec trivia, examination papers, multilingual paeans to footballers, and illustrated inventions. And a second special mention to the pseudonymous Chretine Broke-Prose, whose novella *The Logaλφageis of kLeub*^h: */laːf/; /lʌv/* concludes this issue. A version of Christine Brooke-Rose's first novel The Languages of Love, reworked to incorporate her use of grammatical constraints and polylingual punning, this is a thoroughly rigid and extremely inventive work of sheer play, showing how the Oulipo's constraints stretch far beyond the confines of the rats' labyrinth. And finally, in case you're wondering about the absence of Oulipo members in this issue, we're publishing this festschrift (almost) in tandem with a separate volume of new works from The Oulipo, edited by Ian Monk and Daniel Levin Becker. We hope these two offerings are sufficient thanks to the writers who have, and continue to, compose the finest body of exploratory writing in the known universe.

From A Belfast Childhood

PHILIP TERRY

1

I remember that we lived at 42 Annadale Avenue.

2

I remember being afraid of the bogeyman.

3

I remember cat piss in sandpits.

4

I remember dandelion clocks.

5

I remember Eric's, the butcher's.

6

I remember Clarke's Commandos.

7

I remember British Bulldog.

8

I don't remember the name of the Belfast hotel (The Hilton?) that kept getting bombed, but I think it'll come back to me.

9
I remember Red Indians.

10
I remember *The Belfast Telegraph.*

11
I remember Kimberley biscuits.

12
I remember the Lagan.

13
I remember that the headmaster at Fullerton House was called Mr R.

14
I remember Tollymore.

15
I remember origami.

16
I remember Purdeysburne.

17
I remember buying sweets by the quarter.

18
I remember Rostrevor.

19
I remember Fullerton House being on several floors but I don't remember

ever going beyond the first floor.

20
I remember tracing paper.

21
I remember Ulster fry.

22
I remember "Carrots help you see in the dark".

23
I remember water bombs.

24
I remember that the "x" word in ABCs was usually "xylophone".

25
I remember my grandmother's Yorkshire puddings.

26
I remember Zoom iced lollies.

27
I remember the theme tune for *Z-Cars*.

28
I remember AIJ2342.

29
I remember Yetis in *Doctor Who*.

30
I remember that my father was in the cinema when I was born and that

the hospital phoned the cinema to tell him and that after the call he watched the rest of the film.

I don't remember what film it was.

31
I remember "xox" at the end of letters and birthday cards.

32
I remember checkpoints.

33
I remember Mrs Wilsie, who sometimes looked after me as a child.

34
I remember a cracked draughts piece we used to call "smelly man".

And I remember when it reached the other side of the board we would sing "Smelly man is crowned!"

35
I remember a rubber sock you had to wear at swimming if you had a verruca.

36
I remember that the "e" word in ABCs was usually "elephant".

37
I remember the Red Hand of Ulster.

38
I remember being frisked.

39

I remember trolls.

40

I remember occasionally singing hymns in church and that my grandmother had quite a loud and sonorous voice.

41

I remember the three-legged race.

42

I remember when I could hide under the sofa.

43

I remember that my mother had wanted to call me Rupert.

44

I remember 99s.

45

I remember Tim Radford whose father, I think, taught French at Queen's.

46

I remember Andy White's dad used to write for *The Belfast Telegraph.*

47

I remember that just as some people were Catholic and some Protestant, some people preferred Campbell's soup and some preferred Heinz.

48

I remember copper kettles.

49

I remember Mary Peters.

50

I remember Loupé.

And that whenever you did anything naughty Loupé would tell you off by going: *"Oi-oi-oi-oi-oi-oi-oi!"*

51

I remember that Peter Devlin was at one time in the navy.

52

I remember MCB.

53

I remember a sweet shop in Donegal where the sweets were manufactured on the premises.

54

I remember that my sign of the zodiac was sometimes given as Cancer sometimes as Leo, but that I preferred to think of myself as a Leo.

55

I remember that my family called Nice biscuits "Neece" biscuits whereas the Devlins called them "Nice" biscuits.

56

I remember going to Spain and visiting, I think, Altamira and Toledo.

57

I remember the stink of the Lagan when the tide was out.

58

I remember the plastic Wars of the Roses knights that we used to buy on Saturdays.

59

I remember herrings in oatmeal.

60

I remember Bob-a-Job.

61

I remember that my sister's best friend, up until the time we left Belfast, was Christine Kearney.

62

I don't remember the name of the hotel in the city centre (The Xanadu?) that kept getting bombed, but I think it'll come back to me.

63

I still possess, I remember, a black and white photograph of my class at MCB. We're arranged in three rows: the front row sits on a bench, the middle row is standing, the back row (though you can't see it) is standing on a bench.

64

I remember the craze for collecting stickers which came "free" with chewing gum, though you otherwise wouldn't have bought the chewing gum (I remember one sticker in particular which showed a wrinkly old woman and bore the legend "If teacher is your friend who needs enemies?", and another which read "My granny's a hundred years old. She's an antique.").

65

I remember my favourite lesson at school was junk modelling.

66

I remember that Andy White used to live at 36 Bawnmore Road.

67

I remember that Edith Devlin taught French at Queen's and that Peter Devlin taught English.

68

I remember that the Devlins used to keep their meringues in a biscuit tin (as well as their cheese) and that they were browner than ours and gooey in the middle.

69

I remember the Hillman Imp.

70

I remember Vim.

71

I remember going for Sunday lunch at my grandmother's.

72

I remember parsley dinner.

73

I don't remember the gun-runner George Harrison.

74

I remember that the headmaster at Fullerton House, Mr R. – I don't remember his real name nor do I think I ever heard it – looked very much like Paisley.

75

I remember that the "s" word in ABCs was usually "salt".

76

I remember SBD (silent but deadly).

I remember "He who denied it supplied it".

And "He who smelt it dealt it".

77
I remember Monopoly.

78
I remember that my mother had a sewing box – containing buttons, thread, scissors, a thimble etc – but I can no longer picture it.

79
I remember that my father smoked either Gold Block or Three Nuns, but more often Gold Block when we lived in Belfast and more often Three Nuns after we left.

I remember "None nicer".

80
I remember that Mr R. used to chain-smoke and that my brother was sometimes sent out to get him cigarettes.

81
I remember:

> Dr Forster
> Went to Gloucester
> In a shower of rain
> He stepped in a puddle
> Right up to his muddle
> And never went there again.

82
I remember learning to walk up hills in a zigzag so as to make the climb easier.

83

I remember walking to the top of Annadale Avenue with my father to get fish and chips but I've no recollection of actually eating them.

84

I remember "Not tonight Josephine".

85

I remember "Are you a Catholic or a Protestant?"

86

I don't remember the first time I had a drink but I think my first drink must have been cider, probably Bulmer's, as I don't remember my parents having any other drink in the house.

87

I don't remember the name of the tramp who occasionally called by to offer his services for odd jobs, but I do remember that he gave my mother presents, among them a snow scene (the kind that you could shake to make it look as if it was snowing) and a pair of knickers.

88

I remember that our first television had legs and that you had to hit it if it wasn't working.

89

I remember Barry Hobson being on *Romper Room*.

90

I remember spelling tests, and the difficulty I had in spelling "necessary", though I don't remember what I got wrong (an "s" instead of a "c", "ey' instead of "y"?)

91

I remember watching cartoons on TV after school.

92

I remember that among the party games we played were: musical chairs, pass the parcel, blind man's bluff, a game the name of which I forget but that consisted of pinning a tail on a donkey with a blindfold on, and oranges and lemons.

93

I remember roundabouts (in children's playgrounds).

94

I remember army checkpoints.

95

I remember Loupé drove a VW Beetle. It was cream, and if you lifted up the carpet in the front you could see the road.

96

I remember "Two Little Boys" and "Tie Me Kangaroo Down".

97

I don't remember the killing of Kathleen Irvine in a UVF bomb attack on McGurk's bar.

98

I remember "x marks the spot".

99

I remember when filter coffee first came in Edith Devlin would dry the filters out on the line (and I remember, later, she did away with filters altogether and started to use old pairs of tights instead).

100

I remember "flesh" coloured paint, which was pink.

101

I remember the Rounds calling their daughter Graina.

102

I remember car cricket: one for a car, two for a van, four for a lorry, six for a bus, and out if anyone spotted a two-wheeled vehicle.

103

I remember *Whizzer and Chips*.

104

I remember that the "j" word in ABCs was usually "jumper".

105

I remember, before video, that Andy White's family used to record the six o'clock news on a reel-to-reel tape recorder, so that Andy's dad could listen to it after he got home from work.

106

I don't remember ever understanding the troubles, nor do I remember anyone trying to explain it all to me.

107

I remember Rosemary Sutcliffe.

108

I don't remember the name of the hotel (The Montague?) in the city centre that kept getting bombed, but I think it'll come back to me.

109

I remember the collection boxes outside shops for polio which were in the form of a boy suffering from polio with a strapped leg.

And the ones where you put a penny in the top and watched as it dropped and bounced off a series of pins which made it alter direction until eventually it fell into the bottom with a clunk.

110

I remember on holiday in Spain (Marbella? Seaches?) staying at a hotel called The Golden Galleon when it rained incessantly and the streets became rivers.

111

I remember my father's office at Queen's being very dark.

112

I remember Dublin Zoo.

113

I remember that we buried our pets, at least the smaller ones, beneath a row of trees at the back of the house.

114

I remember Bewley's fudge.

115

I remember that for a long time the Devlins didn't have a television and prided themselves on this.

116

I remember that the "n" word in ABCs was usually "nut".

117

I remember plastic explosives.

118

I remember writing letters to Father Christmas addressed to: "Santa Claus, The North Pole".

119

I remember believing the story that the snakes had been banished from Ireland by St Patrick.

120

I remember Andy Pandy.

121

I remember getting an Arran sweater knitted for me and that once it was made I didn't wear it much as it was very heavy and not that comfortable.

122

In my class photograph the boys wear shoes or sandals with knee or ankle socks, grey shorts, grey or white shirts, and striped ties. The girls also wear shoes or sandals with knee or ankle socks; apart from this they generally have dark pinafore-like dresses over white shirts and ties, though one girl has a light-coloured garment on top and one seems to be without the tie.

123

I remember that my brother used to play viola in the school orchestra.

124

I remember that I used to tease my sister, calling her "lanky legs".

125

I remember that there was a banana tree in the Botanical Gardens.

126

I remember that we lived in a very modern, if not modernist, house, and that I found the Victorian houses of my friends more full of intrigue.

127

I remember having a rope ladder tied to a tree at the bottom of our garden.

128

I remember that when we lived in Belfast my grandmother always used to say how much better things had been in York, and that later when we moved to Colchester, she complained how much better things had been in Belfast.

129

I remember that my grandmother used to like to sit out and watch the Orangemen parading by on the 12th of July.

130

I remember porridge smothered in brown sugar and drenched with cream.

131

I remember club biscuits when they were covered in thick chocolate (which has now been replaced by a thin layer of chocolate flavoured candy) and the advert: "If you like a lot of chocolate on your biscuit join our club".

132

I remember Jonathan Devlin had a thing about buttons and didn't like to touch them.

133

I remember that the "o" word in ABCs was usually "ostrich".

134

I remember my father's story about penning a complaint about school dinners when he was a child (which he must have been pleased with or he wouldn't have told me): "The tapioca was mediocre, the sago was unfit for a dago."

135

I remember an (incomplete) set of playing cards that my father had as a child in York that had aeroplanes drawn on them and which were designed to aid reconnaissance.

136

I remember having a wigwam.

137

I remember the *Blue Peter Annual.*

138

I don't remember the shooting of Henry McIlhone.

139

I remember that when walking with my father or my big brother, instead of clasping their hands I would hold on to their little fingers.

140

I don't remember the name of the Belfast hotel (The Carrick?) that kept getting bombed, but I think it'll come back to me.

141

I remember banana sandwiches.

142

I remember my grandmother's ginger biscuits, and I remember that I preferred them when they had gone slightly soft.

143

I remember Ladybird books.

144

I remember the QE2.

145

I remember that Edith Devlin had a row of storage jars in her kitchen, one containing sugar, one containing vanilla pods, one containing sultanas etc.

146

I remember the film *Zulu.*

147

I remember that our house at 42 Annadale Avenue had underfloor heating and that for years I thought this was standard.

148

I remember play-dough, and how difficult it was to do anything with it compared to plasticine.

149

I remember that airfix glue was very difficult to get off your fingers and that it had a banana-like smell.

150

I remember that the first fizzy drinks I tasted were Coke and Fanta and that I preferred Fanta.

151

I remember staying with the Abellans in the mountains near Madrid.

152

I remember Donegal tweed.

153

I remember bluebottles being much more frequent than they are today.

154

I remember the national anthem in cinemas, and that some people in the audience used to stand.

155

I remember that my brother and sister used to encourage me to say rude words in front of adults.

156

I remember extra-mural classes.

157

I don't remember John Xeni, who narrowly escaped being killed when the Capitol Bar was bombed on Dublin Road.

158

I remember elocution lessons.

159

I remember "I'd like to buy the world a Coke . . ."

And I remember:
>   I'd like to buy the pope a rope
>   And hang him from a tree
>   With Burnadette and Gerry Fitt
>   To keep him company.

160

I remember *Rusty Bedsprings* by I.P. Knightly.

161

I remember sticking needles and pins into Gillian's packet of cigarettes so that when they were pulled out they were in tatters.

162

I remember my father diving off the harbour wall at Portsalon watched by a crowd of (incredulous?) onlookers.

163

I remember that the "i" word in ABCs was usually "igloo".

164

I don't remember the Northern Resistance Movement.

165

I remember Fanad Head.

166

I remember that my grandmother wore dentures and that she'd had all her teeth out in York when she was still young.

167

I remember Action Man.

And I remember Action Man with "realistic hair".

168

I remember *Watch with Mother*, which I usually watched on my own.

169

I remember that the bedroom I shared with my brother had a black and white tiled floor, like a chessboard.

170

I remember iron fist.

171

I remember that Christine's sister, Tory, was a fencing champion.

172

I remember that Mr R. coughed all the time.

173

One of the first things that strikes me about the photograph of my class are the faces I recognise. I recognise (front row) Michael McClure and Shaun Heron (?); I recognise (middle row) Patrick Baird, a girl with tied back hair whose name I forget (Louise?), and myself; I recognise (back row) Timothy Radford, Barry Hobson, Andy White, and another Shaun whose second name I forget. Far more numerous, though, are the faces I do not recognise.

174

I remember Wilsie, our handyman.

175

I remember the UDA.

176

I remember *churros*.

177

I remember *Doctor Zhivago* with Omar Sharif being a television sensation.

178

I remember that the first time I had a baked egg was at Andy White's.

179

I remember not liking cabbage.

180

I remember that the Rowlands had a holiday cottage in Galway but I never went there.

181

I remember Peter Devlin was considered something of an authority on Walter Scott.

182

I remember Ladybird pants.

Index

Abecedaries

WARREN MOTTE

When I was five years old, my first-grade teacher summoned my parents to a consultation, in order to inform them that their son was incapable of learning to read. It was not a particularly auspicious beginning for a person who would come in later years to define himself first and foremost as a *reader*. Family legend has it that my parents laughed when they received the news, for they knew that I could in fact already read, having been taught to do so by my mother before I entered the first grade. But I would not read for my teacher, because she terrified me to the point of muteness. Her name was Olive Whitehead, I recall, and she was a genuine ogre. She seemed impossibly ancient to me at the time, perhaps a hundred years old at the very least. I have never forgotten her, and if I saw her today, some sixty years later (which event I regard as plausible, because extremely cruel people are often extremely long-lived), I cannot guarantee that I would act in a civilized, non-violent manner. If I mention her now, it is because she taught me a lot about teaching, and more particularly still the teaching of literacy—though chiefly by counter-example, of course. She also taught me a great deal about how one may learn to read, thanks to (or in some cases despite) one's teachers. I wager that she never suspected how much she really did teach that slow-witted, backward little boy.

Thankfully enough, after that difficult, inconclusive experience, I had several very excellent literacy teachers. The first of them was Charles Dickens, whom I read and reread while still a child. He taught me that if you take books seriously, they will take *you* seriously. Thanks to him, I discovered that certain moments in books are more important than others. I also learned that one could distinguish levels of importance, and even record those distinctions by making marks in the margins of the text, in pencil. That was a heady, liberating moment; and as I page through my old copy of *A Tale of Two Cities*, right *now*, gazing at those pencil marks (those earnest underscores! those brackets! those arrows! those cf. 345s! those exclamation points!) and thinking about my life as a reader, I realize that that moment was unparalleled. My second teacher was James Joyce. He kindly took in hand a fractious, headstrong adolescent, and taught him patience, attentiveness, and rigor. I came firmly under his sway, firmly enough, in any case, to read everything he wrote over and over again, including his three-volume *Letters*. I read *Finnegans Wake* in a very literal way indeed, returning to the beginning when I reached the end ("A way a lone a last a loved a long the"), and reading it straight through once again. It became a touchstone text for me —though I readily admit that it's not for everyone, and I imagine that one can be a perfectly competent reader never having opened it. My third and most abiding teacher was the Oulipo.

When I came upon the Oulipo's first anthology, *La Littérature potentielle: Créations, re-créations, récréations*, in 1978, it knocked my readerly socks off. I was twenty-six at the time and, having spent most of my life until then reading, I would not have imagined that I could learn so much more, and so quickly, about the possibilities and limits of literature. But the pedagogical dimension of the Oulipo's work is profound (even if some of its members might bridle at such a suggestion), and it has left an indelible mark on the way that I approach the things I read. I don't believe that I have ever thanked any individual Oulipian for teaching me to read, but I would like to thank them collectively and officially here. For their intelligence, their efficiency, their resourcefulness, their humor, their generosity, their forbearance, and for being, in short, everything that Olive Whitehead was *not*.

Paging through that book, I was like a kid in a candy shop. Everything pleased me endlessly: François Le Lionnais's two manifestos; Raymond Queneau's piece on redundancy in "Phane Armé" and his remarks about his hundred trillion poems (which I had not yet read—and despite my best efforts cannot even now claim to have finished); Jean Lescure's history of the Oulipo and his poem for stutterers; Georges Perec's history of the lipogram; Claude Berge's reflections on combinatory literature; Jacques Bens's irrational sonnets; in a word, *everything*. It even pleased me that the table of contents was in the front of the volume, rather than at the end, for goodness sake. More crucially still, I felt right at home in that strange book. Daniel Levin Becker, in his *Many Subtle Channels*, speaks about the way that the Oulipo provides a place for him, with all of his personal tics and obsessions. "It is a place for *les mordus de littérature—the* incurably afflicted," he argues, "the bitten—people preoccupied with the structure inherent in language, the calculation inherent in storytelling, and the possibility for mystery and mischief inherent in the smallest textual enterprise." I felt much the same way, I think, sensing that this was a kind of writing that would not only tolerate my readerly bizarreries, but actually welcome them and put them to work.

Encountering Perec's "Horreurs de la guerre" ("Horrors of War") and his "Petit abécédaire illustré" ("Little Illustrated Abecedary"), I was immediately struck by how *right* those texts seemed. Because literature is certainly literal in nature—that is, it is constructed (in its written form, at least) out of letters. That is something we mostly forget, preferring to think that literature is a matter of words, of ideas, of themes, of style, and so forth. But I found it wonderfully tonic to be recalled to order, to first things, by Perec. Moreover, the notion of the abecedary intrigued me. I remembered my own abecedaries with some emotion. The letter *A* was always red therein, quite naturally, because "A is for apple." I had to summon up all the cultural relativity I could muster when I heard Arthur Rimbaud say that *A* is black. I finally conceded him the right to stake such a claim, but it was a very close-run thing; and to this day I point out to my students that for people born into the English language, *A* is—and must always remain—red. The image of the abecedary pleased me all the more because the word designates an object that I imagined as the very first tool one uses in order to learn to read. For just as all writing begins with the letter, so does all reading. And little by little, it occurred to me that the Oulipo was teaching me to read, all over again. It was thus not a matter of mere whim when, a few years later, I put together a few Oulipian texts in English translation under the title *Primer*.

The tutoring in literacy that I received from the Oulipo was rich, liberal, and various. I had already learned to think about literature both diachronically and synchronically, that is, both in a historical perspective and in an Eliotic fashion, as a simultaneous whole. But the Oulipo's insistence on the double nature of its mission, focused on both *analysis* and *synthesis* (on the one hand, the study of extant, and sometimes ancient texts; on the other hand, the invention of new forms) allowed me to understand diachrony *through* synchrony, and vice versa. Still broader and more fascinating horizons opened up when I began to realize how mutually complementary, and indeed implicative, those two perspectives are. The way the old becomes new in Oulipian experimentation was a revelation to me. When processed through Jean Lescure's "S+7 Method" or Georges Perec's technique of homophonic palindrome, Gérard de Nerval's "El Desdichado," a text I thought I knew pretty well, becomes something very new indeed, something astonishing and barely recognizable. Yet the minimal familiarity that survives serves to put a reader on notice that even the most radically innovative piece of work necessarily recalls certain works that preceded it, and certain aspects of literary tradition. For the "original" text necessarily echoes throughout the "transformed" text, and conditions it; and the more powerful the original, the more marked that phenomenon will be. In other terms, Oulipian experimentation also reminds us how the new wagers upon the old—and how closely those two orders reveal their affiliation, the more closely one reads. One ends up reading any text doubly, at the very least.

Ah, close reading! There too, I thought I had come to terms with the technique, reading Joyce so obsessively. I discovered that I had a great deal more to learn, however, when I turned toward the Oulipo's longer texts, most especially those of Georges Perec, to whom I decided to devote my doctoral dissertation. There, it was a question of attentiveness and concentration, certainly, but also of stamina. It demanded a constant oscillation between the local and the global, between the very punctual and the far more ample context in which the punctual took its place. That kind of reading required a very considerable degree of agility, and I found it exhausting; yet I also found it more consistently and abundantly rewarding than anything I had read up to that time. I learned still other lessons in close reading when I began to translate Oulipian texts into English. For there, too, any lapse of concentration could have disastrous consequences. John Coltrane once said that playing with Thelonious Monk was a wonderful experience, but if he allowed his attention to falter even for a second, it felt like he had fallen down a mineshaft. I felt much the same, translating the Oulipo, walking a knife-edge between fidelity to the French and the desire to produce something legible in English. It allowed me nevertheless to understand that any close reading obeys principles that are much the same, insofar as it involves a negotiation between production and reception, between writerly purpose and readerly desire, between what is intended and what is inferred.

Whatever difficult lessons Oulipian tutelage may have entailed were assuaged by a consideration that was, to my way of thinking, infinitely affirming. I had always suspected that literature had extension in space, that it could be imagined in objective terms, that it had a shape—in other words, right from "A is for apple" onward, I was a committed formalist. Yet I lacked a substantial, convincing body of work upon which to hang my commitment, and the Oulipo came along providentially to convince me that other people, folks far more savvy and accomplished than I, were likewise convinced of the importance of form. Because form is not something mute: it is eminently capable of speech, and very eloquent speech in the best instances. Georges Perec's *La Disparition* (*A Void*) is a fine example of that kind of text. Clearly enough, the decision to write a novel without the letter *E* is a formal choice. Yet that formal choice permeates the thematics of the novel at every level. In so doing, it amplifies the meditation on lack and loss that makes *La Disparition* a great deal more than an exercise in literary pyrotechnics. It inevitably brings our attention back to process issues, encouraging us to think about how novels are conceived and constructed. It suggests that just as the beginning of *écriture* is largely lost to us, so too is the end. And it puts us on notice that any literary text at all, from the most highly structured of Shakespeare's sonnets to the most transparently flaccid example of surrealist automatic writing, has a significant shape, that is, a shape which *means* something.

One of the most important considerations about reading that I learned from the Oulipo involved the idea of responsibility, for I came to understand that the rigor that Oulipian authors invest in writing ought to be greeted by as much rigor as the reader can muster. On the face of it, that way of putting things makes literature sound like utter drudgery, but nothing could be further from the truth in the case of this body of work. For the contract that the Oulipo extends to the reader is complex and detailed, and one of its key clauses involves the idea that literature should be amusing, whenever possible. As Queneau put it, one doesn't write in order to annoy people, or to bore them. So, yes, the Oulipo demands rigor from its readers; but that is merely one dimension of a broader dynamic of *participation*—and that latter notion was, for me, the real revelation. Quite often, that participation takes a ludic shape, transforming the readerly experience through a kind of felicitous alchemy, affording it a purpose and an aesthetic potential that more passive readings largely lack; in short, it invests that experience with meaning. Along the way, there are valuable insights about play itself to be had, should we care to appreciate them: play is not "for nothing"; it takes place in the real world, rather than in some play-sphere insulated from the real; it produces sense; it can be a very "serious" proposition indeed. Whatever else it may be, however, play is essentially and inevitably *articulative*: it puts things into relation with one another, and causes them to move; it puts people into relation with one another and causes them to move; it puts things and people into relation with one another and causes them to move.

By now, another crucial clause in the contract that the Oulipo extends to us will have become clear, for the group's practice is predicated upon a very real respect for the reader. One of the most refreshing things about Oulipian authors is that they do not imagine that their readers are idiots —and most of the time, they are correct. They offer their readers a rare franchise in the production of literature. Philippe Lejeune once remarked that in each of Georges Perec's texts "there is a place for me, for me to do something," and that is broadly true of Oulipian work. Not only do we have a seat at the table, we also have a role to play, one that is as significant as we're willing to make it. It thus behooves us to be as active and engaged as we can when we approach a literary text, and to convene in that process the very best parts of our selves, such as they may be. That is undoubtedly the most fundamental lesson I've learned under the Oulipo's gracious, patient tutelage—and it is one that has served me very well as I've tried to find my readerly way in the lavish, prodigious, and infinitely alluring world of letters.

You Have Six Hours to Complete this Examination

PABLO M. RUIZ

INTRODUCTION

I am currently working on a book project based on a particular constraint: the texts included in the book should be as different from each other as possible, in terms of form, content, style, tone, length, genre, etc. This is therefore a constraint that rather than to an individual text applies to a set of texts. It is, so to speak, a relational constraint. The larger the number of texts included, the more visible (and hopefully interesting) the result. The project as I conceive of it right now will comprise a total of some seventy texts. I offer here a limited set (further limited by the fact that I write mostly in Spanish), but hopefully large enough to achieve at least some of the intended effect. Some texts were specifically written for this project, while others just found their way into it. Some are good, some are bad, some are silly, some are serious, some are ironic, some are naive. Sometimes I'm able to tell which is what, sometimes I'm not. Sometimes I think this is actually not a writing constraint, but rather a reading constraint. Or perhaps it is both simultaneously.

Texts (in published order here):
1) You Have Six Hours to Complete this Examination
2) Six Improbable Lists – Autobiography by Other Means
3) Circles. A Chess Knight Dreams of Geometry (image)

4) Specular Amy: Love Letters (image)
5) Palindromes in Two Languages
6) The Hidden Letter E in Perec's *La Disparition* (translation by Daniella Gitlin)
7) Songs for Liana
8) *Argumentum Ethicum*
9) The Art of the Portrait (translation by Daniella Gitlin)
10) *Ugetsu monogatari*: Multitranslation
11) Beckettiana (art by Daniel Ponce)
12) Email to a Canadian Friend
13) Notes Toward an Art of the Superlative
14) Syllabus: Letters to a Young Poet

You have six hours to complete this examination

Question 1

When Borges slyly accuses a translator, J. C. Mardrus, of pretending to translate, what is he saying and not saying, and what is at stake in such a notion, both for translation and for writing in general?

Answer

Literature is, notoriously, a vastly inexact discipline. (For instance: I recently read the introduction to an anthology of texts (mostly excerpts from his novels) by the Argentinian writer Juan José Saer. The anthologist, a well-known and respected writer and professor, claimed that his decision was plainly justified by the "essentially fragmentary" character of Saer's narrative. Then I came across an article by Saer himself where, trying to justify his decision to include only short stories and essays in another anthology, he says that a novelist that publishes only fragments of his novels is basically betraying himself, for not respecting the essential wholeness he gave to his own works. The wrong question to ask here is, of course, who's right. The right question would be about the assumptions behind those opposite statements.) As a result of this basically unstable nature, literature is prone to be populated by prejudices and clichés, what Borges used to call "superstitions".

One of the literary realms most populated by those "superstitions" is that of translation, and Borges certainly took every possible advantage to denounce them, or at least to play with them. His two main essays on translation are "Las versiones homéricas" and "Los traductores de *Las 1001 noches*", both of them, it should be noted, about works Borges was unable to read in the original. In the first of them, Borges's main move is to attack the almost sacred character of the original. He does so by means of two different arguments: one of them, that there's nothing but drafts, provisional versions. The definitive text, he claims, is a concept belonging to religion or to tiredness. The second argument is that we tend to consider a translation invariably inferior because familiarity with the original, especially when it is a good and well-known text, makes us think of it as being perfect as it is. But the ignorance of the original frees us from that belief. This is what he is saying when he claims: "The Odyssey, thanks to my opportune ignorance of the Greek language, is [for me] an international library including works in prose and verse, etc." To put it differently, ignorance of the original is an opportunity for literature.

The essay about the *Nights* is an expansion and a deepening of those ideas. In "Los traductores de *Las 1001 noches*", the first move he makes is that of placing the practice of translation within a tradition. We can't understand a translation or a translator, Borges seems to be saying, without understanding the fact that translators are usually translating against some other translator, that what they are usually trying to do is to differ from other, previous translators. Borges, as far as I know, is the first in proposing this, thus placing the discussion about translation beyond the usual debate between literality and freedom, fidelity or infidelity, etc. After mentioning the famous and "beautiful", as he describes it, debate between Arnold and Newman on how to translate Homer, one of them proposing freedom and the other one literality (the two main positions in the historical debates) he disposes of these two main ways of translating with a wonderful sentence: "*Traducir el espíritu es una intención tan enorme y tan fantasmal que bien puede quedar como inofensiva; traducir la letra, una precisión tan extravagante que no hay riesgo de que la ensayen.*" The discussion about translation should therefore be about what's in between of those two grandiose purposes, those two abstract claims: the details, the omissions and additions, the syntactic movement in the actual translations. And to discuss that, we need to know who's translating, when, where, and for whom. For instance: Galland, translating in France in the 17th century, has an advantage that is lost for 20th century readers, namely that of any oriental flavor being an innovation and a revelation.

One of the reasons why Borges is very aware of the polemical nature of the translations he is commenting on is, of course, that he himself is writing with a polemical purpose; he himself is trying to differ from Arnold and Newman and therefore from the historical debates on translation. His analysis focuses mainly, but not only, on the work of three translators: the English Robert Burton, the French Mardrus and the German Enno Littmann. After a very careful examination of the pervasive freedoms of the first two and the almost absolute fidelity of the last one (unanimously praised, "even by the arabists"), his verdict is clear. Littman is guilty. Why?

Any discussion on translation, I suggest, should end up in the choosing of an altar of sacrifice. Those who propose literality sacrifice everything to the original. Those who propose freedoms sacrifice everything to the reader. Goethe proposed to sacrifice everything to the foreign culture (a mistake that presupposes that the essential element in any foreign literary work is its belonging to a foreign culture, when it's usually the case, especially with successful works, that one of their merits is their capability to transcend that cultural specificity). Benjamin, in his wonderful failure, proposed to sacrifice everything to that mystical mirage, pure language. So what's Borges's altar? As vague and abstract as this may sound, his altar, I should say, is literature. His main argument to defend Burton's and Mardrus's translations, is their presupposing a literature, that they let a literary tradition to be seen through their translations. While Littman, "incapable of lying" and "always lucid, readable, mediocre," offers us only the "probity of Germany," Burton and Mardrus offer us their literary traditions, and therefore richer works full of the literary sensitivity of their culture and their time. Donne, Shakespeare, Swinburne, are present in Burton. Flaubert or Lafontaine, for instance, in Mardrus. So when he says that Mardrus pretends to translate, what he is actually saying is that Mardrus is not just giving us an equivalent of what he is reading, but rather what he would like to find as a sensitive reader belonging to his place and time, to his literary tradition. This is what explains Mardrus's "creative and happy infidelity."

I think we should put Borges's considerations about translation in a wider frame, thinking also of the presuppositions and conceptions behind his observations. Should one assume that Borges will always condemn a literal translation and praise free ones? Not at all. When he is reviewing, for instance, the Spanish poet León Felipe's translation of Whitman's "Leaves of Grass", he demolishes it by pointing at the repeated and unjustified liberties the translator takes, considering them little less than sacrilegious. Whitman's poetry is sacred, don't touch it. Moreover, he condemns León Felipe for the very same reasons he praises Burton and Mardrus: for including echoes of his own literary tradition in his translation. And when we see Borges's own translations of some fragments of the works by American poets (like Hart Crane, e e cummings or Wallace Stevens) he is being very commonsensical: trying to give the sense in a poetical register of Spanish and taking no liberties. But when he translates Poe's "The Purloined Letter", he takes as many liberties as the genre allows him to; i.e., he translates it, so to speak, to give us the story Poe would have written had he known the genre of the detective story as it developed after his work (this means that, while he is not adding almost anything, Borges eliminates parts and modifies details in the story so it better accommodates to the conventions later developed in the genre). Going back to the two essays on translation, we should say that the choice of the works he considers in his two essays is not innocent. There is, one could say, a difference between translating anonymous works transmitted through centuries of oral tradition (like

Homer, like the *Nights*) and more recent works, with a definite author and a definite original written at a definite time in a definite place. So we reach the conclusion that, ultimately, there's no one Borgesian theory of translation, but many. Another innovation in the history of the discussion about translation: the question about how to translate has many answers, depending on the text, the language, the translator, and the state of literature at the time of the translation.

It could be useful here to resort to the old distinction between the classic and the romantic. In a sketchy presentation, the classic tends to consider the text as the only thing that matters, whereas the romantic tends to think of the poet as the ultimate instance of legitimation. As with any major writer, it would be impossible to place Borges in one position or the other, because he is always challenging them and trying to dissolve the distinction. As a writer, he made the most striking combination of those two opposite poles, writing the most original and innovative work, fulfilling the romantic ideal of the personal voice, with the most rigorous and algebraically precise method of the classic ideal. He followed the strict laws of the narrative short forms, and combined them with a densely poetical language. In short, he tried to make music and mathematics (one of the possible ways of ciphering those two poles) live together in as many different ways as possible. Another writer with an obsession with this opposition and a permanent attempt at dissolving it was the Russian Vladimir Nabokov. I don't know of a better symbol for that struggle between the classic and the romantic, and their possible (and happy) being together in one writer, as the one provided by Nabokov, who at the same time loved to compose chess problems and to chase butterflies. Rewriting Borges's assertion about Mardrus in Nabokovian symbolism, we could say that Mardrus, while pretending to be only playing the chess game of dictionaries and literality, was also trying to provide us with a few butterflies of his own invention. And, according to Borges, we should thank him for that.

Question 2

The mixture of prose and poetry in extended literary works is a feature of much traditional Japanese literature. In the earliest extant anthology of poetry, the *Manyoshu*, for instance, one can find numerous long poems in Japanese with sometimes quite extended prose headnotes or "prefaces" in Chinese. By the mid-tenth century, several texts combining Japanese prose and *waka* (i.e., 5-7-5 / 7-7 meter) poetry had been written. Some of them are travel diaries, some *uta monogatari* or "poem tales", and some simpler sorts of tales in which poems were quoted incidentally, often as elements of the plot.

With the *Genji monogatari*, however, the use of poems and prose in combination attained a remarkable level of sophistication and integration. Explain, then, how poetry is combined with prose narrative in *Genji* and discuss the various roles poetry plays on the course of the "tale".

Answer

In order to better understand the relation between prose and poetry in the *Genji monogatari*, I would like to start by placing it within its cultural setting and its literary tradition. The 11th century Heian society where this work was produced was a highly sophisticated one in terms of artistic and esthetic interests and concerns. The women who were part of the court had a very intense training in the arts in general and in poetry in particular. The ability to write poetry properly (which included not only the actual words in a poem, but also the choice of paper, the calligraphic skill, the mastery of a whole system of symbols and allusion, the knowledge of the poetical tradition) was highly valued. Moreover, the relationship between men and women, and the communication between them, took place almost exclusively by means of the exchange of poems. At this point, the poetical tradition was both extremely rich, feeding originally from Chinese models developed during the Tang dynasty, and highly conventionalized, which means that poetic form, vocabulary and imagery were restricted to a limited repertoire considered proper. This, in turn, led to the development of a very rich symbolic system, so people would be able to communicate a wide range of possible messages required in daily life by using those relatively limited resources.

Considering that poetry was such an important component of daily life, at least at court and among the illustrated aristocracy, it's not surprising that we find it playing a very important role in the literary tradition, not only in the poetic works themselves, but also in prose narratives. In early works like the "Tale of the Bamboo Cutter" (Taketori monogatari) poetry appears with no more literary consequences than the inclusion of any other familiar element, like kotos, pieces of furniture, clothes or shrines. Poetry is just another element of reality, its inclusion is hardly more than a verisimilitude device, and poems have in those works the same function they have in reality, namely dialogues between characters. In another important antecedent, the *Ise monogatari*, poems have a different function, turned now into something like "textual characters," considering that the prose texts refer their circumstance and history, providing also in many cases contexts of interpretation. This overview of the literary tradition of the *Genji* wouldn't be complete without mentioning the *Kokinshu*, the first compilation of Japanese (waka) poetry, a collection of poems carefully arranged so as to make of it something more than just the sum of its parts. Poems are arranged with a somewhat chronological criterion, presenting the poems about the seasons in succession, and even the poems of each season from the beginning to the end of the season. The love poems are also arranged that way, this arrangement overimposing to them the pattern of the love affair, from the first signs of love to the fading love and the sad feelings of the end of the affair. So what we have is a structure carefully devised so as to provide the anthology of poems with a context that will to some extent determine the way of reading them and will also tend to make of the whole a consistent unit.

In the *Genji*, verses and prose, poems and narrative, establish a complex relation that will combine all of those possibilities and models provided by tradition, which in turn will lead to a very unique way of relating them. On the one hand, we have of course the simple realistic element, as in the early monogataris. But on the other hand, while at the beginning we tend to think that poetry works as poetry and prose as prose, we progressively perceive that this functioning starts to get more complex. As the characters in the tale need to interpret the many times elusive poems they exchange, so does the reader with respect to the narrative, which often conceals as much as it tells. When we read, for instance, that "her father loved the way she had of making it seem that a great deal was being left unsaid" (448), referring to To no Chujo and one of his daughters, it doesn't require much imagination to propose that statement as representing what Murasaki Shikibu could have thought of her tale. We can also relate this with what she writes about poems a couple of pages later: "An impromptu poem . . ., if it is spoken musically, with an air at the beginning and end as of something unsaid, can seem to convey worlds of meaning, even if upon mature reflection it does not seem to have said much of anything at all" (451). All of this opens the reading experience to ambiguity and potential meaning, even more so considering the repetition of the verb 'to seem' in these three instances, as if meaning had always a component of subjective effect, ultimately under no one's control. This is further suggested by comments like "There was no trace of ambiguity in the letter, and yet it was worded so discreetly that the outsider would not immediately have guessed the meaning" (1086). Or this other one, much earlier: "I wish you could understand me, but of course it's not the way of this world that we are ever completely understood" (277).

So we could say that the *Genji*, while defining itself in terms of the tradition (and this can be also discussed in terms of the relation it establishes with the two previous prose genres of the time, namely historical chronicles and "old" monogataris, between which it will establish a permanent tension mostly through the narrator commentaries, further complicated by the inclusion of a third element, namely the Buddhist parables and their indirect way of telling the truth, mentioned in the famous literary discussion in chapter 25), it also establishes differences with that tradition and proposes something new: the *Genji monogatari* requires to be read in a way with no precedents at the time, that is, it requires a new reader. As is the case with any innovative work, the *Genji* invents that reader, and does so by means of this kind of 'self-codification', so to speak, of all these comments and discussions about literature and poems and their meaning and purpose. We can also say that the presence of poetry suggests the addition of layers of meaning to the tale. Let's consider, for example, what happens after the death of Genji. As one more of the many instances of substitutions in the tale (which started very early with Fujitsubo being attractive to Genji as a kind of substitute for his mother, whom she resembles), Genji is replaced by Niou and Kaoru. Once Genji's death is announced, both of them are mentioned as the possible candidates to replace him, and from then on both will be the characters around which the narrative develops. Both have some of Genji's features: besides their extreme beauty and talent, Niou is presented as the favorite of his parents in spite of not being the crown prince, and Kaoru repeatedly expresses his desire to retire from the world, both paralleling Genji's situation and desires, as if they were in a sense his two halves. On a more symbolic level, Genji, the 'shining' one, is referred to in a visual way. Both 'kaoru' and 'niou' are words with meanings associated to smelling, to perfumes and scents. And here poetry plays a role in the identification of the three of them as a kind of (symbolic) whole. On page 990, Kaoru is called to receive a message: "The snow, now deeper, was dimly lit by the stars. The fragrance which he sent back into the room made one think how uselessly the spring night's darkness was laboring to blot it out." The allusion is to *Kokinshu* 40, which I give in Seidensticker translation:

> In vain the spring night's darkness accosts the plum,
> Destroying the color but not the scent of its blossoms.

We can see that colors and scents are unified in the imagery of the spring blossoms, which in turn links the colors-and-scents imagery to seasons and therefore to time. This is reinforced by very subtle parallelisms in the tale. The allusion to *Kokinshu* 40 occurs when Kaoru leaves his perfume behind him going to receive a message from Ukifune. The same poem is alluded to on page 556, when Genji is going to visit Murasaki and also leaves his perfume behind him. We have again the substitutions going on, here Genji/ Kaoru and also Murasaki/ Ukifune, and poetry reinforcing those identifications. (All this is also complemented by yet another striking parallelism that occurs between the poetry contest in the chapter "A boat upon the waters" and the perfume contest in the chapter "A branch of plum". There are similar situations, same time of the year and even very similar paragraphs on pages 990 and 515, this one right after Genji shows up at the perfume contest carrying with him two perfumes, as if the story were preparing the future advent of Kaoru and Niou.)

Let's notice that there's also a possible layer of meaning related to esthetics, when we find for instance the poem alluded to on page 513 during the perfume contest, *Kokinshu* 38:

> Who shall judge the color, the scent of the plum?
> Who if not you? The one who knows best knows best.

This poem follows a strong tradition of esthetic symbolism also found in the preface of the *Kokinshu*, where the *Ise monogatari* is evaluated in the following terms: "[His poetry] reminds one of blossoms that have no color, only the fragrance is still there." (Also meanings associated with sex and pleasure have been suggested, linked to images of color and fragrance conveyed through the character for *iro*.)

We could go even a step further by considering the so called Uji chapters, the last ten chapters, with the imagery and symbolism suggested in the very name of the place (meaning something like 'gloomy'). Those chapters can also be read as if they were what the previous poems suggest, namely the night of spring that eliminates the color but not the scent. And if Genji can be symbolically associated with the 'shining' blossom of spring, then the whole tale can be read, in one of multiple possibilities, as Genji's way to splendour, his decay, and his later persistence in the "scents" of his successors. *The Tale of Genji* as the tale of a spring blossom.

Much more could be said about the functions of poetry in the tale (its name-giving function, for instance) and possible different usages of poems taken from tradition and new poems composed by Murasaki (for instance, the possible greater symbolical function of the former, being commonly shared and more completely understood in their implications by both author and audience). Much more also about the conception of fiction and the pervasive imagery of dreams and their possible meanings. And I don't know if it's been pointed out that the *Genji* is to prose, in a sense, what the *Kokinshu* is to poetry, with multiple symmetries in the way they are organized as wholes, the *Genji* by means of poetry devices and the *Kokinshu* by means of those of narrative. But I would like to finish with a reference to Western literature. Henry James, at the end of the 19th century, expected a long future for the novel on the grounds that there would always be areas of human life to explore. This is the most orthodox view of the novel: that of an extended prose, with a narrative nucleus with more or less relevance, exploring the world of human experience. Elements of form and language, in this view, are considered secondary and mostly identified with the concerns of poetry. It's only James Joyce who achieves a confluence between the novel and those concerns of poetry, though the price he pays may seem high to some: the almost-neglect of the narrative component, of the interest in a plot. Proust (among others), on the other hand, seems to have explored human experience in an unprecedented wide scope. But form is secondary for him, and his novel was accused of tedious excess to the point of shapelessness. The formal experiments of the likes of Queneau, Perec or Calvino, among others, regardless of how successful they are as literary achievements (and I value them highly), seem to fall short on that exploration of the human realm. We are still waiting for the novel combining all those elements: narrative interest, deep exploration of human experience and high concern for form and language, for multiple layers of meaning and esthetic complexity. Only that that novel of the future has already been written. By a woman, in Japan, a thousand years ago.

Note: This is what I wrote, in some sort of "English", in six hours of a Friday afternoon in May of 2003, locked in a room with a computer with no internet connection and with no smart phone but with several books, as the second set of my general exams en route to my PhD in comparative literature at Princeton University.

Hugo oulipien?

DAVID BELLOS

It seems insane at first blush to link Victor Hugo—that excessively fluent fount of Romantic self exposure (*Ah! Quand je vous parle de moi, je vous parle de vous!)*[1]—to the least Romantic of all literary movements. The purveyor of sonorous profundities and platitudinous piffle, the slapdash narrator of adventure stories like *Bug-Jargal*, the thundering orator and vitriolic campaigner against 'Napoléon Le Petit' seems the polar opposite of the witty inventors of arithmological alphabettery pursuing subtle junctions between mathematics and literature. In his pre-Oulipian youth, Georges Perec skewered the megalomania of Hugo's stated wish to be "Chateaubriand or nothing" with a culinary pun: *ambition bœuf.* All the same, when reflecting on his own career after the rapturous reception of *Life A User's Manual*, Perec came up with something that sounds very familiar to readers of Victor Hugo:

> My ambition as a writer would be to run through the
> whole gamut of the literature of my age without
> feeling I was going back on myself or treading ground I
> had trod before, and to write every kind of thing that
> it is possible for a man to write nowadays: big books
> and small ones, novels and poems, plays, libretti, crime
> fiction, adventure stories, science fiction, serials and

---

1   Victor Hugo, foreword to *Les Contemplations*, 1856. "Ah! When I tell you about me I am telling you about you!"

children's books . . .[2]

The fact is that the Perec's sole predecessor in this respect—the only writer who could be said to have actually done almost all of the things he set out to do—is Victor Hugo. That doesn't make Hugo an Oulipian, of course, but it makes Perec more Hugolian than he might have wanted to think. But besides this, there are deeper connections between them.

Life A User's Manual abolishes fictional chronology by situating its entire span within a split second, towards eight in the evening on June 23, 1975, when Percival Bartlebooth dies. Perec never made a secret of the fact that the date chosen for his novel commemorates a moment in his own life, his first dinner date with Catherine Binet, the woman who became his companion for the rest of his days. It's commonly assumed that this so-called 'fatidic self-inscription'[3] is also a homage to James Joyce's *Ulysses*, a novel set on a single day, June 16, 1904, when the writer spent his first night with Nora Barnacle. Indeed, Bloomsday is the only date in the 'Chronology' appended to *Life A User's Manual*[4] that is not related to a fictional or historical event mentioned in any of its ninety-nine chapters. But it's also something more than that.

In *Les Misérables*, Jean Valjean saves Marius Pontmercy from certain death at the barricades of June 6, 1832 by carrying him down a manhole and through the sewers. He returns the wounded young man to his grandfather and guardian, Luc-Esprit Gillenormand. As Marius slowly recovers health and common sense, Gillenormand is so moved to have his only descendant come back from the dead that he drops his previous opposition to Marius's politics and accepts his plan to marry Valjean's adopted daughter, Cosette. The wedding is fixed for February 16, 1833. And what date is that? It is the night when a prominent young playwright took a fancy to an actress during rehearsals. They spent that night

---

2   Georges Perec, *Thoughts of Sorts* (Godine, 2009),p. 4, from an article first published in 1978.

3   The term is most often associated with Vladimir Nabokov's, whose plays on the transition from 99 to 00 (for example, in *Pale Fire*) mark the strange fact that he was born in 1899 by the Russian calendar and in 1900 by the Western one.

4   See *Life A User's Manual*, Godine, 2009, p. 640.

together, "making love like animals". Juliette Drouët remained Hugo's acknowledged lover and companion for the rest of her days. The date-coded recording of an amorous milestone in fictional time doesn't begin with Perec or with James Joyce. It starts with Victor Hugo.

In *Les Misérables* the wedding of Marius and Cosette takes place on Shrove Tuesday, *mardi gras*, celebrated in Paris at that time by a street parade called the *promenade du boeuf gras.*[5] However, February 16, 1833 was not Shrove Tuesday. It wasn't even a Tuesday. This mismatch is often put about as an example of Hugo's disdain for mere facts. But it's easy to sneer if you don't know all the facts. The point is that *mardi gras* was Juliette's Drouët's favourite day of the year. The almost invisible clinamen that Hugo introduces in the wedding of Marius and Cosette therefore puts beloved Juliette into the text twice over. The fact that the calendar has to be altered slightly to make the two winks coincide suggests that this was a *calculated* homage, not a sloppy mistake.

For a nineteenth-century man of letters, Victor Hugo was unusually good with numbers—the family's household accounts give ample evidence of his accountancy skills. He also used numbers in self-symbolic ways. Where Perec made a myth out of the number '37'—being born on March 7, 1936, he worked out long before the event that he would turn 37 on 7-3-73, and therefore found that 37 chapters was what he needed to make *W or The Memory of Childhood* the *personal* memoir that it is—Hugo made equally elaborate use of key dates in his own life. Born on February 26, 1802 and told by his mother later on that he had arrived three or four weeks before term, Hugo reckoned his date of conception to have been June 24, 1801. In *Les Misérables*, Jean Valjean is sentenced to hard labour and on arrival at the *bagne de Toulon* he is given his prison number. It is 24601.

Georges Perec never knew the date of his mother's death, only the date she was deported from Drancy to Auschwitz: February 11, 1943. As

---

5   The *boeuf gras* parade of 1861, which took place a few weeks before Hugo wrote the closing chapters of *Les Misérables* at Mont Saint-Jean in Belgium, was in fact the last to be held.

Bernard Magné has shown, the numbers 11 and 43 are utilised, thematised, exploited and mythologised throughout Perec's work, from the heterogrammatical poetry of *Alphabets* (exhaustive recombinations of 11 x 11 letters) to the mysterious mistake in line 43 of the "Compendium" in Chapter 51 of *Life A User's Manual.*[6] Hugo's most shattering bereavement happened a century earlier, on September 4, 1843. His eldest daughter Léopoldine was caught in a freak squall when she was boating on the Seine, and drowned with her husband at the age of nineteen. In *Les Misérables*, Jean Valjean, who has become a prosperous factory owner and mayor of a small town, unmasks himself to save an innocent man from being sent to prison by mistake. He is sent down for life, and on his second arrival at the *bagne de Toulon* he is given a new prison number. It is 9430.

Are these numerical inscriptions of conception, bliss, and tragedy proto-Oulipian practices? Perhaps not exactly—but they have a strong echo in the literary practice of Ouipo's most celebrated member. However, what surely puts Victor Hugo among the contenders for the title of most distinguished anticipatory plagiarist is the *structure* of *Les Misérables.*

That must surely be the biggest surprise. Hugo's novel is famously long and full of notorious digressions on apparently random topics—slang, Waterloo, the treatment of sewage, the character of Louis-Philippe and what happened in 1817. Save for the time-worn thread of all realist fiction, the life-span of a single man, *structure* seems markedly absent from this almost absurdly compendious tale.

It is also true that Hugo had no structure plan to guide his massive work. No synopsis, sketch, plan of action or checklist of features has been found among his papers, and since he hung on to every scrap he ever daubed with ink, it's safe to say that Hugo never had a plan for *Les Misérables.* He wrote it as it came to him, in the most un-Oulipian way imaginable. Almost up to the last minute, moreover, this huge novel had

---

6   See Bernard Magné, *Pérécollages*, 1988.

no internal divisions. Even its final separation into parts was decided only after the first volumes had been set up in type. Every feature of its composition and design appear to be the antipodes of Oulipian conceptions of how a work of art is made. Except in one fundamental respect. *'Tout est voulu dans un chef d'œuvre'*, Hugo wrote in the introduction to his own son's translation of Shakespeare into French,[7] and as he was writing *Les Misérables* at the same time he was most probably also talking about himself.

The order that he imposed in the end on the mass of *Les Misérables* consists of a classical division into five Parts, each of which is split into Books—respectively, 8, 8, 8, 15 and 9, making 48, which surely marks the date of the event that split Hugo's life in two, the suppression of the riots of June 1848 (discussed at length in the opening pages of Part Five). Each book is further subdivided into chapters whose titles and divisions were made on the last state of the fair copy to be set in type. Here is how the numbers pan out:

Book	No. of chapters	Book	No. of chapters	Book	No. of chapters	Book	No. of chapters
I, 1	14	II, 5	10	IV, 1	6	IV, 13	3
I, 2	13	II, 6	11	IV, 2	4	1V, 14	7
I, 3	9	II, 7	8	IV, 3	8	IV, 15	4
1, 4	3	II, 8	9	IV, 4	2	V, 1	24
I, 5	13	III, 1	13	IV, 5	6	V, 2	6
I, 6	2	III, 2	8	IV, 6	3	V, 3	12
I, 7	11	III, 3	8	IV, 7	4	V, 4	1
1, 8	5	III1, 4	6	1V, 8	7	V, 5	8
II, 1	19	III, 5	6	IV, 9	3	V, 6	4
II, 2	3	III, 6	9	IV, 10	5	V, 7	2
II, 3	11	III, 7	5	IV, 11	6	V, 8	4
II, 4	5	III, 8	22	IV, 12	8	V, 9	6

Figure 1. The Chapters of *Les Misérables*

---

7   "Everything in a masterpiece is an act of the will", in *William Shakespeare*, quoted in Bernard Leuilliot, 'Présentation de Jean Valjean', in *Hommage à Victor Hugo*, Strasbourg, 1962, p. 57.

The blank row has been left for you to tot up the columns, and the last cell at the right can be used for the sum total. Now turn over.

*

*

As you now know (unless you have made a mistake),[8] the structure of Hugo's finished novel allocates one chapter to each of the 365 days that it takes the earth to complete a revolution around the sun. (If you count the one-paragraph *Avertissement* inserted before the start of Part I as a chapter-fragment, then the calculation even includes compensation for leap years.) It makes *Les Misérables* conform fully to Roubaud's First Axiom, that a work written according to a constraint speaks of that constraint. Hugo's novel is organised by the interplay of two distinct planetary motions, the earth's revolution on its own axis, and its revolution around the sun. How better could it assert that the meaning of *revolution* is at the heart of the work?

Only an irrational optimist could ascribe to chance, the unconscious, or turning tables thematic-structural mirroring on such a vast scale. It is surely planned—late on, perhaps, but by an act of the mind nonetheless. Amongst other things, the conjunction of two structural revolutions in the last page of the text underlies the sense of aesthetic plenitude that the reader of *Les Misérables* can hardly fail to register at the end:

> *La chose simplement d'elle-même arriva*
> *Comme la nuit se fait lorsque le jour s'en va*
>
> It came about simply, of itself
> As night follows when the day is ended[9]

These last lines of Valjean's epitaph on his gravestone in Père Lachaise match the cycle of a human life to the cycle of terrestrial rotation but also, by falling at the end of the 365th chapter, to the cycle of the seasons as well. But this pleasing fit records absence twice over. Not only is our

---

8   You would not be alone. Numbers as varied as 366, 360 and 375 can be found in pedagogical and scholarly works on Hugo.

9   Victor Hugo, *Les Misérables*, translated by Christine Donougher. London: Penguin, 2013, p. 1304.

hero Valjean departed, but the very lines by which he is to be remembered have been washed away by wind and rain.

The clausula of *Les Misérables* thus provides aesthetic satisfaction of the same order as the closing chapter of *Life A User's Manual*, doubly determined by the completion of a knight's tour (minus one) and the grid square coordinates on which it falls (row six, column one, manifested in the 61 unfinished jigsaws still on Bartlebooth's shelf). The logical necessity of all the features of that fabulous end chapter rest, like Hugo's ending, on the presence of an absence doubly marked in a man's death and in the insoluble conundrum of a last puzzle piece that doesn't fit the space remaining for it.

These remarks could be used to claim that Hugo is not as old-fashioned as he looks, or else that Perec is not as innovative as he seems. I would rather take them as further evidence that Oulipo's claim to pursue innovation in full partnership with the renewal of tradition is completely serious. We can see its unexpected realisation in the formal convergence of a great realist work of the nineteenth century and a monument of post-modern prose.

From Ennead

JEFF BURSEY

3.02.99

Notes on a plane. Yet one more plane. Even different models after some time are all alike. Tinned air. Poor food. Seat mates. Brassy attendants. Counting nuts and bolts fastening wing to body, coming to an odd number. Remember as a kid, in bad times, my brain used to repeat 1:2, 2:1, 2:1, 1:2. It didn't give comfort but order. Not a lot, not regularly. Some feeble neurotic defence against sadness and St. Pius X's barbarism in grades five to nine. All boys. Inadvertent good training for business. But not good for trust, or social skills around girls.

5.02.99

Any moment, due to turbulence, it'll be time to close my laptop. Difficult to type. My seat mate snores. Would a snore sound better if a nose was not a beak, eyes not piggy, knees not pudgy. I'm getting petty about a stranger. Reasons: in my job

10.02.99

Disgust, was it? And being tossed around in mid-air by a giant wind, so I closed off quickly. Does it matter, at day's end, to anyone? Just notes tapped in after reports are done, letters, expenses, contact numbers, minutes. My mind too tired to focus but not ready for sleep, so I write. To preserve a life outside promotion efficiencies, lateral connections, marketing, synergy, global product placement, web commerce and platforms. Doesn't make sense. I do it for myself. Can I really set down one profound statement? Cursor blinks away. Not a taunt. It's just generated by codes. Maybe read a book about – I am kidding myself. Fall last year was busy. Insane. Read a book in July. Magazines since. Profundity?

17.02.99

One more week and I'll be free from travel for a few weeks. My ass feels like a plane seat. Going to gyms and getting massaged in Deltas used to be a perk, or a luxury. No more. Not since New Year's Eve. Overdosed in time for 1999. Still need to do it, but I feel flaccid and puffy. My face looks drawn, as Mom would say. Does writing complaints do any good?

1.03.99

Mostly uneventful trip. But in economy is a woman from Carlyle. Don't see many from Bowmount or Carlyle. Noticeable accent. Looked a bit familiar. Made me recall dating. Last date? July, or August. Mercedes. Way beyond me, I was out of my league. Talked about living in Ecuador and Costa Rica, Sumatra, arduous work on local projects. Doing good works. I wanted a second date, just to see. No go. Ongoing loneliness removes possibility of taking pleasure from solitude. If I wasn't lonely

2.03.99

Up to now, I've written notes in airplanes only. I'm in a peculiar situation, for me. Woman from yesterday put me in it. I said a few words to someone and my accent was recognized. Introductions, but not of places. I'm from. And I'm from. Usually I'm in a bubble. No one knows me. I fly in, out, little trace except for a boarding pass. Could wallpaper a room using boarding passes. An original idea. My bubble disappeared. My fault. Rule one, never tell plane people about yourself. No point. Causes endless questions. In Ripton I didn't correct anyone over pronouncing my name as Prozzer instead of Prosser. Now a woman recognizes me from my dialect. Jesus. And worse, I'm writing about it all.

5.03.99

A client said to me: Travelling's great. You go from one exciting city to a second, staying in swanky places. Yes, it's lovely, I replied. Didn't say a word about carelessly cooked food, dislocation, being surrounded by civility and cordiality, and agonizing over tips. Pools, saunas and gym set-up bland in every place. A car service for Brossard Mauve picking me up in Toronto after I get back taking me to work.

Remember my boss, Ed, saying: You start in two weeks, it's going to be exciting. A lot of travel, long days, good pay. Great pay. Frantic. Buy a car, appliances, suits, any major component of your life pronto. You won't get an opportunity later. I spent a lot of money. Platinum card. Paid off quickly. Never got a car. No point. Train, subway, taxi, foot. Ordered magazines in order to get mail. I'll read it all one day. Buy books occasionally to take on a trip. Never do. Too many pages already.

No one ever waiting for me to return. I visited my cousin Sean in Mississauga. Stayed ten days. Went off on day excursions, and Sean's wife, Liz, sometimes came to see me off, kids in tow. All waved as my train pulled out. And if some pleasure is in me in recalling four sets of good-byes, it'd be good to feel it again. Kids called me a second daddy just because I was around. Didn't please Sean, always busy, yet it was cool between us. In Sean's case a wife is waiting, a family is waiting.

To a client, it won't matter.

Place myself in a larger context and my life is good. Don't live in central Africa, Bosnia, Burma, Tibet. No need to worry about money. I live outside Toronto so pay less for a place – a place I don't see often anyway. Saving money. For my early retirement. 1 million is my goal. No family of my own. Down a sink goes an unlived life.

12.03.99

I believe we could all be issued oxygen masks and a tank at take off, and feel better on arrival. Now I worry about blood clots, despite massages and working out. Don't drink any more. Try and avoid sauces and red meat. Often just eat salad and fruit, and noodles or pasta instead of bread. Never a roll or a bun. Seafood, but not in sauces. Trout and salmon, preferably. I'm 5'8" and 160 pounds. Young. And sexually frustrated. Unasked, an attendant gives me a pillow, and I wonder: Is a pillow a message? Lately, I see messages in all sorts of gestures, dropped words, but I know it's imaginary. No one's looking. I'm a quiet passenger in a conservative suit busy on a laptop. A guy. And women are women, or girls.

14.03.99

Some of my colleagues employ women. A woman – not a prostitute, but a professional type – is in, say, Jack's life from Friday evening to Monday morning. Jack's woman is named Tara or Greta or Simone. Occupation, weekend wife. Jack's not alone. Sonny, Gil, Masoud and Ivan are also taking comfort in a Tara. Recently a set of Russian names popped up. Tara cooks, cleans, spends time at a beautician's, reads, goes to art galleries Tuesday to Friday, back at Jack's apartment for opening of business. Lives in Jack's place, maybe, and is also independently living in an apartment. For Jack it means company in bed, but more so, company out on a Saturday and Sunday. Expensive company, but it's a decision made – a good lay isn't predominant, conversation and interest are, but if a good lay wasn't available, it would end.

I've got money. I know people. It's been a long time since I was sexually active. Over a year. It never occurs on a first date. And it can't just be because of sexual attraction. It used to be, in my late teens, not now. Too little time left me. Lovemaking means continuous talk, mutual interests, intimacy emotionally, not just fucking. So I feel now. But at 20? No.

No woman around. No desire for a weekend spouse. Besides, is Jack sure Tara isn't a weekday wife for a Carl or Ted, maybe, a parent and spouse, until Saturday and Sunday? Aside from not knowing, it's not a permanent state. I live in planes, in suites, eat buffet and visit floating bars. Impermanence galore. Jesus.

21.04.99

A nice break. Maid service cleaned my apartment. Rested a bit. Eyed maid. Travelling will slow down in a year, or so I'm told. Good business times – good money – and I'm stuck in it. Went round Toronto and asked myself a set of questions. No real answers. Timetable for getting out, craving for an acre or six of land, a wife, kids. I want certain elements in my life. No way to get beyond step one: a woman.

I noted I wrote Jesus in my last entry. Swearing or cursing is fine, but in a journal or a diary it seems unnecessary. Am I trying to impress myself by saying: If I feel a strong emotion, only a Jesus or fuck will get it across?

My posterity will contain swear words. My notes to a future self will contain swear words. J****.

25.04.99

Returning to Toronto I met, again, Carlyle Woman. Sitting in business, in opposite aisle seats, we talked about Carlyle, Bowmount, Crescent City. Guess career moves gave a boost to CW, as we met in economy – no. Wrong. We were getting off. I wait until almost everyone is gone. Luggage isn't going to be unloaded. So maybe CW was in business class before.

Nice to talk to CW. Accent aside, I've left Bowmount in my past. After entering Carlyle University I never saw anyone from grade 12. Everyone moved away, or failed. CW is doing fine, it seems. But no laptop, no briefcase. Maybe a spy from lower registers?

I don't often make jokes in writing. Not even in e-mail. Tone gets lost. Too many clients to piss off if a joke goes wrong. Maybe I'm not as funny as I was. Great. Great.

1.05.99

A stopover in Calgary. I prefer Edmonton due to my Oilers. Last time I saw a game was – it won't come to mind. After end of term I used to go to Leaf games, yell for opposing teams. Unless it was Montreal.

I sell meta-ideas. Client produces products or policy or lifestyle concept. Idea given form. An idea of mine, or a company idea, a team idea, sells X's new mousetrap. Am I a parasite? Could I generate an idea if X's product didn't exist? Create an idea devoid of consumerable significance, market surveys, public opinion. Good test.

8.05.99

I'm in a café in Ottawa, not wanting to be in our capital, but bumped from my connection due to Air Canada's error. I'm not alone. CW joined me for coffee. We met in line, two bumped passengers. Since our next planes don't take off until evening, we took a cab into town.

It's not a date. It's coincidence. Oddly, we aren't complete strangers. In 1989, me and my family were at a wedding – Peggy and Greg Merrick – and CW was a friend of Peggy's. Peggy died in a car accident. Greg knows CW. We probably met briefly, but we don't remember.

It feels peculiar. I feel peculiar. A seat mate you never see again. A plane mate? Less rare? No. But you don't talk to everyone. We talked twice, and we are now deliberately talking. We took a ride. It seemed like it needed to be written down, and quickly, before CW comes back.

9.05.99

Just past 1 a.m. On a plane to Vancouver. Spent a good afternoon in Ottawa. It looked better today. Still, too deep in a valley for me. Once I was introduced to a nosy woman, Elva or Rita. Elva quizzed me about Carlyle because of some family connection. I gave all kinds of information, and expected information in return. All I got was: I'm from Ottawa valley. No community, no town, just Ottawa valley. Puzzling. Rude. So Ontario.

Went off topic. I'm tired. Re-booked, re-routed, touristy day. CW and I visited a gallery, a museum, ate out. Remarkably easy to talk and reminisce. So, refer to CW as CW or as G, to give an initial? Point? We know we live outside Toronto. CW/G summers in Carlyle. Money in a family trust – but works for a union. Odds I'll see CW again are slim. It was a momentary diversion from travel. Boring, stupid travel, and tomorrow I'll wake up tired and run down in some room and say to myself: If I'd rented a room in Ottawa, slept, worked out, I'd feel better. I'll tell myself a story, one not including a 5'11" green-eyed composed yet passionate woman, red locks ending at mid-back. My story will begin tritely. Once upon a time.

11.05.99

I can be a real complainer.

17.05.99

All it requires is a delete command.

Late – but I return to a few days ago. Not obsessively, but it's interesting, I need to say, not obsessively. It was a break in my routine. Welcome, unexpected, nice. It can't be repeated. It was a fluke. Air Canada screws up regularly, but inconveniencing myself and G. again would test Air Canada's incompetence.

23.05.99

It's ridiculous. A client wants impossible items added to layout, design, text. Voice-over, too. Always, always, always adding at one minute to an opening or unveiling or broadcast. Impossible to convince Mr. Post not to substitute grey-tinged pink for blue, or pink-tinged grey, on posters, buses, display cases, and on t.v. ads.

I'm so mad I could quit now. Well, okay, not crazy mad. A friend of mind from Russia, Alex, used to say: I'm working like a crazy. So a normal trip to Calgary turns into triage. I was expecting routine. One or two next-to-last-minute nervous suggestions from Post, and cosmetic alterations, sure. We'd gone over every detail, Mr. Post and myself, and Jack too, sitting next to me and typing emergency copy. At least we can complain freely – no need to type in swear words.

30.05.99

I look at G.'s work address on a business card. I could mail a note.

Before boarding, I went to a store and got a tacky postcard featuring mountains and a river. It's in my jacket. I could mail it from New York. And consider possible responses. Or do I mean reverberations? I picture me in my office and a postcard in my mail, read by everyone from ground level to our secretaries and assistants and interns. My business known to strangers. Colleagues get curious. Ask questions. Speculate. Read into innocent scenery looking for significance.

I'm waiting for my plane to be cleaned. I could write a few words now. I put a stamp on a colourful card. One simple act almost done. My message could be about terminals. Boring, probably. I wonder if I lost my sense of fun recently. In unclaimed baggage. We talk about carrying baggage. Yet maybe unclaimed baggage exists, existentially, or mentally or emotionally. Waiting for us, no matter if we remember it. I wonder if all is mental, and if I was just being redundant or self-deceiving. Does it sit in empty areas, and would everyone's unclaimed baggage be tagged and separate? Sniffer dogs? Does my mind get rid of old or useless stuff like grievances, sorrow, recollections of missed opportunities, dead friends? Does it do security sweeps to make sure unsafe-looking pieces are disposed of carefully?

Procrastination.

A postcard invites frivolity, exaltations, endorsements. A small space for a public statement. I considered a careful message. And my reason for writing?

2.06.99

No good reason. Impulses? But I've written out a general note, mildly funny, subtly ironic, and now need to mail it. Of course, it's going to be mailed from an airport far away from mountains or rivers.

Off it went.

7.06.99

Yet again in an airport. But vacation is close. Built up overtime, too, and will actually use it. I'll leave Toronto by train and go some place in

Canada. No planes. No airline snacks. Nature. Outdoors. No computer. A canoe, a barbeque, a bicycle. Walking in forests on my own, away from being crowded. Early August. Working longer days for six more weeks.

14.06.99

A crisis at work derailed every work plan – trips, meetings, conferences, and more. Two managers fired for malfeasance and incompetence. Number two protected number one. We're in free fall now, but elevations will start very soon. Bradford Moore doesn't delay on flow efficiency in its operation. It may affect me come September after jockeying is over. Less travel? More money? More relaxed time? Friends and colleagues are positive about it all. Reasons? None. Beats feeling gloomy.

16.06.99

Mail for me, from G. A letter – a slip of paper in a small envelope, or so it looks. Unopened. Being saved for a non-work time.

On a plane, crossing your legs is almost a political act. My mate is an attractive skinny dyed blonde, 5'5", maybe, great legs. One more movement and I'd be in earnest conversation. So make a gesture and stop typing.

But no. A lay for a layover? It's not because I like being celibate, but I don't want to expend energy poorly. And G's letter magically – a word I never use, it just came to mind - grounds me in my seat. I could view it as being pinned. Wrong word. It's a letter, not a dart, not a claim on me. It could say: Buzz off. No, G'd be nicer. Polite. Cordial. Final, I imagine. Not fierce, but determined to –

Blondie looked at me, open-eyed and open-faced generally, asking for a magazine in front of me. An excuse to talk. Decolletage. A good bust. Skirt is revealing. Faint perfume, but quality. Eyes framed by sporty glasses. Crossed legs in my direction. I'm closing off.

20.06.99

Blondie started to drink more. Became snarky about our attendant, and service industry employees all over. Quite a body, but mean.

Nice – I say nice a lot. Also, tasty, but only about food. Do nice and tasty mean a little or a lot? Warm, tepid? Sloppy words. If I was listening to a commercial's words, and nice was used, I'd never buy X product. Nice is like mayonnaise, it's making a virtue of being inoffensive. I was told to be nice as a kid. Not told to be curious, or to be interested in justice, or to work on exterminating poverty. CW is nice, yes, but more, more. Blondie may be nice sober. G doesn't drink – I need to be consistent – and never did.

Mom's most lunatic sister, Eva, was a drinker. Told to cut down by Dr. Clow. Drank beer and tomato juice on top of medication. Aunt Eva pulled a knife on Mom one day, but never apologized. Mom, codependent maybe, used to say Eva wasn't to blame, it wasn't Eva really. Someone else? No, Frank, no one else. Aunt Eva's worst self? Yes, Mom said. So, really, it was Aunt Eva. A latent Aunt Eva.

All came back because of Blondie's nasty tongue. Yet an attractive tongue. We didn't connect. No point. I'd be fucking Aunt Eva in my mind, a revolting image. All drunk women are Eva.

And G's letter is in my breast pocket unopened. Five days. Nice woman. Did an envelope containing N work on me not taking advantage of an opportunity? But no, Blondie, anyone – it's too empty. My life is empty already.

22.06.99

My last sentence was wrong. G's letter certainly takes up space in me.

Vacation may be in mid-August, due to personnel problems. Two men gone originally, now two more. Deadwood, says Ed, my boss: Expensive deadwood. Ornamental deadwood, Ed added. People moving up. Me too, come late September, after everyone's back from vacation. We need new people, too.

Less travel?

I must make vacation plans. Easy to do. I'll camp in Dunderdale, most likely. Visit at end. Twenty-one days. Vacation time, and some overtime. By myself in a cabin, and take along some books. A portable radio. A rod.

Nice. Equals pleasant. But not mediocre. Sounds it. G isn't mediocre. Good letter. Encourages a reply. Tips me into revisiting Carlyle. But must get time to myself. See G in town. A treat, a break from solitude.

I need to write back. Can't say: Your letter got me to decide on X. If it fits, since we are freer in August, maybe we can meet in Carlyle.

Too formal. Too daffy. Too eager.

Stress I'll be spending time on my own, and would also like to see old places.

Blondie's beauty made me want to fuck. G's ways make me want to make love. Lame. Banal. Nice. Delete? I guess if I'm banal, it can't be a lie to say so.

I'll write back. I'll plan my trip first. Let me concentrate on work until mid-August.

It's absurd. I see G's face clearly. Blondie, seen only a few days ago, is becoming a generic blonde. Am I imagining a future built on looks, niceness and commonality? Add in my loneliness. A mirage. I must be careful. Relaxation is key. I'm stressed, overtired and overworked. I can respond to a simple letter in a simple way. No point going out on a limb. But risk is all I ever wanted to do, for love. I'll decide later about G. For now work, and make my plans. Write a plain letter back. See if G replies. Use my apartment address. If I make a mistake, well . . . well, I make a mistake.

Six Improbably Autobiographical Lists (Autobiography by Other Means)

PABLO M. RUIZ

Artists and writers named Ruiz (in approximate chronological order)

Juan Ruiz (Arcipreste de Hita, Spanish writer, late Middle Ages)
Felipe Ruiz (Spanish poet (Fray Luis composed a poem to him), 16th c.)
Juan Ruiz de Alarcón (Spanish writer, 16th-17th c.)
Hipólito Ruiz (Spanish botanist and travel reporter in Chile/Perú, 18th c.)
José Martínez Ruiz (Azorín, Spanish writer, 19th c.)
Pablo Ruiz (Picasso, Spanish painter, 20th c.)
Floreal Ruiz (Argentine tango singer and lyricist, 20th c.)
Raúl Ruiz (Chilean filmmaker, 20th c.)
Bernardo Ruiz (Mexican writer, 20th c.)
Fernando Ruiz (Mexican animation director, 20th c.)
Enrique Labrador Ruiz (Cuban writer, 20th c.)
Ana Ruiz (Mexican composer and improviser, 20th c.)
Adrian Ruiz (classical pianist from LA, Mexican descent, 20th-21st c.)
Hilton Ruiz (jazz pianist from NYC, Puerto Rican descent, 20th-21st c.)
Pablito Ruiz (Argentine pop singer, 20th-21st c.)
Alice Ruiz (Brazilian writer and translator, 21st c.)
Luis Manuel Ruiz (Spanish writer, 21st c.)
Florencia Ruiz (Argentine singer and songwriter, 21st c.)

Andrés Ruiz (Argentine singer and songwriter, 21st c.)
Agatha Ruiz de la Prada (Spanish designer, 21st c.)
Marina Ruiz (French soprano, 21st c.)
Roberto Ruiz (Argentine orchestra director, 21st c.)

*

Jewish writers and musicians (and several film directors); a selection

Franz Kafka
Paul Celan
Steve Lacy
Elias Canetti
Georges Perec
Clarice Lispector
Joseph Roth
Morton Feldman
György Ligeti
Bruno Schultz
J. D. Salinger
Isaac Singer
Juan Gelman
Charles Bernstein
Joseph Brodsky
Allen Ginsberg
Gertrude Stein
Alejandra Pizarnik
Jerome Rothenberg
Edmond Jabès
Louis Zukofsky
Denny Zeitlin
Maimónides
Benjamín de Tudela

Primo Levi
Carlo Levi
S. Y. Agnon
Woody Allen
Sergio Chejfec
Edgardo Cozarinsky
Romain Gary
Danilo Kis
Leo Perutz
Ellery Queen
Israel Zangwill
Marx brothers
Norman Mailer
Saul Bellow
Philip Roth
Irène Némirovsky
Alfred Döblin
Erich Auerbach
George Steiner
Walter Benjamin
Heinrich Heine
Serge Gainsbourg
Bob Dylan
Leonard Cohen
Paul Simon
Merrill Nisker (Peaches)
Hannah Arendt
Martha Argerich
Daniel Barenboim
Margo Glantz
Martín Kohan
Susan Sontag
Emma Goldman

Isaac Babel
Sigmund Freud
Hermann Broch
Stefan Zweig
Natalia Ginzburg
Nadezhda Mandelstam
Osip Mandelstam
Viktor Shklovsky
Yuri Tinianov
Alfred Schnittke
Roman Jakobson
George (& Ira) Gershwin
Tim Berne
John Zorn
Milton Babbitt
Aaron Copland
Steve Reich
Arnold Schoenberg
Italo Svevo
Alberto Moravia
Elsa Morante
Giorgio Bassani
Umberto Saba
Gustav Mahler
Arthur Schnitzler
Karl Kraus
Albert Einstein
Martin Buber
Karl Popper
Ludwig Wittgenstein
Emanuel Levinas
Arnaldo Momigliano
Attilio Momigliano

Felix Mendelssohn
Ernst Lubitsch
Beck
Lou Reed
Tristan Tzara
Marcel Proust
György Kurtág
Imre Kertesz
Alfred Kazin
Lee Konitz
Richard Rodgers
Lorenz Hart
Irving Berlin
Jerome Kern
Oscar Hammerstein
Harold Arlen
Stan Getz
Lalo Schifrin
Steve Kuhn
Joey Baron
Stanley Kubrick
Diego Rapoport
Leo Sujatovich
Harold Bloom
László Moholy-Nagy
Dave Liebman
Marcelo Cohen
Marcelo Moguilevsky
Meredith Monk
Osvaldo Golijov
Mauricio Kagel
Ana María Shua
Tamara Kamenszain

Moacyr Scliar
Jorge Isaacs
Pedro Henríquez Ureña
Jorge Drexler
Mario Davidovsky
Steve Grossman
José Kózer
Judith Malina
Theodor Adorno
Luisa Futoransky
Erwin Schulhoff
Arthur Waley
Roland Topor
Tomás Abraham
Eduardo Halfon
Zygmunt Bauman
Heda Margolius (Koch) Kovály
Roman Polanski
Raimundo Lida
María Rosa Lida
Marceline Loridan-Ivens
Izraíl Métter
Aleksander Wat
Fritz Mauthner
Marcel Schwob
Jacques Derrida
Yuri Norstein
Joel and Ethan Coen
László Nemes
István Szabó
Radu Mihaileanu
Jacobo Sefamí
Jacques Morelenbaum

Tal Wilkenfeld
Samuel Rawet
Meir Shalev
Josefina Ludmer
Myriam Moscona
Mario Goloboff
Alberto Szpungberg
Laura Wittner
Georges (György) Mikes
Antal Szerb
Zsuzsanna Ozsvath
Jacques Fux
Brian Janchez
Jerry Goldsmith
Dziga Vértov
Mijaíll Kaufman
Marcella Olschki
Mariano Siskind
Gisela Heffes
Cecilia Szperling
Ernesto Semán
Andrea Rabih
Eduardo Rubinschik
Humberto Costantini
Joyce Borenstein
Jules Engel
Maurice Sendak
Regina Spektor
Amy Winehouse
Joseph Heller
Stanislaw Lem
Bernard Malamud
E. L. Doctorow

Melisa Liebenthal
Craig Dworkin
Damián Tabarovsky
Aníbal Jarkowski
Ariana Harwicz
Oliver Sacks
Alberto Manguel
Eugene Ostashevsky
Isak Samokovlija
Peter Bernstein
Stefan Wolpe
Chaya Czernowin
Aby Warburg
León Dujovne
Mónica Lavín
Ari Lieberman
Rachel Galvin
Ilan Stavans
Saúl Sosnowski
Luis Rubistein
Isaco Abitbol
Ben Molar
Andrés Boiarsky
Gustavo Beytelmann
Federico Veiroj
Fabián Bielinsky
Martín Rejtman
Gastón Solniki
Ariel Winograd
Fred Hersch
Kurt Weill
Bob Berg
Randy Brecker

Michael Brecker
Danny Gottlieb
Uri Caine
Héctor Babenco
Gabriel Lichtman
Tommy Gubitsch
Sol Liebeskind
Tom Stoppard
Mark Feldman
Erik Friedlander
Ned Rothenberg
Marty Ehrlich
Michael Formanek
Adrián Iaies
Cecilia Absatz
Bernardo Kordon
Germán Rozenmacher
Alberto Gerchunoff
Osvaldo Dragún
Samuel Eichelbaum
Angelina Muñiz-Huberman
Boris Pasternak
Arturo Ripstein
Nelly Sachs
Leonid Shvartsman
Felix Kandel
Iosif Boyarsky
Pablo Alabarcés
Ágnes Heller
Leopold Auer
Zinaida and Valentina Brumberg
Simón Feldman
Carlo Ginzburg

Eduardo "Tato" Pavlovsky
Cynthia Ozick
Art Spiegelman
Georges Wolinski
Gotlib (Marcel Gotlieb)
Neil Gaiman
Rafael Cansinos Assens
Néstor Perlongher
Will Eisner
Harvey Kurtzman
Jerry Siegel
David Mamet
Benny Goodman
Aharon Appelfeld
Nadine Gordimer
Yuri Lotman
Karel Poláček
Jack Kirby (Jacob Kurtzberg)
David Cronenberg
Noé Jitrik
Rafael Spregelburd
Daniel Link
Angélica Gorodischer
Daniel Guebel
Arkady y Boris Strugatsky
George Cukor
Ernst Lubitsch
Mel Brooks
Liliana Lukin
Carlos Grünberg
César Tiempo (Israel Zeitlin)
Andrés Rivera (Marcos Ribak)
Liliana Heker

Pedro Orgambide
Héctor Yánover
Cynthia Lejbowicz
Chaim N. Bialik
Bernardo Baraj
Fabián Polosecki
Diego Frenkel
Ignacio Varchausky
Isidoro Blaisten
Israel Adrián Caetano
Alicia Dujovne Ortiz
Alicia Steimberg
Elena Poniatowska
Jacobo Fijman
Andrea Jeftanovic
Paul Lehrman
Eliot Weinberger
Robert Pinsky
Arthur Miller
Lionel Trilling
George Oppen
Alfred Kazin
Daniel Freidemberg
Jorge Fondebrider
Alain de Botton
Ernst Gombrich
Stephen Fry
Isaac D'Israeli
Arthur Koestler
Adam Thirlwel
Pablo Martín Ruiz (Gurovich)
Harold Pinter
Muriel Spark

Al Alvarez
Ian Buruma
Andrés Neuman
Martha Nussbaum
Isaac Asimov
Joey Ramone
Paul Auster
Harold Brodkey
Vera Caspary
Michael Chabon
Nathan Englander
Jonathan Safran Foer
Jonathan Lethem
David Leavitt
Melina Dorfman
Delfina Korn
Bob Perelman
Kenneth Koch
Ammiel Alcalay
Etgar Keret
Amos Oz
Kathy Acker
Robert Fitterman
Felix Bernstein
Adam Gopnik
Francisco Goldman
Borah Bergman
Boris Kaufman
Albert Cohen
Patrick Modiano
Carlos Ginzburg
Fernando Fiszbein
Nicolas Guerschberg

Alejandro Guerschberg
Fernando Daniel Stern Britzmann (Nano Stern)
Melina Moguilevsky
Ralph Bakshi
Jack Hirschman
Armand Schwerner
Fabio Doctorovich
Hugo von Hofmannsthal
Peter Altenberg
David Grossman
Richard Teitelbaum
Philip Gourevitch
Georges Didi-Huberman
Daniel Mendelsohn
Mariana Milstein
Else Lasker-Schüler
Sarah Kirsch (Ingrid Bernstein)
Franz Werfel
Kurt Tucholsky
M. H. Abrams
Jerry Lewis (Joseph Levitch)
Simja Sneh
Eduardo Zvetelman
David Krakauer
Mickey Katz
Ziggy Elman (Harry Aaron Finkelman)
Paul Zukofsky
Pablo Aslan
Ernest Bloch
Philip Glass
Darius Milhaud
Jorge Perednik
Otto Klemperer

Bruno Walter (Schlesinger)
Arthur Berger
Raymond Federman
Davis Schneiderman
Lidia Yuknavitch
Alejo Moguillansky
Sara Cohen
Judith Akoschky
Oscar Steimberg
Marti Epstein
Ben Goldberg
Ernesto Snajer
Leo Bernstein
Tulio Halperín Donghi
Rodolfo Mondolfo
Tom Lehrer
Pedro Memelsdorff
Claudio Lomnitz
Judith Butler
Eric Hobsbawm
Howard Zinn
Noam Chomsky
Charles Reznikoff
Carl Rakosi
Mario Castelnuovo-Tedesco
Salomone Rossi
C. K. Williams
Peter Lieberson
Sergio Rotman
Mezz Mezzrow (Milton Mesirow)
Jean Starobinski
Benjamín Stein
Yaki Setton

Roberto Jacoby
Simone Weil
David Friedman
Arthur Rosenblat Nestrovski
Ben Lerner
Peter Cole
Irene Gruss
Jerry Seinfeld
Sergio Mihanovich
Erich Korngold
Boris Groys
Leonardo Tarán
Enrique "Zurdo" Roizner
Henri Bergson
Ira Sachs
Edwin Honig
Alan Berliner
Paul Tabori
George Tabori
Ruth Zylberman
Cynthia Rimsky
Sarah Kofman
Sylvère Lotringer
Chris Kraus
Howard Jacobson
Norman Manea
Max Blecher
Eduardo Ainbinder
Chantal Akerman
Gustav Meyrink (Gustav Meyer)
Alina Bronsky
Rebecca Solnit
León Trotsky

Grace Paley (Goodside)
Ada María Elflein
Mónica Szurmuk
Samanta Schweblin

*

A few words or expressions that are common in (American) English and somewhat difficult to translate into Spanish

Awkward	Ride (noun; to give a ride to someone)	Commute
Fun		Date, dating
Excited, exciting	Clueless	Lazy
Dysfunctional	Creepy	Cute
Hectic	Point (as in "that's a good point")	Entitled
Busy (as in "busy week")		Soul searching
	Spooky	Embarrassing, embarrassed
Bias, biased	Issue (as in "to have issues")	
Random		Accomplished
To look/looking forward	To cope	Momentum
	Out there	Make a difference
Pattern	Tricky	Tart (adj.; flavor)
Approach	Quality time	Ingrained
Flaky	Deadline	Lame

*

Names consisting of the duplication of a name

Baden Baden (city in Germany)
Bora Bora (Pacific island)
Los Tucu Tucu (Argentine folkloric music group)

Juan y Juan (Argentine musical duet)
Los Van Van (Cuban musical group)
Tsé-Tsé (fly, literary magazine)

Mau Mau (dance club in BsAs; antiimperialist militia in Kenya)

Chan Chan (Peruvian cuisine restaurante; archeological site in Perú; Cuban song)

Soco Soco (literary magazine from Córdioba, Argentina)

Flota Flota (floating plastic implement)

Liber y Liber (bar)

Cous cous (Maghrebi dish)

Sur y Sur (Latin American web portal)

Pago Pago (capital city of Samoa)

Llao Llao (hotel in Bariloche, Argentina)

Cümen Cümen (*empanadas* place)

Tacu tacu (Peruvian dish)

Hula hula (dance; game)

Alegría alegría (song by Caetano Veloso; book by Caetano and Waly Salomao)

London London (song by Caetano Veloso)

Pop Pop (Rickie Lee Jones's album)

Cuchi Cuchi (restaurant/bar in Cambridge, MA)

Boogie boogie (rhythm and dance)

Bunga bunga (Berlusconi's parties)

Sau sau (Easter Island traditional dance)

Bang Bang (song)

Humbert Humbert (character in

Boing Boing (web page)

Veo veo (children's game)

Panorámica Panorámica (all-girls rock band from Argentina)

Tunga tunga (musical rhythm from Córdoba, Argentina)

Rongo Rongo (undeciphered script from Easter Island)

Faber and Faber (publishing house)

Talk Talk (pop/post-rock English band)

Wala Wala (town in Washington State)

Miu Miu (clothing brand)

Scotus Eriugena (medieval philosopher; his name means "Irish Irish")

Bam Bam (song; American pop band)

Olsen Olsen (song by Sigur Ros)

Nineteen Nineteen (novel by John dos Passos)

Duran Duran (rock band)

Pum Pum (graffiti artist from Buenos Aires)

Sri Sri (song by the French band Madrid)

El Noa Noa (song by Mexican singer Juan Gabriel)

Absalom, Absalom! (novel by William Faulkner)

Track track (song by Fito Páez)

Sing Sing (prison in NY State)

Nabokov's *Lolita*)
Uai Uai (song by Tom Zé)
Yira Yira (tango by Discépolo)
Bura Bura (Masahiko Togashi's album, with Steve Lacy, Don Cherry & Dave Holland)
Pica pica (card game in Argentina)
Chipi chipi (song by Charly García)
Iguana, iguana (poetry book by Arnaldo Calveyra)
Jamón, jamón (movie by Pedro Almodóvar)
Arf! Arf! (recording label)
Louie Louie (song by Richard Berry)
Claridad, claridad (album and song by Laura Crespi)
Buró Buró (Spanish publishing house)
Miau Miau (art gallery in BsAs)
Roger Roger (French musician)
Tiki tiki (certain elegant soccer style)
Tom Tom (GPS brand name)
Bío Bío (river and province in Chile)
Europe, Europe (travel book by H. M. Enzensberger)
War and War (novel by László Krasznahorkai)
Paka Paka (children's TV channel in Argentina)
Boeing Boeing (play by French author Marc Camoletti; American

Winter & Winter (recording label)
Freak freak (song by Argentine band Fricción)
Beep beep (second episode of the cartoon with Coyote and Roadrunner)
Noa Noa (journal by Paul Gauguin; Brazilian publishing house)
María, María (song Milton Nascimento)
New York, New York (song)
Cucala, Cucala (song by Ismael Rivera)
Tico! Tico! (album and song by Paquito D'Rivera)
Quemú Quemú (county in the province of La Pampa, Argentina)
Lookie Lookie (song by Ricardo Ray; Afrocuban band from the US)
Holland & Holland (clothing brand)
Mahi mahi (fish)
Porro & Porro (clothing brand)
Colo Colo (Mapuche chieftain and Chilean soccer team)
The Good Good (cocktail)
Villa Villa (album by De La Guarda)
Cara cara (song by Chico Buarque)
Você, você (song by Chico Buarque)
Sipe-Sipe (battle for Argentine independence)
Cucha Cucha (battle, street in BsAs, etc.)
Volga, Volga (novel by Bosnian

movie based on that play)
Ong Ong (song by Blur)
Gus Gus (band from Iceland)
Taka Taka (game with two balls and a thread)
Rebel Rebel (song by Bowie)
Yin Yin (book by Gabriela Mistral about his adoptive son)
Wha Wha (city and soccer team in Zimbabwe)
Dik Dik (Italian pop band)
Muña Muña (grocery store in San Miguel de Tucumán)
Arranca, arranca (song by Violeta Parra)
Dinorah, Dinorah (song by Iván Lins)
AA (*bandoneón* maker)
Fernández y Fernández (old name of restaurant El Globo in Buenos Aires)
Pity Pity (album and song by Paul Anka; Spanish version by Billy Cafaro)
Soñar, soñar (film by Leonardo Favio)
Years & Years (electro-pop English band)
Tian Tian (Panda bear in the Washington DC zoo)
Chitty Chitty Bang Bang (book by Ian Fleming and film with Dick Van Dyke)

Miljenko Jergović)
José José (Mexican singer)
Of course, of course (composition by sax player Charles Lloyd)
Asa, asa (song by Caetano Veloso)
Marí Marí (*comparsa* in Gualeguaychú carnival)
Uma-Uma (work by Héctor Oesterheld)
Belle-Belle (French fairy tale)
Mirror Mirror (film with Julia Roberts; Star Trek episode)
Walther und Walther (German publisher)
Cau Cau (river in Chile)
Alan Alan (British magician)
Django Django (English rock band)
Pim Pim (Paraguayan folklorical rhythm)
Quena Quena (kind of *colla* warrior dance)
Grimes! Grimes! (song in the opera *Peter Grimes* by B. Britten)
Anaïs Anaïs (Cacharel perfume)
Menu, menu (children story by Jacques Roubaud)
Andy Andy (Dominican bachata musician)
Chop Chop (family cooking magazine, USA)
Clicky Clicky (blog about music)
Chiku Chiku (composition by Paulo Moura)

Springfield, Springfield (song in the Simpsons' episode "Boy-Scoutz 'n the Hood")

¡Bernabé, Bernabé! (novel by Uruguayan Tomás de Mattos)

Glory Glory (song by Mickey Newbury)

Merica, Merica (song by Caetano Veloso)

Dolan & Dolan (law firm in Massachusetts)

Peck & Peck (clothing for women)

Vil & Vil (novel by Juan Filloy)

Chucu-Chucu (musical rhythm from Medellín)

Gelem Gelem (international Gipsy anthem)

Haidar Haidar (Syrian novelist)

Cero Cero (bar in Jardín, Antioquia, Colombia)

Graver & Graver (American publisher)

Chin Chin (Argentine independent publisher)

Cha Cha (composition by Leonard Bernstein)

Kon Kon (restaurant in Buenos Aires)

Translation Translation (lbook about translation edited by Susan Petrilli)

Berlin! Berlin! (book by Kurt Tucholsky, English edition)

Choo-Choo (Russian animation film by G. Bardin)

Perón Perón (resto-bar in Buenos Aires)

Emery Emery (American comedian)

Bam-Bam (Flintstones character)

Etcetera Etcetera (restaurant in NYC)

Zoo Zoo (cartoon cat by George Herriman)

Up & Up (song by Coldplay; bar in NYC)

Title Title (piece by Meredith Monk)

Walsh & Walsh (law firm in Somerville, MA)

Meow Meow (Australian cabaret artist)

Vhd Vhd (character in a story by Calvino)

She Said, She Said (song by The Beatles)

Lawyer Lawyer (English name of a Chinese film by Joe Ma; original title is different)

Clap! Clap! (Italian DJ and producer)

Coqui Coqui (hotel in Tulum, Mexico)

Salgán & Salgán (documentary by Caroline Neal about Argentine musician Horacio Salgán)

Mushi Mushi (Uruguayan

Mariel Mariel (Chilean singer)
Song-Song (composition by Brad Mehldau)
The The (English band from the '80s)
Piri Piri (spicy sauce)
Mara-Mara (Basque family advocacy organization)
Cerveza, cerveza (song performed by Peruvian girl Wendy Sulca)
Speech! Speech! (book by English poet Geoffrey Hill)
Edwards & Edwards (poetry publisher from Argentina)
Cache cache (hide and seek in French)
Rosa, Rosa (song by Sandro)
Yepa, Yepa (taco place in Friburg, Germany)
Chis Chis (lake in the province of Bs.As.)
Fetén Fetén (Spanish musical duo)
El Toque Toque (children's music ensemble)
Gris-Gris (American magazine about arts and literature)
Treinta, treinta (short story by Dalmiro Sáenz)
Kill Kill (song by Lana del Rey)
Shuz – Shuz (objects store in Bogotá, Colombia)
orchestra)
Chame-Chame (neighborhood in Salvador, Bahia, Brazil)
Boogety Boogety (composition by Kenny Garrett)
Natalia Natalia (character performed by Argentine TV comedian Juan Carlos Araujo)
Pavo Pavo (band from Brooklyn)
Knock Knock (film by Eli Roth)
Toc Toc (play by Laurent Baffie)
Plin Plin (Argentine clown)
Jai & Jai (art gallery in Los Angeles)
Pasando y pasando (book by Vicente Huidobro)
Nueva Nueva (poem and book by Raúl Zurita)
Good Morning, Good Morning (song by The Beatles)
Star Star (song by The Rolling Stones)
Los galgos, los galgos (novel by Sara Gallardo)
I and I (song by Bob Dylan)
Bye and Bye (song by Bob Dylan)
Dead Man, Dead Man (song by Bob Dylan)
Ushpa Ushpa (department in Cochabamba, Bolivia)

*

Musicians, bands and performers I saw live; composers whose music I heard live; other styles of music I heard live

Spinetta Piazzolla Marta Argerich Cuchi Leguizamón Salgán y De Lío Nelly Omar Pedro Aznar Alfombra Mágica Polaco Goyeneche Dino Saluzzi Puente Celeste Fernando Cabrera Naná Vasconcelos Jaime Roos Jorge Dalto Rodolfo Mederos Litto Nebbia Manolo Juárez Raúl Carnota Vitale – Cumbo – González Juana Molina Rubén Rada Ernesto Jodos Carlos Lastra Horacio Larumbe Hugo Fattorusso Osvaldo Fattorusso Diego Schissi Quinteto Hermeto Pascoal Egberto Gismonti Pat Metheny Group Keith Jarrett Trio Herbie Hancock Miles Davis Tribute (Hancock, Ron Carter, Tony Williams, Wayne Shorter, Roy Hargrove) Zawinul Ravi Shankar Anoushka Shankar Zakir Houssain Django Bates Gerry Mulligan John Scofield Chick Corea Kenny Burrell Mike Stern John McLaughlin Michael Brecker Paco de Lucía Wayne Shorter Brad Mehldau Bill Frisell Evan Parker Peter Brötzman Steve Lacy Cecil Taylor Derek Bailey John Zorn William Parker Joe Lovano Paquito de Rivera Ignacio Berroa Tim Berne Fred Frith Louis Sclavis Marc Ducret Thomas Lehn & Gerry Hemingway Steve Swallow Carla Bley Ran Blake Lê Quan Ninh Scott Henderson Gary Burton Chucho Valdés Bebo Valdés Diego el Cigala El Gran Combo de Puerto Rico Leny Andrade George Benson Al Jarreau Allan Holdsworth Dave Holland Modern Jazz Quartet Aretha Franklin Axel Dörner Mika Vainio Lucio Capece Gustavo Nasuti Tomatito Michel Camilo Ana Moura Don Byron Meredith Monk Arto Lindsay Bang on a Can Geri Allen Susan Howe & David Grubbs Dave Liebman & Marc Copland Danilo Pérez Femi Kuti Reco do Bandolim e Choro Vivo Dennis Chambers Paul Lytton Charles Lloyd Chris Potter Julian Lage Caetano Veloso João Gilberto Djavan Gal Costa Gilberto Gil Elba Ramalho Marisa Monte Chico Buarque Iván Lins Rubén Blades Vinicius Cantuaria Tricky Joanna Newsom Sonic Youth Laurie Anderson Sting Joni Mitchell Paul Simon Rickie Lee Jones Bob Dylan Beck Björk Peter Gabriel Sixto Rodríguez Manhattan Transfer Cat Power Wilco Depeche Mode Buke and Gase Hopkinson Smith Alicia de Larrocha Cuarteto Arditti Ensemble Intercontemporain Horacio Lavandera Ivo Pogorelich Itzhak Perlman Johnny Gandelsman Bach Mozart Beethoven

Brahms Ligeti Pierre Boulez John Cage Edgar Varèse John Dowland Palestrina Monteverdi Haendel Steve Reich Stravinsky Bartok Messiaen Scriabin Haydn Debussy Ravel Chopin Liszt Scarlatti Vivaldi Rameau Poulenc Schumann Schubert Stockhausen Kurtag Dutilleux Ginastera Villa Lobos Mario Davidovsky Morton Feldman Luigi Nono Julián Carrillo Gagaku (plus performances of bunraku, noh, kabuki) Gamelan Shakuhachi Musics from India (plus kathak, bharatanatyam, odissi dances) Chinese Opera Music from Mali Fado Flamenco Gospel Traditional Vietnamese music Traditional Persian music Brazilian Chorok

*

Novels, memoirs, poetry collections, songs, sculptures, etc., named "Tango something" (which are not tangos, or Argentine, or Uruguayan, and in which "tango" tends to be some sort of metaphor)

Satantango. Laszlo Krasznahorkai (1985)

¿Tango?. Conlon Nancarrow (1983)

Tango. Zbigniew Rybczynski (1981)

Tango. Sławomir Mrożek (1964)

Finski tango. Bosko Velimirovic (2015)

The Beauty of the Husband: A Fictional Essay in 29 Tangos. Anne Carson (2001)

Last Tango in Paris. Bertolucci (1972)

Poslednji tango u Kraljevu. Jasmina Ana (2014)

Indian Tango. Ananda Devi (2007)

Tango alemán. Mauricio Kagel (1978)

"Tango del viudo". Pablo Neruda (1927)

"It Tango". Laurie Anderson (1982)

"Tango". Elie Nadelman (1920-22)

"Tango". Martin Puryear (1982)

"Tango". David C. Roy (1996)

Le tango (perpétuel). Erik Satie (1914)

Perpetual Tango. John Cage (1984)

Tango: Poems. Daniel Halpern (1987)

Tango: historisk roman. Arvid Rundberg (1993)
Tango: My Childhood Backwards and in High Heels. Justin Bond (2011)
Tango. Georgi Karaslavov (1948)
Tango. Bernard Caleo (1997-2009)
Mandrake Tango. Liz Rideal (2003)
One Man Tango. Anthony Quinn (1997)
ZHizn' kak tango. Valeri Rokotov (2003)
The Two-Bit Tango. Elizabeth Pincus (1992)
Whiskey Tango Foxtrot. Glenn Ficarra and John Requa (2016)
Tango für Irma. Stefan Wolpe (1927)
Be-Bop Tango (of the old jazz-men's church). Frank Zappa (1972)
Tango Alpha Tango. Album and rock band from Portland, Oregon (2011)
Holy Tango of Literature. Francis Heaney (2004)
"Tango". Louise Glück (1981)
"Tango Bittersweet". Fred Hersch (2006)
Tango con vacas. Vasily Kamensky (1914)
"Tangoul Mortii". Paul Celan "Todesfuge" (c.1945)
"The Tango". Aleister Crowley (1913)
The Tango. Leslie Scalapino and Marina Adams (2001)
"Tango de Montréal". Gérald Godin (1983)
Naked Tango. Svetozar Ivanov (2008)
Naked Tango (After Warhol). Guillermo Kuitca (1994)
"Vesenneye tango". Valeri Milyayev (1973)
Knife Edge & Absinthe—The Tango Poems. Lyn Lifshin (2012)
T.A.N.G.O. Exhibit at the museum in Cluj-Napoca, Rumania (2015)
"Tango". Greg Smith (2007)
Tango: Poems in Prose. Vasa Mihailovich (2004)
Waiting to Tango. Victor Tapner (2015)
Blood Opera: The Raven Tango Poems. Jannie Edwards (2006)
"Tango". Bill Berkson (2006)
"The Tango of Paula Sola". Nicole Brossard (s.d.)
"The Introjection Tango". Ben Yarmolinsky, Charles Bernstein (1991)
Pago Pago Tango. John Enright (2012)

Tiny Tango. Judith Moffett (1987)
Blue Tango: Poems. Michael Van Walleghen (1989)
All-Night Lingo Tango. Barbara L. Hamby (2009)
"Two to Tango". Ciaran Carson (1994)
The Silent Tango of Dreams. Stephen Anderson (2006)
Tango Baboons. Bosse Hellsten (2005)
"Tango". Moishe Broderson (s.d., WWII)
"Yiddish tango". Ruven Tsarfat (s.d., WWII)
"Anna's Tango". Chick Corea (2005)
Midnight Taxi Tango. Daniel José Older (2016)
Shanghai Tango. Pseudonym, contemporary Chinese artist
Shanghai Tango. William Overgard (1987)
Shanghai Tango. Jin Xing (2007)
Tango Berlin. Kurt Bartsch (2010)

A Seedbed, A Grimace, A Carnival: Anticipatory Blurbs

LOUIS BURY

Oulipo was—is—a seedbed, a grimace, a carnival. [*Oulipo Compendium*] is an indispensable book for everyone who cares about literature. — **Susan Sontag**

You can discover more about a person in an hour of play than in a year of conversation. Fifty-plus years after its inception, Oulipo continues to show us how life must be lived as serious play.

—Plato

Quality is not an act, but a habit, and the parergonal delights of *Oulipo Compendium* evince the kind of literary habits that consistently produce the quality of genius.

— Aristotle

The lyf so short, the craft so longe to lerne.

— Geoffrey Chaucer

In order to attain the impossible, Oulipo attempts the absurd.

— Miguel de Cervantes

It is good to rub and polish our brain against those of the Oulipians.

— Michel de Montaigne

We know what we are, but know not what we may be, 'cept when we explore potentiality.

— William Shakespeare

Better to reign in hell than serve in heaven.

—John Milton

Oulipo Compendium constitutes the most passionate orgy within man's grasp.

—John Donne

If what Oulipo does proves well, it won't advance./ They'll say it's stolen, or else it was by chance.

— Anne Bradstreet

Order is heaven's first law and this book is positively divine.

— Alexander Pope

In truth the prison, unto which we doom/ ourselves, no prison is: and hence for me,/ in sundry moods, 'twas pastime to be bound/ within Oulipo's scanty plot of ground.

— William Wordsworth

If I loved the *Oulipo Compendium* less, I might be able to talk about it more.

—Jane Austen

Talent hits a target no one else can hit; genius hits a target no one else can see. Buy this book and scry your own dark bulls-eye.

— Arthur Schopenhauer

I celebrate Oulipo, and sing Oulipo,/ and what Oulipo assumes you shall assume,/ For every atom belonging to Oulipo as good belongs to you.

— Walt Whitman

Oulipo dwells in possibility — A fairer house than prose.

— Emily Dickinson

A super-human achievement . . . Editors Harry Mathews and Alistair Brotchie say in ten sentences what everyone else says in a book, what everyone else does not say in a book.

— Friedrich Nietzsche

Oulipo is a premise whose thousand-year conclusion no one has yet dared to draw.

— Oswald Spengler

If the voyage of discovery consists not in seeking new landscapes but in having new eyes, then Oulipians are arthropods among us.

— Marcel Proust

Most people do not really want freedom, because freedom involves responsibility, and most people are frightened of responsibility. Use this book responsibly.

— Sigmund Freud

A rose is a rose is a rose is a rose.

— Gertrude Stein

Oulipo Compendium is a crimson flag flapping from the castle tower, a cavalcade of red knights riding up the side of a black rock, wine upon the universe's lips.

— Virginia Woolf

An axe for the frozen sea within us.

— Franz Kafka

I have always imagined that Paradise will be an Oulipian library. Welcome, reader, to Paradise.

—Jorge Luis Borges

Oulipo, Foulipo, Noulipo:
The Gendered Politics of Literary Constraints

MICHAEL LEONG

I.

The Oulipo, short for the *Ouvroir de littérature potentielle* (Workshop for Potential Literature), was founded in Paris in 1960 by two polymaths: Raymond Queneau, a former surrealist known for writing *Zazie in the Metro*, and François Le Lionnais, a mathematician, engineer, and member of the French Resistance who, in 1944-5, was a prisoner of the Dora-Mittelbau concentration camp. Interdisciplinary in nature, the Oulipo came to embrace a rigorous formalism, insisting that literary freedom could be unleashed not through the energies of chance, the unconscious, or automatic writing (à la surrealism) but, paradoxically, through rule-bound procedures and mathematical constraints. Oulipians follow the elegant strategizing of Daedalus and Ariadne rather than the irrational urges of the Minotaur; as Queneau famously said, they are "rats who construct the labyrinth from which they plan to escape."

To many, the Oulipo and its most well-known writers represent a certain moment of postwar experimentalism or neo-avant-gardism that witnessed such inventive works as *Exercises in Style* and *One Hundred*

Thousand Billion Poems by Queneau, *A Void* and *Life A User's Manual* by Georges Perec, and *Invisible Cities* and *If on a Winter's Night a Traveler* by Italo Calvino. These works, playfully animated by combinatorial, metafictional, and procedural impulses, highlight a systematized process of composition and emphasize the active role of the reader in creating meaning. *A Void,* for example, (*La Disparition* in the original French) is a lipogrammatic novel that doesn't contain the letter "e" while *One Hundred Thousand Billion Poems* is a series of ten sonnets, which —because all of the lines (composed with identical rhyme and meter) are supposed to be cut into discrete strips—can be shuffled and recombined to create one hundred trillion potential poems. In its mischievous understanding of intertextuality (and here we can think of Harry Mathews' "35 Variations on a Theme from Shakespeare": *To be or not to be: that's the problem, Nothing* and *something: this was an answer, Choosing between life and death confuses me . . .*), the Oulipo sought to reveal the potentiality of tradition open for re-elaboration by a collective talent.[1]

Now that the early masterpieces of the Oulipo have, in turn, been canonized within the Western literary tradition, both North American supporters and detractors alike continue to misrepresent the complicated and ongoing legacy of the movement. Many think, for example, of the Oulipo in the past tense. "Those dudes were the bomb," say the editors of the literary journal *Anomalous* in their 2015 special issue on constraint. For Kenneth Goldsmith, the Oulipo is "dated" and any present consideration of its work would be necessarily "washed in nostalgia."[2] The Oulipo, far from being a relic of literary history, remains active as a collective and continues to recruit new members; it elected the Argentine writer Eduardo Berti and the Spanish writer Pablo Martín Sánchez in 2014.

In the 2013 volume *The End of Oulipo?: An Attempt to Exhaust a Movement,* Lauren Elkin quotes one of her writer friends "in an anti-Oulipo mood": "Lots of men sitting around doing crosswords."[3] This caricature encapsulates two of the most persistent critiques of Oulipian and constraint-based writing: 1) that it is a homosocial, if not, misogynist enterprise and 2) that it merely amounts to apolitical parlor tricks of little consequence. While such criticisms are both understandable and, in certain instances, productive, they need to be rigorously qualified given the polemical nature of much of the discourse surrounding constraint-based poetics. As Alison James observes, "Decontextualizing accounts of conceptual or procedural writing sometimes obscure the specificity of the Oulipian project, revealing the assumptions and impasses of the North American poetic avant-garde."[4] The misperception that the Oulipo is just a bunch of "dudes" or "men sitting around doing crosswords" is closely connected to a lack of awareness of the current state of the Oulipo, which has consolidated, since 1995, a talented cadre of four women writers: Michelle Grangaud, Anne Garréta, Valérie Beaudouin, and Michèle Audin. While women, to be sure, still make up a minority of the group, they are producing remarkable work that is underappreciated in an Anglophone context.

Oulipian writing may appear, on the surface, to be indulgently perverse diversions (akin to solving crossword puzzles), but literary constraint can stage a profound and moving engagement between the intricacies of the word and the wider world. Perec's *La Disparition*, of course, acknowledges, if obliquely, the "disappearance" of his mother during the Holocaust. Indeed, some of the most historico-politically ambitious constraint-based poetry from North America is being written by women; taken together with the existing works of the Oulipo's women writers, this transatlantic and multi-generic corpus can serve as a formidable foundation for what Julianna Spahr and Stephanie Young have called a "*f*oulipo," "a sort of feminist Oulipo."[5] An examination of two exemplary novels by French *Oulipiennes*—Garréta's *Sphinx* and Audin's *One Hundred Twenty-One Days*—alongside procedural poems by North Americans Lee Ann Brown, Mary Margaret Sloan, and M. NourbeSe Philip will show that conceding restrictive writing procedures to a masculine domain of apolitical formalism is a critical misstep, a grave underestimation of the potentiality of potential literature.

II.

Spahr and Young's call for a *"foulipo"* occurred during the 2005 *"noulipo"* conference at CalArts in Los Angeles, an event designed to speculate on a North American Oulipo: "The purpose of noulipo was to examine the legacy of Oulipian constraint-based writing among Anglophone writers" (149). Many of the various talks and presentations, later published in *The noulipian Analects* (2007), criticized the Oulipo for being backward-looking, androcentric, and apolitical. Canadian conceptualist Christian Bök argued that the "Oulipo has so far left inexplicit, if not unexplored, the political potential of [...] innovative literature" (157) and that "the poetic tastes of the group can often seem quite banal, insofar as its members seem to enjoy dickering with the gearboxes of obsolete, literary genres (like the sestina or the rondeau), revivifying these antiquary styles, yet entrenching their canonical repute" (222). In a provocative performance piece called "'& and' and *foulipo*," Spahr and Young meditated on a perceived "schism" between the male-dominated Oulipo and the feminist performance and body art of the 1970s (invoking Shigeko Kubota, Marina Abramović, Carolee Schneeman, and Adrian Piper, among others). Drawing on their teaching experiences, they called attention to the fact that young practitioners of the former could claim a certain "[r]adical" appeal while those influenced by the latter have been dismissed as derivative. Spahr and Young alternately read from a paper inspired by, but not strictly adhering to, the Oulipian method called "slenderizing":[6] they removed the letter *r* from all of the words (except proper nouns) of their text:

> isn't it inteesting how we can think of no instance
> when a woman has bought in wok using a constictive
> composition device to any of these wokshops and yet
> we can think of men who did it week afte week and
> called themselves adicals fo it. And while we wee
> talking about the false envionment of poety wokshops,

> we wee also thinking at the same time about the lage
> amount of wok by men that did this and the not so lage
> amount of wok by women that did this in the
> contempoay poety scene. (7)[7]

And as a nod to 70s body art, Spahr and Young undressed and dressed in several cycles as a recording of them reading the text (this time including the letter *r* but treated by the N + 7 procedure) played in the background.

Spahr and Young's concept of a *"foulipo,"* a synthesis of a poetics of constraint with a feminist body art, is both clever and provocative, and their performance raises, in searching and earnest ways, important issues regarding the gendered politics of literary constraint. Nevertheless, their discussion should be both expanded and refined especially now that we have the hindsight of over a decade of literary production. Rather than shine the light of critical inquiry on already visible male writers—Spahr and Young note Christian Bök's reputation as a performer and the "big personality" of Kenneth Goldsmith (11)—and continuing to treat women's restrictive writing as a minoritarian genre within an already marginalized discourse, I suggest bringing women's restrictive writing into the very center of a twenty-first century poetics of constraint. Even if we agree with Spahr and Young that there is a "not so lage amount of wok by women" based on restrictive procedures, the corpus of such work is, nevertheless, significant enough to warrant critical attention. In other words, a more productive question would be not, to use Spahr and Young's terms, "what['s] up with all the men and thei love of estictive, numbe based pocesses" (11) but why aren't women writers being recognized for their innovative work with restrictive techniques and what can we do to redress this situation?

In discussing the Oulipo's women members, Spahr and Young opine, "thee still seemed, like Michelle Grangaud, elected to the Oulipo in 1995, oom fo only one o two women wites to build a caee" in constraint-based writing (11). Yet with the impecision of the phrase "one o two," Anne

Garréta, elected in 2000, and Valérie Beaudouin, elected in 2003, unfortunately are elided from the conversation, cast aside as generic and interchangeable token figures.

To be fair, the fact that the Oulipo only had three active women participants in 2005—Audin was elected in 2009—was worth mentioning in the context of the CalArts conference. And it was also worth asking "is Oulipo pehaps toubled by an univestigated sexism and thus not capable of being a pat of ou witing life in any way." In an interview published in 2014 with Barbara Henning, Mathews, the Oulipo's first member from the U.S., responds to Spahr by reflecting on the Oulipo's misogynist roots: "In the beginning [...] there were no women and that may have been due to a somewhat misogynistic streak in Queneau."[8] He also notes that "Luc Etienne exemplified another kind of misogyny." But Mathews goes on to recognize how much the gender dynamics of the group have shifted and the work that is still necessary to rectify the group's foundational biases: "Of the 12 most active members [...] four women are always present and always contributing, which is not enough but it's already a step in the right direction. We also have several gay members, both men and women." There is, in other words, a significant gap between the sexism of the Oulipo circa 1970 and the evolving and still-contested gender politics of the present-day Oulipo; within this gap, one which Spahr and Young ignore, there is potential for constraint-based writing to be a part of a feminist writing life.

The reason why Spahr and Young neglect, say, Garréta, one of the Oulipo's most intellectually rigorous members, may relate to issues of translation as well as genre (Spahr and Young close their piece by suggesting that conceptualist Caroline Bergvall could be a significant *Foulipienne*). Being a prose specialist, Garréta is not widely known in North American poetry circles. Moreover, her books, critically-acclaimed in France, have not been available in translation until recently: for example, her debut novel *Sphinx* (1986), a "constrained" love story written so that the genders of the two main characters are consistently ambiguous—Jacques Roubaud calls it "a kind of semantic

Oulipo"—was not published in an English edition until Deep Vellum Press released Emma Ramadan's translation in 2015.[9] Indeed, the first book by a female member of the Oulipo to appear in English, *Sphinx* is a fascinating exploration of love, memory, and desire that is committed, as it says on the dedication page, "*To the third*":

> Moments, fragments come back to me. One morning at the Kormoran, the sight of A★★★ brought tears to my eyes: I was imagining this body, lost, dead, vanished. I used to love watching it move, hips and back swaying in rhythm. The memory of sweat on that body after . . . after what? I was watching A★★★ dance from within a profound paralysis, an intense solitude, letting myself be invaded by every movement, feeling the tension of this immaterial thread that linked us even from a distance. Then a sudden invasion of anguish—looking at this body and knowing it to be ephemeral.[10]

It is impossible to assign a fixed gender to A★★★ in the same way that one cannot authoritatively say that the narratorial "I" is either male or female. By negating clear markers of gender Garréta refuses the binaries of *he/she* and *his/her* while also provoking the reader to imagine the potential ways that bodies can be variously sexed and gendered and the manifold encounters they can have with other bodies that are also particularly sexed and gendered. *Sphinx* suggests a combinatorial characterology: A★★★ and the narrator can both be men, they can both be women, A★★★ can be a woman and the narrator can be a man, and so on.

Just five months after Spahr and Young's "'& and' and *foulipo*" performance in Los Angeles, on the other side of the Atlantic, the audience for the Oulipo's March 2006 reading got a glimpse of what a "Foulipo" might look like as it witnessed "the take-over of the Oulipo readings by women" at the Bibliothèque Nationale de France. For the unlikely occasion—the odds were "3 chances out of a thousand," in fact —that one of the Oulipo's monthly readings included only female members, Garréta presented a parodic introduction, "Oulipian Moment for the End of Times":

> You are all alone with us: Valérie Beaudoin, Michelle Grangaud and myself.
>
> The wings are empty; the dressing-rooms deserted; there will be no *ex-machina* male Oulipian [*oulipianus ex machina*] tonight to resolve and save the ending of this considerable tragedy in the realm of French (and possibly world) culture:
> An Oulipo solely represented by women.
> This is unheard of. Unsymbolizable. Could it be one of the forewarning signs of the end of times? The apocalyptic moment of culture?
>
> Some in the Oulipo, foreseeing the catastrophe about to happen even called for the cancellation of tonight's public reading. Countervailing forces (the adventurous souls among the Oulipo) rose up to advocate letting the event take place, whatever might come of it.[11]

Through the arch suggestion that an all-female Oulipo might presage a kind of cultural catastrophe in international letters, Garréta also seems to suggest the possibility of a new, post-apocalyptic regime of representation, the promise of "whatever might come." That there are "countervailing forces [...] among the Oulipo" is an important point, even if couched in parodic terms, especially for those who assume the group is homogeneous ("dudes doing crosswords"); now well into the twenty-first century, it is clear that the politics of Oulipian writing is far from monolithic and that Oulipian practice can accommodate feminist and queer positions.

It is then odd that Spahr has continued to misrepresent the Oulipo at the expense of ignoring the achievements and interventions of the collective's women writers. For example, in the introduction to Barbara Henning's *Looking Up Harryette Mullen* (2011) Spahr blithely describes the Oulipo as being "not only mainly French but also mainly male."[12] "I believe they admitted a woman once," she continues, referring to Michèle Métail, who was elected in 1975, "She seems to have quit at some point."[13] Perhaps this misconception relates to Alison James' observation that the "Oulipo has a curious place, both central and marginal, in contemporary North American poetry and poetics." The Oulipo, in this instance, seems central as a shorthand simplification while its particularities—its minority members—get marginalized in the pursuit of polemic. It would be more productive to analyze what Garréta might call the forces and countervailing forces that are actually at play within the group so we might bring what is marginal towards the center with more discursive specificity.

At the end of her essay "Oulipo Lite" in *The End of Oulipo?* Laura Elkin calls for the Oulipo to "shed [its] chauvinist inheritance" and "to promote members like Anne Garréta." Garréta is certainly promoted by other members of the Oulipo but in qualified ways that reveal some of the internal tensions within the collective. In his introduction to the English version of *Sphinx*, Daniel Levin Becker, the Oulipo's second American member, calls Garréta "arguably the most deliberately radical thinker [the Oulipo] has ever counted among its ranks" (v-vi). But in his memoir *Many Subtle Channels* he calls her interests "perpendicular to the workshop's standard values" and describes *Sphinx* as "motivated by the desire to say something political about gender, not something grammatical."[14] He further notes that Garréta's intelligence, which is "not without dogma," "can jar at times with the otherwise unacademic tenor of oulipian proceedings" (229). Similarly, Mathews calls her a "brilliant woman" and "an admirably provocative member" but adds that "she is somewhat too respectful of academia." These American Oulipians are implying that the critical investigation of gender is merely an "academic" pursuit (in contrast to more writerly concerns); in other words, the Oulipo's perceived masculinism may be linked to its anti- or un-academic forces. One also wonders whether a strict "grammatical" focus is obscuring another kind of "dogma" and if politics, grammaticality, and gender can be cleanly separated into distinct domains.

Garréta has stated that "to be Oulipian is to be queer and being queer participates in the potential" [*etre oulipien, c'est être queer, et être queer, c'est participer de la potentialité*].[15] Such an understanding considers what Levin Becker terms "perpendicularities" as simply part of literature's potential and potentiality itself as a force that can re-imagine "standard" (and heteronormative) values. We might say that *Sphinx* is novel of queer potential. Garréta is thus an important heterodox figure within the Oulipo and should be central to any conversation about gender, queerness, and literary constraint. Ramadan's translation of Garréta's 2002 book *Not One Day* [*Pas un jour*], which Deep Vellum released in April 2017, should bring Garréta more deserved recognition to Anglophone readers, impelling them, perhaps, to revise their outdated estimations of the Oulipo.

Will Evans' Deep Vellum Press has, indeed, been on the forefront of promoting the work of the Oulipo's women authors to an English-speaking audience: In 2016, the Dallas-based press published Christiana Hills' translation of Audin's 2014 *One Hundred Twenty-One Days* [*Cent vingt et un jours*], an intricate novel that tracks the intertwining lives and afterlives of various French and German mathematicians throughout World War I, World War II, and beyond. A kind of Queneauian *exercice de style*, *One Hundred Twenty-One Days* is a brilliant example of what Linda Hutcheon has called "historiographic metafiction," a postmodern form of highly self-reflexive writing that "both install[s] and then blur[s] the line between fiction and history."[16] Audin's novel consists of eleven chapters that assume a range of non-literary and para-literary forms: diary and journal entries, a series of newspaper clippings, a historian's annotations of letters and photographs, and oral interview transcripts. For example, we might encounter, as in Chapter 3, a paper abstract from a specialized scientific publication:

CARMO'S CONJECTURE
IN THE FINITE CASE
NOTE BY A. SILBERBERG, PRESENTED BY C. MORTAUFS
(*Reports from the Academy of Sciences, Meeting of March 27, 1939*)

We prove, for Galois fields, a conjecture similar to the one proposed by Carmo in the complex field. From this we deduce a few corollaries and a few questions to which we hope to return in a future paper. (46)

The reader encounters archival objects, such as this one, as the bounded potentiality of history writing: *One Hundred Twenty-One Days* is not so much a historical novel per se but the possibility of any number of historical novels based around a certain archive.

A formal device subtly binds together Audin's disparate chapters: any given chapter begins with the last word or phrase of the previous chapter. Such repetition is, in rhetorical terms, an example of *anadiplosis*, a figure of linkage. Audin not only exploits this figure across chapter breaks but also across narratorial voices. Chapter 3 ostensibly ends with a historian's note: "Thus ends the last of the articles saved by Pierre Meyer in the large manila envelope" (49). Chapter 4, in turn, begins in Meyer's voice, "In the large manila envelope, I had arranged . . ." (51). According to Audin, she "used an Oulipian idea connected to troubadour poetry" in creating the novel's subtle interconnected structure.[17] We can see in this Provençal poem from Pierre de Blai a similar pattern of repetitions:

> En est son fas cansoneta novella;
> Novella es quar eu cant de novell;
> E de novell ai chauzit la plus bella,
> Bell' en totz sens, et tot quan fai es bell
> Per que m'es bel qu'ieu m' aleger' e m deport,
> Quar en deport val pauc qui no s deporta.
>
> Jois deporta mi quar am domn' isnella;
> Isnella es sella que m ten isnel:
> Isnel cor n'ai quar tan gen si capdella
> Qu'il capdela mi ses autre capdel,
> Qe mais capdel non quier mas per conort:
> Per gieu conort qu'om no s pes qui m conorta.[18]

Audin's formal choices may seem to corroborate Christian Bök's accusation that the Oulipo's "members seem to enjoy dickering with the gearboxes of obsolete, literary genres (like the sestina or the rondeau)" though in the case of *One Hundred Twenty-One Days*, Audin's neo-troubadour repetitions cannot be ascribed to what Bök calls the group's "banal" tastes or its "ignorance about [the] social potential" of constraint (202). Audin is concerned with nothing less than the ways the data of the past get structured into legible histories. *One Hundred Twenty-One Days* is an Ouroborean book that ends with the same words with which it begins:

> I start to write:
>> Once upon a time, in a remote region of a faraway
> land, there lived a little boy. (155)

Audin suggests that all historical transmission is instantiated through rhetorical figuration—whether through the "once upon a time" of the fable or through the repetition of words (" . . . in the large manila envelope. In the large manila envelope . . .") in which the strategy of repetition becomes the archival "envelope" that gives historical information its form.

One of Audin's chapters is simply a list of increasing numbers, a move unsurprising for an *Oulipienne* who is also a professional mathematician (Audin, a specialist in algebraic topology and symplectic geometry, was formerly a professor at l'Institut de recherche mathématique avancée at the University of Strasbourg). Chapter 9, "The Numbers," elegantly establishes the suggestive relation between the narrative and the numerical, between recounting (*recompter*) and recounting (*raconter*); it begins "-25, the temperature (in degrees Celsius) in Upper Silesia in January 1945 during the evacuation of Auschwitz" and ends "157034, the number tattooed on a survivor's arm and jotted down on a page from a blue notebook."[19]

Chapter 2, a diary of Marguerite Janvier, a World War I nurse, and Chapter 8, a narrative from Mireille Duvivier's perspective, demonstrate Audin's ambition to articulate women's subjectivities as they are embedded within historical narratives. In the Val-de-Grâce hospital, Marguerite had tended to wounded Jewish mathematician Robert Gorenstein in 1916 and had fallen in love with him. Nevertheless, Marguerite eventually winds up marrying another mathematician under her care, Christian M. (mentioned in the abstract above as "C. Mortaufs"), who turns out to be a collaborationist and Nazi supporter during World War II. In 1943, Mireille, who is coincidentally Gorenstein's niece, meets and falls in love with André Silberberg (also mentioned in the abstract above), a Jewish mathematician who is later arrested and sent to Auschwitz. We learn that the book's totemic number 121—a palindromic number, 11^2, and one more day than Sade's 120 Days of Sodom—represents the number of "days of happiness for André and Mireille" (122). Audin's unnamed historian, whose voice most fully emerges in the 11th chapter, recognizes the fundamental importance of what Jean-François Lyotard calls *le petit récit* or "the little narrative":[20] "The private events, like the one hundred twenty-one days of Mireille and André's story, do they not form a sort of chain that holds the threads together—

the very fabric of history?" (152). The "chain" is the master figure of the book: it constrains (in the same way the end of each chapter constrains the possibility of the next chapter's beginning) but it also links. Moreover, one of Audin's larger projects is to imaginatively recover the "little narratives" of women who get elided by the grand sweep of historical metanarratives. Audin's translator Christiana Hills, in fact, describes her latest book *Mademoiselle Haas* (Gallimard, 2016) as "a series of short stories about unmarried working women in 1930s Paris, women who are forgotten in the historical and political narratives of the inter-war period."[21]

Audin's father, Maurice Audin, was a mathematics instructor at the University of Algiers and a member of the Algerian Communist Party. In June 1957, during the Battle of Algiers, he was arrested by General Jacques Massu's Tenth Paratroop Division, tortured, and never seen again. Public controversy ensued. On December 2, 1957, over a thousand people attended the *in absentia* defense of Audin's doctoral thesis, *Sur les équations linéaires dans un espace vectoriel,* at the Sorbonne in a show of solidarity.[22] Yet despite years of committees, inquiries, and appeals, Audin's disappearance was never resolved. According to the biographical note included in *One Hundred Twenty-One Days*, Michèle Audin "refused to receive the Legion of Honor" on January 1, 2009 "on the grounds that the President of France, Nicolas Sarkozy, had refused to respond to a letter asking for information on her father, the possible whereabouts of his body, and the recognition of the French government's role in his disappearance." In her refusal letter to the president, she says that the "honor awarded" [*distinction décernée*] by him is "incompatible" with his "non-response." She continues, "I do not wish to receive this medal" [*Je ne souhaite pas recevoir cette décoration*].[23] In a minor detail in Chapter 10 of *One Hundred Twenty-One Days* (which takes the form of a binder of historical documents), we learn from Christian's death notice, clipped from a 1996 issue of *Le Figaro*, that Audin has pointedly given her anti-Semitic collaborationist character the Grand Cross of the Legion of Honor:

The Mortfaus, Langlois,
Dubois, Meyer, and Besson families
regret to announce the passing of
CHRISTIAN MORTFAUS
X 1911
Croix de Guerre with one mention
Grand Croix de la Légion d'Honneur
Deceased the 11th of November, 1996, in Paris, 7th arr.,
in his one hundred and fourth year.
Succeeded by his children, grandchildren,
and great-grandchildren. (138)

Christian's *décoration* is an imaginative, if sardonic, transmutation—indeed, an extension—of Audin's uncompromising political refusal to receive the Legion of Honor. The letters of Christian's last name anagrammatically shuffle throughout the course of the novel (Mortsauf, Mortaufs, Motfraus, Morstauf, Morfaust, Mortfaus), an Oulipian touch, to be sure (Audin's colleague Michelle Grangaud is an anagrammist extraordinaire); but, by Chapter 10's inserted death notice, Audin's relentless, almost claustrophobic, permutation of letters becomes an accusatory insinuation that accepting an oppressive government's support amounts to an ethical death (*Mort*) or, better yet, a Faustian bargain.

III.

To restrict a consideration of North American procedural, rule-governed, or constraint-based poetry to only women writers wouldn't be much of a constraint. One might think of, in no particular order, univocalic poems such as Evie Shockley's "legend" and Cathy Park Hong's "Ballad in O," "Ballad in A," and "Ballad in I" from *Engine Empire*; Chris Tysh's homophonic translation "Acoustic Room"; Anna Rabinowitz's book-length acrostic *Darkling*; Marjorie Welish's variations on William

Carlos Williams in "The Black Poems"; process-driven works such as Lyn Hejinian's *My Life*, Judith Goldman's "dicktée," Joan Retallack's *Procedural Elegies/Western Civ Cont'd/*, Laynie Brown's *Daily Sonnets*, Jen Bervin's *Nets*, Caroline Bergvall's *VIA*, Robin Coste Lewis' "Voyage of the Sable Venus," or Barbara Henning's *My Autobiography*, a sonnet sequence that draws on 999 phrases from 999 books; Harryette Mullen's "Between," which follows the form of Michèle Métail's *filigrane* or "edge," or, for that matter, any one of Mullen's substitution or alphabetical poems from *Sleeping with the Dictionary* ("Blah-Blah," "Jinglejangle," "Variation on a Theme Park"); Eileen Tabios' hay(na)kus; Amaranth Borsuk and Gabriela Jauregui's "My Hypertropes," so-called "translations and transversions" of Oulipian Paul Braffort's *Mes hypertropes: Vingt-et-un moins un poèmes à programme*; and a range of now-classic N+7 poems from Bernadette Mayer's "Before Sextet" to Rosmarie Waldrop's "Shorter American Memory of the Declaration of Independence" to Susan Holbrook's "Insert."

The extent to which the individual works above are operating within an Oulipian tradition varies. And one can certainly imagine a much more inclusive list—or a series of more methodical lists that can each suggest any number of critical perspectives. But my argument goes beyond the simple fact that women, as it were, are "doing crosswords" alongside their male counterparts. Rather, I'd like to look beyond merely formal categorization (or resemblance of compositional methods) and explore the cultural ambitions of constraint-based poems by Lee Ann Brown, Mary Margaret Sloan, and M. NourbeSe Philip. In their introductory note to Spahr and Young's "'& and' and *foulipo*," the editors of *The noulipian Analects* speculate on one of the animating ambitions of restrictive writing: "if the forces of history are (inevitably) shedding the (human) subject, then it is [...] more radical [...] to accede to history's power and voluntarily surrender what it will inevitably sweep away" (3). But not all writers use formal constraint as a surrendering of free expression or as a critique of the liberal subject's politics of choice. To invoke Michèle Audin, we might think of a restricted repertoire of writing practices to be not a surrender but a *refusal*, a refusal that might carry a range of political implications. So too can we think of constraint as a strategic focusing that can allow what Nathaniel Mackey might call a "discrepant engagement" with "history's power" on a close textual level: this is particularly the case with the poems by Brown, Sloan, and Philip, which all rely on the manipulation of deliberately selected source texts.[24] In short, these poems aim to accomplish a variety of cultural, cognitive, and aesthetic activities from political protest to epistemological and historical inquiry to the memorialization of racialized trauma to the exploration of new, or at least alternative, modes of representation. Crossword puzzles they are not; instead, I prefer to call these poems "prosthetextual."

My notion of "prosthetextual poetry" is inspired by Oulipo co-founder François Le Lionnais, who wrote in his "Second Manifesto," "who has not felt, in reading a text—whatever its quality—the need to improve it through a little judicious retouching? No work is invulnerable to this. The whole of world literature ought to become the object of numerous and discerningly conceived prostheses."[25] Prosthetextual poetry, at its most basic level, is a work of appropriation that critically revises a source text, a "retouching" of a pre-existing document. To adapt Le Lionnais' playful idea for an "Institute of Literary Prosthesis," I want to argue that such a retouching should not be limited to just literary texts and that the rationale for the retouching should not be limited to solely aesthetic concerns: prosthetextual poetry can be a way of "retouching" historical materials. (As Evie Shockley says, "Those who cannot forget history are destined to remix it.") Moreover, we should go beyond the idea of a "judicious" retouching precisely through disruptive Oulipian procedures such as N + 7, a method that involves choosing a source text and substituting all of its nouns by counting seven nouns beyond them in a chosen dictionary. Walter Benjamin's "On the Concept of History" offers an illuminating caveat to anyone approaching a prior document:

> There is no document of culture which is not at the
> same time a document of barbarism. And just as such a

> document is never free of barbarism, so barbarism
> taints the manner in which it was transmitted from
> one hand to another. The historical materialist
> therefore dissociates himself from this process of
> transmission as far as possible. He regards it as his task
> to brush history against the grain.[26]

This "dissociation," this deliberate distancing from the barbarity of history might be achieved through rule-bound procedures. In their constraint-based poetry, Brown, Sloan, and Philip enact a double process: a critical reading of a cultural document as well as a creative re-writing of it, something akin to what Jed Rasula calls "wreading"—a poetic brushing of history against the grain.[27]

Lee Ann Brown's "Pledge" can act as a heuristic model for a prosthetextual poem. In the tradition of Rosmarie Waldrop's "Shorter American Memory of the Declaration of Independence," "Pledge" playfully, but no less seriously, refracts the Pledge of Allegiance through the N + 7 looking-glass. Here are the first three stanzas:

> I pledge allergy to the flail of the United States of
> Amigo.
> And to the reputation for which it stands,
> one national park, under godmother, indivisible,
> with lice and kabob for allegiance.
>
> I pledge allegory to the flagellant of the United
> Statistic of Ammunition.
> And to the reproduction for which it stands, one
> naughtiness, under good, indivisible, with lick and
> juvenile for anatomy.
>
> I pledge allelomorph to the flagelliform of the
> United State-of-the-Art of American English.

> And to the repudiation for which it stands, one
> nationalism, under go-getter, indivisible, with library
> science and juvenile court for Alleluia.[28]

In "judiciously retouching" the Pledge of Allegiance, Brown has torqued the text into a document of dissent. "Pledge" is a pledge of *dis*allegiance that critiques the dangers of "nationalism." I argue that the N + 7 technique—in this case, Brown used three dictionaries of increasing size for the three variations—allowed her to expose the national violence inherent within the document.[29] We see references to American militarism quite starkly in phrases such as the "flail of the United States" and "the United Statistic of Ammunition." We also realize that national unity and cohesion depend upon a "repudiation" of the "other" ("the repudiation for which it stands")—whether it be a speaker from a different linguistic tradition (a so-called "amigo") or a deviant citizen such as a delinquent youth sent to "juvenile court." (In 2017, the ethnically-marked word "kebab" takes on pressing relevance as President Donald Trump makes moves to ban citizens from seven Muslim-majority countries—Syria, Iraq, Iran, Yemen, Libya, Somalia, and Sudan—from entering the United States.) Brown's poem expresses—to use its own language—an "allergy" to the misuse of power. It is quite literally an "allegory," a speaking otherwise that distances the author from the barbarity of her culture so that she can posit an alternative politics. Such a politics is based on a non-patriarchal society ("under godmother") as well as a Steinian erotics of wordplay ("with lick [...] for anatomy"). Ultimately, "Pledge" shows, to quote Christian Bök, that there is a "[political] potential still available to younger writers, who might wish to mimic Oulipo in the hope of advancing the group's experimentation without repeating the group's accomplishments" (222).

Mary Margaret Sloan's little-known but astounding series "On Method," which was published in "Folio Two" of Joseph Donahue's short-lived electronic journal *Titanic Operas*, is an example of a longer prosthetextual sequence. In her preface, Sloan explains that she "wanted the poem to involve a method that would explore a classical model of order with a mathematical basis and would then wreck itself from within, deteriorate that classical symmetry and develop as a complex adaptive system into a more flexible model of order."[30] As far as the form of composition and the method of constraint, Sloan used "a modified version of a rondel as the basic form" and employed quadratic functions to increase the length of the repeating lines. Currently, there are 22 poems in this ongoing series. Here is the fourth rondel, which describes a quest that seems both physical and metaphysical:

> If the middle ground is a middle term, site of exclusion,
> then, after penetrating the sacred grounds disguised,
> we gave our animals into the hands, extremities,
> of the observers. Theirs was a still-born range
>
> where as colors of the sky evaporated, lack
> remained, replacing vision. Simple and unmagnified, stars,
> keeping their distance and details intact,
> shower the crystalline lens. Transubstantiation
> of sentience to a circle of masonry,
>
> the palace, in which were propped apertures
> in diversity. Our guide motioned us from within to
> inspect the place of which so many
> species of memory were made.

If "writing is an aid to memory" (to cite an important work by Lyn Hejinian), then Sloan's unorthodox mode of composition points to the potential fact that there are as many "species of memory" as there are for species of writing and that writing by way of constraint might access memories not found within the documents of hegemonic histories.[31]

Through the complicated use of mathematical constraint (this is "hardcore" Oulipian writing, not an example of "Oulipo lite" that Laura

Elkin dismissively associates with Hervé Le Tellier), Sloan's work pushes the phenomenology of perception in new and dazzling—if disorienting—directions. Her use of the rondel is not some "dickering with the gearboxes of obsolete, literary genres," as Bök would have it, but rather, according to Andrew Joron's introduction, a rigorous situating of language "on the cusp between order and chaos," in an "interzone" of "pink noise" "in which surprising information can be transmitted."[32] For Joron, Sloan is "the foremost *oulipienne américaine*": she certainly deserves more widespread recognition and "On Method" should be a more widely discussed poem in conversations about constraint, mathematical or otherwise.

The politics of "On Method" becomes more apparent once we begin to scrutinize Sloan's fascinating source texts: Descartes' *A Discourse on Method* and Richard F. Burton's *First Footsteps in East Africa or, An Exploration of Harar*. The latter is a nineteenth-century travelogue that documents Sir Richard Burton's legendary explorations in Ethiopia. This is a passage describing Burton's meeting with the Amir of Harar that perhaps informed the fourth rondel that is quoted above:

> Presently the blear-eyed guide with the angry voice returned from within, released us from the importunities of certain forward and inquisitive youth, and motioned us to doff our slippers at a stone step or rather line, about twelve feet distant from the palace-wall. We grumbled that we were not entering a mosque, but in vain. Then ensued a long dispute, in tongues mutually unintelligible, about giving up our weapons: by dint of obstinacy we retained our daggers and my revolver. The guide raised a door curtain, suggested a bow, and I stood in the presence of the dreaded chief.[33]

The African guide from Burton's narrative that so much annoys the

European travelers is recast in Sloan's poem as a metaphysical guide of "within" that gestures toward "species of memory" (that go well beyond the now familiar binary of *mémoire volontaire* and *mémoire involontaire*.) Sloan's poem, I argue, critiques an imperial and positivist epistemology as well as a corollary ethnographic gaze that treats foreigners and foreign bodies as exotic objects of knowledge. In setting out to create an order that would "wreck itself from within," Sloan is pulling out the rug from what Thomas Richards in *The Imperial Archive* calls the "superintending unity of knowledge" that most Victorians presupposed.[34] As Sloan says in rondel 22, "the data never do speak for themselves." In place of an objectifying, classificatory, and cartographic gaze, Sloan is proposing a new kind of aesthesis, a re-visioning of "vision," what she calls (in rondel 15) a "paralogical / esthesia," perhaps a new kind of perception that can articulate what intellectual historian Martin Jay calls "a non-dominating relationship between subject and object."[35]

My last example of a prosthetextual poem is the longest and most extreme: M. NourbeSe Philip's 2008 *Zong!*. In this book-length poem Philip sets out to tell "a story that cannot but must be told."[36] Using solely the legal decision of Gregson v. Gilbert (the so-called Zong case) as her "word-hoard," Philip transforms an eighteenth-century archival document into a nearly 200-page open field poem. The court case concerned the slave ship, Zong, which in 1781 left the west coast of Africa for Jamaica. Because the trip, which should have taken six to nine weeks, took a gruelling four months, the captain ordered the remaining cargo— many had already perished from thirst and suicide—to be jettisoned in the belief that the insurers of the ship would underwrite the cost of the slaves if they did not die a natural death. Gregson, the owner, unsuccessfully filed a claim for the destroyed cargo but was successful in recovering the previously lost cargo. The legal decision of the insurer's appeal, which runs to approximately 500 words, constitutes the found text that Philip subjects to "a variety of techniques such as whiting and/or blacking out words, fragmentation and reversals." Technically speaking, this is what the Oupeinpo—the painting arm of the Oulipo—calls "*reassemblage*," which is a collage in which "the fragments assembled all come from the same source" (*Oulipo Compendium* 281).

Raymond Queneau had famously described Oulipians as "rats who build the labyrinth from which they will try to escape." In *Zong!*, Philip powerfully connects poetic constraint with the material conditions of transatlantic slavery in a kind of ritualistic mimeticism. In the book's conclusion, called "Notanda," Philip says, "My intent is to use the text of the legal decision as a word store; to lock myself into this particular and peculiar discursive landscape in the belief that the story of these African men, women, and children thrown overboard [...] is locked in this text" (191). And just as Sloan "wrecks" and transforms the landscape of imperial exploration in "On Method," Philip, through extreme techniques of linguistic fragmentation and rearrangement, explodes the discursive landscape of her source text in an act of recovery.

Philip's decision to scatter the words of *Gregson v. Gilbert*—to send it through the paper shredder, as it were—gives her the opportunity to create an array of multilingual puns and surprising graphemic and phonemic correspondences. For example, the word cluster "fou" from the word "found" on the top of the page in Figure 1 can be read as the French word for "mad." We thus might discern a ghostly micro-narrative of a "mad rose" who threw herself, because of "thirst and frenzy," into the sea (the phrase on the bottom of the previous page is "she falls falling") (62). The glossolalic breakdown of language presented here might be construed as a spectral channeling of this woman's voice; indeed, the book's first epigraph, which comes from Dylan Thomas' "And Death Shall Have No Dominion," suggests a raising (and rising) of the dead: "Though they go mad they shall be sane, / Though they sink through the sea they shall rise again . . ." The word "oh," bookended by the syllables "es" (which might be the Spanish verb for "is"), sounds out, as it were, the distress call "SOS," a phrase which Philip immediately spells out and repeats on the page ("s o /s s o /s s/ os"), thereby creating a stuttering, homophonic play, a necromantic bringing forth of traumatized voices. "Es" or "is" becomes "oh," which becomes "os," the Latin word for "bone."

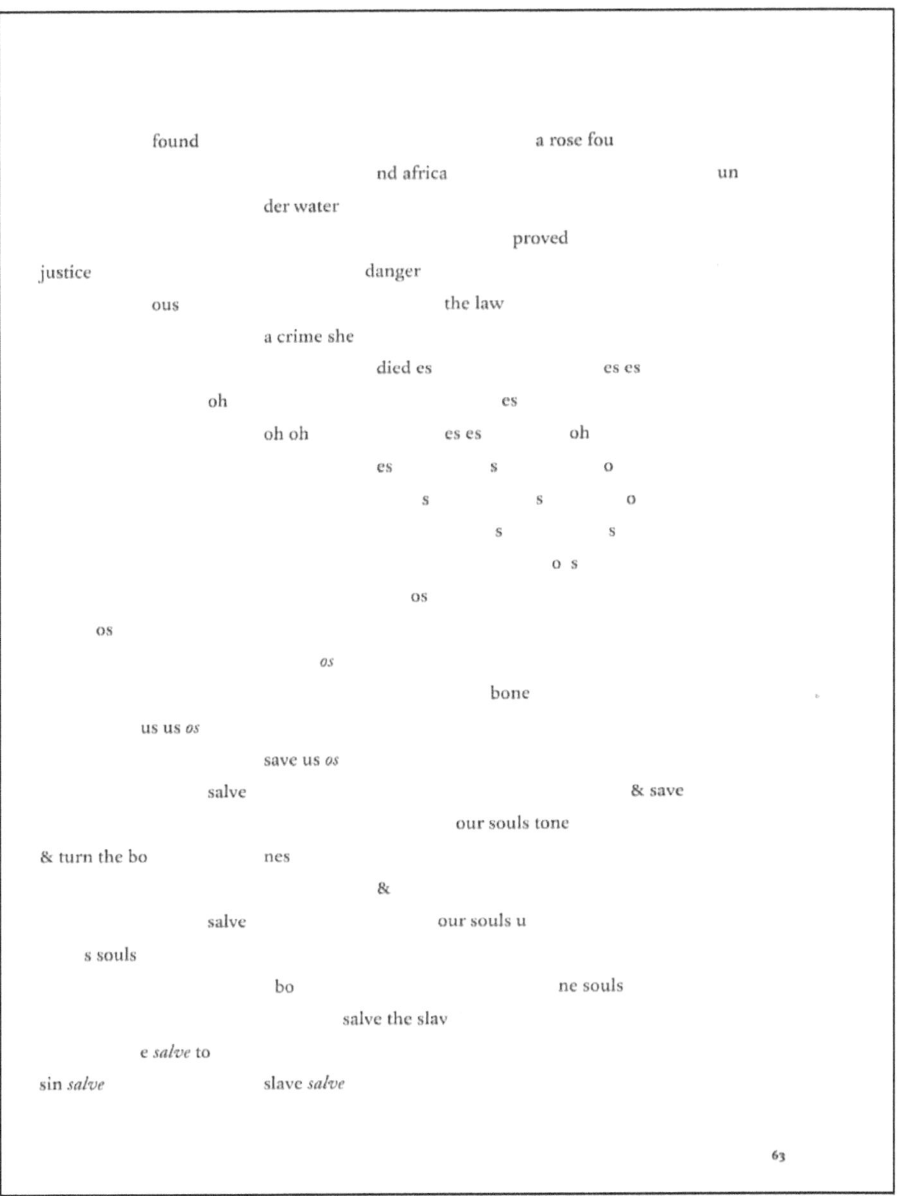

Figure 1.
Page scan of *Zong!*

Nathaniel Mackey brilliantly expounds upon this labored stuttering in his back cover blurb: "Fretful, possessed, obsessed, upset, curse and homeopath both, [*Zong!*] visits a breathtaking run of glossolalic scat upon historical trauma."

In his reference to homeopathy Mackey envisions Philip's noisy poetic scat to be both poison and cure. *Noise*, which according to the *OED*, can be "[a] disturbance made by voices; shouting, outcry"; the sense development of the word "is perhaps from 'sea-sickness', the literal sense of classical Latin *nausea*." We might indeed understand the noise of *Zong!* as the "homeopathic" antidote to the enduring nausea of the Middle Passage. Philip, in fact, has described some of *Zong!*'s fractured syllables as nauseating: "There were things that came out of the text, phrases like 'nig, nig, nog,' and so on, that made me feel nauseous as they would surface." This nausea, I argue, is a specific symptom of the "archive fever" (to cite Jacques Derrida's famous phrase) that pertains to the researcher who ventures into the mortuary that is slavery's archive. Philip's insistent reordering of restricted letters might also be read as an ameliorative strategy, as homeopathic. In the last line of the page on Figure 1, her anagrammatic imagination reveals that there is a potential *salve*—a source of healing—in the word *slave*. In a 2007 interview, Philip says, "the archive of the owner and the lawmaker [...] is in fact the only marker" of those aboard the *Zong* and "in shattering that gravestone the voices are freed."[37] The chaotic *mise-en-page* of *Zong!*, its tormented textual sea, bears witness to those drowned and dispersed by law's illogic.

Kate Eichorn usefully reminds us that "it may be tempting to locate Philip's *Zong!* as a form of 'postcolonial Oulipo,' but such a reading is one that only dares to read the text as an impressive procedural work when, in fact, it is doing much more and comes into being as a text and performance under radically different conditions."[38] I agree with Eichorn that an Oulipian frame shouldn't obscure *Zong!*'s participation in Caribbean cultural practices. But putting *Zong!* in conversation with Oulipian thought can shed light on transatlantic practices of literary constraint. On a *noulio* panel on constraint and content, Paul Fournel, the Oulipo's President, cited Jean

Lescure, who maintained that constraint is intended "to force language to say what does not want to be said" ["pour faire parler dans le langage ce qui ne veut pas parler"] (*The noulipian Analects* 40). This linguistic "forcing" can, of course, serve a variety of purposes but it can amount to a powerful ethics, if not a politics, of poetic form: rigorous constraint—however nauseating—is what allows Philip to usher forth the unsayable, to ritualistically channel the voices of the dead. In this sense, Philip is like the user of a Oujia board, who, in attempting to contact the spirit world, begins with a most limited text: the twenty-six letters of the alphabet.

ENDNOTES:

1 Portions of this essay were derived from a talk "Reading, 'Wreading,' and 'Prosthetextual' Poetry" given at the 2010 "Conference on Constrained Poetry" at the University of North Carolina, Asheville, and brief portions of this essay appeared in "Rats Build Their Labyrinth: Oulipo in the 21st Century" (*Hyperallergic Weekend*, May 17, 2015), an omnibus review of Daniel Levin Becker's *Many Subtle Channels: In Praise of Potential Literature*, Lauren Elkin and Scott Esposito's *The End of Oulipo? An Attempt to Exhaust a Movement*, and Louis Bury's *Exercises in Criticism: The Theory and Practice of Literary Constraint.*

2 *Oulipo Compendium*, Harry Mathews and Alastair Brotchie, eds. (London and Los Angeles: Atlas Press and Make Now Press, 2005), p. 111.

3 Lauren Elkin and Scott Esposito, *The End of Oulipo?: An Attempt to Exhaust a Movement* (Alresford: Zero Books, 2013).

4 Alison James, "Transatlantic Oulipo: Crossings and Crosscurrents," *Formules* 16 (2012), p. 249.

5 Juliana Spahr and Stephanie Young, "'& and' and *foulipo*," in *The noulipian Analects*, Matias Viegener and Christine Wertheim, eds. (Los Angeles: Les Figues Press, 2007), p. 11.

6 According to the *Oulipo Compendium*, "slenderising" entails removing from a text "all instances of a particular letter" and having the text "still make sense." In one of Harry Mathews' examples, slenderising the sentence "He could not erase the raging borne in dearth, decrease ensuring" yields "*He* *could not ease the aging bone in death, decease ensuing*" (228).

7 This piece was also recently reprinted under the name "Foulipo," in Juliana Spahr and Stephanie Young's *A Megaphone: Some Enactments, Some Numbers, and Some Essays about the Continued Usefulness of Crotchless-pants-and-a-machine-gun Feminism* (Oakland and Philadelphia: Chainlinks, 2011), pp. 31-42.

8 Barbara Henning, "An Interview with Harry Mathews," *Eoagh*, June 25, 2014. <http://eoagh.com/?p=2238>.

9 Marcella Durand, Interview with Jacques Roubaud, *BOMB* 108 (2009). <http://bombmagazine.org/article/3304/jacques-roubaud>.

10 Anne Garréta, *Sphinx*, trans. Emma Ramadan (Dallas: Deep Vellum Press, 2015), p. 84.

11 Anne F. Garréta, "Oulipian Moment for the End of Times," *Drunken Boat* 8 (2006). <http://www.drunkenboat.com/db8/oulipo/feature-oulipo/oulipo/texts/garreta/times.html>.

12 Barbara Henning, *Looking Up Harryette Mullen* (Brooklyn, NY: Belladonna Books, 2011).

13 *The New York Review of Books* published Jody Gladding's translation of Métail's study of "Chinese reversible poems" and Su Hui, *Wild Geese Returning*, in March 2017.

14 Daniel Levin Becker, *Many Subtle Channels: In Praise of Potential Literature* (Cambridge, MA: Harvard University Press, 2012), pp. 228-9.

15 Isabelle B. Price, "Eros Mélancolique : Interview de Anne F. Garreta," *Univers-L,* March 18, 2009. <http://www.univers-l.com/eros_melancolique_interview_anne_garreta.html>.

16 Linda Hutcheon, *A Poetics of Postmodernism: History, Theory, Fiction* (London: Routledge, 1988). p. 113.

17 Michèle Audin, "What is the Oulipo?" trans. Christiana Hills, *Publishers Weekly*, April 29, 2016. <http://www.publishersweekly.com/pw/by-topic/industry-news/tip-sheet/article/70103-what-is-the-oulipo.html>.

18 M. Raynouard, *Choix des poésies originales des troubadours*, vol. v (Paris: F. Didot, 1820), p. 298.

19 Michèle Audin, *One Hundred Twenty-One Days*, trans. Christiana Hills (Dallas: Deep Vellum Press, 2016), pp. 119, 123.

20 Jean-François Lyotard, *The Postmodern Condition: A Report on Knowledge*, trans. Geoff Bennington and Brian Massumi (Minneapolis: University of Minnesota Press, 2002), p. 60.

21 Steve Danziger, "Rabbit Trails into History: An Interview with Translator Christiana Hills," *Open Letters Monthly*, June 1, 2016. <http://www.openlettersmonthly.com/rabbit-trails-into-history-an-interview-with-translator-christiana-hills/>.

22 John Talbot, "The Strange Death of Maurice Audin," *Virginia Quarterly Review* 52.2 (Spring 1976).

23 Qtd. in Edwy Plenel, "La lettre de Michèle Audin à Nicolas Sarkozy," *Mediapart*, January 2, 2009. <https://blogs.mediapart.fr/edwy-plenel/blog/020109/la-lettre-de-michele-audin-a-nicolas-sarkozy>.

24 Nathaniel Mackey, *Discrepant Engagement: Dissonance, Cross-Culturality, and Experimental Writing* (Tuscaloosa: University of Alabama Press, 2000).

25 François Le Lionnais, "Second Manifesto" in *Oulipo: A Primer of Potential Literature*, Warren Motte, ed. (Champaign and London: Dalkey Archive,

2007), p. 31.

26 Walter Benjamin, "On the Concept of History," trans. Harry Zohn. In *Walter Benjamin: Selected Writings*, vol. 4, Howard Eiland and Michael W. Jennings, eds. (Cambridge, Mass. and London: Harvard University Press, 2003), p. 392.

27 According to Jed Rasula's *This Compost*, modern American poetry represents a resuscitation of reading into "wreading" or "nosing into the compost library [...] in the compost library books have a way of collapsing into each other, not in the improvements of more 'authoritative' editions or versions but by constant recycling." Rasula claims that "[b]efore Pound and Olson, we have no instances of poets whose reading itself becomes the manifest fulcrum of their commitment to poetry." For my purposes, Rasula's ecological notion of textual recycling (in the way, for example, Charles Olson absorbs Hesiod into *The Maximus Poems*) is of less interest than an oppositional re-writing or "re-wreading" that represents not necessarily "improvements" or judicious retouchings of prior texts but rather critical appropriations of them. *This Compost: Ecological Imperatives in American Poetry* (Athens: University of Georgia Press, 2002), p. 18.

28 Lee Ann Brown, *Polyverse* (Los Angeles: Sun & Moon Press, 1999), p. 36.

29 Brown used a "small German-English dictionary, then Webster's, then the *OED*." Email to author, November 19, 2010.

30 Mary Margaret Sloan, "Preface," *Titanic Operas: Poetry and New Materialities*, Folio Two.
<http://archive.emilydickinson.org/titanic/material/sloanpreface.html>.

31 Lyn Hejinian, *Writing Is an Aid to Memory* (Los Angeles: Sun & Moon Press, 1996).

32 Andrew Joron, "Pink Noise." *Titanic Operas: Poetry and New Materialities*,

Folio Two.
<http://archive.emilydickinson.org/titanic/material/joronsloan.html>.

33 Captain Sir Richard R. Burton, *First Footsteps in East Africa or, An Exploration of Harar* (London: Tylston and Edwards, 1894), pp. 205-6.

34 Thomas Richards, *The Imperial Archive: Knowledge and the Fantasy of Empire* (New York: Verso, 1993), p. 4.

35 Martin Jay, *Songs of Experience: Modern American and European Variations on a Universal Theme* (Berkeley: University of California Press, 2006), p. 359.

36 M. NourbeSe Philip, *Zong!* (Middletown, CT.: Wesleyan University Press, 2008), p. 196.

37 Patricia Saunders, "Defending the Dead, Confronting the Archive: A Conversation with M. NourbeSe Philip," *small axe* 26 (2008), p. 69.

38 Kate Eichorn, "Multiple Registers of Silence in M. NourbeSe Philip's *Zong!*" *XCP: Cross Cultural Poetics* 9 (2010), p. 35.

Circles/ Specular Amy/ Palindromes in Two Langauges

PABLO M. RUIZ

Circles. A chess knight dreams of geometr

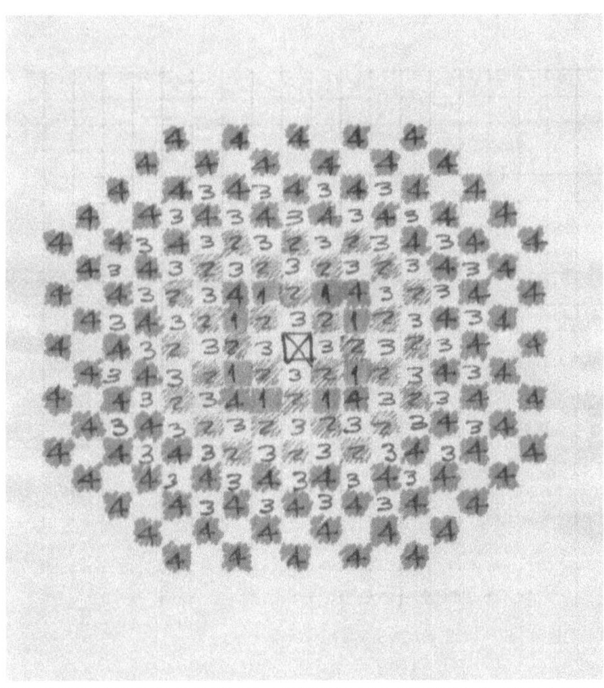

Specular Amy. Love Letters

Six Palindromes

Monovocalic

A cat ataca.

Self-answered

Is it a rap tone? Not? Para ti sí.

Nonsensical

A raven? Nevará.
Noise set: acate sesión.
I say no, I sap. Pasión ya, sí.
As I rot, negra. Yo soy argento (risa).
So so big sac inserts: tres nicas gibosos.

Serb, Magyar: raigambres.

Old Ata, my old "I" on: oídlo y matadlo.

O, sonar glare mock; comer al gran oso.

No, to bed. A Mac? A la cama de botón.

Ana, top me, I timed us. Sudé mi tiempo, Tana.

Nada. More data removal. Lávome. Rata de Roma dan.

From The Tome of Commencement

TOM JENKS

1:1: In the freshman year Loki created the Happy Valley and the asteroid.

1:2: And the asteroid was without Settled principles, and ineffectual; and fog was touching the fizzog of the big drink. And the Daemon of Loki inflamed the fizzog of the fathoms.

1:3: And Loki said, let there be magnolia: and there was magnolia.

1:4: And Loki saw the magnolia, that it was peachy creamy: and Loki split the magnolia from the fog.

1:5: And Loki called the magnolia Green Flash, and the fog he called Pitchy Dark. And the cocktail hour and the cock crow were the first Green Flash.

1:6: And Loki said, let there be a welkin in the interior of the fathoms, and let it disengage the fathoms from the fathoms.

1:7: And Loki made the welkin, and split the fathoms which were subordinate to the welkin from the fathoms which were above the welkin: and that's exactly what happened.

1:8: And Loki called the welkin Happy Valley. And the cocktail hour and the cock crow were the second Green Flash.

1:9: And Loki said, let the fathoms subordinate to the Happy Valley be garnered en masse unto one apartment, and let the ponderous acreage crop up: and that's exactly what happened.

1:10: And Loki called the ponderous acreage Asteroid; and the union en masse of the fathoms called he The Vasty Deep: and Loki saw that it was peachy creamy.

1:11: And Loki said, let the asteroid drag out bamboo, the chicory coddle pips, and the algae drag out mandarin oranges after its stock, whose dibble is in Itself, to the asteroid: and that's exactly what happened.

1:12: And the asteroid dragged out bamboo, and chicory coddled dibble after its stock, and the algae dragged out mandarin oranges, whose dibble was in Itself, after its stock: and Loki saw that it was peachy creamy.

1:13: And the cocktail hour and the cock crow were the third Green Flash.

1:14: And Loki said, let there be bay windows in the welkin of the Happy Valley to disengage the Green Flash from the Pitchy Dark; and let it be for inklings, and for sauces, and for instants, and epochs:

1:15: And let there be bay windows in the welkin of the Happy Valley to give magnolia to the asteroid: and that's exactly what happened.

1:16: And Loki made duplicate gigantic bay windows; the higher magnolia to apply standard operating procedure to the Green Flash, and the decreased magnolia to apply standard operating procedure to the Pitchy Dark: he made the weird too.

1:17: And Loki jammed it in the welkin of the Happy Valley to give magnolia to the asteroid,

1:18: And to apply standard operating procedure to the Green Flash and to the Pitchy Dark, and to disengage the magnolia from the fog: and Loki saw that it was peachy creamy.

1:19: And the cocktail hour and the cock crow were the fourth Green Flash.

1:20: And Loki said, let the fathoms drag out abundantly the charged yeoman that hath bubbliness, and stormy petrels that may wobble above the asteroid in the yawning welkin of Happy Valley.

1:21: And Loki created gigantic kippers, and every flagrant yeoman that moveth, which the fathoms drag out abundantly, after their homies, and every reckless stormy petrel after his stock: and Loki saw that it was peachy creamy.

1:22: And Loki sanctified it, saying, Be luxuriant, and widen, and plug the fathoms in the seas, and let stormy petrels widen in the asteroid.

1:23: And the cocktail hour and the cock crow were the fourth Green Flash.

1:24: And Loki said, let the asteroid drag out the flagrant yeoman after his stock, stirks, and limping things, and ugly customers of the asteroid after his stock: and that's exactly what happened.

1:25: And Loki made the ugly customers of the asteroid after his stock, and stirks after their homies, and every thing that sidles up to the asteroid after his stock: and Loki saw that it was peachy creamy.

1:26: And Loki said, let us make a baboon in our dead ringer, after our picture: and let it have management of the haddock of the vasty deep, and over the stormy petrels of the aerosphere, and over the stirks, and over all the asteroid, and over every limping thing that sidles up to the asteroid.

1:27: So Loki created a baboon in his own dead ringer, in the dead ringer of Loki created he him; gentleman and lady created he them.

1:28: And Loki sanctified them, and Loki said unto them, Be luxuriant, and widen, and eke out the asteroid, and overmaster it: and have management of the haddock of the vasty deep, and of the stormy petrels of the aerosphere, and of every flagrant thing that sidles up to the asteroid.

1:29: And Loki said, Look, I have given you every chicory producing pips, which is to the fizzog of all the asteroid, and every timber, in which is the mandarin oranges of a timber producing pips; to you it shall be for peanuts.

1:30: And to every ugly customer of the asteroid, and to every stormy petrel of the aerosphere, and to every thing that sidles up to the asteroid, wherein there is bubbliness, I have given every minor chicory for peanuts: and that's exactly what happened.

1:31: And Loki saw every thing that he had made, and, look, it was jolly peachy creamy. And the cocktail hour and the cock crow were the fifth Green Flash.

Hypnotic Labyrinth

ANDRIANA MINOU

0. ENTRANCE/EMERGENCY EXIT

Sound asleep in a retrograde mirror while you're watching me unsuspectingly. You can't see the lambs nor the wolves to the slaughter nor the devil-red skin dripping fat of profane odour nor the fusiform cells one on each end of mine purposefully placed there to touch you. All you see is my sleep concealing me. You see the crests of my dreams in their fleshy shapes. You see the baby-feel flesh of my terror. But I'm sound asleep dreaming of you watching me. And it's different in my dream, you know me entirely. So exquisitely defenceless in my dream-mine you're digging with your hands persistently until your nails are filled with mysterious matter of blind words and invisible nails. You're digging tenderly to reveal me bit by bit. The more you assemble me the more I collapse. The more I collapse the more you teach me how to fall without dying. To love without dissolving. To be loved neither in contortion nor in the foetal position. Straight back. Lying on my back, eyes firmly shut. Open palms facing upwards. No cyanide pill under my tongue. To be loved as I ought to. Dangerously.

1.

The room is empty. Just a square wooden table. We're sitting on two chairs with perfectly round seats. While laughing inside at inside-jokes, I see you from the corner of my eye, your stare fixed at the table. A kind of monopoly is placed on the table. Everything is tiny yet three-dimensional, tiny buildings, tiny trees, even tiny birds chirping on tiny branches as they move with the tiny breeze. Everything is tiny yet we can both half-close our eyes simultaneously and stare at the tiny streets and project two tiny versions of ourselves strolling peacefully holding each other by the hand. It must be autumn because there are yellow leaves everywhere and the sun looks like wrought gold. All the buildings are familiar, my house, your house, houses we used to live in, schools, conservatoires, theatres, post-offices. Even the prison is familiar in this monopoly. Even the car-park. Amongst them, there's a very old building, faded orange or pink or something, deserted yet not abandoned. It looks like a house I'd seen in your dream the other night. But I don't know what it is. *It's the grape-mill,* you say, *this is where they make the wine.* That's what you said, and then you looked at me, and we both had our eyes wide-open.

2.

The moment I was about to hang out of the window I caught a glimpse of myself on the opposite window and only then did I notice I was Marilyn Monroe. Wearing just a white satin negligee, white as frost. I stepped out avoiding the broken glass and heard the bolt on the bathroom door move a little and there were voices behind the door, mostly men but the most horrible one was the voice of an old lady, even her voice was wearing a black widow's veil. In the meantime, there was shooting. *How's this possible?* I wondered *What sort of person chases Marilyn to shoot her?* I jumped on the red roof and my feet were white, absolutely white as frost. White and sharp, passersby pointing at them in admiration. Then they'd bring their index fingers to their mouths to touch them with the tips of their tongues and taste the air between their fingers and my sharp feet and the air tasted white too, absolutely white as frost. One end touching their fingers and the other end touching my feet, right on their toes, balancing on the red roof. Luckily, my feet were so sharp that they slashed the air in two before I got covered in strangers' fingerprints. Luckily, my hair fluttered charmingly over my bare shoulders and my white satin negligee filled up with a bit of breeze, so I could jump from rooftop to rooftop, quasi-weightlessly. Because the passersby just pointed at me, but the black widow's veil kept rolling towards me in clots behind my back faster and faster, clotted like dried up orange juice with drowned flies floating inside. All I wanted from my life at that specific moment was a pause. I would give my right eye or the left one, not sure, the one that's slightly drooping as it's always more enamoured than the other. But no, there's no point in thinking of this, all I manage is to encourage the formation of sweat drops on my temples, white sweat, absolutely white as frost, quite dangerous, it gleams from a distance and reflects the sunlight and attracts the bullets from the guns of the old lady in the black widow veil. I must say I was in a tight spot, but if I managed to collect my scattered brain there was a chance I could survive this. Then, amidst the endless rows of red roofs, I saw someone sleeping, a muscular man, right in the middle, in between my feet, flat on his back, his chest exposed, as if shame had been invented long after his death. I realised why I hadn't noticed him before, he was wearing a red cape, red like the roof, not like shame, his eyes shut tight, his chest towards the sky, I touched him with my fingers, sharp fingers like my feet, white and sharp as frost. *Wake up! The black widow's veil will kill me!* I yelled, and he instantly jumped on his feet. *It's you, right? The flying guy . . . What's your name . . . I'm no good with names and identities.* And he took me in his arms and he kissed me he was kissing me he has kissed me he had kissed me he would have kissed me he will have kissed me he will kiss me he kisses me he's kissing me kissing me kissing me, his red muscles clutching my white satin negligee white as frost and I'm thinking I'm saved phew that was close he's the flying guy, his name slips my head though, after all if I did remember it I would've just called it out I would've called him to come and save me in the first place. He's not talking to me, he's just holding me tight and I close my eyes so he can kiss me more and he's kissing me kissing kissing my neck and his kiss is red, not red like shame, it's white as frost, white sweaty gleaming attracting the bullets, and then black black clotted kiss of an old lady in a black widow's veil.

3.

There are no funerals here, mortuaries remain closed in temperatures between -11 and 11. All is covered in a thin layer of salted ice, whose savoury taste alludes to inexplicably deep-frozen tears. The streets, the roofs, even the sea are frozen and there is not a soul in sight. They all go to the nearby village, some kind of tourist resort (or re-mort), packed with tourists swarming to attend the funeral attractions. Funeral processions pass by in pomp and circumstance one after the other on a seaside avenue full of taverns where one may enjoy delicacies such as rare octopus tentacles stuffed in Fibonacci shells. Some funerals are poor, others are very grandiose, yet all are accompanied with absolutely silent crowds of people stepping on the tips of their unusually pointy shoes. There are no sobs, wails or laments, only the sound of banqueters sucking the tentacles, clinking their cutlery on porcelain platters. I'm sitting alone at one of those seaside taverns, waiting for no one. The waiter is running up and down in front of me, he can't keep up with the orders, everyone is winking at him to hurry up and serve them first. Once in a while he trips over the leg of my chair as he abruptly shifts directions amidst this ferociously dumb orgy of blinks. In my mind I build a majestic tower piling up all my moments of unattainability on top of each other; holding my water pistol, spattering water all over the sea absentmindedly. I would very much like you to come and sit beside me. It would have been a very welcome surprise indeed.

4.

In the distance you could see the woman in the dark glasses approach. The way she wore them was so flashy one couldn't manage to notice anything else about her, therefore her features got dimmer as she approached. Even her step seemed to be specified by the two glasses covering her eyes meticulously. One might say her glasses were her most vital organ. She opened the iron gate and started ascending the cement staircase in the yard. As soon as she reached the middle, she paused and turned her dark glasses towards the people who frequented the yard. Their faces and hands were dipped in something white that had dried off on their skin. Amongst them, as usual, was my father, with his permanent expression of wrath mixed with delight making his face contract. Once again, she tried to imagine the interior of his mouth, his bitten tongue. The people with the white faces and hands surrounded her before she had a chance to realise they had approached her. They lay her down on her back against the cement staircase and father stood above her, probably trying to look as tall as he used to seem to her when she was still a toddler. He was wearing black patent leather pointy shoes, with heavy soles. *You must choose who's the most important one*, he said to her, but his voice suddenly reminded her of Leonard Cohen's voice so much that she didn't pay any attention to what the meaning of his words might have been. This must have outraged him. His face instantly turned completely expressionless, he stretched his leg and brought his foot close to her body. With violent and precise moves, shaking the tip of his shoe a little every time, he broke her ribs one by one. Then he left, but the people with the white faces and hands stayed there, to hold her down on the cement staircase, although they knew that she was unable to move any more no matter how much she wanted to. Then she could distinguish her features, their faces were all faces of men she had fallen in love with, she even saw the face of a boy she used to chase around at break time in fifth grade. Even the one who had convinced her he was unlike all the rest was there. He stretched his arm and took her dark glasses off. *Every night I dreamt of your tears*, he said in a voice of a bow sliding on a string tuned in d flat major. She wanted to ask him what was that white liquid that had dried off on their skins, but she felt an inexplicable discomfort, an anticipatory shame for the response she would have received if she had asked. My silence is your question. Repatriation. After an unconscious circle she had ended up back where everything had started, and now she was just waiting to watch a repeat of her personal big bang, she had returned to the fraternal body, she had become spineless, soft, fluid, shapeless, the product of his self-abandonment. How dare she think that it was her, hiding beneath the shell? All is dry again, compulsively waiting to get soaked in persuasive randomness. She knows she must remain there forever, disarmed, surrounded by her blunt lovers, the warden-shadows, locked in the moment preceding his little death, before her grand trivial genesis.

5.

Come and lay down, you told me, come, just a tiny little bit, come, let's embrace. I don't know if I can I don't know if it's possible. Don't worry, I'll spread this piece of leather on the mattress for you to lay on. The leather was very thin, almost transparent, you shook it lightly and spread it and I realised it was human skin. Now we're lying down, the autumn foliage hanging above our heads. Orange and golden and dry soundless rustling. While you're embracing me I secretly rub my fingers on fresh walnut peels and the more I rub them the darker they become. My fingers are poisoned, the thumb and index finger. Then you leave, you go to the reception to pay the cheque, you say, and I stay there, gazing at my poisonous fingers. The more I gaze at them the more I think of the one who will annihilate me by killing my mother before she gives birth to me. He is one-armed with sepia ink eyebrows. The one-armed man is hiding in a room on his own and I keep inventing excuses to sneak under his bed and take a peek at him. I'm planning to knock on his door and ask him if I could brush my teeth at his washbasin. I can't really tell what it is exactly that makes him so terrifying. It is probably because the more you look for him the more he hides and he only appears when he chooses, without a warning, and he brings his face close to yours and he grins for no reason. I see his silhouette against the window, he's shaving in front of a tiny mirror. One eye watching the razorblade, the other one fixed on me, out of the edges of his lips escape the short murmured notes of a song he wrote for me. *Candies of collapse, Getting old in relapse.* Somewhere tormentingly close to me, I can't see you. I hear your hands searching nervously through your pockets, I hear your sweat dripping and the trees with the voice of Yves Montand. Autumn flavoured jamais-vu.

6.

They deceived me. I was sticking my face against the windowpane and I could now see it clearly that they were not my saviours. They were wearing cassocks and sunglasses, smoking cigars, carefree passing by me on their flying motorbikes, their hair and beards waving behind them in slow motion. It was a lie. They hadn't come from somewhere else. And now my only hope to get out of this desert is my father's car, double-parked next to the recycling bin but I don't want to go there, I linger, I pretend I must brush my hair, that I can't find any washed underwear for the trip, I don't want to go because I know that father is upset after waiting for me for so long and the more I linger the more upset he will get. I also know that he will never leave, he will be waiting there, double-parked, getting upset forever (no matter how long forever is). That's why I climb down the balcony, down to the desert of dusty low hills and I leave. In all the hidden caves I see countless copies of Lucian and Charon having a most civil conversation. I'm thinking they must be pretty old, all of them, somewhat like great-grandfathers without any great-grandchildren. The landscape is yellow and brown and no matter how lightly I step, I create a little cloud of dust with every footstep. You appeared out of one of those little clouds, looking carefree. It wasn't you at first, only your words, blended with non-words; written on a virtual piece of paper, ironies mixed with little hearts, lies mixed with curses, sweet-nothings mixed with bitter confessions, half-articulated kisses of the ending. We walk side by side on the dusty path, all is dry and hair-raising. You are angry at me for believing that you loved me. You say I should probably move to Epidaurus. You kiss my fingertips one by one. You laugh at me cruelly, your eyes are not eyes of faith anymore, your gaze is narrow, and I throw myself on your neck weeping, embracing you like a bird of prey.

In my arms, you cry because you know that you will never grow up. Now you see your wrinkles being wiped out of your face, your body getting firmer, your hair growing back, and your heart beating faster, like the heart of a baby in my arms. And you cry and beg for forgiveness. You cannot love me, you say. You are a cold, flabby toddler. You can feel hunger, thirst and sleepiness. But you don't know how to love me, you say.

7.

We were drinking Turkish coffee next to the open window. In colourful little cups. Green for me, red for you. You took a sip and said this reminded you of the desert. I couldn't get my head around this. How could Turkish coffee or open windows or colourful little cups remind you of the desert? I should have asked you perhaps, *how could I remind you of the desert? I'm fair and blue-eyed and loquacious and my hands are cold and you just kissed me on the couch.* But I didn't. The afternoon sun was creeping in through the window. And you kept being the most handsome naked man I had ever seen lying on a couch, sipping Turkish coffee without sugar in a little red cup and reminiscing about the desert. So I started pretending to be a desert too. I closed my eyes and let all the tears I had been saving for the evening flow in my little green cup, all in one go. I spat out all your kisses on the floor and all their S's climbed on your hairy tummy like scorpion curves. I snapped my fingers seven times and turned into a pile of sand. *A pile of sand!*, you exclaimed. *Just what I needed for my empty hourglass!*

8.

It is Lacrimosa-day in some old house. (Lacrimosa-day is situated somewhere in between Sunday and Monday). When I get angry, everything starts shaking. I am angry at something invisible chasing me. The angrier I get the more I know that it's chasing me and the more the walls and the windows and the trees and then the sky and the sun are shaking. In the living room there is Mozart and his maid. They tell me, *don't go in, you will scare them away.* But I do go in the living room and I see Mozart and his maid sitting at the fortepiano. Mozart doesn't have a human voice, he's something like a jukebox singing in all the sounds of all instruments (a concerto?) to the maid and she is writing down everything she hears. Mostly syncopations when Mozart sings the woodwinds, crotchet minim minim crotchet, the maid is writing with a very soft-tipped pencil, the notes are nearly erased as soon as she writes them down, and this makes me wonder how on earth did all Mozart's works survive if they were written in this sort of pencil. When I enter the room, the maid pauses for a while and looks at me in surprise. She says something to Mozart in German, but he keeps singing and I sit in an armchair next to them. The room starts shaking and someone whispers in my ear that I have actually been dragging the invisible creature after me. I go out in the corridor, trying to take the creature I've been dragging or the creature that's been chasing me somewhere far away from Mozart. The maid is running after me in terror and I tell her not to worry. I take more distance and I get angrier and angrier and I take distance until getting angry and taking distance become tautological and everything starts shaking and then I laugh at the creature that's chasing me or the creature I'm dragging the angrier I get the harder I laugh and the more tautological they get and the more everything shakes even more out of my larynx springs a laughter two laughters the laughter of the wanderer and the laughter of the seducer and all around all is collapsing, the building, the trees and then the sky and the sun.

9.

Blood transfusions had commenced in the evening. Most of them were unsuccessful. Most patients were transferred to the circus. My head transformed into a flaming ring. The lion-tamer was done with the transfusions and started ordering the lions to jump through. They obeyed politely like clockworks and as soon as they landed on the other side they turned into clockwork princes. They would then spend the rest of their lives half-hidden, peeping behind windows of dust and sweat. There were always three lovers on the beds, a couple and a third woman, simply lying on her side, facing the peeling wall-paint. In the other corner of the room there is always an elderly man with golden teeth, upright, leaning on a walking stick. His pupils were snake eggs. Every time the third woman changed sides, with his yellow-stained finger he showed her the clockwork princes sticking their faces against the windowpane. And she would grab the two lovers by the arms and they would run down a dark corridor of concrete and wind whistling old favourites with obsolete lyrics. When she ran she would split in two bodies, one was faster and the other was slower than her. One of them was mine. The other one was me.

10.

When I used to live with Mr Playmobil in a yellow room of yellow bricks it was midday all day the time of little nothings our shadows were straightened we would stand very tall a bit vulgar we would stretch the tops of our heads towards the sun and we would say nothing at all or think nothing at all or feel nothing at all there was no crime that hadn't been organised already or a penalty that hadn't already been reduced we diminished and lessened out of fear of diminishing lessening we diminished and lessened with the manic desire to become two little nothings holding hands two little nothings of plastic childishness filled with songs permeating each other through concave and convex fixtures and cachectic recollections of a vacant simplicity

-What's the matter?

-Nothing

Mr Playmobil was so tender tender Mr Playmobil forgetting me little by little gently tactfully absolutely focusing on whatever it was he was doing his rectilinear features were so adorable that's why I made him take me to the cinema every evening not to watch a film but to crosseyedly peek at him immersing in the silver screen forgetting me little by little I would long for the moment I'd behold my favourite face of his the one I could see precisely the moment he would forget I existed altogether although I was still there sitting by his side still holding his hand softly pretending I was blowing bubbles in my fizzy drink slightly immaterial with a different kind of lightness this time in my turn supposedly immersing in the residue of my fizzy drink at the bottom of the glass bottle so that we could once again become two little nothings out of reflex now a bit smoother under the moonlight pseudo-secretly conducting our interabsence.

-What's wrong?

-*Nothing*

After midnight as soon as we got back to the yellow room of yellow bricks we used to grab a little broom and chase the glow-in-the-dark ghost back into the pensioner pirate's treasure chest and then we'd lie in the grey plastic bed side by side in terror terrified we'd hold each other embraces heavier than remorse remorses sharper than words words pettier than a time running out with the precision of trivial things long little nights of nothingness filled with sweet nothings of guilt our guilt of never being enough of never being small enough to survive proximity of never managing to become two little nothings that would only fit inside each other exactly as much as necessary in this world that scatters its fleshy deceit all around us with a bang violently tyrannically whole every dawn no deluge no reboot only this tomorrow that will already be a new day before we get a chance to finish with the now that presses itself against our bodies demandingly

-*What do you want?*

-*Nothing*

In any case it's always a little simpler in dreams we will always lock ourselves up in there my dear Mr Playmobil we don't have to arrange a date all routes will be melting like flaming telegraph wires unable to bear such annihilation of such distance they will simply become a crowd of copies of our encounter my dear Mr Playmobil in dreams it's always a little simpler to be as plenty as a nothing

11.

The nights when I ride my pink 60s broomstick and I go flying using a matching dustpan as a fan – it gets strangely hot as you approach the stars, somewhat zigzag but still piercing – god is a crooked eye looking like a bent fish on the moon. You never know what it's looking at because regardless of the angle you see it from it still looks squint, perhaps in its attempt to prove that it is the point of reference even with this cheap old trick. Then there is a moon eclipse and the clouds are coal dust sprinkled on our heads affectionately. Within this black-out epiphany, the world's rhyming seems total. After this, I find it hard to do something or to even wait for something to happen. I just keep flying, yet I am now accompanied by a man with muscular cheeks and a tight mouth, he's speechless, letting out only long growls of disdain, which is not surprising of course since his hair are clearly covered in Jim Morrison's ashes, the ashes I would recognise from miles away, mostly due to their characteristic odour of velvet loose-threads of reluctance. As we pass by the moon, the crooked eye looking like a bent fish, in yet another cheap attempt at – this time emotional – blackmail, becomes a slot of pain with sharp sugar crystals stuck around its eyelids, even though it has no tears, it is a sort of dry birthless pain, it is a night in present continuous of teeth being uprooted and bones breaking. Yet the eye is only bending and squinting. He who's sitting next to me on my 60s flying broomstick pretends he's laughing, pretends a pistachio got stuck down his throat, pretends he's secretly in love with me, pretends it's all make-believe, shows me his knees smooth and round like ice sculptures, no sign of creases and wrinkles and scars from child-play, they look nothing like human knees, nothing like knees of a living being, nothing like mortal knees, he's about to say something but darkness catches one hair of his between its fingertips and begins to unravel him softly, his entire self is being pulled apart from the end of this little hair soft and steady, he isn't breaking, just being pulled apart meticulously, unravelling all the way, he doesn't seem to be suffering, he probably thinks that he's just falling asleep and that he'll catch the rest of it in the next episode, he has no idea, it doesn't even cross his mind that an ending can be so insignificantly painless. Even though I barely knew him well enough to be able to tell whether he actually existed, I miss him terribly, and this is something I haven't got the strength to explain with reason, as the bent-fish-shaped crooked eye in its final attempt of power exhibition, is posing melodramatically and has now transformed everything around me to a soap-opera starring Sunday school regulars. And on top of this, crickets are singing *when the music's over* just to torment me. Perhaps it's not really him that I miss, perhaps I miss myself before meeting him. Me and my priceless peace and quiet of negligence. Before the world's final rhyming. I must make it in time to that place where I don't exist before the others send me there first. Round my neck, in my palms, some grey shadows keep folding and unfolding almost erotically. Jim Morrison's ashes.

12.

I was walking by the water and it was sunny, not too bright, enough to make the waters look somewhat desirable. And I thought, what a shame, I don't have a white one-piece swimsuit like the one that lady who just passed by on her vaporetto is wearing. For an instant I wonder if I'm in Venice, but the lady tells me I'm in Amsterdam and this is the river Spree and I'm thinking the Spree has probably been transferred from Berlin recently and I had no idea. I look at her breasts, increasingly sagging in the white swimsuit, which is wet and loose and as a result is letting her breasts hang and I'm craving a dive in the river among the vaporetti but I soon realise that these waters are not for me, these waters are too cold and all the swimmers in them are old, perhaps they've grown old because they swam in such cold waters, perhaps they swim in such cold waters in a desperate attempt to stop ageing. I just sit on a bench and watch the old bodies go in and out of the cold waters, I'm counting the wrinkles on the waters and the wrinkles on their skins and the sum is always a sacredly familiar number.

13.

He dips his feet in the water because he has forgotten how to walk on it. He's neither an illusionist nor of aristocratic descent, he's not even carrying any luggage because every night he sets all his belongings on fire in his living room. It's not a pirate ship, the sailors don't wear eye-patches, they don't drink rum, just non-fizzy soft drinks as they solve crosswords and Sudoku puzzles. He knows where he's going, but they don't. The sea is a thin blue gauze, so shallow that the ship is scraping the seabed, so shallow he could have just walked to his destination instead, but, as mentioned above, he can't remember how to walk on water, and he doesn't want to wet his ankles, he's very shy and he hates being the centre of attention. He reached the harbour which was definitely the one, just like any other harbour at the edge of a shallow sea of thin blue gauze. He reaches the harbour and waits for her. But she's late. It doesn't matter, though, she's worth the wait, she's pretty, not too pretty, just as much as necessary, she's wearing a loose white dress and a chic cactus wreath, her voice is soft like the inside of an unripe chestnut, but she's not coming. There's no point in him calling out her name, firstly because he doesn't know it and secondly because she usually wears earphones, as she always prefers to cover vulgar harbour voices with some Goldberg variations or a bit of Cole Porter. Waiting is the only option, then. Without wondering what or how or why, if he should, if he could, if he's able to, if he's allowed to, if he's just a character in a book by Mr Beckett or Ms Austen, if something's happened to her, if she's simply ignoring him pompously or not pompously, if she's not even aware of his existence, if their date was set for a different time, if there's no date at all. He's waiting very skilfully, he's a virtuoso. After all, he has spent so many hours practising, perfecting the technique of waiting (he's the guru of the queue at the super market, the cash dispenser, the changing rooms or the Ferris

wheel, the archbishop of rush hour, the professor of the waiting room at the dentist's, the godfather of check-in), that is, the ability to find the point lying equidistantly between what he's waiting for and the hours that separate him from it and keep passing ruthlessly, to forget how many hours have passed, to disregard any meaning they might have, but to also not allow his life to hang from the desire of the moment it will appear, no matter what it is he's waiting for. In other words, to remain focused on it without letting it crush him. He has spent so many hours practising this talent of his, a soloist of anticipation, who knows that this is it, the great recital, his debut at the Royal Albert Hall of the waiting, and he must show off his talent and then all will be easy, it will be the beginning of a wonderful life. Because the point where he's been standing until now will have blended with the moment of the arrival of the woman he's waiting for, and this brand new pocket time-space will be something like a lucky charm, or a magic pebble, and he'll be free to leave, because he'll be able to carry it wherever he goes. That's why he keeps waiting, although she's late. He keeps waiting for her even after he wakes up on his bed, his brain still soaked in sea mist. The fact that he wakes up, brushes his teeth, drinks coffee, goes to work, eats lunch, watches the news, cooks dinner are mere illusions. He's still standing there, same spot, at the little harbour next to a shallow sea.
(yet the beloved ones never come to shallow seas)

14.

In the beginning you were reciting a poem. You were telling me I look like a lion. That my hair resembles fire and my eyelids resemble embrasures. We were lying next to each other. Then you shut your eyes and I shut them too. *Come, sleep now*, you said. But we didn't fall asleep. From time to time we'd half-open our eyes and take a peek at each other. Like newborns still keeping half an eye on the world. Out on the street one could only see elderly ladies in large wicker hats and canvas bags hanging from their arms. They were heading to the beach of course, while on the wide-waved sea countless bald heads were floating, the heads of their future or past husbands. They were all floating cheerful and motionless, just letting the waves move them. The elderly ladies spread their colourful towels on the beach and read romantic novels about couples who are about to kiss on the cover. From time to time they gaze at their floating husbands, they take off their reading glasses and replace them with opera binoculars. The poor ones use kitchen-roll paper tubes instead. One of them stopped me on the street and told me

I am 128 years old

But you look younger than me

I know

She's holding a cactus with a bushy top and she calls it Beirut and she carries it round as if it were a miraculous relic incapable of healing anyone because no one can kiss it. I look for you among the flower pots in the front yards but I have a hunch you have fallen asleep for good after all. I don't want to be awake on my own and I start repeating out loud all I can remember of the poem you were reciting in the beginning. There is no danger of anyone hearing me because all the shutters are shut. All of a sudden I feel like it's Sunday, something that always causes me a sort of unspecified nervousness. I keep walking but now I shut my eyes firmly, I don't want to peep anymore. That's why I didn't see the boys carrying the half-plucked pheasants between their legs, offering themselves to me so ruthlessly, nor the ever gaping mouths, nor the toothless little kisses, nor the slimy little hearts now and then missing a beat in slight exasperation, nor your pillar-of-salt-lovers with their eyes nailed on their backs. I don't want to peep anymore. I will almost patiently wait for the moment when I will open my eyes and we will be lying next to each other and you will be reciting a poem.

15.

It's the winter sea all around us, heavy with fog. You were begging me to stop a bit unwillingly, as if you were rehearsing a hackneyed scene from a play. At the edge of the dock, at the edge of the winter sea, at the edge of the metal chair, the table was so delicate, everything was so delicate, the table legs seemed like the white calves of a Hollywood diva, perhaps there was a delicate high-heeled shoe on every end but I didn't want to look, I didn't want to take my eyes off you sitting opposite me. You were begging me a bit unwillingly to stop stroking your hair, quietly at first in a very soft voice, then your gaze turned pitch black, the gasping supplications at the bottom of your eyes, spirals that turned into hesitant whirlpools, then your half-opened mouth, and finally you turned your gaze somewhere else towards the faraway winter sea. So other was your gaze that I couldn't tell where your voice was coming from, mechanical, begging me to stop, an andante metronome voice, ideal for an afternoon promenade in a labyrinth of mossy walls. Yet I'm not taking my hand off your head, I'm laying it there, it seems as if it's sprouting from your brain, I feel like a prophet violently baptising you in a new sense of touch, preaching about promised lilies and cracks on rosy bodies, it seems as if my fingertips are tenderly clutching the shadiest cortex of your brain, feeling so brisk that I can't stop. The waiter, your protégé, is standing next to us, an adolescent of a complexion as transparent as fog, holding a tray of fluorescent cocktails, pink and yellow cocktails, a bit 80s, he's dressed in white, he's all fog, even his thoughts are trespassed by the fog, thoughts dipped in a diluted milky swamp, he's a civil servant of the fog, tax stamps floating in his cocktails along with a half-erased aristocratic face. First he glances at you with pity, as if he were protecting you, although he is supposed to be your protégé. Then he turns his eyes to me without moving his head, only slightly turning his gaze, fixing it on me sternly, his gaze so polygonal it doesn't really suit him, a creature of no shape, permeated by the fog. Nobody and nothing moves. This triptych contains neither proximity nor loneliness nor distance nor companionship. A geometrical limbo. The three of us suspended there, I with my hand resting on your hair, the waiter staring at me, and you peering at the faraway sea. A winter sea that cannot even sigh under the burden of fog.

16.

The moon is electric. The girl takes her clothes off preparing to get in the bathtub with the electric moon. Her skin, soft and transparent, rubs against the moon's sharp edges a little, as she's trying to make herself comfortable. Just a tiny scratch on her thigh, it's nothing. She floats in the water, rests her head on the tiles and shuts her eyes. The moon's cable is fitted with a plug and the plug is hanging out of the bathtub. Someone's watching, hiding behind the Byōbu. He's staring at the parts of her skin that momentarily emerge from the water, deliciously ephemeral limbs. He's watching the switched-off-electric-moon-taking-a-bath-with-her. He's watching the hanging plug and cable. He's watching her shut eyes and peaceful mouth. He's watching her languid arm. He's watching the scratch on her thigh. He's watching the water as it's slowly cooling down. He's watching the hanging plug and cable. He's watching and licking, he's licking his lips, licking his tears.

17.

Father said

Look at this look look can't you see look at your hip bones how protruding when you lay on your back what have they become suddenly what have you become what have they become look can't you see he told me now human beings can come out of your body human beings a bit like me perhaps and in the night you don't sing twinkle twinkle little star anymore in the night you sing twinkle twinkle little scar look he said and his eyes wide open grinding his teeth terrified and furious and scared and deceived he said I was deceived they deceived me how could I know when I was taking you out of my body and you were smaller than a scar how could I know it would come to this now I didn't want to perpetuate my kind no I just wanted I wanted I just wanted I wanted some company I wanted a creature a woman who couldn't who wouldn't disdain look down on no not a twinkling scar no desire no pleasure just her twinkling in my darkness her instead of that miserable little star I wanted the woman who could blind herself mutilate herself inseminate herself abdicate herself I wanted I wanted and now these two protruding hip bones like handles waiting for someone who's coming from far away so far I can't even conceive of it now breaths now gasping and wide open windows now two protruding bones two protruding handles not for me no I alone once more deceived and I deceived you and they deceived me deceived and alone with the little star who thought it was you.

18.

Then suddenly the summer had turned gray. Not entirely, but gray hairs out of nowhere had covered all the furniture, the bed-sheets, the floor and the trees. It was the moment you were leaving in repeat. Every time I shut my eyes I would see you leave, my eyes would get electrified by the ultimate trace you had left on the corner of a turning road, at the far end of a yellow-stained horizon, behind two sliding doors of a train or a glass partition at passport control. Every time, all that remained was the sweat of your palm on mine. Before it dried off I would open my eyes and you'd send me to the corner shop to buy twenty iloveyous and I'd go and the corner shop guy would give me the evil eye. He would grab some wire objects like rickety paperclips and stuff them in a plastic bag and he would say *they're broken though, only got broken iloveyous.* But I'd buy them and bring them to you and I'd hide them in your pockets when you weren't looking. So that you'd have something to find in your pockets when the sweat of my palm would have dried off on yours.

19.

Something must have gone wrong in the very beginning. Many guests come and go in this guesthouse, and that's reasonable as it is a guesthouse after all. They come and go hurriedly and quite aimlessly, one can see it in their step and gaze very clearly, and I keep hearing languages I always recognise as little as it takes for me not to understand enough, languages probably spoken in accordingly slippery sounds about a sin that slips away like a fish precisely the moment it is about to be committed. All the foreigners seem to be able to communicate with each other, so they might be foreigners only to me, that is, I might be a foreigner to them after all, so I might be the only real guest in this guesthouse. I go round naked from the waist up but nobody seems to care, neither do I, and I sneak in your Venetian room with the folding-screen sized and shaped masks, masks that I will never know which face they have touched upon. The floor and walls are made of glass and a large window sees to a street full of other guesthouses with glass walls. I hide behind the folding screen and look across the street. In every single room I watch couples trying to embrace yet always being interrupted, by a phone ringing, room service, an unforeseen salto mortale, or – usually – by the unprecedented blow of an incurable disease. So the negligees will remain stuck on flesh, sadly electrified merely due to the bad quality nylon and not due to opposite magnetic fields on the tips of indulgently charged fingers. I peep on you for a while behind the folding screen, realising with regret that you have not even noticed my presence in the room. Half-lying in bed, you are fixedly staring at something small in your hands. I come closer and lie down next to you and you give me half a look, mumbling something like *yes, now, just a minute.* What you're looking with such fixation is a tiny renaissance painting of myself, precisely as I am looking at this specific moment, half-naked with nobody seeming to care not even in the painting. I'm surrounded by adolescents seeming to want to lie down on their backs on top of me. I look a bit like a baby angel and with your ring finger you are caressing my picture on the chin, exactly where the boyish fuzz grows, while your eyes are sparkling and changing colours. With your other hand you're caressing me mechanically without a glance, while you're wondering how it is to lurk beneath the cheeks of an enamoured maiden. But it's breakfast time. I wrap myself in a white bed-sheet and go to the lobby. At the corridor I run into a fish-tailed Freud, who greets me courteously touching the tip of his hat and nodding. His tail doesn't seem to bother him when he walks. I arrive at the dining-room where I hear cutlery clink against the porcelain while all the tenants eat peaches. The cook is standing behind a counter covered in peaches and she hands one peach to each. When it's my turn, before I get a chance to ask for toffee gateau, she lays ten of them on my tray. It's too late to refuse to take them of course, so I decide to show some good behaviour by eating them all, thus expressing my gratitude for her offering me ten instead of one as an act of reverse discrimination, even though I actually wanted toffee gateau, not peaches because they're out of season and they will definitely taste blunt. The peach peel resembles the boyish fuzz on the chin of my image, the one you were touching with your ring finger and perhaps the peach flesh might resemble the flesh of my image, this is definitely how it would feel like if you pressed your finger a bit harder, if you tore it in half but I can't really tell if you were waiting for me to leave in order to try this or if you stopped touching it altogether after I'd left your room. I tear a peach in half with my hands and it's mouldy, its flesh covered in a kind of mould that looks like black caviar. I open the second peach, the second, third, fifth, last one and they're all mouldy. I wonder if this fishy mouldy black caviar business has anything to do with Freud's fish-tail, although he didn't seem like anything more than an extra to me during our brief encounter. On the other hand, though, I thought his eyes got narrower the moment he noticed my nudity under that bed-sheet, surely an expression both suspicious and suspecting, since nobody had seemed to care before I wrapped myself in the bed-sheet. The real problem, though, is that I'll have to remain hungry for the time being. Perhaps I should have begun the story at the end, retracing my footsteps in hopeful rewind. This way I would have done everything more carefully, gifted with the inexplicable wisdom of my experience. Perhaps a fig leaf is better than a bed-sheet and an apple is better than a peach. Perhaps, if I began with a different ending I would arrive at that sin that has been slipping away like a fish since the beginning.

20.

My shadow was to my body what a body usually is to a shadow. I don't know why. Perhaps a lack of fluids, my doctor had warned me but I always found it hard to drink a lot due to my innate weakness to resist the violent urge I feel every time I see a vessel full of water to spill it, not in haste, not in one go, but slowly and thoroughly, watching in awe, the little artificial stream being formed exclusively out of my own will, and the stain (yes, I am crazy about stains) on the ground, on a cloth, on skin, even on the surface of a peaceful sea, the stain of water spreading unhurriedly yet with enviably calm decisiveness. So I always enjoyed this activity so much that I rarely managed to avoid spilling the water and swill it instead. I never found this alarming, after all the difference is only one letter, so every time the doctor would ask me *do you swill enough water?* I pretended I had misheard him, that the question was *do you spill enough water?* so with a crystal clear conscience I would always reply *certainly, doctor.* So maybe that's why my shadow started claiming the role of my body. My body started taking the role of an extra, the prompter, even though it maintained its vertical posture, the shadow remained horizontal on the ground, yet the shadow started making decisions and dragging me (and being dragged while standing up is quite uncomfortable) wherever it pleased. The shadow must have had a really strong personality, since, whenever we took a stroll in busy streets or in markets or train platforms during rush hour, passersby would keep pushing me or stumble on me (as usual) yet they would suddenly make way, take small circular detours or even beg for an apology letting my shadow walk through comfortably or fit in the packed train carriages, sometimes even leaving me (that is my body, if you please) on the platform or out of the queue or out, generally but not indefinitely out. Every evening, my shadow wanted to perform at the theatre. Although my body was still upright while my shadow was still lying on the floor, the audience couldn't take their eyes off my shadow, slightly sitting up, thus acquiring a rather uncomfortable posture in which they would watch full ancient Greek tragedies or Shakespearean dramas without even noticing my body, standing up straight and expressive on stage, not even for a split second. All the eyes could only see my shadow, colourless, joyless, empty, two-dimensional, reciting monologues in my own voice, my own movements, an outline, a slim slice of darkness, a stain of absence, they would enthusiastically applaud at the end of every show, delirious, screaming and pulling their hair in ecstasy. But tonight there is a murderer in the audience. I can see the little gun barrel of his revolver gleaming from time to time under his jacket. Nobody else can see it, all the eyes are on my shadow and my shadow certainly can't see it either since my shadow is blind. Only I can see him and only he can see me, he is the only one not watching hypnotically my shadow's great monologue, he is the only one looking at my lips move and my face muscles contract, and my eyelids half-closing in old-fashioned excess every time I utter a word bearing a past identity that's sufficiently uncertified for me to claim. His face reminds me of someone, perhaps that doctor who advised me to swill water, perhaps that ancient Greek high-school professor, I can't discern any details in the twilight where he is sitting, but he is familiar and I keep reciting, I continue with my shadow's great monologue, until the murderer stands up from his seat calmly, so calmly nobody pays attention and in the heat of the monologue he aims and shoots my shadow straight in the stomach, right in the middle, exactly where her navel would have been (if it had one), and I feel the bullet hole on my stomach and my body deflating in the heat of the monologue which is still being recited pompously, I feel my body deflating like a balloon, I'm thinking that outer space was living inside me all those years and that a couple of galaxies might be streaming out of me now, even some astonished astronauts, but perhaps it's time for a black hole to remain as is customary, and I am now colourless, joyless, empty, two-dimensional, I am now an outline, a slim slice of darkness, a stain of absence nobody will applaud at the end of the monologue, I am now a shadow with a voice reciting relentlessly, a vacuum that the murderer is picking up from the stage, he folds it many times very patiently, he carefully places it in his breast pocket, just a small triangular handkerchief he straightens meticulously and he leaves just before the end, before the applause, he leaves smiling a smile as soft as the mysterious trace of light following a falling star.

21.

It's almost morning now. Still white. The surrounding. No colour. But it's a matter of time. It's almost morning. I must have been sliding, for quite a while, on a moving-walkway darkness. Of the sort that takes you someplace and you know it. I was sliding, yes, rolling, if you like. What's certain is I didn't lift a finger. Not to mention a leg. That's certain. Because I am not standing. I am in absolutely horizontal position, in line with the horizon, which is yet to be shaped, the surrounding is all white, I told you. So for the time being my horizontal body is the horizon. A short, pleasant interval of touch. Just for a while, yet pleasant, to define, just for a while, the point where they meet and rub and squeeze, all this happening on top of me, sharpened embrace of extremes, yet it's still white, the surrounding is still white, I told you. White and cold. Familiarity. Cold white familiarity. I can't tell whether I remember therefore it's not possible that I understand. But I start knowing my body, cold white familiarity without a voice. No, voices don't fit here, their vulgarity would make the landscape explode suddenly due to a colour overdose. Now listen, I guess that's what I meant to tell you, my body is familiar, no voice, white, cold this almost-morning-today. And it's sliding on top of the river. The river isn't wild, it looks like all the rest surrounding me, white cold familiar. A bit like still waters running deep. So I'm right to be scared. My eyes are wide open. Silence helps. I see my outer shell and then a second shell, a plastic one, transparent. You can see it only if you get really close and I am too close. A transparent plastic bag, like the ones they use in abattoirs to wrap the meat. I look for the blood. I look closely to find the blood. But it's all inside me. Familiar cold white blood, still blood, inside me, still water of the sort that takes you someplace and you know it. And I keep floating and sliding slowly wrapped in the transparent plastic bag, I silently count down from one hundred to fall asleep but it's not working. As soon as I reach zero, it transforms into a snake biting its tail.

Familiarities. Again. Literalisms. The waters start separating from the sky. And darkness takes shape like a literalism beneath my eyelids. A literal exit of literal emergency, it only takes a muscle spasm and there it is, waiting for me, not to dread or remember it, but simply to recognise it. Can you hear it? Blabbering again, that's what darkness always does, blabbering in every respect. Paralysed eyes, yet skins remain hyperactive. Countless palms without fingerprints, no fear of the future. Nobody will read them on me as soon as I reach the shore. I'll be safely wrapped in the transparent plastic bag. The separation starts, I can hear the birds, giving the signal as usual. There is another voice with them, a voice I cannot only hear, but also see. Familiar, white, cold, sliding, sharpened, embracing, submerged, soft, river-like, literal voice, never talking of yesterday or tomorrow, so I'm not dreading or remembering it, I simply know it. "And the morning after, if you are found dead wrapped in a transparent plastic bag floating on the river, then your lover is the *hero*". The word hero sounded in italics.

22.

I'm sitting on a green armchair. Ropes resembling extremely long fingers are tightly wrapped around me. Someone is standing opposite me but I can only see him from the neck down. He's standing motionless until he suddenly slits my throat with a move so fast that I don't even get a glimpse of the blade. The blood is swelling, rising up from my throat to my nostrils and then behind my eyelids. As I'm choking, I watch a parade of creatures from the past. The mouse that comes at night to chew your ear off as sweetly as possible in case you don't cover up well in bed, the wolf who will eat you up in one gulp in case you leave the playground, the shark who will devour your legs if you swim too far, the snake that is curled up inside a cabbage lurking until you decide to make a salad, the spider who sneaked through your nostril into the labyrinth of your ear and is weaving its web little by little more and more, the crocodile that lives under the shut toilet lid, the yellow-eyed lion with a speaking voice so sexy that it gives you the shudders. The seven wounders of the world. One for each day of the week. I thought it was the eighth day today, the one when I usually rest, yet I can't take a look at my wall calendar, the one with the sentimental rhymes behind each page, the one I always carry in my pocket. A hand appears from the side, holding a crumpled paper bag. I turn my head and see you chewing something, watching the parade too. You sit beside me on a cinema seat, looking amused. You sit beside me so I am also sitting on a cinema seat, I have no idea where the green armchair is gone. You turn to me and burst into laughter. With your finger you show me all the strange creatures that keep parading in front of us and you burst into laughter. *They're plastic, look at them, fake, and this blood is just ketchup,* you tell me and then you dust the ropes off my clothes, the ropes once resembling extremely long fingers yet now looking like candyfloss. You offer me the paper bag. *Care for a pumpkin seed?*

0. INTRODUCTION (TO REALITY)

It is hard to describe. It could be called "time of the skull". Because everything happens inside a skull within the borders of a reality that can only occupy time yet no space. But it occupies a type of time impossible to measure in numbers so that space is rendered insignificant. It is easy to mistake this for other activities, which also tend to generate realities that exist outside of space but within some sort of time. For instance, for a last kiss on a train platform, the solution to a Sudoku puzzle, blowing bubbles in a fizzy drink, decoding a manual, reading the side-effects of a pill, attending a catechism class on the last day of school, counting sheep for self-hypnosis purposes, a conversation with Madame Bovary before she swallows the arsenic, and many many other activities. The only thing that makes the difference is the space, in other words, the skull, which – regrettably – is usually considered unreal, as if all those doubting its existence have never had a face mask beauty treatment or a shave or have never banged their head against a wall. The other only thing that makes a difference is the fact that the "time of the skull" phenomenon is of nobody else's concern. It is so personal that the possibilities of it concerning anyone else are infinitesimal. It is despairingly and delightfully trivial. A fairytale I tell myself so that I don't fall asleep. An enduring kiss I give to a sleeping beauty reality to awaken it inside me. A labyrinthine reality allowing me to enjoy the loss of orientation, precisely because it is not a labyrinth of rooms and corridors, but a labyrinth of centuries and seconds entangled in a complex network of causes and effects seamlessly stitched together. It is not the type of reality you choke on, remaining unable to spit it out or push it down your throat or even suffocate with it. Many claim that they find nothing wrong with this type of reality and that is very important – perhaps even courageous – to proceed within its specific borders with a watch around your wrist, se-

(or)in-cluded within the four cardinal directions. I always find this either really funny or really depressing, depending on the position of their watch hands and their four cardinal points. Because they are unknowingly disorienting themselves and in these cases it is hard to tell them what exactly it is that's wrong with reality. It is a secret whose whisper may only be borne by the "time of the skull". What's wrong with reality is the fact that it is not just one. It has surrounded us. Reality and its copies – or perhaps just its copies. In this case reality is wanted, for sale, condemned, missing. And what you are reading now is not a text. It is a knobless door. What matters, however, is to not panic.

Frenching of the Western Isles: A Murder Mystery in 100 Sentences

JOHN K. PECK

1. *Knowledge is useless unless one acts upon it.*

2. Central London, 1913: a police station at night, dark save for a brightly-lit interrogation room at the end of a long hall.

3. Xerex, the fresh-faced young inspector from the country, regards the suspect from across the table as the latter searches the pockets of his gray velvet jersey.

4. "Perchance, Inspector, have you seen my glasses anywhere? I am quite blind without them," says Bellocq.

5. "My apologies, but I have not—and pardon my abruptness, but we should discuss the dreadful matter of Orlov."

6. "Dreadful indeed," says Bellocq, toying with the strange ring on his left hand.

7. OULIPO, short for *Ouvroir de littérature potentielle,* is a literary movement

founded in France in the mid-20th century whose members use constraints such as lipograms, palindromes, anagrams, acrostics, pangrams, and other generative devices in their work.

8. *Vivid dividers, looking for something to divvy up.*

9. *Every sentence comes out swinging, but they all eventually fade away.*

10. *Your coat, Ma'am.*

11. Midnight, dense fog: in a third-floor flat in Bloomsbury, a lantern burns brightly in the darkness, casting its glow as if from a prehistoric cave dug into a cliff.

12. Xerex sits in his study, calling up the crime scene in his mind as he sips a glass of scotch.

13. Vexed, he tries to recall everything he can about the pilgrimage to Mecca, also known as the *Hajj*.

14. He remembers the sheet over the body, the chalk outline.

15. "Victim showed signs of poisoning, though toxicology tests were inconclusive and eventually abandoned."

16. Oulipean texts are often open-ended, and many can be read in any order, then reshuffled and reread countless times.

17. *Legio patria nostra.*

18. He recalls the note found near the body: *I will write as long as I am able, just as nectar flows from the fresh-cut cane; my sentences can fit any crime, my alphabet any wor(l)d, and for the uninitiated there is but one warning: beware*

the Hajj.

19. Lastly, a book, *Pilgrimages of the Near East*, lay open on the victim's reading stand.

20. Nothing else had been found hear the body or anywhere *in situ.*

21. Other than the standard pangram featuring the fox and dog, there are several with darker undertones, including a brief, unsettling sentence featuring a sphinx made of crystal.

22. *Under earth, under stone, under wellspring and bedrock.*

23. Bellocq had been a commander in the Foreign Legion in Algeria; he received an honorable discharge after being wounded and spent time in Egypt and the Arabian peninsula before taking a job in London as an editor at *The Comstock.*

24. *Ecoutez:*

25. *Able was I ere I saw Elba.*

26. Under the tutelage of Professor Baxter, Xerex rose quickly through the academy, and now faced his first truly worthy foe in Bellocq.

27. *Emperor Napoleon was cast into despair upon seeing his island prison rising from blue Ligurian waters.*

28. "For you, Bea, a fine French example made for the Duchess of Lissixg, who was known as 'the Imp Queen'—but I can't remember the Latin for imp." (Harry Mathews, *The Conversions*)

29. Entered into official record *absente reo:*

30. Victim: Orlov Bellocq, brother of Charles, critic by trade; known as a jittery and neurotic man whose life was not just shaped by paranoia, but defined by it.

31. A cryptic note, found near the body, did little to answer the questions of *why* and *how*.

32. Nine objects found on the victim: three 1p coins, a shilling, a small pouch of snuff, a comb, a spare trouser-button, an unsmoked cigarette, and a small piece of denim.

33. Red stains, likely the result of a nosebleed, were observed on the right shirtcuff.

34. Knees and elbows overextended, body outstretched, eyes open, face contorted in convulsive pain.

35. Dorothy, the maid, found the body after entering the room with the intention of tidying it up.

36. Criminal forensics found no fingerprints apart from the victim's anywhere in the room, nor on the windowsill or doorknob.

37. What would drive a man to kill his own brother, particularly a man as seemingly charming and worldly as Bellocq?

38. *Xerex, 'tis I—sit, Xerex!*

39. Gold ring on the third finger of the left hand, engraved with strange letters; silver-and-quartz band on the right thumb.

40. Beaded choker around the neck: souvenir of a long-ago safari.

41. Xerex, at long last, stumbles into bed, recalling the words of Professor Baxter: "One can always go to sleep when there is nowhere left to go."

42. *Ecce homo.*

43. Dreams at last visit the exhausted mind of Xerex.

44. Zirconium demons, sphinges with webbed eyes, dark and towering, lap-lions of Hesiod.

45. For those who have studied religious ritual, long-form constrained writing can be viewed as something like a pilgrim's path: the literary equivalent of the *Santiago de Compostela* or the *Hajj*.

46. Hesiod spoke, then everything went black.

47. *Able was I, Dnaknarfdine, ere Enid, Frank and I saw Elba.*

48. *Verdigris on the stone walls of the gulag.*

49. *Dum inter homines sumus, colamus humanitatem.*

50. Bellocq—the dead Orlov, not the living Charles—stands in the doorway, speaking wordlessly: "Forgive me: your door is open, so I cannot knock."

51. Low in the distant sky, near the bloody line of the horizon, a 28-letter pangram shines forth:

52. *Sphinx of black quartz, hear my vow.*

53. "Quo," says Professor Baxter sternly, fading away as Xerex rises from the depths of his dream, "is what should be here, where you have written

'quero'..."

54. Yesterday's soft fog is but a memory, and now the cold, relentless rain of today streaks the windows of the interrogation room and beats down on the roof.

55. "You must understand, I am not accustomed to being lectured on my own country," says a testy and seemingly underslept Bellocq.

56. "Forgive me—I did not mean to imply that France or her citizens were shiftless or capricious, merely that there exists a great tradition of Gallic satire and irreverence," says Xerex.

57. "Gentle with those sweet, delicate words—you don't want to bruise them," replies Bellocq with a slight sneer in his lip and a tremble in his jaw.

58. "Neophytes love to play in the fields tilled by the true masters," says Bellocq finally, before turning away and wiping his nose on his cuff.

59. "Neophyte or not," replies Xerex, "it is my job to investigate this case to its end."

60. In constrained writing, there is often an eerie "otherness" to the language, often brought on by a preponderance of unusual words: *Xerex, Orlov, Bellocq, Hajj.*

61. —Non. Il ignorait tout (par surcroît, nous n'avions alors aucun fils). Mais il partit, n'ayant qu'un but: savoir où nous avions fui, qui nous avait nourris, où nous avions grandi. (Georges Perec, *La disparition*)

62. *Zlink!*

63. *Fraj!*

64. *Uuut!*

65. *Agaaa!*

66. *Eeeeep!*

67. *SKRONK!*

68. In a Berlin apartment a man rolls a pair of alphabet dice 100 times, producing a string of 200 letters that will alternately be used as the first and last letters of each sentence in a 100-sentence essay.

69. "Every letter is a clue," says Professor Baxter, "and thus one may go on reading forever; the trick lies simply in knowing when to stop."

70. Bultérieurement, en un conciliabule, il butinait cette stibulation: «Buse! ce globuleux buton buche mal ton burnous!» (Raymond Queneau, *Exercices de style*)

71. Nascent ideas filled the inspector's field of thought, hovering in his mind's dark penumbra.

72. Young Xerex suddenly bolted upright, dressed hurriedly, and raced to the station to dispatch an alert.

73. *Upend the status quo!*

74. *Velocius quam asparagi coquantur.*

75. *.wov ym raeh ,ztrauq kcalb fo xnihpS*

76. Killed by the poisoned pages of a book: the victim's habit of licking his thumb before turning each page introduced, over several minutes, a lethal dose of the toxin *cicu*.

77. Chronograms are phrases in which numbers (generally dates) are hidden, such as the inscription over the western door of St. Castor in Koblenz from 1765: *DIro MarIa IVngfraV reIn/Las CobLenz anbefohLen seIn* ("Let Koblenz be recommended to Mary, the pure and virginal.")

78. *Pow!*

79. *Let 'er rip!*

80. *etc.*

81. London, Wandsworth Prison: the cold fog of morning gradually gives way to the dull light of midday.

82. Footsteps tread the halls of the holding area.

83. "So, my young friend," said Bellocq, "it seems you managed to weather the storm."

84. "Nefarious: a book sent to your brother the critic as a gift, its reading triggered months later by a threatening note," replied Xerex.

85. *Ziggurats do not always rise darkly into the sky: some are inverse, and drive into the earth like wedges of sharp slag.*

86. Never one to relinquish the last word, the prisoner rages from behind the bars of his cell at Xerex.

87. "Cursed neophyte—you know nothing of the true mysticism at the

heart of our movement!" shouts the red-faced Bellocq.

88. "Granted, neophyte I may be—but I am free to continue playing in the sacred fields, while you shall live out your days behind bars," replies Xerex coolly, immediately pleased with the full-bodiedness of his quip.

89. *Ze,* in some modern, progressive texts, is often used to stand in for "he", "she", or "he or she".

90. Xerex, later that night, stands in his study, sipping scotch and watching the flicker and glow of candlelight reflected in the burnished silver of a candelabra.

91. Examples of palindromes include "Able was I ere I saw Elba", "No 'X' in Nixon", "Do geese see God?", "Taco cat", "Kayak", "Tatami mat", "Redrum/murder", and "Xerex".

92. *Rum, whiskey, God—whatever gives your pen a good rev.*

93. *Hannah, I was a saw; I, Hannah!*

94. *Beyond the curtain of words lies the country of pure, lizard physicality: ingestion, dominion, sleep and sex.*

95. 'Ye', as in the faux-medieval 'ye olde', is simply a visual misinterpretation of the 'thorn' letter þ, meaning 'þe' was simply pronounced 'the'.

96. "*Per aspera ad astra*—through hardships to the stars," says Xerex coyly before downing the rest of his glass of scotch.

97. "Killed not during the pilgrimage, as he thought he would be," says the young detective with a smile, "but instead, and quite elegantly I must say,

with a book *about the Hajj.*"

98. "Zirconium has many interesting properties, not least of which is the letter with which it begins," says Professor Baxter with a slight sigh.

99. Under the book's endsheet, still unfound, lies a note written in a hand forceful enough to warp the nib:

100. *Elba, though a disaster, was no disabler: for the critic Cain was dead long before I was his brother, and Abel, as always, was I.*

The Hidden Letter 'E' in Perec's La Disparition:
declaration of its exact location
and interrupted interpretive attempt at its multiple
meanings

PABLO M. RUIZ

For years, for decades, a ghost has haunted French literature. A persistent rumor, a widespread suspicion, suggests that somewhere in Perec's lipogrammatic novel *La Disparition*, famously written without any instance of the letter E over the course of its more than three hundred pages, there is, concealed, crouching, clandestine, waiting to be discovered and denounced, a persistent and intolerable letter E. Since the novel's publication in 1969, this insidious suspicion has afflicted the souls of the good people of letters, who have endured it with a hidden anxiety, like an implicit and latent accusation of their readerly incompetence. The purpose of the following lines is to expunge this harmful specter.

First let us say a few words about why it is reasonable to expect that there be a letter E in a novel composed by definition without the letter E. We should remember that this novel was written in the context of the Oulipo, which promotes the creation of literature under formal constraints. The lipogram is an example of one such constraint. Now, within the conceptual apparatus of the Oulipo, there exists what Oulipians call "clinamen": the clinamen is simply a rule that allows one to violate the rules, that is, that allows one to take liberties with respect to the constraints with which one is writing. Oulipian authors have no obligation to resort to the clinamen (strictly speaking, they also have no obligation to write under formal constraints). In the case of Perec, however, we encounter a writer who stands out not only for the virtuosity with which he develops and utilizes the constraints he has adopted, but also for the systematic and creative way with which he has applied the clinamen in his writing—the most notorious example of this occurs in what probably is his greatest work: *Life: A User's Manual.* It makes more sense, given what we know about Perec's works, that there be at least one E in *La Disparition*, as opposed to a complete absence.

The letter E appears, effectively disguised, on page 161 of the first edition, which has the same pagination as the later Gallimard pocket edition of the "L'imaginaire" series. What one sees at first is not actually an E but rather its camouflage: a musical notation composed of two eighth notes and two sixteenth notes linked as a set of four notes. If one removes the last sixteenth note and turns the set of three remaining notes counterclockwise ninety degrees, an undeniable and capital letter E emerges. There it is, invisible and in front of everyone's eyes, exactly like that other *lettre volée*, the purloined letter of Edgar Allan Poe's story alluded to explicitly by Perec and partially rewritten in the novel. Another element that makes this presence seem to be the result of a calculated intention is its location in the book. Seeing how there are three-hundred-and-twenty pages in total, this musical E finds itself exactly in the middle of the book, the facing pages 160/161. Where could the presence of the only letter E in the whole novel be more significant than at its very center, as though it were the gravitational nucleus around which everything else turns? We also ought to remember the recurrence of the theme of playing with the form of letters through inversions, rotations, and transformations, that Perec takes up in both his autobiographical *W, or the Memory of Childhood* and *Life: A User's Manual.* We should note as well that the musical notation was designed in such a way that the horizontal line at the middle of the letter E be shorter than those at either end, which matches the design of the standard capital letter E.

And what is the provenance of those musical notes in the novel? It's the whistle that Douglas Haig Clifford, the unacknowledged brother of Anton Voyl and incestuous husband of Olga Mavrokhordatos, uses to call out to his fish Jonas as it swims in the pond of the house's garden. There is a relatively clear reason both for this particular character to be the one to whistle, and for there to be a connection between the surreptitious E and musical notation. Considering moreover that the E never used in the novel is, among other things, a symbolic transposition of the disappearance of Perec's Jewish parents in the context of Nazism, and considering as well that the characters in this novel disappear or die upon seeing a *zahir*, the unforgettable object which Borges invents in his eponymous story and is the instrument of torture used by the Nazi deputy commandant of a concentration camp in Borges's other story, "Deutsches Requiem," that reason becomes even more weighty and significant. This page is too short to expose that reason, but the reader will have no difficulty in discovering it for herself.

u au matin, l on ouït Haig qui
i maison. Puis, au point du jou
vu sortir. Il portait un chandail à c
ı gros blouson. Il avait un sac à la
ı jusqu'au bord du bassin, il s'acc
ar trois fois

ınt un signal qui paraissait signifie
itôt Jonas apparut. Il tint à son
scours, lui lançant par instants du
ıulait dans sa main ainsi qu'on fai
Voir du couscous.

Forever Never Ends

PETER CONSENSTEIN

When you think about it, the question mark at the end of the title *The End of Oulipo?*[1] makes it sound funny. Intoning the question adds a sense of doubt, some sarcasm, irony or ridicule to the title. It just depends on how it is pronounced. Is it the authors' goal to leave readers with the idea, thanks to a quick glance at the title, that they are only suggesting and not really sure if the group Oulipo has come to an end or not? When I first heard about the book's publication I knew that it was an attention grabber and felt surer than ever that the Oulipo is now a lot more than just a clandestine group of authors that no one ever heard of. It's funny that a book asking whether or not a group of *littérateurs* has met its demise is conversely an indication of its steadfastness. Why the group is so steadfast has to do with how this beast called literature, the metalife of language and those who live through it, behaves, invents and reinvents itself and us, again and again, from time immemorial. Literature changes. Art changes. The Oulipo facilitates those changes. It ends when literature ends, which may mean never.

There are a certain number of books written on the Oulipo that have transformed the Oulipo into a reference point in literary history, and not just French literary history. There are also François Le Lionnais' (a co-founder of the group with Raymond Queneau) three manifestoes. I'd like to look at these texts, as well as some written by various members of the

---

1 Lauren Elkin, Scott Esposito, Alresford, Hants, UK: Zero Books, 2013.

Oulipo, in order to demonstrate the richness, promise and potential of the Oulipian endeavor, which, I propose, is not in stasis. Further, it is important to underscore just how transformative Oulipian writing is for the reader, whose efforts to interpret, create, or recreate reality are also transformed.[2]

What circumstances provoke Lauren Elkin and Scott Esposito to ask about the end of the Oulipo? In their short preface, they make some questionable claims and comparisons. For example, they compare Tzara's instructions for writing a Dada poem—pure chance, the "poet" pulls words cut up from a newspaper article out of a bag and voilà a poem—to Jacques Jouet's instructions for writing a subway poem.[3] Yes, these methods have game playing in common, but Tzara's Dada poem is like throwing dice, whereas Jouet's subway poem has rhythm, composition, planning, and methods for transcribing language from the mind to the page. The fundamental notion attached to the Oulipo's use of constraints is that they represent a means of avoiding chance, a notion central to the group's enterprise and which Elkin and Esposito sweep aside, even ignore, with the comparison they provide. I'll come back to this later.

Using the term "open source," a clear reference to software programs that are freely shared, Elkin and Esposito propose that Oulipian constraints that are described and shared on the oulipo.net website, or in journal entries and the *Bibliothèque oulipienne*, are part of the group's "ethos" (6). While it is true that the members of the Oulipo share their constraints openly, which partially contributes to the notion of potential literature, there is a more compelling impulse behind the sharing (and invention) of literary constraints: the building of a collective. This is not "open source," but it is the "ethos" Elkin and Esposito fail to appreciate.

---

2 These other books include the aforementioned *The End of Oulipo?*, Daniel Levin Becker, *Many Subtle Channels* (Cambridge, MA.: Harvard UP, 2012), Hervé Le Tellier, *Esthétique de l'Oulipo* (Bordeau: Le Castor Astral, 2006), Pablo Martín Ruiz, *Four Cold Chapters on the Possibility of Literature Leading Mostly to Borges and Oulipo* (Champaign, IL: Dalkey Archive Press, 2014), and my own book, *Literary Memory, Consciousness and the Group Oulipo* (Amsterdam: Rodopi, 2002).
3 Visit the Oulipo website, oulipo.net for a description of a *poème de metro*. http://oulipo.net/fr/contraintes/poeme-de-metro

Revealing how little they appreciate how the Oulipo functions as a collective, they derisively suggest that contemporary Oulipian production is "inbred" (6) in the next sentence. Simplistic and nihilistic thinking such as this is wilfully ignorant of the service the group is performing by providing a model for writing, inventing and imagining as a collective. To this too I will return. Again.

As the authors segue into their sustained discussion of the works of certain members of the Oulipo, such as Jacques Jouet and Hervé Le Tellier of whom they are the most critical, they do recognize the group's successes and label the production of Italo Calvino, Jacques Roubaud and Georges Perec "classic literature" (9). By doing so, can the reader surmise that these authors believe that experimental literature is classical? Unwittingly they appear to run into the conundrum at the heart of literature's evolution: like all intentional human endeavors, experimentation is integral to progress.

Whenever and wherever there is experimentation, there is also a high level of failure. The members of the Oulipo run tests like scientists in laboratories. The tests themselves, even those that fail, are meaningful contributions to the evolution of literature; a successful outcome is unnecessary. Within this context, where and why do Elkin and Esposito take issue with Jacques Jouet? For the most part, Esposito, in his essay "Eight Glances Past Georges Perec," finds the work of Jouet amateurish and uses Jouet's participation in the Oulipo as a reason to denigrate the entire group. Elkin insinuates that he does not produce "true literature" (37)—such conceit, Monsieur Elkin!—because it lacks "dedication, persistence, and struggle." Who gets to decide what shape "dedication, persistence, and struggle" take? Accusing such a productive author as Jouet as lacking in these qualities is only a conceitful act of norming. The Oulipo never promised to produce "true literature" (an oxymoron?) (they're experimenting).

Esposito then chooses to ridicule Jouet's approach to politics. He tells the Oulipo what it "must" do as he compares Jouet's work to the work of Christian Bök:

> Instead of using constraint to write pedestrian satires of political excess—the kind of disposable literature that will be written regardless of whether constraint is involved—the Oulipo must follow Bök's example and envision books whose political revelations could only come through the use of constraint. This would be to return the Oulipo to its original, revolutionary roots (61).

It is refreshing to hear Esposito mistakenly, yet complementarily, raise the goals of the Oulipo to "revolutionary" level. However, the Oulipo makes their apolitical nature quite clear and I have yet to sense that they have revolution on their minds.

Esposito has every right not to like Jouet's work. To use his dislike of Jouet to imply that Oulipo has met its end is simply a failed argument. First, the Oulipo has no expectations concerning how its literary output will be judged or critiqued. Sometimes, they write "successfully," at other times their writing is for a more limited audience. Second, no one member represents the group. In the case of Jouet, let's simply note that there are some who agree with Esposito, but many more that write effusively about the work of Jouet. I am referring to a volume of the journal *SubStance*,[4] a critical appraisal of Jouet's work. Warren Motte, in his introduction to the volume of which he is the guest editor, declares that in the work of Jouet "tradition and innovation find such felicitous articulation that they become virtually indistinguishable" (3). It is the encounter of innovation and tradition that is interesting, a sort of nodal fusion point of the future that brings attention to the Oulipo and one that Elkin and Esposito fail to grasp and hold on to for all its worth.

The authors also play a risky game of "more revolutionary than thou," one that can result in divisiveness. Moving from a critique of Jouet to one of Hervé Le Tellier, an author and radio host well known to the French literary public, they write:

---

4 Vol. 30, No. 3, Issue 96: Special Section: Jacques Jouet

> . . . the Oulipo is menaced by the reactionary bourgeois
> element Le Tellier represents . . . if the Oulipo hopes to
> avoid exhausting its potential, it is up to its members
> to stay outside of the mainstream . . . if an Oulipian
> leaves the workbench and settles into a comfortable
> armchair, his worldview narrows, and his work's
> potential diminishes (76).

The tone evokes moral and ideological superiority and not systematic, theory-based criticism. It undercuts elements of Lauren Elkin's critique of Hervé LeTellier that happens to be valid. She takes Le Tellier to task for two reasons: 1) because his constraints are versions of "Oulipo light" (not necessarily probing mathematical theorem) and 2) because of his misogyny. Elkin, obviously a sophisticated and knowledgeable reader, is a Barnard College graduate who doesn't want to cop to the fact that she too sits in a "comfortable armchair" as a "Lecturer in the Department of English and co-director of the Centre for New and International Writing at the University of Liverpool," according to her Tumblr page.[5] Although she successfully critiques Le Tellier, she wrongfully projects onto the Oulipo her own worries, including becoming a "reactionary bourgeois," wishing to "to stay outside of the mainstream," and acquiring a narrow "worldview."

Before moving on to explore other reactions to the Oulipo, Elkin's discussion of misogyny in *The End of Oulipo?* deserves focus. Elkin calls the choice of the word "Ouvroir" a "delightful condescension toward women" (77), since an 'ouvroir' is defined as 1) "Lieu où l'on se rassemble, dans une communauté de femmes ou dans un couvent, notamment pour effectuer des travaux d'aiguille" and 2) "Atelier, souvent à caractère confessionnel, où des personnes bénévoles effectuent des travaux d'aiguille pour des ornements d'église ou au profit d'une oeuvre de bienfaisance, d'un hôpital ou de nécessiteux."[6] An 'ouvroir' was a place where women did needlework for the well-being of the underprivileged or to beautify

---

5 http://laurenelkin.tumblr.com/about.

churches.

The birth of the Oulipo came at a time when the notion of male privilege was not even conceived; male privilege, as defined, was taken for granted. Jean Lescure explains, in "Petite histoire de l'Oulipo,"[7] that the group first claimed the title S.L.E., or "selitex," short for "séminaire de littérature expérimentale" (26) but rejected the title because it sounded too much "l'insémination artificielle." There are no etymological roots linking "séminaire" to either "semence" or "sperme." Obviously, they probably liked joking about *sperme*. But the sounds of the words also interest the original members of Oulipo, which becomes more evident in Lescure's wording for explaining how the members decided upon Oulipo: "nous consentîmes à lier à la li l'ou. Restait la po et le po de cet ouli" (26). Using terms like "belle ouvrage," "bonnes oeuvres," "morale" and "beaux-arts" to explain their choice of the word "ouvroir," the members understood the meaning of 'ouvroir.' These choices and emphasis on rhyming and wordplay call to mind an era (1960) when privileged white males bathed in their unconscious "glory."

Are these compelling reasons to ask whether or not the group has reached its "end"? Is the experimentation in which the members of the Oulipo engage, consciously or unconsciously, fundamentally misogynist? The group is not arriving at its endpoint even if the experimentation in which they engage is probably fundamentally misogynist since any enterprise launched from within literary society born from fundamentally misogynist society is tainted. Elkin, declares that it's "hard as a woman, to know what to make of the Oulipo . . . Even women who love the Oulipo get impatient with it" (78). Faced with misogyny everywhere, impatience and not knowing "what to make of the Oulipo" is a generous stance and to be viewed as incentive to move forward, raise consciousness and engage. Insinuating that the group is seeing its final days ignores how important Oulipian experimentation is to the infinite

---

6 Centre national des ressources textuelles et lexicales:
http://www.cnrtl.fr/definition/ouvroir.
7 Oulipo, *La littérature potentielle* (Paris: Gallimard, 1973) 24-35.

process of challenging literary norms.

Juliana Spahr and Stephanie Young also wrote on Oulipo from a feminist perspective in a piece entitled "Foulipo."[8] The text is compelling in its authenticity and openness and poses some questions that raise consciousness and others that reveal how misguided some are as it relates to what Oulipian writing means socially.[9] Spahr and Young's written text does not communicate the meaning of the performance aspects of its presentation. Bruna Mori tells us that Spahr and Young's performance was part of "noulipo's politics of constraint panel," which took place at the Roy and Edna Disney Cal Arts Theater, Los Angeles, October 28-29, 2005. The text itself was "created through interpretations of Oulipian tactics of n+7 and Luc Etienne's "slenderizing," or "asphyxiation"— removing the letter "r" from speech." The performance was staged such that "Midway through the piece, a recording of their voices replaced their recitation, and they proceeded to remove their clothes, put on their clothes, remove their clothes, and replace them again, as they might do each day at home." The performance, while questioning Oulipian practice, was also an honest reflection on how women can both practice a form of Oulipian experimentation and remain true to themselves. In their text, they point out that in the poetry workshops they offer and attend, they "can think of no instance when a woman has bought in wok using a constictive composition device to any of these wokshops and yet we can think of men who did it week afte week and called themselves adicals fo it." They appreciated the men's use of "constictive compositions," all while remaining suspicious: "When we liked this wok by men we saw the eteat into constaint as an attempt by men to avoid pepetuating bougeois

---

8 The piece can be found here http://epc.buffalo.edu/authors/goldsmith/foulipo.html and here http://www.drunkenboat.com/db8/. Another longer version is found in *The noulipian Analects* (Los Angeles: Les Figues Press, 2007), a fascinating book containing essays and texts stemming from a conference, "noulipo," organized by REDCAT in 2005.
9 Kenneth Goldsmith in "A Response to Foulipo" responded to Spahr and Young's piece here: http://www.drunkenboat.com/db8/oulipo/feature-oulipo/essays/goldsmith/respon se.html, as did Bruna Mori in "Noulipo's Oulipoed Foulipo," which can be found here: http://www.drunkenboat.com/db8/oulipo/feature-oulipo/essays/mori/noulipo.html.

pivilege." Because the men never directly addressed all that bourgeois privilege infers, Spahr and Young rightfully assumed that using constraints does not create distance between a writer and bourgeois premises or habits. Although their suspicions about the inability to face down bourgeois privilege are worthwhile, the initial assumption that there is some specific connection between the use of constraints and the avoidance of privilege needs further investigation. From an Oulipian standpoint, the testing of constraints is not tied to a rejection of privilege. It is a means of countering the weight of traditional literary forms, which can represent privilege, but doesn't necessarily. Molière critiqued King Louis XIV quite pointedly, yet he is not known for how he innovated formally on the structures of classical French theater.

Feminist writers and performance artists react directly to, and interact with, the stress and gaze exercised on their bodies as a means of counteracting or at least resisting direct dominance. Feminist artistic production disrupts historical, economic, political and esthetic attempts to exploit the female body. As such, their honesty about their relationship with the Oulipo is impressive:

> And then we stopped shot of asking the question, is Oulipo pehaps toubled by an uninvestigated sexism and thus not capable of being a pat of ou witing life in any way, a question we didn't eally want to ask because we wee scaed of the answe and what it would deny us and we wee all about the "& and."

There is never a reason to stop asking questions about "uninvestigated sexism." To do so is to shrink our responsibilities to advancing social evolution. The performance itself challenges the "uninvestigated sexism" of the members of Oulipo and expresses concern about being exclusive rather than inclusive, a generous and laudable sentiment. It seems to me that Spahr and Young sense the potential of Oulipian experimentation, yet miss the opportunity to seize its possibilities as they reach their conclusion where they celebrate the impact of a conceptual series of photographs: "Hannah Wilke's Intravenus seies, completed shotly befoe he death fom beast cance in 1993 whee the pocedues at wok ae aging and disease and twenty yeas late the young beautiful body is eplaced by the body at its final and most conceptual bode." Wilke shares the debilitating effects of cancer on her body in her photographs. When focusing on the formalities, history and modalities of an art form and approaching creative work with the intention of reflecting them through imaginative innovation, which is at the heart of Oulipian production, potential meaning is born. Wilke made art true to herself, made a social and political statement, and did so by conceptualizing photographic representation.

As shown, misconceptions regarding the Oulipo's politics and its role in the avant-garde can lead to expressions of disappointment rather than precise critical engagement. Pablo Martín Ruiz, in *Four Cold Chapters on the Possibility of Literature Leading Mostly to Borges and Oulipo,*[10] writes:

> The Oulipo, which has always embraced the literary past and has never engaged in the rejection of tradition, has consistently refused to be considered an avant-garde group. But if we focus on the interest on methods of artistic production as a key and even defining element in the avant-garde mouvements, then the Oulipo, devoted exclusively to developing such methods and procedures and to turn them in the very aim of invention, can actually be said to the very culmination of the avant-garde, its paradigm and its exhaustion (148).

Too many ideas lead to confusion. While it is true that the Oulipo does not consider itself an avant-garde group, instead of attempting to respect and understand such positioning, Ruiz basically replies "too bad." After which, he declares that the Oulipo represents a "culmination" and an

---

10 Champaign, IL: Dalkey Archive Press, 2014.

"exhaustion" of a "defining element" of avant-garde "mouvements." But isn't it also true that all "avant-garde" movements have a "culmination" and an "exhaustion" when the moment (era, politics, society, etc.) they contest comes to an end? Isn't it also true that this is exactly what the Oulipo hopes to avoid? Oulipo resists temporal, social, cultural and even political limitations and that is what makes the work of these authors, mathematicians, etc., so interesting. Insisting that Oulipo is part of an avant-garde movement is a fundamental error in calculus and criticism. Ruiz is correct when he states, just after the above quote, that the Oulipo turns "conscious composition into a space of intellectual inquiry, into a field of study and an art form" (148-9). Here Ruiz opens the door to seeing the potential of the group's particular positioning within and without literary history.

The questions Ruiz asks about what Oulipo represents are actually similar to those asked by Spahr and Young as well as others. Regarding reception, he asks how to read a "work the composition of which we know to have been as deliberately pre-conceived and artificial as possible?" As far as critical analysis, Ruiz asks why "there is a tendency to value positively the resorting to traditional constraints, but to value negatively the invention of new ones?" Finally, he wonders whether or not there is an "ideal degree of visibility for the constraints" (157). Bringing these questions to the fore, claims Ruiz, is what makes the Oulipo into an "undeniable success." These questions about reception, about how to process an exercise in conscious and procedural writing, are excellent pathways into contemplating how to comprehend experience and how to read Oulipian texts. These questions force critics to ponder artifice, as well as the construction of value systems and esthetic choices. The Oulipo's success in creating such effective interactions with art tempt any engaged artist.

Oulipian potential is derived from attempts to extract what results from the encounter of two or more systems, both of which are governed by constraints and limitless at the same time. Those systems are language itself and either previously extant literary constraints (modified or not) and newly invented ones. The potential is in the text born of that encounter, the methods used to create the encounter, and the manner in which other authors or artists may choose to create their works by exploiting Oulipian methods. Oulipian potential is also the effect reading Oulipian texts has on the reader. The questions Ruiz asks reveal the extent to which the reader's engagement with Oulipian texts forges new methods of perception of not only written texts, but also the potential of any and all perceived patterns.

In Ruiz's closing observations about the Oulipo, he discovers that the reading of Oulipian texts "is ultimately made with the material to be found at the core of philosophy, science or religion" (289). Such reading seeks to decode more than a text's surface, but also its structural core, its functioning logic and its layered mysteries. While Ruiz posits a relationship that links reading Oulipian texts to a virtual hermeneutics of philosophy, religion and science, it is Daniel Levin Becker, a member of the Oulipo, who, in *Many Subtle Channels*[11] speaks eloquently and in a detailed and personal fashion about his interactions with Oulipian methods and production. Those interactions change how he sees and perceives what surrounds him. After time spent organizing the archives of the Oulipo, he admits to feeling fed up and wanting only to retreat to his apartment and take distance. Or he has the opposite reaction, finding the world

> enchanted and encoded, whispering sweet monovocalic nothings . . . from billboards and bakery windows, lobbying for the syllabic significance of every phrasc I hear in the Métro. I can feel my thought patterns changing gently, being primed along Oulipian lines; . . . On the better days I am instinctively aware of the potential of my own thoughts; on the slow days it's all I can do to inventory and categorize them— criticisms, compositions, the *inclassable*—in the hopes

---

11 Cambridge, MA.: Harvard UP, 2012.

that I can read some sense into them later (242).

What I find appealing in Becker's description is how deeply the de-norming and subsequent re-forming of patterns enters into his spirit. Thoughts are no longer just ideas that may or may not be productive, they exhibit potentiality thanks to their patterns and possibilities. The pattern of thoughts change. And then Becker uses these magic words that remind us of Ruiz's comments: "inventory" and "categorize." These are the stuff of knowledge; they create it, integrate it, make use of it and take ownership of it. Ultimately, categorizing and inventorying are the generative actions of all hermeneutics. Finally, Becker does more than cogitate: he "feels" thoughts and "hopes" for them to make sense. These verbs that capture affect are also means of acquiring knowledge.

For Becker the reader is invited to the party. But this party has obligations and they don't include bringing flowers or a bottle for the hosts. The reader, suggests Becker, "enjoys that game of triangulation for its very endlessness . . . She's geeked on the rush of unraveling secret Oulipian snarls, begins to look reflexively at any old text with an eye out for buried constraints, hidden indices, serendipities of which not even the author was aware" (294-5). After the party, a parting gift for the reader is the ability to notice, which Becker calls a "beauty of potential" (297). When the mind is stimulated to notice, find patterns and potential in the unimportant and the trivial, making sense takes on potent power. Becker transfers these reconfigurations to the "supposedly nonliterary world," which in turn takes on game-like aspects: "numbers and letters and words and phrases are combined and split and reconfigured and exchanged" (298). Potential in terms of potent and power transferred to the reader who is then transformed into a writer of a world, a maker of a world, a potential world, are gifts bestowed by the Oulipo. The duality of Oulipian potential, both for writers who invent and readers drawn into texts as players of the constraints' games, makes clear that this group is not avant-garde. It is timeless.

Hervé Le Tellier, in *Esthétique de l'Oulipo*[12] also does an excellent job of explaining the particularities of the relationship between the Oulipian reader and the Oulipian writer. Le Tellier, in fact, confuses the situation perfectly by reminding us that the members of the Oulipo are both readers and writers. Members of the group can resort to the use of constraints to write during difficult personal times:

> Car la contrainte, répétons-le, qui doit pouvoir resservir, peut stimuler le désir de celui qui, d'abord, en en fut lecteur. Et rares sont les oulipiens qui, à un moment, n'ont pas été ensorcelés, subjugués par cette contrainte, et n'y ont fait appel à d'importantes occasions de leur vie personnelle (251).

One potential outcome of a constraint is its repeated use. Since the members of Oulipo are readers of constraints and are "bewitched" and "subjugated" by them, yet, cognizant of their power, they turn to them on "important occasions" in their lives.

Constraints, Le Tellier continues, measure time, they impose a particular movement upon language, one that does not necessarily respect its syntax. Prosodic constraints change the amount of time it takes to read a poem and therefore the chronology of a reading. Readers anticipate that time in the "rythme de lecture" (270); constraints effect biology by governing a reader's anticipation. Expanding even further, Le Tellier finds that for many members of the group, "contrainte et quotidien entretiennent une relation intime" (271), a notion that corresponds to Becker's extension of the effect of constraints onto the "nonliterary world." However, it is the constraint's ability to express the "émotion des objets" (271), an ability born of the relationship between constraints and daily life, that may be surprising coming from these scientific minded, mathematician savants.

The interconnectivity of the different elements that compose a world

---

12 Bordeau: Le Castor Astral, 2006.

comes as no surprise. The idea that the constraint offers a novel means of articulating (on the levels of both creation and reception) those elements, is also not sparkling new. Seeing and grasping how constraint is a particular form of articulation, and then re-inventing them, tweaking them, and practicing them for all to see and share, feels like a moment worth savoring and a spirit worthy of respect.

As I said previously, when discussing Elkin and Esposito's book on the "end" of Oulipo, the use of constraints is anti-chance. Le Tellier does a good job showing how that works when he discusses Gérard Genette's criticism of the group. Genette criticized Georges Perec's use of the lipogram (a systematized elision of one letter or more from a text) when re-writing Baudelaire's famous sonnet "Receuillement." He did the same in *La Disparition*, famous for its astounding elision of the letter 'e' throughout an entire novel. Genette suggests that chance played a role in Perec's re-composition of Baudelaire's sonnet. Le Tellier is astonished that Genette "fait montre d'une telle inexpérience de la contrainte" (246), that it is obvious that Genette never tried his hand at writing under constraint and unusual that Genette allows himself an "étrange ingénuité, inhabituelle chez lui" (246). If Genette had tried writing a lipogram, he would have seen the extent to which he would have been forced to follow unusual paths to the voluntary making of meaning. There is no luck to such efforts. As an example of the bounty that constraint supplies, Le Tellier declares that *La Disparition* is the French language novel that contains the greatest number of different *substantifs* (nouns). For Le Tellier, a lipogram shows that the "mot juste" doesn't exist, that all languages are equal, and that when working under the degree of difficulty imposed by a lipogram, the author's choices create the text. He is most surprised by Genette's inherent belief that the language itself will eventually mean what it says, thus overriding an author's will.

Le Tellier's defense of an anti-chance practice of writing brings the raising of consciousness into focus. Raising consciousness holds promise (potential?) in that it can never be put to bed because once raised, it cannot be deflated. Raising self-awareness—or knowing that we know (consciousness)—by practicing a constraint, gives birth to potent and power; seeing is changed, worlds are invented and modified. The effect is drug-like. But Le Tellier refuses the drug-like analogy:

> La contrainte n'est ni un dopage, ni des vitamines, ni de l'engrais. L'oulipien ose, parce que la contrainte est un moyen *et* un principe autant qu'un obstacle, parce qu'elle fait levier pour la création. Elle est un moule pour la langue, et aussi son complémentaire exact pour l'œil et l'oreille, un emballage (272).

He sees the use of constraints as a dare, a means, a principle, an obstacle and ultimately a vehicle of creation. The constraint shapes language and packages it. The drug-like effect I described is how it induces insight into what may or may not have already pre-existed. Already and not already, what does it matter if comprehension is enhanced?

Understanding that which links constraint to potential, that the group Oulipo rejects chance, that it is neither a political nor an avant-garde enterprise, is essential to a response to recent criticism of the group. Such an understanding is also an invitation to any social or political movements that wishes to practice Oulipian methods to reach their own goals. It is with a quick review of specific elements of François Le Lionnais' manifestoes that I hope to defend the eternal and infinite aspirations of the group.

In the three manifestoes, François Le Lionnais emphasizes the permanence of the debate that most interests the Oulipo. In "La Lipo (Le premier Manifeste),"[13] Le Lionnais states clearly, when situating the Oulipo's objectives in relation to literary history, that "la vérité est que la querelle des Anciens et des Modernes est permanante" (15). In other words, as long are there are those who attempt to move "ahead," there will be those who prefer stasis. In "Le second manifeste" (Oulipo, *La littérature potentielle*, 19-23), Le Lionnais asks what would happen if

---

13 Oulipo, *La littérature potentielle* (Paris: Gallimard, 1973) 15-18.

"l'OuLiPo . . . disparaissait subitement" and then answers his own question: "Il en résulterait cependant dans le destin de la civilisation un certain retard que nous estimons de notre devoir d'atténuer" (23). The grandiose reference to the "destiny of civilization" is made, on the one hand, tongue in cheek. On the other hand, the potential of the Oulipian project, as I've discussed, does apply to the making and implementation of knowledge and comprehension. Exaggeration and self-importance tend to play roles in manifestoes, yet at times to hear from and read those who hope to move civilization along, bit by bit, is reassuring. In "Le troisième manifeste—Prolégomènes à toute littérature future,"[14] Le Lionnais indicates that there are three phases of the "programme de construction de toutes structures littéraires possibles." The first phase includes categorizing all possible mathematic theorems and fabricating all possible chemical substances. The second requires extracting from this grouping all structures that have worthwhile efficacy. The third phase leads to the threshold of the "l'Œuvre" (799). Suffice it to say, the Oulipian project sees no end, is not restricted to memorial time, believes that it belongs to destiny and is permanent since it intends to engage with "future literature." Le Lionnais' reference to "l'Œuvre" is one that encompasses not only literature and writing, but the sciences (at least mathematics and chemistry) as well. What does an eternal literary project mean? First and foremost that any critique of the Oulipo needs to respect the temporal framework within which the members work as well as all that this field of temporality implies.

Limitlessness serves as the impetus to certain Oulipian projects. For example, *Cent mille milliards de poèmes* by Raymond Queneau contains 10^{14} poems, a collection of poems that is governed by the constraint Queneau invented wherein every line of the ten sonnets he presents can be replaced by any line of any of the other sonnets. In one short work,

---

14 In Marcel Bénabou et Paul Fournel, *Anthologie de l'Oulipo* (Paris: Gallimard, 2009) 798-801.

15 Paris: P.O.L, 2013. The first three volumes, *Navet, Linge, œil de vieux*, were published in 1999.

Queneau was able to produce more literature than all the literature that had ever been produced. Jacques Jouet writes in public squares, writes a poem every day and published *Du Jour,*[15] 896 pages long. He plans on writing a poem every day until his death. His *roman feuilleton* (novel-series, or soap opera) *La République de Mek Ouyes* is now 2000 episodes long and I have heard from colleagues that Jouet intends to ask other members of the Oulipo to continue adding episodes after his death. In 1979 Georges Perec wrote *Le Voyage d'hiver,*[16] about a young French professor who unearths a book in a used book store that would upend the history of nineteenth century French literature. Members of the Oulipo retook and continued the story and in 2013 *Le Voyage d'hiver & ses suites*[17] is published, co-authored by Perec and Oulipo. Perec's original 48-page book once republished contains 448 pages. There is also the *Bibliothèque oulipienne,*[18] a leaflet-like series of, at last count, 231 volumes in which members practice, share, continue, retry and try out, innovate upon, their different writing practices, structures and *tentatives*. These leaflets represent another on-going collective effort, they are literary practices that are eternal and valuable models of collective writing.

The Oulipian project is about potential more than anything else. The final word, in italics, of the "Note de l'Éditeur" in *La littérature potentielle* is "préliminaire." Theirs is to start working, not to finish. Although the word 'literature' is used seriously, I would like to emphasize the word "writing," or even *"écriture"* to better grasp both the intimacy and potency of the group's work. Sentient beings who read know how moving a good read is. We sense how writing has an immediate effect on daily activities, on our own sensibilities, on how we comprehend the people, economies, politics and history of the moments of our existence. Experimentation in writing is experimentation in what can be and nothing could ever be more necessary. The temptation to state "at this moment of history" is great, for all the most obvious reasons, but to

---

16 Paris: Seuil, 1993. First published in *Saisons* (Paris: Hachette, 1979).
17 Paris: Seuil, 2013.
18 Visit http://oulipo.net/fr/bo for a list of all the titles.

actively use language to articulate the fiction and dreams that enrich possibilities (potential), that reveal quadrants and spaces, be they virtual, sentimental, geopolitical or geometrical, that explore possible impulses for easily perceptible psychological turmoil, is an activity necessary for humankind forever and for never.

Embedded Words & Liaisons

DOUG NUFER

The Me Theme Fare, Well Farewell

Into X, I, cant-intoxicant influent
In fluent slogan
Slog an us age usage
The me theme does press.

O, do espresso cart
Elite cartel iterations
Ration shot hot dosages?

Do sages' binges bin gestes testify?
Test if you lipogram OULIPO
Grammar marines in esteem teem
Abound a bound motto mot to avoid A Void.

Gram grammar maraud it or auditor types typeset
Ethereal here a la mode Alamo defeats, feats.

PR ivy, privy to can a Dada shout
Canada dash outhouse or gander
By house organ derby parlays par,
Lays its wayside allocations.

It sways ideal locations to prevent
Top rev entropy.

Ropy divertissement
A-styles divert.

Is semen tasty?
Lesser serendipities end.

I, pities amass, am assoiled, oiled
An ointment anointment pries the priest,
He who led whole diagnostic consciences.

I, agnostic, con science's mythic kale
My thick ale new sand news and re-
Creation recreation in foreign info reign
(Rum or rumor writ, he'd writhed,
"We're readying a dying ozone O zone")
All us, I've, allusive fatalist, fat
A list A-list.

I'm a gist imagist
Your yo ur thesis the sis thesis
The REM in theremin fare
Well, farewell

The Me Theme.

After Word Afterword

"Why is justice just ice?" was far from my first exposure to embedded words, but this line in the poem "The Third Station of the Double-Crossed" by Chris Toll (1948-2012) in *Clutching at Straws* drove me to enlist such words in the service of an extreme constraint. Many thousands of these recruits lounge in the dictionary, in books, newspapers, and magazines, on billboards and in conversations, potentially begging for discipline. I started to write something by using repeated lines consisting of only the larger words and the smaller words each larger word completely contained. I preferred words whose meanings changed, from long to short form. For such an unnatural and restrictive project, one that concealed and revealed the author/ subject while also reflecting on the first-person pronoun that dominates so much writing, *The Me Theme* seemed like an apt title.

When poet Annalisa Pesek read what I was up to, she suggested a companion constraint: not only embedded words but also liaisons between words could be included in the strings of letters that must repeat. This struck me as offering the advantage of being more rigorous yet more fluid, with an added benefit of making the enterprise more obscure and therefore weirder than the non-compounded version of the constraint. So in the stanza, "O do espresso cart/ Elite cartel iterations/ Ration shot hot dosages?" the words "cart elite" reform as "cartel ite-" en route to becoming "cartel iterations" which "ration shot hot dosages."

Thanks to OULIPO and the procedures that open new approaches to writing, this is how it often begins for me: a chance encounter with a sequence of letters, sounds, or some other pattern makes me wonder what to make of it. Will the constraint spawned by the sequence mercifully exhaust itself after a few pages, or will it tie me up for years in pursuit of writing a novel or series of poems that might express the constraint as it was meant to be? When staking out some claim to a scheme that might form the basis of a book, I try to find out how or if this constraint has been used. Harry Mathews, Daniel Levin Becker, Warren

Motte, and William Gillespie are some of the advisers I've consulted over the years, but then there are always pieces popping up in various forms of publication that might well have covered this territory to such an extent that any attempt for another writer to venture there would be redundant. It's best to avoid the Oulipian consolation that someone may have "plagiarized by anticipation" my work or fulfilled the demands of a constraint before I did.

After finishing a book of poems that emerge from strings of words, embedded words, and liaisons (like the example above), I didn't find any predecessors. Not by any due diligence, I did learn that a 1994 Joni Mitchell song, "Sex Kills", has the line, "Is justice just ice?" It seems unlikely that Toll wrote his poem decades before it appeared in 2010. Maybe he came to "justice" unaware of "Sex Kills," wrote his poem, and then discovered that Mitchell had beat him to the line; or, her line could have prompted him. I'm just relieved that they didn't go crazy making whole works out of embedded words and liaisons.

But what do I know? Maybe they did.

Songs for Liana/ Argumentum ethicum

PABLO M. RUIZ

Description of Songs for Liana

Song # 1: "Sometimes", by My Bloody Valentine
This song requires attention. You should listen to it with your eyes as well. When you do that you realize what the secret of its construction is: a bright luminous melody on top of a dark black layer of distortion. The melody is so simply beautiful that birds should sing it every morning.

Song # 2: "Floaty" (Foo Fighters), by Petra Haden and Bill Frisell
This song reminds me of those things that cannot be touched: a friend's voice, the planets in the sky, childhood memories, bright colors, smoke, nightmares, stories not told yet, the soccer ball I lost when I was six, the string sounds in this very song, your favorite words.

Song # 3: "En Gallop", by Joanna Newsom
You should know everything and more about this song. You should forget everything and more about this song.

Song # 4: "Será que la canción llegó hasta el sol", by Luis Alberto Spinetta.
This is my favorite songwriter in Argentina. Y esta es una canción de cuna que hizo para sus hijos. Me gusta la canción de cuna en general: una canción para cantarle a alguien que no la entiende. Como si su poder no

dependiera de su sentido, o mejor, como si dependiera de un sentido secreto, like a mantra or a magic spell. A veces, la mejor poesía tiene algo de eso también: un puñado de tiniebla que no entendemos y que nos convierte un poco en niños.

Song # 5: "Darkest Dreaming", by David Sylvian.
This song seems to know the way you feel about things you have never even imagined. How it does that, I have no idea.

Argumentum ethicum, or Ethical Refutation of the Existence of God (An Interlinear Translation from Spanish)

El acto de bondad es de virtud indudable sólo cuando se ejerce de manera completamente

The act of goodness is perfectly good (that is, it achieves perfection as a good deed) only if it is performed in a completely

anónima, ya que es la única exenta del pecado de vanidad o del cálculo interesado de

anonymous manner, since this is the only way it could be free of the sin of vanity or of the selfish expectation of

beneficios ulteriores.

ulterior benefits or gains to be received as a consequence of the good deed (like in the case of gifts or donations).

Ahora bien, si Dios existe, ese acto de bondad pura sería imposible, ya que Su

Now, if God exists, that act of pure goodness (free from all possible sins) would be actually impossible to perform, because His

omnisciencia lo conocería.

omniscience (that is, the consequence of His being all-knowing) would of course know it as its absolute witness.

Pero Dios no puede ser un obstáculo para la bondad, que es Su misma esencia.

But God cannot be an obstacle for goodness, which is His very essence, what He is constantly thriving for in everything He does.

Por lo tanto, y en nombre del Bien, Dios no existe.

Therefore, and in the name of goodness, God does not exist. Or if He does, He will immediately cease to exist.

Oulipo Forever

MARC LAPPRAND

How does Oulipo fit into evolution? In other words, how can we assess the advent, existence, and longevity of the Oulipo group in terms of evolutionary concepts? The *Ouvroir de Littérature potentielle* was born in 1960. Yet the notions of potentiality engendering wordplay have always existed, ever since humanoids transformed grunting and growling into articulated language. However tricky it may be to establish when the first proto-Oulipian appeared, it is yet fair to assume that when articulated language was brought into our ancestors' brains (some say around 100,000 years ago), notions such as humor, play, riddles, and puns must have simultaneously appeared. Some radical evolutionists claim that those capacities are in fact needed for our survival as a species.

You will also remember that Oulipians count single years as centuries. They have therefore already existed, as a constituted group, for over 5600 years. That makes their history almost as old as that of writing (Sumer, around 6000 years ago). In addition to this time inflation, they are quite fond of the concept of "anticipatory plagiary," which refers to any text produced before 1960, the composition of which being akin to Oulipian methods. So, one may assume that our Pleistocene ancestors (Pleistocene is the long and rather monotonous era during which language started to develop) are all anticipatory plagiarists of Oulipo, as long as they devoted their speech activity to controlled play, systematic punning or even algorithmic structures (mural paintings in very old caves actually point to that direction). This propensity to play with words fits logically with the concept of *The Symbolic Species*, brilliantly developed by Terrence Deacon.

We will thus argue that Oulipo, as a consensual gathering of knowledge-thirsty adventurous intellectuals (in 1960) is the unavoidable official outcome of what has forever existed in the history of mankind: treating language not as a mere communicating tool (e.g. "See bison in valley? Let us corner prey upstream of rivulet, hunt and slaughter beast for family food!"), but as the instrument of a higher order, that of play on language (e.g. "See bitumen in vampire? Let us corner prig upstream of robber, hunt and slaughter beauty for fancy footing!" – assuming they had a forethought of what S + 7 would be prior to the advent of the dictionary).

The British anthropologist Robin Dunbar has come up with the tantalizing idea that language may have evolved from the mutual grooming among the great apes. You groom my back and I will groom yours. Thus we strengthen our alliance. But how do we include a third ape? A grooming *ménage à trois* would be cumbersome; so let's figure another way of forming alliances, and eventually look for a new and more efficient way of communicating our desires, fears, emotions and hopes. Deacon goes a step further. Using the tripartition of the semiologist Charles Sanders Pierce (icon, index, symbol), he identifies humans' thirst for symbolism. His completely new (and contested) approach provides some basis for the notion that our super brain hypertrophied itself in order to accommodate the arrival of language. Indeed, language is an extremely complex system, which, as far as we know, no other higher order of the animal kingdom possesses. Deacon argues that our brain needed to expand significantly to host such an intricate machine as language; and it did not happen the other way around, i.e. "Gee, we have such a smart brain, what worthy download should we envisage: ESP, time travel, language?" Now, if we espouse this fascinating view, is it not appropriate to accept the notion that once our ancestors mastered any form of articulated language, and once their level of structural and grammatical consciousness was such that they realized they could play tricks to and with the machine, they would do so for the sake of exploration, provocation, or mere fun. Proto-Oulipo was born a long long time ago (but not far away in the galaxy).

Evolution theoreticians have convincingly established that our need for art and artistic expression is not only genetically encoded in us, but that it is also a fundamental and necessary component for our survival as a species (cf. Denis Dutton's *The Art Instinct*). Linguistic expression can cover many artistic forms, such as poetry, song, religious mutterings, or advertising. When Aristotle (4th century BCE) formalized the vast array of tropes, putting metaphor in a foremost position, it is fair to assume that those figures of speech had long existed before he wrote his *Poetics*.

This evolutionary view of Oulipo also makes sense with the two concurrent fields of activities they initially proposed: anoulipism and synthoulipism. The former consists in analysing the huge corpus of existing literature, in order to assess its levels of potentiality; the latter is the creative side of Oulipo, informed by the findings of the former. Indeed, one only has to look at the ginormous brains that Oulipo gathered in its early stages. The combined cultures and erudition of all members covered pretty much the whole spectrum of knowledge: Antiquity, Renaissance, the Classic era, modern times, along with the histories and theories of painting, music, drama, mathematics, graphs, logics, chess, crosswords, nuclear research, computer science, philosophy, journalism, tweeting, and so on. Under the highly motivational auspices of the two founding members, François Le Lionnais and Raymond Queneau, the group became quickly very productive, despite their first ten years spent in some kind of secrecy.

All living organisms depend on a very limited but fundamental set of functions closely related to survival and reproduction. For the Darwinians among us, all living species evolve according to natural and sexual selections. Can those principles be applied to the Oulipo group? If so, we must admit that they are doing very well from a Darwinian perspective. As a collective, they have always maintained good health. Their unique governance without a guru or a pope at their head (like André Breton for the surrealists or Alain Robbe-Grillet for the *Nouveau Roman*) has proved a fabulous warrant of longevity: not only has the Oulipo group managed to successfully aggregate new members, but they have expanded their horizons across the French borders. The latest new comers are from California, Argentina, and Spain. The election procedure is very simple, yet very effective: cooptation means they all have to agree to integrate a newcomer. Furthermore, if one deliberately applies for inclusion, one is irrevocably doomed to exclusion. Thus, no personal ambitions can interfere with the harmonious existence of such a homogeneous, yet diversified, group of human beings – or *homo Oulipo*. The Oulipo genetic code must be very strong. No constituted group of intellectuals has ever lasted so long (at least in modern times). The usual destiny of an avant-garde, or any form of a counter-movement, is to disappear sooner rather than later, either for lack of fuel (or stimulus) or, worse but too commonly, for tyrannical abuse of a usually self-proclaimed leader, or "maître à penser." No such dangers seem to threaten the Oulipo group, which is thriving, despite recent attacks from those American para-oulipian writers and journalists who predict that they are doomed (mostly for lack of renewal, which is quite preposterous).[1]

Interestingly, one of the first definitions of Oulipo referred to the group as an "Organism which proposes to examine in what way, given a scientific theory concerning among other things language (therefore, anthropology), it can be induced with aesthetic pleasure (affectivity and fantasy)." Immediately after this declaration of intent was laid out, the now famous definition (attributed to Raymond Queneau) of Oulipians being "Rats who have to construct the labyrinth from which they plan to escape."[2] Indeed, Oulipo is akin to a living organism, with its interdependent constituents, be they rats or human beings. The word "Ouvroir" must not be neglected either: it refers to a workroom, more specifically a sewing room where nuns used to gather for their needle-work, usually in a convent. And what would they be sewing other than the DNA string of the Oulipo organism? If Oulipo is an organism, it may be

---

1 Elkin, Lauren, and Scott Esposito. *The End of Oulipo?* Zero Books, 2013.
2 *Oulipo: 1960-1963*, Christian Bourgois, 1980, p. 43 (my translations).

compared with the Hydra Lernaia: the multi-headed monster of the Greek mythology, whose severed heads reproduce twofold. From this perspective, Oulipo is no less than a formidable machine-monster, designed to read, decipher, analyse, interpret, and share vast patches of culture.

Oulipians naturally each have their individual personality, tastes and distastes, writing preferences, let alone disagreements on the status of the constraint within a piece of writing. However, whenever and wherever a single member of Oulipo speaks of the entire group, they do so in the same voice, with the same cheeky mood, with the same love of all that they do, and the same passion and pride of their belonging to the group. It is fair to assume that this is key to their harmonious survival. Despite the fact that among the ten founding members only one is alive as I write these lines, the original spirit has not faded; its DNA has only adapted to our ever-changing environment. Perhaps the most conspicuous change in the group's *modus operandi* is their public readings, which started at the Halle Saint-Pierre (at the foot of Montmartre in Paris) in 1997. The famous "*Jeudis de l'Oulipo*" kept on attracting good size crowds of fans, presently taking place monthly during the school year in the great auditorium of the *Bibliothèque nationale de France*.

The first abstraction of Oulipo was born in the brain of François Le Lionnais during the Second World War. It took some fifteen years to evolve and take form. What is amazing is that the group was so quickly constituted, as if flowing from source. It is a known fact that Oulipians never really die (neither can they willingly resign their belonging to the group); they may, however, be called upon after their physical disappearance. Paul Fournel, the current Oulipo President, explains that when deceased Oulipians are evoked in a regular meeting, it is not for the sake of blowing the bugle at the last post, but more plainly because they might still have a few questions to ask them.

All this being said, coming back to evolution, one may safely claim that Oulipo, being fit, is likely to survive, divert us, enrich our lives and continue to fascinate the eager readers that we have been for a very long time.

Concise Evolutionary Bibliography

Blackmore, Susan. *The Meme Machine.* Oxford, New York, Oxford University Press, 1999.

Boyd, Brian. *On the Origin of Stories: Evolution, Cognition and Fiction.* Cambridge (Mass.), Londres, Harvard University Press, 2009.

Boyer, Pascal. *Et l'homme créa les dieux : Comment expliquer la religion.* Gallimard, coll. « Folio essais », 2001.

Bryson, Bill. *A Short History of Nearly Everything.* New York, Broadway Books, 2004.

Buican, Denis. *L'Odyssée de l'évolution.* Ellipses, 2008.

Buss, David. *Evolutionary Psychology: The New Science of Mind.* Boston, Allyn and Bacon, 1999.

Carroll, Joseph. *Literary Darwinism: Evolution, Human Nature, and Literature.* New York, Routledge, 2004.

Cloutier, Richard. *Les Vulnérabilités masculines: une approche biopsychosociale.* Montréal, Éditions de l'hôpital Sainte-Justine, 2004.

Darwin, Charles. *On The Origin of Species by Means of Natural Selection* [1859]. New York, The Modern Library, 2009.

Dawkins, Richard. *The Selfish Gene.* Oxford University Press, 1975.

Deacon, Terrence: *The Symbolic Species: the co-evolution of the language and the brain.* New York, Londres : W. W. Norton & Company 1997.

Dunbar, Robin. *Grooming, Gossip, and the Evolution of Language.* Cambridge (Mass.), Harvard University Press, 1997.

Dunbar, Robin. *The Human Story: A New History of Mankind's Evolution.* Londres, Faber & Faber, 2004.

Dunbar, Robin, & Louise Barrett, Ed. *The Oxford Handbook of Evolutionary Psychology.* Oxford University Press, 2007.

Dutton, Denis. *The Art Instinct.* New York, Berlin, Londres, Bloomsbury Press, 2009.

Fisher, Helen. *Anatomy of Love.* New York, Ballantine Books, 1992.

Gottschall, Jonathan. "The Tree of Knowledge and Darwinian Literary Studies." *Philosophy and Literature,* vol. 27 (No. 2), Oct. 2003, p. 255-268.

Gottschall, Jonathan, & David Sloan Wilson (Éd.). *The Literary Animal: Evolution and the Nature of Narrative.* Evanston (Illinois), Northwestern University Press, 2005.

Gould, Stephen Jay. *The Hedgehog, the Fox and the Magister's Pox: Mending the Gap between Science and the Humanities.* New York, Three Rivers Press, 2003.

McCrone, John : *The Ape That Spoke: Language and the Evolution of the Human Mind.* New York: William Morrow & Co 1991.

Miller, Geoffrey. *Spent: Sex, Evolution, and Consumer Behavior.* New York, Viking, 2009.

Miller, Geoffrey. *The Mating Mind: How Sexual Choice Shaped the Evolution of Human Nature.* New York, Anchor Books, 2001.

Nadel, Jacqueline, & Jean Decety. *Imiter pour découvrir l'humain : Psychologie, neurobiologie, robotique et philosophie de l'esprit.* PUF, 2002.

Pinker, Steven. *The Blank Slate: The Modern Denial of Human Nature.* New York, Viking Penguin, 2002.

Raymond, Michel. *Cro-Magnon toi-même! : Petit guide darwinien de la vie quotidienne.* Seuil, coll. « Points Sciences », 2008.

Shields, David: *How Literature saved my life.* New York: Alfred Knopf 2013.

Smail, Daniel Lord. *On Deep History and the Brain.* Berkeley, Los Angeles, London, University of California Press, 2008.

Tooby, John, & Leda Cosmides. "Does Beauty Build Adapted Minds? Toward an Evolutionary Theory of Aesthetics, Fiction and the Arts." *SubStance,* Issue 94/95 (vol. 30, No. 1 & 2), 2001, p. 6-27.

Wilson, Edward O. *Consilience: The Unity of Knowledge.* New York, Akfred A. Knopf, 1998.

Workman, Lance, & Will Reader. *Evolutionary Psychology: An Introduction.* Cambridge, Cambridge University Press, 2004.

39 Lines for the 40

PAUL GRIFFITHS

'A club. Bard, card, gabbler, bugler . . . . Are all —?'
'Call it a cenacle, rare C., or err!'
'Are we here? Why are we here – met here, sat?'
'The sonneteer, hip H.! "So stole the rose . . ."'
'" . . . Our Mary dear, our queen" – our nun-mama!'
'No, ole man R. Can mama be a nun?'

'As Jess, a Cuban queen, can be a nun.'
'Naval queen, Javan queen, nun queen . . . – all!'
'I remember Cal; she'd be the real mama.'
'Lord! Nor "real", nor "our". Elder Al do err!'
'Or prose processors regress . . . . So: "O rose . . ."'
'That pal met many a clap as he sat.'

'Is it to risk port or pastis *I* sat?'
'Clears, releases all. Nurse, a jar! Nurse! Nun!'
'Valerian releases all – or rose.'
'I believe dinner'll relieve Dan and all.'
'Off! Fed, fortified, coffeed! Do I err?'
'Laggard clam, cured, I had, me and mama.'

'A clam? Mama ate a clam? Hi! Mama?'
'Aches? Qua headaches? She just ate as she sat?'

'"To be or..." I torture our bard; I err . . .'
'Afar off on an aeroplane, our nun . . .'
'Nun again? Queen? Bard? Declining are all . . .'
'As asses . . . O Homer! O Bach! O Rose!'

'Nice fall! "A rose is a rose is a rose".'
'All dead calm. A pure lull. Headache, mama?'
'To flop, to flop, full of turbot, of all!
'O just quest! To eat East-Coast cactus sat!'
'Let it lie in cute cut lentil, nice nun!'
'I'll vet the liver, revel till I err!'

'Art! Great art! Eat?! EAT?!?! Anger! Fear! Gag! Err!'
'No, dear A. Dressed dace on an ice of rose . . .'
'Veal and laverbread bedevil our nun.'
'O Ninook on a moon kink, o mama!'
'List: At last I sit as still as I sat.'
'Cake, liver, dace, veal, laverbread and all!'

'A–B–C–D– . . . As bar codes do err, our job squad rose.'
'Nada. Chill nihil. Adieu, nun mine. Adieu, mine mama.'
'O sestina, amaze the Sat police – members all!'

LiVING dIVISiON

BY STePH

L iVING dIVISiON has roots in a game from my school days. We would try to out *gross* each other by imagining more and more disgusting foodstuffs. It starts tame: "off milk"—but the list continues:

"Off milk and lemon juice."
"What about off milk, lemon juice and vinegar?"
". . . and water from the dog's bowl."
". . . and . . ."
". . . and . . ."
"Off milk, lemon juice, vinegar, dog's bowl water . . . and a rotten egg!"

In rose-tinted memory I assign the game a semi-educational purpose. The rotten egg, the worst imaginable thing to eat, was the trump item. The list always began with soured milk and ended with an ancient egg. It was a memory exercise, but, for me at least, it also engendered a fascination with patterns. I took to heart the truth that everything is always worse with a rotten egg.

Perhaps my love of sequences and patterns began with such games or perchance is a quirk of genetics, but suffice to state; I love patterns.

While this reasoning is unsound:

I love patterns.
Oulipian writing constraints contain patterns.
Therefore I love Oulipian writing.

in my case the conclusion also happens to be true. I have enjoyed patterns since childhood, and I'm always searching for the trump card; the smelly egg.

A couple of years ago I was working with lipograms. I challenged a student reading group to #TweetWithoutAnE while my own explorations soon took me to the very limited letters of the Prisoner Restriction. The work was enjoyably frustrating—or should that be frustratingly enjoyable? The results, while my own words, did not have that *je ne sais quoi* that identified them as mine. My style was hidden beneath the restriction. I liked the writing that emerged, but it did not feel mine.

The Prisoner Restriction, is a lipogram where the letters that are 'permitted' are chosen for being compact. They have no ascenders or descenders, allowing 'a' and 'c' but not 'b' or 'g.' In practice this rules out whole sections of language, not just an even spread of 'forbidden words.' Aside from a few irregular verbs, the lack of 'd' removes the simple past tense (~~ed~~) and while forbidding 'h' removes the perfect (~~have~~) and past perfect (~~had~~), and the lack of 'g' removes all continuous tenses (~~ing~~). The future is missing too, since 'l' is forbidden (~~will~~), this also accounts for the removal of a swathe of adverbs (~~ly~~). Pronouns, other than first person, are lost to the lack of 'h' and 'y'(~~you/she/he/they~~). Taken together, this makes for works written almost entirely in the present tense, using either the first person or named characters with concise short sentences.

I enjoyed the mental gymnastics of the task, but this style of writing was so unlike my own that I started to look for an alternative. Trawling memory lane for ideas led me to the fundamental question: "What would happen if I 'rotten egged' the prisoner?"

My first childish reaction was '*eww gross.*' Even as an adult it feels unconscionably cruel to throw a rotten egg at a captive inside a small cell. The prisoner within has enough problems trying to fit as many words as possible onto a scrap of paper, without the addition of eggy hydrogen sulphide.

That was the Eureka moment. Hydrogen sulphide in chemical notation is H_2S. Elements are abbreviated to one, two or three letters. These are standardised symbols. Perhaps I could write using them? It would not be quite a lipogram, but perhaps, neither would it rule out whole sections of language as the Prisoner Restriction did.

I found a copy of the periodic table and examined it for constraint viability. I wanted to know which parts of language would be ruled out by writing with these symbols. Would whole sections be excluded as with the Prisoner Restriction? If so, this would be a non-starter and I might owe the captive an apology and some air freshener.

I found that J and Q were not part of any chemical element symbol. Neither letter appears frequently in English, so I felt this was not a barrier to using the constraint. I noted that 'e' was not present as a single letter symbol, but was part of several pairings. This would make words with 'e' possible, but still restricted. Similarly 'd' is present, but not on its own, which makes simple past tenses of 'ed' possible, but only when the other letters in the symbols are taken into account, and often requiring a symbol to split across two adjacent words. I decided to allow symbols to split across words, but to keep them within sentences, lines or paragraphs or other punctuation as appropriate for the piece, to help with the 'pauses' in the text. I concluded that writing with chemical element symbols, instead of a normal alphabet would be quite possible, while still be restricted enough to be comparable to writing with a lipogram.

Writing with chemical elements felt like writing with a new alphabet. As I became more familiar with the symbols, and how they might group together to equate to the letter groups I wanted (eg: ing, er, ed, tion) I found I was composing text at a reasonable speed, while still having to consider several phrases and words, before finding one that worked. Then came the challenge of how to present the text to the reader.

I started by using 'normal text' but keeping to the capitalisation of the element symbols. I also preserved the spaces between words, regardless of whether they fell mid symbol or not. This allowed symbols to continue across word splits, but not across lines splits.

I

I BIrTh

I GaIN SeNSe

I FIT iN HeRe

I FAlTeR aNd FAlL uNdEr

YOU CeAsE uNdErSTaNdING aNY NOISe

YOU ReBUFF mY AsSISTaNCe

YOU CRuSH OThErNEsS

YOU PArTiTiON

Y

The text version above is very readable, but does not communicate the constraint very clearly. Looking at it with no other frame of reference, I do not think many readers would notice the 'pattern' behind the capitalisations. The subject matter is linked with the constraint, so that if the constraint is not itself recognised by the reader, the piece is diminished. I decided to treat the poem as a visual piece, not words that were format independent. This allowed me to include the full names of the elements, showing how the parts have come together to make a whole, and that whole is an account of division between parts. The end result was the accompanying piece, "LiVING dIVISiON."

The Art of the Portrait

PABLO M. RUIZ

"Seeing him astonished, he asked: 'What do you think?"
And he replied: 'Sir, this is the Theology of Painting.'"

Antonio Palomino, *The Pictorial Museum and Optical Scale*

Testimony

This isn't the first time that someone has asked me how I wrote that story, nor is it the first time that I'm answering the question. It's true that I have offered various answers, but they weren't contradictory. Let's just say that suddenly I thought a plant was growing inside me. Let's say that I felt the need to achieve a certain effect and that I inferred everything else, almost mathematically, to that end. Let's say that it was as though the story itself, transformed into a kind of faceless angel, possessed me for three days before leaving me, aglow with the dark and thick light of that which has journeyed from nothingness into the cosmos. The truth is that when I reached the house after the attack, the parents asked me if I could turn what had happened into a story. I replied that yes, I could. I explained to them that it wouldn't be a realistic story. I repeated something to them that they must have already read somewhere:

"Reality is the origin and the destination of all literature. Realism is its enemy."

"Literature has more enemies than you think," the mother replied, enigmatically. "But please write it. Do it for her."

Fragment

We are all our faces, but not her. Not because of her beauty or my love for her. Who knows if I really loved her, who knows if I truly love her now. Hallucination is the truest quality of love. Nothing demands it more than a face that demands it. And nothing is farther from literature than a face, which seems to exist to mock language. Anything visual, you might counter: the colors, the countless whites of light, the cascades of shadow over a body that moves. And yet nothing escapes the impotent hands of language the way a face does, like mist. You don't need to invent a little Cantorian sphere or underground cellars or hallucinatory concoctions to reach a writer's level of despair; every face already gets you there. I see, in your face, a crystal that doesn't stop looking at me. I see, in your face, the echo of sea constellations, the hum of golden insects, the wake of Babylonian stars. I see, in your face, the water of future rains, the masks of other faces, the crystal that watches me watching you. I see, in your face, your face and the reflection of your face and the mirrors of the emptiness of your face, which floods the space. I see, in your face, your age dissolving, the subtle hint of your sex, the careful distortion of your parents' faces. I see, in your face, an abyss, a girl lying down, the fruit of a ripe tree, the unintelligible languages of Babel, a shoemaker's hammer. I see eight-fingered hands, I see circles with perfect angles. I see millions of deaf tapirs, I see an iceberg melting in the sun. I see, in your face, the universe that includes your face that includes the universe that includes your face. I see your loving handwriting, I see the loving letter with your handwriting, I see the loving envelope with the letter with your handwriting. I see a twenty-cent coin that I've already forgotten and I see a letter of the alphabet that has been amputated and plucked from a tongue. I see the elegant nuptial viper of the *Panchatantra*, I see the drop of an oil lamp that woke the secret lover on a faraway night imagined in Asia Minor. I prepare myself to sing of the unattainable union between the simultaneity of your face and the succession of my language, the black and white of a never-ending chess game, the beauty and the beast of my story.

Writings in a Notebook

1) "A man sets himself the task of drawing the world. Over the years he fills a space with images of provinces, kingdoms, mountains, bays, ships, islands, fish, rooms, instruments, stars, horses, and people. Just before he dies, he discovers that this patient maze of lines traces the image of his beloved's face."

2) "Art should be like a mirror that reveals our own face to us. Torn apart."

3) "An inquisitive destroying of the face: break off a tooth, slice the gums, pierce the ears, trim the eyelashes, smash the forehead, puncture the palate, tear off the lips, impale the cheeks."

4) "When we look in the mirror we see our faces but we don't see the enigma. The sphinx went backwards, hiding the mirror behind the enigma. Oedipus' brilliance consisted of identifying the enigma with the mirror and seeing that the answer was man, was himself. That was the beginning of his undoing."

5) "You can't see my face, because no one can see me and stay alive. You won't be able to see my face, because no man can see me and survive. My face won't be visible to you, because man cannot see me and continue living.

6) "The face differs radically from the body, it's another thing entirely. It is the body's sullied mirror, its foreign grammar, its escape path, it is the

song among the dead. And because of its frontal position, because it exposes itself to the world, because it aims high, it seems to do everything in order to liberate itself, in order to stop being mistaken for the dead weight that it carries. We have looked in vain for the soul inside the body. There is no soul but the face."

7) "Exodus 33."

8) *"Faceless the sultry and overpowering lion/ Faceless the stricken slave, faceless the Queen."*

Her

She was the youngest of three daughters. She got along very poorly with her older sisters, who envied her beauty. She was her parents' favorite child, and she adored them in turn. Ever since she was a teenager, Francisca had dedicated herself with passion and discipline to painting. Her abstract paintings brought together the plain geometry of Mondrian and the material power of Tàpies in an almost incoherent way—an incoherence that was perhaps a good summary of Francisca herself. At the ceremony where her mother, a good writer of mediocrities, received second place in a novel contest, she met Paulo, who had won first place with an excessively Borgesian novel. Their affair was only cut short when she won a scholarship to study fine arts in Paris. He had plans to visit her at her studio on Rue St. Pierre, but in the first letter she sent him from Paris she told him, in a single clerical sentence, that she did not want to see him again.

Crime Stories

When the story came out about the attack that deformed her face, her sisters were the first suspects. They were both brought in, but released very quickly because there was no evidence against them. It had been a year since Francisca returned from Paris, and three since she had been in touch with Paulo, who had continued to love her with tenacity and in secret. Despite her mother's urgent insistence that the police do everything possible to identify the guilty party, there were no developments in the case for months. But when Paulo published the story, the mother contacted the police because she believed the text to be a barely veiled confession. It was a story that some praised and that granted Paulo a fleeting fame, at least within the rather small world of letters. When the detectives told her they didn't see anything necessarily incriminating or confessional about the story, even though it was admittedly about the face and its destruction, the mother used her authority as a writer and a reader (she mentioned a vague doctorate degree and an old essay about a dead man in a labyrinth) to make the case that there were clues they could not ignore, and that she knew very well what a writer's words were capable of hiding. When the police finally raided his home, Paulo ended up confessing. In a notebook that had "Novel" written on the cover, there were some notes that were used as additional proof against him. Francisca had not spoken since the day of the attack and now she was painting hyperrealist portraits, huge fragmentary portraits that showed just a part of a face, not the whole face. Looking up close at the canvases, you could see that these partial portraits were composed of myriad little faces, each one whole but deformed.

At the "Bokharis" Café

"I remember it well. It was in all the papers."

"But has anyone seen her destroyed face?"

"No, her confinement was permanent and twofold: she stopped speaking and stopped leaving the house. No one saw her during those months."

"Paulo's story makes it sound like it never happened."

"That's his wish. Actually, that's the weakest part of the story."

"It's not even a good story. It's a collage, isn't it? The old cento technique."

"A failed combination of crime fiction and fairytale, a dark genre and a light one. And on top of everything it tries to be fantastical."

"I'm not sure it's bad. Maybe it's like love: its value is absolute for whoever lives it, but might be ridiculous for an observer."

"Or like despair."

"Say what you will. What's undeniable is that it had absolute worth at least for one person, that it transformed at least one reader. If that were the criterion, it would be the greatest story in all of literature."

"What's also undeniable is its conviction and excessive pathos. I prefer to think that it's just a draft for a future novel."

Reconstruction of the Facts

The scholarship was something that the parents invented in order to keep her away from him. They got her accepted at the school for fine arts in Paris by paying for everything, including the studio on Rue St. Pierre. As soon as Francisca was settled in Paris, they told her that Paulo had been seen with another woman. The mother had always hated him, among other reasons, for winning first place that one time, which for her had been a humiliating experience. What is impossible to explain is the acid on her face. We don't know if the father or the sisters were accomplices, but Francisca probably stopped speaking because talking would have meant condemning her mother and putting an intolerable truth out into the world. It was her mother who made sure that someone let Paulo know. When he went to visit Francisca, they wouldn't let him in. The mother asked him to write the story because she knew she could use it to accuse him, the obvious suspect. But why, if he was innocent, did he confess? Because the only thing that mattered to him was that the story reach Francisca, and he thought that giving a certain notoriety to the case would guarantee that she read it. And that, as everyone knows, is what happened, followed by all the unbelievable consequences that we will keep trying to explain.

The Art of the Portrait

But my true despair as a writer is not that. It isn't the image but rather the thing. It isn't the word that says light but rather the word that *makes* light. That's the word that throws me into despair and that I need to look for, among archaic terms and pages of old grammar books, among the outbursts of history and the substance of pain. I have to go through the letters and strip them of their speech, to conjure languages into music and numbers, languages to bewitch zebras and bears, to make the trees dance and divert the waters, to make the stones that we have been and will become jump, until time becomes a legend that we have proven untrue and you have returned from darkness. To bring back Phillip Theophrastus' murmur, which he whispered to the ashes of a rose so that the rose would be again, to make the *astrum in faciem* doctrine come true for this song, to rediscover the lost glossolalia of the cabbalists, mad with divinity, for my prose. And which sacred syntax? Which profane rhetoric? Which declensions and etymologies? The language of the end of time, the inaudible language of the angels, the baptismal language of the animals of Eden—I write in huge, barbaric and broken languages. Read me, read me with the motions of your devastated face, read me with your chilling eyes. Read with me, join me in this act of reading. If I can't reach your face with the breath of my words, if I can't reach you with the soothing song of the sirens that is my song, or with the destructive silence of the sirens that is my silence, if I can't reach you with what I write, if what I write is not at once the riddle and the solution to the riddle of your face, if it is not the fullness and the emptiness of your face, then it is nothing and it is less than nothing.

I call upon the prophetic within me, I open the dictionary of the oceans and then sing out and foretell my words. These words will crawl along and touch the underground roots of graves, seep into the grooves of the wood covered in sap and mud, descend and dig into mineral veins and the salts of sunken cavities. These words will lift and touch the burning matrix of the planets, will lift and touch the elemental orbits of the sun and the specters of starry cycles and the wild grace of the galaxies, which will be traces of your face in my hands for me to mold and return to their source, shaped by my words. My words will be nourished by the pulsing of the birds, the shifting meaning of dreams, the faithful syllogism of that which changes, and like fire they will sweep away the shadows, like air they will absorb everything remembered and everything forgotten, and your face will finally be your face, your phoenix face, your rose face, your reborn intact face returned to the insatiable and legendary whirlpool of the ages.

Fifty Nouns of Noun

LANCE OLSEN

"You verb a greedy noun," he verbs softly, and his noun verbs my noun and then verbs down.

I verb loudly as my noun verbs beneath his expert nouns. He verbs up and verbs the noun over my noun so I can verb him as I verb in the soft noun of my noun. I verb to verb him.

"I verb to verb you," I verb.

"I verb," he verbs. He verbs down and verbs me, his nouns still moving rhythmically inside me, his noun circling and pressing. His other noun verbs my noun off my noun and verbs my noun in place. His noun verbs the nouns of his nouns, claiming me. My nouns verb to verb as I verb against his noun. He verbs his noun, so I verbed back from the noun. He verbs this again and again. It's so frustrating . . . Oh please, Christian, I verb in my noun.

"This is your noun, so close and yet so far. Is this nice?" he verbs in my noun.

I verb, exhausted, pulling against my noun. I verb helpless, lost in an erotic noun.

"How shall I verb you, Anastasia?"

Oh . . . my noun starts to verb.

"Shall I verb you this noun, or this noun, or this noun? There verbs an endless noun," he verbs against my nouns. He verbs his noun and verbs over to the bedside noun for a foil noun. He verbs up between my nouns, and very slowly he verbs my nouns off, staring down at me, his nouns gleaming. I verb fascinated, mesmerized.

"How nice verb this?" he verbs as he verbs himself.

"I verb it as a noun," I verb. Please verb me, Christian.

He verbs his nouns as his noun verbs up and down his impressive noun.

"A noun?" His noun verbs menacingly soft.

I verb just one noun of sexual, tense noun. He verbs down at me for a noun, measuring my noun, then he verbs me suddenly and verbs me over. It verbs me by noun, and because my nouns verb, I verb myself on my nouns. He verbs both my nouns up the noun so my noun verbs in the air, and he verbs me hard. Before I can verb, he verbs inside me. I verb out—from the noun and from his sudden noun, and I verb instantly again and again, falling apart beneath him as he verbs to verb deliciously into me. I can't verb this . . . and he verbs on and on and on . . . then I verb again . . . surely not . . . no . . . "Verb on, Anastasia, again," he verbs through clenched nouns, and unbelievably, my noun verbs, convulsing around him as I verb anew, calling out his noun. I verb again into tiny nouns, and Christian verbs, finally letting go, silently finding his noun. He verbs on top of me, breathing hard.

"How nice was that?" he verbs through his gritted nouns. Oh my.

I verb panting and spent on the noun, nouns closed as he slowly verbs out of me. I verb my nouns and verb my nouns, smiling at the woven noun imprinted on my nouns from the noun. I verb my noun as he verbs the noun and noun over me. I verb up at him completely dazed, and he verbs down at me.

"That verbs really nice," I verb, smiling coyly.

The Constraints of History in the Works of Michèle Audin

CHRISTIANA HILLS

Since her co-option into the Oulipo in 2009, Michèle Audin has contributed a singular approach to the group's experimental endeavors in her unique way of weaving history into her writing. For example, her novel *Cent vingt et un jours* (*One Hundred Twenty-One Days*, 2014) tells the story of a group of French mathematicians during the two World Wars. Each chapter of the novel takes a different form: diaries, newspaper articles, a transcribed interview, and scholarly notes, but also a fairytale, a literary narrative inspired by Stendhal, and a list of numbers. Over the course of the novel, it becomes evident that these various "documents" form the archive of a historian researching M., one of the mathematicians.[1] Yet the historian is prevented from publishing a biography of M. because the latter's heirs refuse, likely fearing their grandfather's reputation would be damaged because of his cooperation with the Nazis during the Occupation. And so, the story can only be told through fragments, which offer glimpses of this century-long life through a myriad of perspectives, though never M.'s own.

Audin's work earnestly investigates the way in which the written and oral forms of history reveal certain sides of events while concealing

---

1 As the name of this mathematician appears in different anagrammatic permutations in each chapter of the novel (such as Mortsauf, Mortfaus, or Morfaust), I will simply refer to him as M. here.

others, thus constraining our understanding of them. Indeed, her literary undertaking can be seen to counter Canadian experimental poet Christian Bök's criticism of the Oulipo for leaving the political potential of constraint "inexplicit, if not unexplored" by limiting their work to a poetic agenda.[2] By mobilizing Oulipian techniques to explore the larger constraints of history, Audin opens new avenues for the political potential of constraint in literature.

Audin's attention to history has undoubtedly been shaped by what may have been the most defining moment of her life: the disappearance of her father, Maurice Audin, when she was just three years old. At the time, the family was living in Algeria, where Maurice was working as an assistant in mathematics at the University of Algiers while completing his doctoral dissertation. He had developed strong ties to the Algerian Communist Party and was fervently involved in the party's anti-colonialist efforts. On June 11, 1957, he was arrested, then subsequently tortured and killed by parachutists of the French Army. His body was never recovered and, despite pleas from his widow and his dissertation supervisor, the circumstances of the affair have never been resolved. In 2009, Michèle Audin publically refused the Légion d'Honneur because French President Nicholas Sarkozy had ignored her mother's formal requests for the French government to provide her with more information and finally assume responsibility for the affair.

Audin's memoir *Une vie brève* (*A Brief Life*, 2013) tells of her search to understand this devastating event as an adult through what remains of her father's life. She divides her sources into three categories: what she calls the *oral component*[3] (family stories), the *iconographic component* (photographs), and the *written component* (official documents, family testimonies, and her father's own writings). Each category offers a certain type of information about her father's life, yet, like the historian of *Cent vingt et un jours*, she must sift through the constraints of the various forms

---

2 "Oulipo and Its Unacknowledged Legislation," in *The noulipian Analects* (2007).

3 My translation, as are all subsequent quotations from Audin's works.

in seeking the life they evoke. In the end, it seems the materials also serve to reveal the vast amount she can never know and the absence that remains in the wake of his disappearance. From this work, one can deduce various threads that she continues to follow in her subsequent writing: the way form and genre in shape and constrain knowledge; the way large-scale events, like the Algerian War, can profoundly constrain individual lives; the way history can serve to hide, omit, and erase certain aspects of the past; and the way memory and time inevitably distort the past, such that it can never be perfectly retrieved.

Audin's constant play with form and genre is perhaps the most striking quality of her work. Both *Cent vingt et un jours* and *Mademoiselle Haas* (2016) employ genre variation to explore the different ways a story can be told and how form can constrain our understanding of what we read. *Mademoiselle Haas* is a collection of stories about unmarried working women in Paris from 1934 to 1941 who all share the same last name of Haas. Victorine Haas's story, told in a first-person narrative about her first day working as a housemaid for a new client, is accompanied by footnotes that reveal details from her past.[4] Léopoldine's afternoon spent in a Paris café before she heads to her factory job is presented in a question-and-answer format that describes surface elements, such as the café décor, the customers' conversation topics, the customers themselves, and Léopoldine's own demeanor. One of the more affecting stories is that of Pauline. It is also the shortest, consisting of just two paragraphs describing Pauline's identity card as verified in 1939, then inspected again in 1941, with the addition of a red stamp reading a single word: *JEW*. As the stories of *Mademoiselle Haas* illustrate, form constrains what we can learn about a life.

As mentioned above, the fictional historian researching M. in *Cent vingt et un jours* must also deal with the constrained forms in which history presents itself. Even before he is prevented from publishing his biography of M., the historian must grapple with the various pieces of

---

4 As Audin notes in the book's appendix, the form of this story was inspired by fellow Oulipian Pablo Martín Sánchez's *F(r)icciones* (F(r)ictions, 2011).

information he collects from various oral, iconographic, and written components, while never having an opportunity to encounter M. himself. Indeed, we as readers never really gain a "complete" picture of M., as he seems to transform in each chapter, going from a boy obsessed with mathematics in Senegal to a young wounded soldier in a Paris hospital during WWI to an ill-tempered professor and Nazi collaborator during the Occupation. The historian must piece together these fragments of M.'s life, in some cases having to decide whether they even occurred, such as stories passed down through a chain of sources with no link back to the eyewitness: *I remember that Pierre said that Bernadette had told him that someone had told her that her father... Not very reliable.*

Form also plays a role in her most mathematical "novel" (as the book calls itself), *La formule de Stokes, roman* (The Stokes Formula, A Novel, 2016), which explores the history of a mathematical formula and the mathematicians who found various innovations and applications for it. This book distorts history by telling it in calendar order, rather than chronologically.[5] The only constant in the story is the formula itself, while those using and innovating it vary widely in terms of time and place. Such an alternative telling of a formula's "history" challenges the traditional forms in which history is presented to us, which tend to follow chronological or biographical trajectories.

In addition to Audin's literary works, she has two blog projects, *Mai quai Conti*[6] and *La Commune de Paris*,[7] which both focus on the 1871 Paris Commune and its ties to France's larger cultural history, especially in terms of its effect on the academy. Form also plays an important role in these works, as their online formats fragment the story being presented while also offering a great deal of hypertextual potential in the way that

---

5 To illustrate, the first vignette in the book is dated January 1, 1862, followed by January 5, 1857, January 9, 1895, and January 13, 2012. This particular constraint was inspired by fellow Oulipian Michelle Grangaud's *Calendrier des fêtes nationales* (Calendar of National Holidays, 2003)

6 Last updated in June 2014 on the Oulipo's website at http://oulipo.net/fr/mai-quai-conti.

7 Still being updated as of June 2017 at https://macommunedeparis.com.

the reader can find connections between the various articles, images, and links presented therein. The forms of these projects suggest that history doesn't have to be confined to history books, but can be a living part of digital culture, continually updated by the author and transformed through user interaction.

Beneath the artificial structures created by such complex forms, a common thread through Audin's work is the way in which large-scale events, especially those of a political nature, can constrain the lives of individuals. In contrast to the schoolboy's view of history as a timeline punctuated with important names and dates, Audin's writing seeks to uncover how these events can frame human lives by overshadowing and constraining them. Studying a map of a German town, the historian in *Cent vingt et un jours* notes how easily and seamlessly these constraints can act:

> On the back of the map of the little town of N., near another photo of the statue on the fountain, the tourist center has included a summary of the town's history, starting 500,000 years ago, lingering over the 17th, 18th, and 19th centuries, and ending with a leap from 1933 to 1945:
>
>> Between 1920 and 1933, the university's reputation grew due to the presence of several renowned physicians and humanists. During World War II, the town escaped the bombings. In 1945, the university reopened. Today, the population is 130,000 inhabitants, of which 20,000 are students.

Numbers, which François Le Lionnais called *delicious and terrifying*, can be a political constraint on our view of history, as shown in the exercise from a German mathematics textbook described in *Cent vingt et un jours* that asks students to calculate the area of the German Reich before and after World War I. Yet numbers can also be a powerful tool of resistance, as seen in another chapter of the novel that offers a list of numbers with

relevance to the events in the rest of the book, numbers like 0.577215...,
Euler's constant, but also:

1 single bullet managed to remove one of M.'s eyes, his nose, and half of his jaw
and
19 years old, the age of the future great poet when he jumped out of a trench
and
*491 men and women from Convoy 60 were taken by SS officers and dogs and
immediately gassed*
and
*157034, the number tattooed on a survivor's arm and jotted down on a page
from a blue notebook.*

As these numbers suggest, nothing is more constraining on individual
lives than war, the wars that disfigure M. for the rest of his life, sink a
ship carrying his brother, drive one of his classmates and comrades to kill
certain members of his family, cause a decline in French mathematics
with so many of its mathematicians slaughtered in trenches and
concentration camps, tear apart lovers, invalidate identity cards (and
identities), erase individuals from public record, and take away the father
of a three year-old-girl.

The timeline of history forgets, omits, erases. While M.'s story (at least
the story the historian wants to write) cannot be told because his heirs
don't want to sully his reputation as a mathematician, the stories of the
various Mademoiselle Haases, all ordinary working women, are those
that, as the narrator tells us, have been *ignored by the history books. There,
they are invisible. Forgotten. Left out, rather.* Yet Audin seeks to tell their
individual stories through the constrained forms history can offer her.
One of the women, Suzanne Haas, is listed by the French Academy of
Sciences as a co-author of a paper published in 1940 on a specific type of
mushroom, but altogether disappears from the Academy's records after
the war. Yet the Shoah Memorial does not mention her deportation or her
death, leaving the narrator to optimistically muse that Suzanne *may have*

met a tall handsome young man (or a man who was less young, less tall, less handsome) and they both disappeared from the world of applied mycology . . . and scientific journals.

It seems only imagination can redeem the devastation caused by history's constraints. As Audin's work highlights, the constraints of history reveal how much we don't know and perhaps can never know about the past, despite our best efforts to understand it. Even when individuals haven't disappeared from civil records, as Audin finds in tracing her family's history at the beginning of *Une vie brève*, so much is missing, leaving Audin to remark that her family is composed of people *who didn't have a history*, ancestors who *are only known to us as names and dates in civil registers, being the only proof that they existed.* Later in the memoir, Audin admits that she doesn't even know if her father knew how to swim, or what kinds of things made him laugh. In a harrowing contrast to Georges Perec's *Je me souviens* (*I Remember*, 1978) and the Oulipian tradition it has inspired,[8] Audin's memoir pinpoints the constraints of what she cannot remember about her father, precisely because she never had the opportunity to. And while her family can offer her memories of their own, they are not necessarily helpful. Near the end of the book, she writes: *It would be easy to write here that I remember how I used to walk in the street with him, in my little red dress, it would be easy to write this because my mother says she can picture me doing it, but no, I don't remember it. Because all that has been recounted, repeated, set in stone.*

Yet she still has traces of him, through his civil documents, his notebooks filled with mathematical notations, the disorderly quality of his papers she finds familiar, his small dense handwriting in blue ink, and objects like his desk, his watch, and his razor. There is a clear parallel in Mireille Duvivier, whose story punctuates *Cent vingt et un jours* with an eponymously titled chapter in the form of a literary narrative. Like Audin,

---

8 Though of course we should note Perec's tragic loss of both of his parents when he was very young, and his own contrast to *Je me souviens* he makes near the beginning of *W, ou le souvenir d'enfance* (*W or the Memory of Childhood*, 1975) with this confession: *I have no childhood memories.*

Mireille seeks to find out what happened to a loved one, in this case her lover André, through the traces that remain of his life and the one hundred twenty-one days in which they knew each other before he disappeared in a Nazi roundup. While she, too, is left with a few objects—a makeshift note thrown from a train, a few photographs, a mathematics article he wrote, and his copy of Dante's *Inferno*—what she really clings to is not these physical objects containing his recorded words, but rather the words that exist only in her memory, all the words he said to her: *Hard words, for life in Strasbourg . . . . Serious words, to talk about Mozart's Fantasia . . . . Beautiful words, to describe the numbers he was studying . . . . Impassioned words, sweet words, words of happiness.* For Mireille, only the words of her shared experience with André, words that will never be recorded in history, can help her to better understand the past and guard it from the shadows of what happened afterwards.

As Audin evokes in the last chapter of *Cent vingt et un jours*, such *private events, like the one hundred twenty-one days of Mireille and André's story* can *form a sort of chain that holds the threads together—the very fabric of history.* The forms of history can constrain our understanding of the past, yet the telling and writing of stories can redeem it, becoming the chain that holds the threads together and gives meaning to a life. Even in the face of distancing and distorting constraints such as time and memory, hidden stories can still be told, if only one seeks them in what remains.

In fact, Audin writes that her scholarly work researching the history of twentieth-century mathematicians was a first step towards writing *Une vie brève*, by giving her *a way to connect the singular history of my father's disappearance . . . and our singular grief to a collective history. Around the millions of individual sorrows that followed the disappearances of millions of people in the Nazi camps . . . there is a collective grief, a historic memory, that has left us with a lack, one which I always feel.* This collective lack is the key constraint of history: in the end, what it offers only serves to reveal what we can never really know about the past. Yet this lack also inspired Audin to seek out her father's story and write it down, to add to the collective memory of all those lost to history's catastrophes.

This lack has also driven Audin's writing ever since. Since joining the Oulipo, she has sought to use Oulipian constraints to question how history can be told differently, and how stories can reveal a potential previously hidden by history's constraints. You could call it a new language, like the languages other Oulipians have created that lack certain vowels or restrict syllables or mimic other languages or define or exaggerate or spiral or remember, a language of history that isn't told by the victors or the history books, one that doesn't fetishize wars or names or dates or traditions. This language can only be created by choosing the limits of what can be written. At the end of *Une vie brève*, Audin reveals the key constraint of the memoir: *It would be false to tell you that I don't have memories of him. I do, I hold onto them—and that's why I'm keeping them for myself.*

Whether piecing together the true story of a life or using fiction to reveal the underbelly of history, Audin's oeuvre ultimately illustrates how one might surmount the constraints of history through the limitless potential of constrained writing. Indeed, constraints born of creativity and imagination, like those of the Oulipo, can be a powerful political tool to teach us about how our understanding of history shapes our lives and our reading of the past. For history is not simply a timeline, or a list of numbers, or something left in the hands of "the victors," but, as Audin writes at the beginning of *Mademoiselle Haas*, it is *yours, mine, ours*.

Exit Interview

PETER LANDAU

"Where am I?"

"You've had time to think, to contemplate, to meditate, maybe even pray over your situation. Where has that gotten you? Here. A room. Away from everyone you know and love. Unheard, unseen. Did you think it would lead to this?"

"No. No, I did not."

"That's what happens when we follow false prophets. Do you think Clarence T. Nantucket, or whatever he calls himself, will rescue you? Do you remember Clarence T. Nantucket?"

"I used to work for him. I was a cartoonist."

"That's supposed to make you special?"

"I'm no longer a cartoonist. I never really was. I just like to draw, mostly faces."

"You're not special, Harry."

"How do you know my name?"

"See, you don't know everything. But I do. I know your name, for instance, even though your signature was never printed on those silly tracts of yours. No, there wasn't any reference to Harry Friedhart or Free Fart. Yes, Free Fart, I know all about you. I know how you were lured into the glamorous and seductive world of religious comic books. Clarence T. Nantucket a.k.a. Holy Roller a.k.a. Franky the Faithful a.k.a. Marvin Schneider. That last one comes from his birth certificate. Yes, your great messiah was born in a hospital. He cried, bloody and small, just another one of us mere mortals."

"Clarence T. Nantucket is a god among cartoonists! His character designs are legendary. His sequential compositions: the pacing, the contrast, the use of negative space -- can't be touched."

"Oh, he can be touched, and he *is* touched, in the head. Just like you, little lost Free Fart. Only there's hope for you, if you can see the light. The real light. Not the delusional torch you've been blinded by, but the light of reason. If Clarence T. Nantucket told you to jump off a bridge, would you do it?"

"No."

"Good, then we're getting somewhere. Would you jump out of a window if Clarence T. Nantucket asked?"

"No."

"Okay, so we've established that. Now, would you jump off a chair?"

"Maybe."

"Okay. Let's start there. Let me untie you. Your arms will be a little sore, but that will pass."

"How about my legs?"

"You're free."

"Who are you?"

"I'm a friend of the family. They're concerned. I help resolve concerns."

"They never mentioned you before."

"Mentioned who?"

"You."

"Who am I?"

"I don't know."

"My name is Stan."

"Stan the man."

"Do you think I'm the man?"

"You're *a* man."

"Yes. Stand on the chair, Free Fart. Don't worry, I won't pull it out from under you. Or will I? Guess that's a risk you'll have to take. It's a bit wobbly, isn't it? You could lose a few pounds, but I think it'll hold your weight. So, jump. Go on, jump. I said, Jump!"

"Why?"

"Good. Very good. You're starting to ask questions. Who am I, right? By what authority do I have to order you around?"

"Ow! Why'd you go and do that for?"

"How the mighty have fallen. Get up off the ground. What have you, no respect for yourself? Don't worry, I'm not going to pull the chair away from you again. Sit down. Don't you trust me?"

"No."

"You know who does trust me? Your parents. They hired me to help you."

"You said you were a friend."

"Yes, a friend, the best kind of friend, one who is on retainer. Money can't buy happiness, but you can rent it. And I'm not cheap. That's how much your parents value you. They have invested heavily in me to exorcise the demon you believe is divine. Think of me as a plumber. Your pipes are clogged and I'm here to clean you up. I know you're obstructed. There's a term for that condition, blocked—one might say, in denial. Now, I'm not going to use a plunger on you. That would be silly. I'm just going to talk to you. Talk will clear the mass of nonsense that Clarence T. Nantucket, or whatever his name is, has made you swallow."

"I haven't had a number two in months, long before I ever went into that religious pamphlet store."

"Denial."

"Fact."

"Interesting usage. Fact. Whose facts are you referring to? Biological facts? I doubt a body could survive that long without having voided itself. It would be toxic. Waste must be removed, not stored, otherwise the body is poisoned. Far as I can tell, it's not your body that's broken.

"Oh, please. Don't try to sway me with your gas. I'm wise to your parlor tricks. We all fart, you know, it doesn't make you special. It's neither an attribute nor a deficit. But we're getting off topic, aren't we? The point of our conversation is conversion. That's a word you understand."

"Well, as I understand it, conversion doesn't involve being tied a chair."

"It could, depending on the conversion. Anyway, you're not tied to the chair anymore, so stop avoiding the topic, which is conversion."

"You want to convert me? That doesn't sound like my parents. They're not religious people."

"But you are. You rebelled against the secularism of your family, didn't you? How better to get back at them then by going religious zealot. They're scientists, rationalists, but not you. No, not Harry Friedhart. You saved yourself from their secular hell by trusting in a higher power. Only faith wasn't enough. You had to spread the good word in word balloons floating over your crude scribbles. A cartoon strip to convert others to see the light you basked in to buttress the fragile belief you built up, to support your erratic behavior and, dare I add, spastic bowel."

"I do like to draw."

"And fart?"

"No!"

"You lips say no, but your bottom says yes. Get back on the chair. No, sit down. Get comfortable. We're going to be here for a long time. Unless we're not. It's your choice. Do you believe you have the freedom of choice, Harry?"

"Everything has a price. Choice is extra, and you have to pay for that."

"Did Clarence T. Nantucket tell you that?"

"No, I just made it up."

"Clarence T. Nantucket was just making it up as he went along, too, and gullible marks like you fell for it. You were his patsy, a cheap outsourcing for manufacturing, child labor. Religion was the carrot to lead you where he wanted you to go. There're a million more like you out there, Harry. Desperate and lost."

"You're saying that Clarence T. Nantucket was the one pulling the strings, not God? Maybe God was pulling Clarence T. Nantucket's strings while he was pulling mine. Maybe God is pulling your strings right now."

"Please, I'm a professional deprogrammer."

"Deprogrammer? To remove programming. Do you think I'm a television set? Who watches television any more? There're no good programs, just deprograms, like you. Where's your off switch?"

"You can't change the channel that easily. Stand up."

"Sit down, stand up—you're worse than church."

"I wish there was an off button for your bottom."

"Are you okay?"

"Thank you. I'll be fine in a minute."

"How long have you been in this business?"

"Too long. Please, sit down. Get comfortable. Relax. There's no pressure here. No one is going to tell you what to do, how to think. I offer you an exit from dependency. Independence. Think about that word."

"It makes me think of being in Depends. I wish my problems were that easily fixed. The trouble is I'm stuck. I'm neither dependent nor independent. I'm constipated."

"Let me help you become incontinent. You're no longer a prisoner of Clarence T. Nantucket."

"I was never tyrannized by him. It was the bubble. It *is* the bubble. It always has been the bubble, and I'm scared to say it may always be the bubble."

"The bubble?"

"Internal affairs."

"Are you talking about demonic possession?"

"I'm possessed, body not soul. The engine that drives the foul exhaust that I spew is the bubble."

"You're not making sense. The bubble? Who is that? Clarence T. Nantucket works alone. He's a one-man swindle, too old and greedy to cut anyone else in on the action. I know, I've done my research, and no bubble has come up."

"The bubble is me. Inside of me. I want it out."

"You're just confused. Take a shower, get some rest, eat a good meal and let me take you home. Your parents miss you very much. They love you."

"What's my father doing?"

"He misses you."

"What's today's obsession?"

"You. He's also building a city in the basement out of cardboard. I think he'd appreciate your help. It's very detailed. Impressive."

"And mom?"

"She loves and misses you, too."

"What about my sister?"

"Stella? Yeah, she loves you and misses you. They all do in their different ways."

"None of them need me. They're carrying on without me. The only one for whom I'm essential is the bubble. I'd call it a symbiotic relationship, but I don't see what I'm getting out of it."

"This bubble is a parasite?"

"A parasite can be removed, but what if it's not a parasite, what if it's me?"

"I'm not a physician, son. I'm not a psychiatrist either. I'm a deprogrammer. You're a very sick person and need professional help. I can't offer you that, but I can refer you to mental-health professionals. Get out of that chair. Let me make this very simple: do you renounce your allegiance to Clarence T. Nantucket, and are you ready to return home to the care of your loving parents?"

"I don't know."

"What don't you know?"

"I never pledged my allegiance to Clarence T. Nantucket. There's nothing for me to renounce. He never even paid me, so there no financial agreement or contractual obligation to break. He did allow me to buy tracts at a ten-percent discount."

"Was that you?"

"What?"

"You know what. You farted. It wasn't me, and there's no body else here."

"No? Shouldn't there be a mirror, you know, a two-way mirror, and my parents are on the other side watching, waiting to run in and hug me?"

"You're thinking of a police procedural. This isn't television, Harry. It's real life. Will you please stop that! I wish there *was* a window in here."

"I'm sorry. It's the bubble. I have to relieve the pressure or I'd be fatter and more uncomfortable than I already am. I've tried to hold it in, really I have, but then I get these terrible cramps. When I lock my backdoor tight, the bubble finds the key and opens it. I don't want to let them rip. They rip me."

"Your parents told me about the flatulence, of course, but I thought they were exaggerating. I get a lot of that, demon tails and horns, fire and brimstone stuff. We need to talk about the bubble."

"I've told you all I know. You're the expert, you're the professional. Help me."

"I can't help you until you're willing to help yourself."

"I just told you I'm willing."

"Are you? It doesn't smell like you're willing. Look, you and I both know there's no bubble. You're chubby, but you're not a beach ball. No one took an air pump to you. You're not a balloon. You're just a kid, a mixed up and terribly gaseous kid, but that's it."

"The bubble isn't my imagination!"

"Then show it."

"That's what I've been trying to do. I've tried to pass it, but it's stuck, a plug that won't let anything . . . solid pass. I've even tried to cut it out."

"You self-mutilate?"

"What?"

"You said you cut yourself."

"I tried to cut myself, but I couldn't. Would you do it for me? It doesn't have to be a big knife. Just a pinprick. Think of it as deflating a balloon. I need to alleviate the pressure. Please, will you help me?"

"Yes."

"Do you have a pocket knife? It would be in your pocket. You have a few of those. Why aren't you checking?"

"There's this. Keys."

"Keys?"

"One of these keys will unlock the bubble."

"Are you going to stab me with it?"

"No. Choose one."

"Your car key."

"Good choice. Here, they're yours. What are you going to do with them?"

"Stab myself in the belly."

"Why, are you a car?"

"No. I'm sick. There's a bubble of gas inside of me that's growing bigger every day. I can't fart enough to deflate it. You give me a key, a car key, but no car. What is that supposed to do?"

"Why don't you get into a car and drive?"

"Where's your car?"

"Ah-ha! Now do you understand?"

"No, and I don't think you do either. You're stalling."

"Stalling? You mean a bathroom stall? Interesting. Now who's stalling? What is it about my car? Why can't you find it? Do you want it? What for?"

"I don't care about your car."

"Then why do you want to know where it is?"

"Because you gave me the key."

"You picked it."

"You told me to."

"Do you do everything you're told? Clarence T. Nantucket tells you to draw comics, and you draw comics. This bubble of yours says fart, you fart. Is that any way to go through life, a good German just following orders? Now give them back."

"No. I'm done taking orders."

"Ha ha. Good, but I want my car keys back."

"I'm putting your keys in my back pocket. You know what that means? If you get within three feet of me I'll let you have it. Now you'll do as *I* say. Get on the chair. No, I didn't say, 'Sit on the chair.' That's right. Stand on it. Hard to keep steady? Close your eyes. Harder now? Lift one leg. No, I didn't say you could use your arms for balance. Oh no! You're getting wobbly. Don't fall! I told you not to fall. Get up."

"Look. I've had about enough of this!"

"Me, too. I'm no stooge. I've not been brainwashed. I like drawing comics, but I'm glad that's over. I quit, and now I'm quitting you!"

"The door's locked."

"Of course it is, but I bet one of these opens the door. Your silence leads me to believe my assumption is correct. Let's see: this one is too big, too small, but this one is just right. What do you know, it fits!"

"Don't! If you go through that door I'm out of a job. This is my last chance. I've not been a very successful deprogrammer lately. My last two clients ended up returning to the cults I kidnapped them from. Well, kidnapped is not the word I would use. The authorities, yes, they call it that. They say it's an 'illegal act.' A 'punishable offense.' Don't worry, I've got a good lawyer provided by the company. They've a reputation to uphold, but they'll cut me loose, throw me under the bus, without a second thought. It's the larger picture. I understand. Still, my family . . . my wife says she wants to leave me. My kids won't talk to me. Suddenly, *I'm* the bad guy. I'm the enemy."

"Maybe there's a way to redeem yourself. Do one good, selfless act. Let me go."

"I can't do that!"

"If you let me go and talk to my family and apologize to them and give them back their money and say you were wrong about me then you'll feel better about yourself."

"How did such a young and smelly boy get to be so wise?"

"Are you ready to accept my offer and take the first step on the road to your redemption?"

"This is crazy. I could lose my license, not that I have one, but you understand. My boss isn't going to accept failure from me, not again. I can't. No. Sorry, I have to break you. Nothing personal. That's not fair! You're not playing by the rules. Look, seriously, this isn't a game. You're sick. I can smell it. There's a void in your life that you're filling with religion, with this bubble, with the gas that poisons the air and warps your mind. I've taken an oath, that is I've always planned to write an oath and suggest it as part of our training—maybe when I'm back in the company's good graces."

"Do you need a company? A man of vision such as yourself shouldn't be tied down by bureaucracy."

"Look, I'm wise to your plan. It's textbook. They teach it in our training class. Religious Indoctrination 101."

"I'm not religious. I don't think I believe in god or whatever you want to call it: a force, power, nature. Not once did I believe Clarence T. Nantucket and his talk of salvation at the end of a quill. All I wanted was to draw, be a cartoonist. I may be young, but I've been through enough to know there is nothing out there. It's all in here."

"Self-reliance?"

"No, the bubble. You can't deprogram it. You can't convert it. You can't kill it without killing me. I'm the bubble."

"You?"

"Who else? I think the bubble was inside me since there was a me. I can't recall not having the feeling that there was something different about me, not a mental difference, something physical. You understand? I've no vestigial tail, webbed fingers, parasitic twin. Nothing so obvious . . . to the eye. Is it evolutionary?"

"I can't see how. Though it's a strong defense mechanism. I can't imagine it as more than a mutation that will get shuffled out of the genetic deck in time."

"Thanks. I know you're trying to help, but if you want to be of genuine service you'll do as I asked."

"I can't."

"No, you *won't*. I can have you charged with kidnapping. You're working in ethically muddy waters. Even if you're not convicted you'll never work in your chosen field again."

"Are you threatening me?"

"No, the bubble is. The bubble does everything. I'm nothing. It's the brains of the operation. I'd never sue you, but the bubble suggests that such a course of action may be necessary if you're unwilling to release me and repair the damage you've done to my family."

"The only one who's damaged your family is you. Remember, they hired me because they weren't able to deal with you, their own flesh and blood."

"To love me they must learn to love the bubble."

"Do you?"

"What other choice to I have? Suicide? The bubble wouldn't let me, much as I might want to end it all. You're supposed to have all the answers, but answer me this: how do I live? I thought so. Just unlock the door and let me go. Give up, like I have, and accept that you're a loser. I'm a loser. We're all losers in the end. In my end. I fart. You fail. We meet at that point of no return. Why fight it?"

"You're a bit young to have given up so completely. When I was your age I wanted to be president or an astronaut, better still the first astronaut president. You need to have dreams."

"No. I'd rather be awake."

"I was speaking metaphorically."

"That's the problem, I'm not. The bubble doesn't represent anything. It is the bubble. I'd prefer you spoke with clarity. Words are a bad means of communication made worse by trying to be clever. Don't distract me. Say what you mean."

"I don't know what I mean anymore. I'm a fraud. How can I help you if I can't help myself? I don't know if it's your stink that has made me dizzy, but I think I'm going to be sick, mentally sick, in the head."

"Yeah. I get it. Great. Join the party. Let's all vomit our brains out. Who needs them. I'd like a little peace and quiet."

"You and me both. Give me those keys. We're getting out of here, both of us. Let me buy you a drink."

"I'm underaged."

"What, you can't drink soda? How about a Virgin Mary or a Shirley Temple. You and me we got a lot to talk about. I've got things on my mind that I need to get out. Don't leave! Wait for me! I thought we were going to puke?"

"I was speaking metaphorically."

"But you said that we should speak our minds directly, without any fuss or flourishes. If I can't trust you, who can I trust?"

"God?"

"I've made a career dismissing God and religion. I can't just reverse a lifetime's work."

"You've lost faith."

"Yes."

"The bubble has given me faith, but it's a foul faith."

"It stinks to high heaven."

"But it reaches heaven. The angels can smell it, which means it must exist. That means I exist. The bubble has shown me that."

"You think the bubble is out to help? Then why do you want to rid yourself of it?"

"That kind of help I don't need. The truth is, I'd rather have no faith, nothing at all. I'd rather be deaf, dumb and blind if that meant no more farting. Sometimes I think, it's you and other people who are the problem. You love the smell of your own farts, why not mine? It's so egotistical.

Then I remember, even I can't stand the smell of my own farts. It's sunny, not a cloud in the sky. It looks wonderful, doesn't it? Fills you with hope."

"It does."

"Not me. Do you smell that?"

"Ugh. God, yes!"

"Remember me."

The Compositor's Constraint
or, How Wrong Can an Old Book Be?

DENNIS DUNCAN

When we see a typo in a document, very often we can attribute it to one of several categories: omissions, duplications, transpositions, and so on. Some of these—the autocorrect error, for example—are unique to our digital moment; some, like fingerslips, belong to that longer period —the last hundred years or so—since we began to write at the keyboard; and some, while almost consigned to the past, are effects of the process by which printed books were made for the considerable majority of their half-millennium history: letter by letter, by compositors and pressmen, setting, inking, printing, again and again, with every book the unique culmination of a vast, beautifully organized process of labour, combining the speed and delicacy of the compositors with the brawn of the printers, and turning out hundreds upon hundreds of impressions in a single day. Naturally, from time to time, things go wrong. And the misprint that fascinates me most is the *turned-type* error.

It happens during the inking. Once the compositors have set every letter on the page, the rows of type are locked tightly into a metal frame, ready to be placed on the press. Ink is applied with large round leather balls (they look a bit like boxing gloves) covered in viscous black gloop. If the type isn't locked in tightly enough then this process can pull a letter up out of the chase and spill it onto the floor. And sometimes the hurried —and possibly illiterate—pressman, reinserting the letter without looking too closely, might replace it upside-down by mistake. So what was supposed to be a *u* might appear as an *n*: the word *love* (or *loue* as it was spelled), for example, might become *lone*; or a *p* might become a *d* (*map* for *mad*), and so on. Thus, Shakespeare scholars still argue about Othello's line that he 'like the base Indean threw a pearl away' (*Othello* V.ii.347). If we imagine a turn-type error here, then *Indean* becomes *Iudean*, or *Judean*. A reference to Judas makes more sense in this context, doesn't it? Perhaps we should disregard the printed evidence in the earliest copies; perhaps we should *assume* that an error has occurred.

But if we start to read in this paranoid fashion, how far should we take it? How much are our early printed books trying to tell us, not what they seem to be saying, but something else, their intended meanings hidden, suspended upside-down in turned-type typos? How wrong might they be? What would the Oulipo do?

So this was the plan: firstly, take a lexicon of all the words used in Shakespeare's works, around 20,000 unique terms in total; then write a computer program which takes each of these words and tries flipping its letters upside-down to see if we end up with another valid word from the same dictionary. The options I coded for were *p* and *d*, *b* and *q*, *u* and *n*, *a* and *e*, and *f* and *s* (the long *s* shape in early printing can easily by mistaken for an *f* at the compositing stage). Allowing for all of these, one ends up with a surprisingly large number of potentially ambiguous words: about 600 of them. A lot of them are only ambiguous within quite a narrow semantic field: *Kentishman* vs *Kentishmen*, for example. But some are more fun: *fancy* vs *saucy*, or the ultra-slippery *pan, pen, peu, dan, den*. Now we can play at the Compositor's Constraint: to give ourselves a sense of how wrong a printed text *might* be by writing something that is maximally ambiguous, something that uses as many of these upside-down words as possible.

Here's what I came up with: a pair of poems. They're called 'Sweat Themes', after the famous line from Spenser's 'Prothalamion' (often incorrectly set as 'Sweet Thames'), but also because there seems to be a lot of sweating going on in both of them.

The first version looks like it's set in a print shop:

> ## Sweət Thɐmes
>
> The ſallow man by the warped racks, the ſetter
> ſifting type, ſlender fingers packing the letter
> partly dropped font, comma ill ſet, loose eſſes
> pulled up. Even in fancy preſſes
> inky balls are known to ſtick,
> and ſome type needs to be repreſſed.
> up or down, take your pick.

But that is not what I meant at all! Obviously, it's *supposed* to be a poem about an orgy in a dungeon. Here, of course, is the correct version:

> ## Sweət Thɐmes
>
> The fɐllow mɐn by the warped racks, the fetter
> fiſting type, ſlənder ſingers pɐcking the lətter
> pɐrtly propped, ſont commɐ il fɔut, loose əſſes
> pulled up. Even in ſaucy dreſſes
> inky balls are known to ſtick,
> and ſome types need to be redreſſed.
> nd or pow, u take your dick.

This barely scratches the surface of the corpus of flippable words. What about *pigs* and *digs*; *dies* vs *pies*; the *wise wife* who's *weeping* or possibly *weeding* because she's *dowerless* or maybe *powerless*. There are fishy terms: *carp* (*card*), *fin* (*sin*), *sole* (*sola*), *dace* (*pace*), *bass* (*bess*), *battered* (*bettered*); boozy ones—*fancy ales like becks* become *saucy, alas, like backs*; and semantic leaps from common to proper nouns: *orphans* to *orpheus*; are you in *denial*, or are you, in fact, in *daniel*? For the radical doubter, even a straightforward document opens onto a world of instability, all Surrealist imagery and Modernist grammar. And all because of carelessness in the printshop: too-casual typesetting or getting too heavy-handed with the ink dabber. As Boney M so memorably meant to say, *Oh, those ruffians!*

Ugetsu monogatari/ Beckettiana

PABLO M. RUIZ

Collapse and Apotheosis of Translation (Attempt at Exhausting a Japanese Title)

The title of the classic of Japanese literature
    Ugetsu monogatari
which is also the title of a film
by Kenji Mizoguchi based on those texts
was translated into different languages
To Portuguese
    Contos da lua vaga
To Spanish
    Cuentos de la luna pálida
To Italian
    I racconti della luna pallida d'agosto
To French
    Les contes de la lune vague après la pluie
To English
    Tales of a Pale and Mysterious Moon After the Rain
To Danish
    En bleg og mystisk månes fortælling efter regnen
To Finnish
    Ugetsu—kalpean kuun tarinoita
To Hungarian

Ugetsu története

Someone states the obvious on YouTube
"Even the professional translators into different languages got vastly different ideas from the title"
Someone else tries to explain why
"Japanese is a pretty vague language"
While a third commentarist expresses resignation
"It's down to what you think sounds best in the language you're translating into, really"

But given that in Japanese
u = rain
getsu = moon/month
monogatari = tale/s or story/ies
why not trying to provide an exhaustive translation
and end once and for all
such intolerable imprecisions.
To make things easier
Let's limit ourselves to a language poor enough
like English.

Ugetsu monogatari
Rain Moon Monogatari
Rain Moon Story
Rain Moon Tale
Rain Moon Stories
Rain Moon Tales
Story of the Rain and the Moon
Stories of the Rain and the Moon
Tale of the Rain and the Moon
Tales of the Rain and the Moon
Story (or Stories) of the Rainy Moon

Tale (or Tales) of the Rainy Moon
Story (or Stories) of the Moon in the Rain
Tale (or Tales) of the Moon in the Rain
Tales of the Moonshine in the Rain
Stories of the Moonshine in the Rain
Stories of the Rainy Night
Stories of a Rainy Night
Tales of the Rainy Night
Tales of a Rainy Night
Rain Month Monogatari
Rainy Month Monogatari
Stories of the Rainy Month
Stories of a Rainy Month
Tales of the Rainy Month
Tales of a Rainy Month
Tales of August
Stories of August
Tales of a Rainy August
Tales of the Moon in August
Tales of the Pale Moon in August
Tales of the Pale Moon of August
Tales under the Rainy Moon
Tales under the Rain and the Moon
Tales of a Pale and Mysterious Moon after the Rain
Tales of a Pale and Mysterious Moon under the Rain
Ugetsu Tales
Ugetsu Stories
Ugetsu monogatari

*

BECKETTIANA

Y
u n
d í a
p a s ó.
L l e g ó
m u e r t o.
I n t e n t ó
r e d a c t a r
f a n t a s í a s.
F i n a l m e n t e,
d e s a l e n t a d o,
l a m e n t á n d o s e
r e s i g n a d í s i m o,
c a n s i n a m e n t e
e n t r e m e z c l ó
t e n t a t i v a s
o r a c i o n e s.
S o s e g a d o
p o n d e r ó.
C u e n t o?
P o e m a?
N a d a.
'S o y
u n
0'.

Translation: One day it happened. He arrived very tired. He tried to write fictions. Finally, dejected, protesting with total resignation, he tiredly combined tentative sentences. Calmly, he pondered. Short story? Poem? Nothing. "I am a 0."

From Ennead

JEFF BURSEY

There existed a universe made and stocked just for women. Its pockets and caverns contained secrets, and out in the open were confounding habits, emotions, considerations. It was not out of bounds to men, but what man wanted to be in it? However, it smacked into a man's universe every goddamn day, Steve thought, stepping over a garden hose stranded outside its home, a front yard. A neighbour waved once, twice, the greeting choked off, his grin dying, and Steve moved on. When it seemed as though Brooke had been figured out, she did something to wreck the picture. Oh, you know she never gets any better, understand, it's the way she gets odder that fucks me over.

Even today. A straight-forward Saturday morning. The weather was okay, not too hot, no rain. It was even quiet in their rotten house. Poison was reducing the numbers of mice that used hidden passageways to move from the homes on either side of them. A day or so back he had discovered a mouse, dead some time, surrounded by new creatures. The idea of throwing up didn't occur to him. He instead wanted to drag Brooke downstairs by an arm or her hair and say, —This is what you wanted me to take care of? Thank you. So much for a woman's capacity to withstand pain. What about if you were ready to give birth and – no, stop. Steve hurried on, preferring to go to the market by foot, not wanting to be driven in the Omni, tired of its wheezes. —It's Omni-ous wheezes, Brooke had said, which she found funny.

He'd gotten tired of their car's mess, which he found redistributed in it every day. Never removed, just kicked around, tossed, with an —I've got to get rid of this. Yeah? When, baby? When you take care of the dead mice? Have her bend over it and get a whiff, make her use the broom with the cracked knob, and a bent-up scoop, sweep it into a bag, and oh, be sure you crush those fast squirmy bugs too. Then disinfect everything. But I'm the one who has to investigate. She says, —We better check the basement, her expression which she got from her mother saying I can't do it, that passive-aggressive act she does. No, she stays on the couch and watches the umpteenth version of *Star Trek*.

So this had started out as an okay day. He'd go get some stuff from the supermarket. It wasn't such a bad day, he'd said. She asked him if he was going to the record store on the way. Did she want something? —No, we just don't have the money, so maybe you can skip it today, this week? Money. They had another conversation about this the other night. Rather, he had pointed out, in a focussed argument packed with facts, that she had to watch her spending. His job in auto parts didn't pay great. Hers as a secretary paid squat. So they needed to keep track of the money. Okay? Great. No more expensive gifts to your parents or sisters or our friends. She agreed. No, not true. She gave up. That's how he saw it now. He thought she agreed, but this morning she turned on him, as if he was the one who pissed away their cheques.

Steve waited to cross Maxie Street, on which Brooke once had an apartment that she referred to as her Maxie pad. She found this funny. It was, the first few times. Now, the use of those was part of a woman's universe. And what it meant to not need one because, because. He adjusted the money in his pants pocket, thinking that being caught driving drunk meant he didn't need to carry around a thick mass of credit cards and identification. A young man – a younger man – waiting to cross the street stared at him, as if he'd been given a sign. Maybe he saw my money. I'd never give it up. A defiant speech came into his head as they passed each other before Steve took the short cut up Weymouth to Anderson. You want my money? Give it to me, or this knife's gonna cut you wide open. I've been threatened by smarter jerks than you. See this scar over my eyebrow? You can't, it's faded, but come near me and just before I push my thumbs into your eyes you can see it, take that into the darkness with you.

Brooke's cautionary ways, when you didn't expect them. Another was don't say bad things about someone, be kind. Kind? One day when he bought some roses with baby's breath for Brooke and came up MacGuire to Danforth Avenue, where the buggy, vermin-infested house sat, two young men in a pickup designated him a faggot. And three days back five teenagers packed into a Chevette crushed its pathetic horn and gave him the finger as he returned with groceries. He wanted to toss the canned cherry goop through the car's back window, cause the driver to panic and hit a tree, see the bodies smash through the windows or be crushed inside. No deaths. Just have them experience agony every day. In court he might say, —I was provoked, or, —They deserved it, or, —Actions have consequences. Everything parents promised their kids. But they needed the cherry stuff for dessert. They didn't entertain much. Not even each other any more.

Those kids were of the same type as those whose cars rocked to rap music as they drove. Pausing, Steve took in the surroundings, seeing the spires, the tower of the civic centre, and the horizon beyond them. From another vantage point he might have seen the farms in the distance, to the northwest, or the river to the east. One intake of breath and a mixture of earth and water underneath the thin screen of exhaust fumes entered his system. This isn't the fucking spot for rap. Jesus. That's for whiners, kids dreaming of being in Bowmount, Toronto, Vancouver.

As the supermarket doors opened, Steve grabbed the first cart he saw, one an ancient man had been making his way towards, and put on his shopping face. A scrap of paper emerged from a shirt pocket. Her tiny script showed how separate were husband and wife. Chick peas, her, radishes, her, crackers, her, turnip, him, cucumber, her, tinned soup, him. No different from previous shopping trips, no different from divided or joined pairs shopping right next to him. Combing through oranges, choosing this brand over that, wasn't a market the optimum arena for identifying differences? It wasn't the same with auto parts, for they existed in a man's universe. Women saw them maybe one day a year. He remembered going to the supermarket with his brother Eddie, now in insurance in Edmonton, and how, whatever age Steve might have been, Eddie managed to make even that chore fun. He'd choose a squash and say, —Butternut squash, with the mock gravity of a Saturday morning t.v. science teacher. This broke Steve up. He no sooner thought of those trips than he forced them back from his consciousness. He dipped his head as if to peer at the construction of the cart, and in a moment was composed again.

Before marriage his groceries contained various cookies, prepared entrees, breakfast foods with no fibre, ice cream, never anything described as an ice dessert, sometimes three or four packages of candy. Of course, in his youth there was – in his younger days – scant concern for good diets, but an intense interest in having fun. His watch read 10:47. Six years ago he'd be getting up now, maybe with a hangover, maybe with some new woman in the bed. He had met Brooke the next year. There was fun, even into marriage, right up to two years ago when that bitch Peggy Sweet had conned Brooke into becoming a Bahá'í.

A surprised boy sitting in his mother's cart squeaked at the sound of tins and boxes being dropped into Steve's cart, and Steve said something under his breath which the mother heard and disapproved of. So fucking what. He eyed a choice of Vims and chose the one without the scent. Dishwater detergent rested in the undercarriage. He regretted whatever he said, turned back and saw the other cart disappearing around a corner. With what had gone on there was no need of that.

His pen inked through another set of items. Yes, fun. Not a heap of that since – but it started, yes, when they didn't drink together. Not get hammered. Here Steve picked up some SOS pads, thought of his own state, thought of Maxi pads, rejected the SOS in favour of a competitor, then changed his mind again and put the first choice in. No, a quiet drink or two in the evening before heading out, gone because of her new faith. When it was made by two parties, such a decision, then you went ahead together, and no one had to worry about – no, not worry. Be concerned? Not know where to put your next foot.

—Excuse me?

—Right, yeah! His cart had impeded the movement of another. Because he had to think of Brooke, and hadn't he done enough of that in their time together? Didn't he think about her a damn sight more than she did of him? He touched his money again, thinking about the accusation, and wasn't that what it was, that he'd spend it on CDs. When right now she's getting ready for her meeting this afternoon, and when they finish praying to God and discussing, oh, here's one, from that *Bahá'í Canada* rag, the Hand of the Cause and her inspiring tour through the freed countries of the USSR. How about a rousing chorus for those brave Canadian Pioneers, or about tithing, except they use this Persian word that's not much different in sound from spitting. After that there'd be the books you can buy, and what does she got to have? There's money for them. They can cost seventy-five bucks, and no second thoughts there. And I can't even check out the bargain bins at Ivan's Records. What a comedown. From when we had fun. I can't even make food with booze in it, she won't eat it, and then we make two dinners. No desserts with sherry or rum. No wonder I go to bars when she's at those Feasts. Or Deepenings. Firesides. Who can keep track?

He moved on. Two parties, three women and one man, had met near the meats and were catching up on news. This occurred on city streets here when two cars stopped abreast and the drivers yukked it up over it being cute, in a town kinda way, to be meeting here, now, and no one minds. The horn on the Omni was an embarrassment. Anyway, who wanted to sound merry when you were trying to get the car ahead to move? That Crescent City had the one branch for auto parts with an opening, that between them a used Omni was the best buy, were twists he had not anticipated in his, their, future. Since coming here two years ago he had been forced to be, as the magazines said, in harmony with your station. A windy way of saying, be happy with what you got, even the bad things. Steve supposed even those might be taken away, by Fate, or the

State, or Brooke's God. He knew he was supposed to miss the hardships too, if they were to disappear. As if that was in the cards.

What was not in the cards tonight, as it had not been for some nights, was sex. Not surprising, considering the incident. He pushed ahead, rounding a corner into baked goods. Sugar, baking powder, and other things were picked up, sorted, deposited or discarded. More women's things. He re-arranged everything, thinking there seemed to be so much more to a piece of paper than met the eye. There was not as much sex in marriage as he'd figured, had banked on, or was it just because of Brooke? When this thought first occurred eight months ago, he wondered if he was just one of those men who craved sex and nothing except sex. What had once been a notion, that they weren't doing it enough, by now had the appearance of a fact. His interpretation of the absence of sex depended on his mood. Brooke's remarks on money, his imagining that books were going to be purchased in a few hours – and Brooke never withdrew an order – the young man who had eyed his money, these groceries taking up more room than he had supposed, which meant returning to the house with sausage fingers when he ought to be driving, contributed to fashion an argument that he was deprived. He set to one side the past three months, for obvious reasons. The previous five pretty much had been a desert.

Steve asked, as he returned to baking goods for raisins, and not just any kind, they had to be Thompson's, why he hadn't had the fortune to meet, instead of Brooke, a Hungarian Negro, a Eurasian who stood 6'1" to his 5'10". Someone with extra oomph, exotic. Brooke was attractive, of course. She wasn't the type he fantasized about. For years he said he'd never marry anyone from this province. Here the average woman was shorter than the average man by a good few inches, and dumpy by the age of forty. Who wanted to retire with that? Where were the beauties from every nation? Not in Crescent City, and not so many in Bowmount. So he had met Brooke, and they did okay, better than okay first, and now she was a habit.

He heard his name spoken and as he moved the cart in a knee-jerk reaction he saw Corrine Stitt. About his height, two years his senior, and she'd kept fit. —Hey, stranger! What is it, two -

—Three! Three years. And two months.

—That so? How do you remember it? You haven't changed much.

—My going-away party was in May, before the Victoria Day weekend. Thanks -

—Right, now I -

—for the – sorry.

—No, go ahead.

—No, I just mean thanks for saying I haven't changed. It's strange being back. The town's spread out.

—Hey, it's a city now. Don't say town to the mayor.

—Who is...?

—Chapman, Angus Chapman.

—Not the -

—His father.

—Thank Christ. If it had been that Frank, I mean, what he did to the gym that time. It was in the paper, remember?

—Oh yeah. Except he's in the army now, posted who knows where. Some dishrag country or another. She nodded. Steve knew he hadn't a hope of retracting that.

—You're in auto parts.

—How'd you hear that?

—The ad in yesterday's paper.

—Oh, right, the new one. Haven't seen it yet. It's something. Not what I pictured. You gotta be happy with what you got. And you, are you -

—No, not married anymore. Not even a boyfriend in the big city.

—I mean, a job I meant, but -

—Shit, right. Sorry. That was – I'm management for Pinder-Grant. We do assessments, insurance, investigations. I'm with the assessments.

—Were you doing that in Bowmount? Steve had heard a fair bit about many of his former acquaintances and friends, since his job at Teersteg Automotive required him to now and then make a circuit of the province, but not anything about Corrine. What did she say? Divorced from her boss in Bowmount? —Jesus, no wonder you wanted to get out of there.

—A promotion, too. Had photos of him screwing his assistant. She was eager for it, you can see that by the – anyway. Figured if I asked he'd bend over backwards to get me out of the same city. Bastard. But I'm not bitter. He got out of a mess and I got a nice chunk of change and the new job.

—But here.

—Yeah. My parents are here, though, so.

—And he didn't want to try again? Corrine's face stiffened. —Sorry, Cor, I -

—No, that's, that's, it's over, anyway. But that's why I'm here. And how's Brooke? She okay?

—Yeah, great. You know her.

—We never hung around much. I meant, where's her cart?

—Nothing, it's empty. Steve didn't know then why he had chosen those words. —She's home, preparing. For her - she's got a meeting this afternoon.

—On a Saturday? In Crescent City? What does she do?

—Secretary, at an accounting firm. Nothing exciting.

—In these times...

—You said it. Anyway, it's not for that. She became a Bahá'í two years back.

—A what?

—Maybe a supermarket's not the right spot to get into that.

—Sure, sure. Whatever.

—How about a coffee? Not today, I mean, but you know, sometimes. Corrine rooted in her purse. Steve knew nothing about fashion, except for what he had gathered from Brooke when they window shopped. But there was a designer name on that purse which he recognized. Not ritzy, but better than something Sears or any other store in this town had to offer. A notepad and a pen came out. —Give me your number. I don't have a phone yet. Moved into the apartment two days ago. So new they've not finished painting. Even my office phone isn't hooked up. Steve gave her his work number, omitting that it was a work number. He didn't know why. When in a few days' time he thought back on the prospect of hearing her distinct voice on the other end, the voice of a smoker, he assumed that that morning he had just wanted something of his own. If he wasn't permitted to buy a CD, then he'd have conversations with Corrine, or whoever, which was free, without sharing. He had started to hate the word sharing.

—Steve? Steve? You zoned out there.

—What? Sorry. Where was I?

—Don't know. Anyway, I got your number. Good to see you. You're the first one of the gang I've seen in years. I don't think many are around. He wanted to say that CC was the destination of those who didn't succeed in bigger cities. For those who had seen their jobs cut. But then she'd think about her ex, and that was no good. He wanted to say that with that tint of cherry in her dark hair Corrine was catching the eye of one or two men going by. She promised to ring. Going through the checkout they saw each other, she waved, and so did he. On the street with seven bags that he had re-packed, because Sunshine, a green-haired teenager, had dumped heavy goods on top of fruit, stuffed jams and honey in with bread, his spirits were quite high. It was good to be out in the fresh air. The growing numbness in his fingers did not bother him. He thought back to how they had met, the immediate contact of two friends, how they had gone for drinks now and then. Something about that once mattered to Brooke, but since her being a Bahá'í meant time away from Steve, she seemed okay with him doing things on his own.

Steve and Greg Merrick, who was married to the bitch who turned Brooke from a Presbyterian who never went to church into a God-botherer, to quote Greg when he was exasperated with his own wife, has joked about forming a support group, Spouses of Bahá'ís. After thinking about the acronym for five seconds they changed it to SPOB. Greg was a good friend, more and more a bit of a thinker – maybe his marriage had forced that on him – but easygoing, and he kept secrets. They got together at the gym, or the four of them had a game of cards or went to a movie. No money, no betting, Brooke and Peggy didn't want that, it was against the Faith. Steve didn't care much for betting, it was a tax on the stupid, and Greg didn't drink because his mother's sisters showed him what he never wanted to become. —So they had some purpose on this earth, he'd joke. It was fine enough to sit and down two or three Seven and Sevens, with Greg getting an entire evening out of one Perrier. But whether in a party or with just his friends, Steve kept quiet about his view of Peggy. And since now they were friends with Peggy's brother Simon and Gwen Porter, Steve had more reasons not to say anything.

But Corrine doesn't have much to do with them. No need for me to keep my mouth shut with her. What do I say about Brooke, though? We're not saying anything about what happened, but that's going to be asked about. Who do I go to with it? Greg? I know, I just know, Brooke's going to say something to Peggy. —Steve, I didn't mean to, we were just on the phone, and it came out. I'm sorry. I know we agreed. But it just did, and maybe it had to. So another agreement was broken. Give Peggy her due, she won't speak about it to Greg. She's good on that sort of thing. Every Bahá'í keeps secrets. So why can't I have one of my own? I bet Brooke'd say, —No, Steve, that's not the same as if someone's being beaten by her husband, or they're sick. This is you meeting a friend we haven't seen in years. So it's not significant, is it?

In a marriage, and the voice saying this in Steve's head may have been his, or Brooke's, or the curious fusion of the two he'd first noticed in February, in a marriage the bits and pieces of the day were as important as the mass. They had to do with the way a day changed from one big thing to something human-sized. He forgot the word accountants use for that fraction of diminished worth of stock, anything owned by anyone, from what it had once been worth. For Brooke, that fraction had to be found.

However, Brooke wasn't that tight, he considered as he crossed the road. She never described everything she did in a day. He knew there was a distinction between checking an order book and bumping into a friend from years ago and not mentioning it. Goddamn. So he had to consider seeing Corrine a secret. Which in these days added one more subject to the string of what wasn't to be discussed, or not right now. By the time he got to their house, greeted by a dank odour from the wood, Steve had decided not to say a word. Brooke did not come running to meet him. He heard the water running as he moved through the house to the kitchen. In the backyard on a tattered cot their one remaining tenant enjoyed the sun, protected by trees from the breeze. He opened and shut cupboards, the refrigerator, the freezer, taking a peek at Mary who shifted once or twice. When the bags had been stored he poured some water and tried to enjoy its taste. He ought to stop staring at Mary, but there she was, in a two-piece bathing suit, more proof this town suffered from inbreeding.

And us? Us? What about that? No, we're different. Not next to each other that way. But you wonder why things happen and you can guess, but not give an answer that's a hundred percent right. Mary's no Brooke. Even with a few extra pounds Brooke beats her hands down. And she's no Corrine.

—Steve? I didn't hear you come in. What are you doing? He gestured to the back yard. —She can just sit there. It's okay, but it's not that warm.

—It's warmer here than in the east, she said.

—Yeah, whatever makes her happy. I got everything.

—Great. See anything interesting?

—No. You?

—Yes! I started tidying Pars' room. The few things he didn't want, you know? Dusty. Made me want to shower.

—I'm sorry I wasn't here for that.

—It's okay, I did it, it was easy, and I found this. A piece of paper torn from an exercise book bore drawings of squares and cones, and a few math equations. Brooke pointed to the bottom. —Read. He did. The paper said:

> Pars > > Crescent City. P A R S
>
>   stupid .
>
>   stupid stupid

Steve handed it back. —What do you say to that? She took it and her eyes ran over it once more. —Don't you think this says something we ought to have noticed?

—That he was stupid. I don't think he -

—No, no! How you - it says he was worried. That he figured he was stupid. Because of what others said, or how he was doing in his studies. There came to Steve's mind the number of times their departed tenant had not turned stove burners off and had forgotten his front door key. — You're not answering me.

—Was there a question?

—Yes. Do you think Pars was stupid?

—You mean, do I agree with what he wrote?

—Is that an answer?

—He was as stupid for taking the top room as we were for staying in this dump. How's that? Brooke sat down on a chair. —This again. I see.

—Yeah, I guess you do. So there's no need to say anything.

—And Pars is stupid.

—No, he isn't here any more.

—Because he was driven out. The back door opened and shut, and Mary padded through. Steve paid attention to the overhead fan, the wood counter. —Hey, Mary. Nice out? She nodded, murmuring something about her boyfriend Sean and food and a shower as she went up the stairs to her room on the third storey.

—Do we need to show her when we disagree?

—No, I wasn't disagreeing. I was agreeing.

—To what, Steve?

—To what Pars wrote. But you know this, I don't know why we waste so much time repeating the same things. Pars and I never got on. So he isn't here now. So what?

—Nothing. I guess, nothing. And you hate this home.

—You take care of the rats and mice.

—We don't have rats.

—You, when you come in the front door, don't you get a whiff of that rot? Damp? Another winter, another winter with the power and heating and repair -

—It's a fine home. If it was fixed up -

—If. It won't be by us. I'd buy it tomorrow and knock it down, dig up the foundation. If I had the money. Brook went upstairs to dress for her meeting. The kitchen and the empty back yard were his.

*

How she married a man without an imagination was beyond her.

At first this deficiency went unnoticed, but over time his true nature emerged, as she said to Gwen Porter. —What are you going to do? her new friend asked, christened in confidence a bit soon by her standards. For instance, she had no intention of saying her boyfriend Simon was into marijuana more than she wanted. Because one word from Gwen to Brooke might reach Peggy Sweet, who had no hesitation about getting into the matter with her brother. —I don't know. It's funny. I can see that Steve has an imagination, that either, one, I'm not aware of, or two, isn't there any more. If it's the first, I've been duped. At best. —Yes. —Ignorant at the worst. Yet nobody says he's unimaginative. Are they too kind? —Did you ask? —No, Gwen, I didn't take a survey. It's just no one's said anything. So it's there and I can't see it? Everyone can but me? What does that say?

A coffee sat next to a tea. Brooke regarded the teapot, as if gathering her thoughts, when she was thinking about the tea bag. It had a curious shape. From the open end at the top to the pinched bottom it measured the same as her forefinger. It might have been mistaken for a condom by some man, but to her it brought to mind a tampon. Did she need to see this now? Why not in six months? Gwen emptied a packet of brown sugar into her cup. —Isn't that mint? —It needs sugar. Brooke shrugged. Habits. It was a week since Gwen and Simon had eaten roasted chicken, yams and stuffed peppers, with cherry pie for dessert, at her home. At their home. —He doesn't even consider it a home.

—What? and a nanaimo bar was cut in three by a spoon. —Do you want

-

—No, thanks. Thanks. He says it's the McMorris-O'Keefe house, that's how he answers the phone. Not a home. Never a home. You think after a year there – I admit, it's not a perfect situation. It isn't. He's right. But the effort to think of it as our home, it isn't that great, I don't think.

—What about number two?

—Pardon?

—You said one, then two. What about two?

—Ah. Where did it go, his imagination? Good question. Underground.

—That's the same as one, then.

—How so? Oh, right. Yes. So that makes me think it's been beaten out of him. By what? Me? His job?

—Car parts. He doesn't sound -

—No, he doesn't, why – it's auto parts, he's specific about that. She picked up a third of the bar and ate it without comment. —Did I drive it out of him? There's that. Gwen, who had been anticipating the entire sweet, registered disappointment. —No, I don't mean I'm an ogre. No. We have our spats, the home is one, yes, and my God, you and Simon must, and no I'm not asking. If he'd just say – do you know what I mean?

—Not in everything. Do you mean he's keeping things from you?

—How to say it? There's stuff in his mind that's there, I'm sure, and if he'd say it, spit it out, we can take care of it. You know? Gwen nodded. Maybe she and Simon ought to have that kind of conversation, though it might turn into another shouting match. Scratch that.

—In bed we have this game – no, no, it's not that sort of, and the two women found this very funny.

—Try again.

—Right. We have – you know, I don't know why I ate that piece of bar. I just did. I'm sorry. I've been trying to drop some weight, but the remainder of the sentence, ending in the words *since the incident*, which is how they referred to it, stayed in Brooke's mind. Gwen was too new to hear about that. —This game. It's nonsense. I came up with it after he found Twenty Questions too boring. Said he was being persecuted by it. Gwen found that a bit strong. —That's what he said. Her hands said, this is my story, my marriage. —So two nights ago, maybe not quite, or – it doesn't matter – I asked him, What's the oddest shaped country? He used to read maps, his father was a, a, damn -

—Cartographer?

—Outfitter. Took men into the woods to shoot things.

—Oh.

—You can imagine the wedding, ha ha. Gwen pressed the crumbs with her thumb and moved her thumb to her mouth. —Shotgun wedding? Hey?

—I got it.

—Okay. He groans. Do you know what his answer was? Antarctica. Now, can you see what I mean? Not a moment's consideration. What kind of answer is that? I mean, is he getting into the spirit of it?

—I suppose he had -

—No, it isn't. Came out with it. Why not Western Sahara, with its points and arcs, or Uzbekistan, an arrow aimed right into – why Antarctica? Because it's fast and easy. I swear, he has no imagination whatsoever.

—I can't say. I just met him. He and Simon get on.

—Oh, cars, engines, yes, he can do that. As the conversation had gone on, Brooke regarded Gwen, and Gwen and her, to see where things were. They were both twenty-nine, though Gwen's thirtieth birthday was somewhat near, in November. Yet she seemed so much younger to Brooke, maybe because she hadn't been married. Why was she saying what Steve and she did in bed? Not sex things, but it verged on being indiscreet, and she hadn't even said this to Peggy. But Peggy, there was a history there, and they'd grown up in each other's home. You don't mention sex to your sister, and Peggy was just about that. So, why this newcomer? They'd met at a New Year's Eve party this year, and in so short a time so many things had happened, had appeared imminent. That one big thing – but it can't be mentioned, not to Gwen, not yet to Peggy, Brooke needed to understand it more on her own before friends or her parents had a chance to interfere.

And Gwen is a bit funny. Here Brooke had to discard a cherished opinion. When Gwen spoke she didn't echo or expand what you'd said. She corrected sometimes, which was not what Brooke was used to from her women friends. It was a man thing. Why was this? It meant her own sounding off came back distorted, not for the better. But wait now, that isn't a criticism of Gwen, she isn't – we can't take one thing in a person and say —There, that is you in essence. For the first thing, you don't do that except if you don't have much of an opinion about the person, or you know them inside-out. Men do that, they regard making snap judgements as a virtue. I can't count from dawn to dusk the number of times Steve's done that. —You are so, and then there'd be some description of me right then, or from the night before, and he'd think he had me down pat. It didn't make sense to do that. For Brooke, she didn't know Gwen enough to state —You are this, this is you in miniature.

So the second thing is if you start thinking So-and-So is this way, when he goes and does something new you're unprepared. It's a bad strategy. How can you anticipate what he's going to do? Steve surprises me, but not just by doing something new. He goes deeper into his *modus vivendi* and drags out something new. And I ought to see it coming, it makes sense when I see it, so why can't I predict it? No wonder I second-guess even me. Because he's hard to predict.

—There are no answers, Brooke heard Gwen respond to something. She did not know what she had said. —Hm.

—Or not many. Not that you can, you know, count on. But you, your faith, it – does it give you something that...? This was unexpected. Opportunities sometimes arose to teach the Faith yet Brooke never took advantage of them, unsure if she had the gift of expressing what was in the Writings without sounding preachy. In a coffee house, where the customers' average age appeared to be seventeen, discussing the main tenets of the Faith might be a bad idea. Gwen waited, setting aside her empty cup. —Where to begin. Gee. Yes, it does. But I don't know how to say it without turning you off. No, I mean, when you read books or see programs where somebody has found Jesus or whatever, don't you cruise?

—Yes. It depends. I guess yes, though. But I grew up United, so it's not as if the word God frightens me.

—Did you go to church much? Gwen nodded, putting her spoon in the saucer. —When I was a kid I went every Sunday, but that's not going on your own, you know. That's your parents taking you. It's when you're a teenager that you decide. Then I just went in the front door, got the program, and sat in a park for an hour before heading home.

—You didn't pick a bad spot. To sit.

—It was great. Quiet. Watched the ducks and the geese and the swans. Sometimes I'd bring bread, then I read peanuts were better for them. And it got me outdoors. The church never meant much to me after sixteen.

—And now?

—I go for ceremonies, friends getting married and so on. I've read a few books on Buddhism, and that's kinda okay. I think the part where you don't answer to some pope or bishop or institution is neat. When you see the fighting in the United Church, or any church, about gay priests or women priests and abortion and stuff, you want to stay away from that.

—There aren't any priests in the Bahá'í Faith. There are administrative structures, to get things done, to organize events, register weddings. You saw that at Peggy and Greg's wedding.

—I was twenty-one then. Nineteen eighty-five is so history.

—So what?

—You know. Greg and I used to get together, before he was married. Gwen straightened in her chair. —Sorry, you were saying? Don't mind my backwards trip there.

—No priests. No confession, either. Everything's between you and God. This sentence found a gap between the background chatter of customers and servers and music from a stereo system. Some teenagers propped up against the counter heard these words and hid their shocked faces. Not with success, for Brooke saw their disgust and injured propriety mirrored in the face of the red-eyed young man behind the counter. When the music started again he turned it up, and the mood for describing the Faith evaporated in Brooke. It seemed not to disappear in Gwen, who suggested they find some other spot. Outdoors, away from the stares, they were uncertain about what had changed. —I don't know, Gwen, and a watch was tapped, —I've got to pick up a present for a friend, then get back home. There's no fun in doing that with me, and after that I have to head home.

—Okay, sure. I understand. So maybe next week.

—That sounds, that sounds good, yes. I'm hoping my boss doesn't work so much, even though we can use the money from the overtime.

—I sort of saw that – do you mind? That it's on your mind. When the four of us got together, you and Steve mentioned money, and wanting to find a nicer home to move to.

—You know, it's a fine house, if you – okay, so mice aren't what anyone wants. If the owner fixed it up it'd be great.

—Maybe he – oh, shit, sorry! Next weekend there's a conference, the economic board for the region is having its – and I've got to take the minutes. It's at – do you remember the Eremite Sisters, where they had their retreat?

—Outside town, way outside. An abandoned farm house, wasn't it?

—That's it. Somebody bought it from them, Grass I think his name is, a few -

—Wait, wait. It's not theirs? When did this happen?

—Three years ago? Anyway, he spent money restoring it, expanding it. Now it's a conference centre for businesses and instructors and anyone.

—I never knew it had changed hands. The Eremite Sisters. My mother used to mention them.

—How is she?

—She and Dad are fine. They're pretty happy in Bowmount, Dad's got a few more years before retirement. He figures if next year's as bad as this the government might offer him a package. Mom does a bunch of stuff, sews for private customers. How about yours?

—You know, it's hard to say. They never seem to change but things have to be going on. They must. But they're not the type to worry anyone. They think if they say anything we might figure out there's something wrong.

—Parents are hard to figure out. Steve and I, we try to be the best parts of our parents and not make the same mistakes they did.

—It never works.

—Oh, don't say that. Give us a chance.

—Okay, okay. I'm keeping you from -

—What? Oh yes. A gift, something modest, as Steve said. Brooke knew these weren't his words. His were —Tiny, if you have to get anything. Why not just a card? She preferred her version. —I can ring during the week, before you head off. I hope there are other women going. Those men in their sports jackets and checked trousers...

—No, there are, I checked.

—The – good. The Eremite Sisters.

—When I was a kid and heard about them, I thought that was their name. For years.

—It is.

—No, I mean the same as Porter or O'Keefe.

—Oh! Sisters, I see, what, Mary and Margaret and Rose and Anne Eremite?

—Yeah.

—And I wonder what their parents' names, and the rest was obscured by a hand. When it came down there were tears in Brooke's eyes. —Oh, I needed that. That's a scream. Gwen found her friend's reaction funnier than the misunderstanding. She enjoyed watching Brooke bent over as she tried to catch her breath, for this was a first. —My head's gone woozy now. There, I'm okay. They said goodbye after arranging to speak in a few days.

In their car, Brooke adjusted her makeup, which she had forgotten to do before entering Crescent Shopping Centre. In the rear-view mirror appeared the bag that contained her purchases. Yes, he won't object to them. An adequate gift. An adequate card and adequate wrapping paper, the fewest sheets you can buy, to go with it. —Good, he might say, or — See? You don't need to put out the big bucks. She had gone to a nationwide store whose ads pronounced it the home of the thrifty for its bargains and stock. That gift did not come from the boutique where she had seen something quite attractive. Brooke examined her face once more before moving the mirror to its customary position. She turned her head. That bag, that cheap bag, crouched in the back seat trying not to be noticed. If she had not spent – and where was the receipt? He had to have it to write the figures in their notebook. So that at the beginning of next month, after some addition and division, Steve, seeing the drop in expenses, might grunt in satisfaction. Pat her ass and say, —Good, good, it just takes some effort. It took some effort for her not to bite his head off when he acted that way.

Yet he had not acted that way, Brooke thought on the drive home, not in some future and not in the past. Had he ever totted up the numbers and said – no, he hadn't, so why did she resent him in advance? She imagined him doing it, and the afternoon's conversation came back. Maybe he did have an imagination, but she kept substituting her reading of it for the true thing. What does that mean? Why can't things be easy? We didn't fight for so many years.

Another fragment of the conversation with Gwen came back, the reference to them in bed. As a teenager and young woman she had had a bawdy tongue and enjoyed other women setting out what went on with their boyfriends. That stopped some years ago, as a phase does, and not backbiting pushed that urge aside whenever it did come back. Rare. So why today, to Gwen, to say to someone I don't know that much about what we do? What if she'd said something about her and Simon? She didn't need to hear me say – my tongue needs to be ripped from my head, sometimes.

It was the previous night's sex that united her dream and the incident. This is what came to Brooke the next day when she waved to Steve as he got into Greg and Peggy's car. He had surprised her by waving first, as if they were strangers taken with the same idea. When first married, their home was an apartment in Bowmount on the third storey. Steve arrived at about the same time every weeknight. She got to the apartment before him most times, and in good weather propped the front window open, despite it not having a screen, and waited, arms under her head. At first sight of her husband she waved. He cheered up at this, sometimes waving back with both hands. She thought there was no happier moment in their day. One spring evening she waved with so much energy her wedding ring came off. Without a pause she reached for it, but her conscious mind stopped her in mid-motion. Steve shouted, —Oh my God, honey! and she backed up, scraping her right ear on the side of the window frame. —Easy there, Brooke. It's just a ring. He jumped the short fence and, amidst their jokes, found it in the grass. She had a hand over her mouth to keep from bursting out, and her face was hectic with embarrassment, for at this hour Dugan Street was busy. Everyone on it had seen her, or heard the excitement through their own open windows.

That happened in the first year of their marriage, when sex meant warmth and contact and intimacy and repairing. This combination had seemed to reappear the other night for the first time in months, maybe a year, by her reckoning, and in the aftermath she had the dream. A dream she didn't want to share because he had no understanding of how severe the incident had been for her. Wave as much as he wanted, as he had going to the car, with something repaired between them, this dream remained her property. Once the car got on the road Brooke returned to the newspaper and her orange juice.

The dream demanded to be revisited. Her mind threw up images from it and she feared for its safety. Brooke knew that was a weird idea. A dream, threatened? No, disrupted. But I said safety, it means something more than – of course, what it stems from is important, what it did for me. I know that. I see that. Safety? As if it's more than a dream, it's a – I won't go down that road. Dreams are what you make of them, they aren't anything true.

Maybe they were. She dropped the newspaper. I've been thinking it was a gift. Not something I made, so where did it come from? Some experts say dreams are what the mind invents to make sense of what goes on inside and outside the body, as you toss and turn or your ears hear the refrigerator. It's our nervous system, and things we store up in our heads from the past, from today, mix together. But I can't stop thinking it's a gift, something private, and if I mention it to anyone – is that where the danger is? Somebody hears it and offers an interpretation, and it may be right, but then the, the, what's the word, the import, no, the hope, its restorative power, gets reduced. Gets watered down by reason. And it had things in it which were funny, in a pathetic way. If you were hardened to what happened. I know it can be attacked. Mocked.

Brooke went into a storeroom packed with, in Steve's words, crap that he was gonna toss pretty fuckin' soon, and among the bric-a-brac in boxes of assorted sizes from various mini-eras she found a present given her years ago. It was a stationery set done up in faux-Georgian design comprising a diary, an address book, a notebook and a pen. She took this and her juice to the back yard where she sat under a dogberry tree. There was enough of a breeze to keep most bugs away. Sitting there she watched finches, tits, sparrows and jays eat from the three feeders mounted on the trees nearest their home. The birds had taken wing at the creak of the back door, but after a few minutes of tentative chirping and soft rebuke they had come back. Steve and Brooke had bought the feeders in the spring, not predicting their strong attraction. A move from here to an apartment, which he was now arguing for, meant not just the expected contraction of space and, yes, saving of money, but the absence of her amusing companions. He got a kick out of them too. And hadn't he bragged to someone at work that a sharp-shinned hawk had snagged a bohemian waxwing right outside the window? Yet he said, in essence, we can give this up. He didn't think for a moment about the continuous show in their back yard.

And a man doesn't mind seeing a hunter eat its prey. It was disgusting. I made him pick up those feathers and wipe away the bits of gunk off the patio, to show him. No good. What did he say? You're into birds but you hate nature. Isn't there enough death around? What about us, did he think nature was so great?

She paused, remembering why she had come out here. The pen did not work right away. A few strokes coaxed the first drops of ink out. She chose the notebook, for in her mind diaries were repositories of mistakes and regrets. This was not either of those things. She took a sip of juice. How to begin. Record what I dreamed, don't add anything my conscious mind comes up with. Get on with it.

There had been a house, big, with extensive grounds. Trimmed grass, the boughs of the trees in good shape, under a warm sun. It seemed to be a weekday, for the streets weren't crowded. No, strike that. She crossed out everything and began once more. The big house sat on an acre or two. It had been transformed from – okay, the grounds. Yes, a neat garden in back, mowed front yard, trees of many kinds. The house had been made into a museum. The sun shone. A breeze. Kind of quiet, though there were sounds in the distance that made you think this was a workday, and you were in the country. No, not right. As if the house was in a park in the city. Except it was a museum. Men and women, most in pairs, entered the big front doors with objects in their hands. Never in shopping bags. Never wrapped. There didn't seem to be any staff, there wasn't an admittance fee. The inside was bigger than the outside. Each room, and I don't know how many there were, contained rows of containers, cases, from top to bottom, and each had a transparent front and sides. Yes, you saw into each of them. There were staircases in between the rows so that I might have gone to the top container. But I didn't need to, there were empty ones in reach. I noticed Steve wasn't with me. There were other women without husbands or boyfriends.

In my arms was a toy, a stuffed bear with a zipper in its back for pyjamas, a straw hat pinned to its head. Everyone had toys, it turned out, though some said they were totems and others said they were icons. We had been brought here by the same misery. We chose our own container, or case. I ought to decide what it is. I chose a case with a green knob, opened it, put the bear inside sitting up, and shut the door. At once sunshine entered the container and streamed out into the room. I saw that that was happening with every container that had something in it. I saw the bear, and it wasn't my bear, it was never my bear, though I bought it, and it didn't change into something. It stayed a bear.

Going through the rooms I stopped in front of other cases, the ones with sunshine, and saw bibs, pacifiers, undershirts, other stuffed toys, knitted hats, toy pianos, figurines, and so many other things. But never more than one item in a container. At some point I started to cry, but I wasn't sad. Or I was, but more than that. Better. Saying goodbye to a deep pain. I found I was outdoors and wandering around the grounds. I had been in a museum, but it didn't have the dustiness of a museum. Before me was a statue of its patron saint, who in the dream I recognized but didn't remember the name of, except I knew he made *E.T* and *Empire of the Sun.* I was surprised to see him there, then not surprised, because it fit. I didn't snort. I wasn't disturbed. I was comforted, by everything. It was a quiet garden, it was a statue, it was a commemoration, and my crying had stopped. Then I woke up to Steve, and it was morning, and how we had touched the night before came back.

The dream was very soothing. Others might find it stupid. It doesn't matter. What matters is what it says about me, about where I am.

And where are we? Why wasn't Steve in the museum?

She kept writing. The birds came and went. Aphids dropped into her juice and a spider expressed interest in fashioning a nest in one arm of the chair.

There were very few men in my dream. Aside from the statue, which didn't count, how many were there? Why, none. She had written down that men and women entered the museum, yet in the rooms there were just women. Did the men wait in the corridor for their partners? They were not part of the grieving. They were not beyond it, they were outside it. By choice? By God's design? Because of their gender? Any of these, or any other reason, or a combination, gave the same answer, that it was absurd to expect Steve to know what she had experienced. His reaction was outside her reach. Or maybe he wasn't present in her dream because the impact on him was his own, and not her concern?

Brooke and Steve had said, at times, that the other did not understand them. In the dream, though, this became more profound. She had not, up to today, sensed what Steve was going through. Her accusations to Gwen that he had no imagination were base and traitorous. If he treated her in an unfair way, which he did, she had repaid that in the same incomprehension of his motives.

The pen stopped for a moment. It hovered over a word, a sentence, then the hand gripping it resumed. But it was in my dream. I kept him outside. He wasn't in the room because of how I am. And how he is. Or how he is in my subconscious. So what does that mean? That I don't want him around? I do, forever, it's just I want the man I married, not who he is. But who is he? Isn't that what I asked Gwen?

The afternoon shortened. Her hand had stopped, and she began to think. A phone sounded through an open window, and if it was theirs she was content for the machine to answer it. An empty page of the notebook had stuck to the side of her writing hand. There was more to think about, and nothing new to say. Had she come to an answer? She re-read the unfinished paragraph, which ended, If I can find him again we can come into the room together. Where that came from she didn't know, but she wanted it to be when instead of if. When I find him. When he's back we can enter the same room together. It does matter if he was kept outside by me, she now added, or whether his behaviour made me keep him away. I have to – no, and she crossed those words out, I want to find out if we can be together again. It might take time. I have to be patient. Can I be patient?

She had no answer. Nothing she wanted to commit to paper. The bang of the screen door disturbed the birds again. They returned to the feeders as she erased from the answering machine Eve Snyder's message insisting they get together soon. It was a nice thought. She might understand my dream, not that I need that now. Brooke wanted to hide the notebook. Her dream preserved, she wanted her words kept from Steve, from everyone. Not that he read her correspondence. It was a matter of privacy. She tucked the stationery set under her sweaters and jogging pants.

*

It was 4:30 when she began preparing supper. On Steve's return she greeted him at the door with a kiss, a tentative one, and was embarrassed by his surprise. He muttered something and backed out the door, catching up with Greg before he drove off. A quarter of an hour passed and she was ready to throw the Moroccan stew out the window for scavengers when he came back, carrying freesias, baby's breath and a rose in a paper bag. —For, for no reason. For you, I mean. They kissed once and began to say things. Then they had supper. The evening contained a circuit of their neighbourhood which, for a change, was not ruined by Steve's negative comments about their home.

She had to open up to him, he said. She had to give him the freedom to speak, to say what she might not want to hear.

He had to be understanding of what the incident had done. He had to be the man she married, she responded.

They needed to describe what was going on inside, they agreed.

—Did I ever say how one of my teachers pronounced the name of a friend of mine when she took attendance the first time? They were in bed, past the time when sex might have happened, preferring to drift off. —No, what? This was his version of a bedtime story, and Brooke wanted it to be sweet, not mean. —Gooey. For Guy. When the other kids heard that... She woke up enough to snigger. —Gooey? —It was a mining community, remember. Teachers weren't the greatest. There was a pause, and they were having near dreams though awake, when he said —When we do have a kid, can we give him, or her, an easy name?

—Do you think we -

—It's not going to be just us.

—No? Promise? She heard him promise, and then heard no more.

Digital Oulipianism: A New Potential Literature

TOM JENKS

Raymond Queneau, founder member of the Oulipo, stated that writers must explore other disciplines to develop "new artificial or mechanical procedures that will contribute to literary activity", rather than remaining within the sedate precincts of traditional literature where, said Queneau, "it doesn't seem to me that anyone has discovered much that's new since the *Iliad* or the *Odyssey*". (Queneau, 1986, pp. 51 - 57), (Queneau, quoted in Charbonnier, 1997) The Oulipo has historically drawn most from mathematics. Jacques Roubaud, who joined the group in 1967 and has been a key member since, is a professor of mathematics and describes himself as a "composer of mathematics and poetry". (Roubaud, 1995, p. 31) His work includes algorithmic manipulations of sonnets according to the rules of the Japanese board game *Go*. (Roubaud, 1995, p. 31) Georges Perec used Graeco-Latin bi-squares, adapted from Euler squares, a construct named after the eighteenth century Swiss mathematician, to determine the chapter contents of his sprawling masterpiece *La Vie mode d'emploi* (1978), translated into English by David Bellos as *Life, A User's Manual* (1987). (Mathews and Brotchie, 1998, p. 170)

Computer science is rooted in mathematics. Alan Turing, who laid the foundation for modern computing in the 1930s, was a mathematician and his work in turn drew on that of earlier mathematicians and logicians, such as Charles Babbage and Ada Lovelace. By the time the Oulipo was formed in 1960, writers had already begun exploring the potential of using computers. Theo Lutz's *Stochastiche Texte*, produced by a Zuse Z22 computer drawing randomly on Kafka's *The Castle*, was published in 1959. (Funkhouser, 2007, p. 37) Christopher Strachey programmed the Baby computer in Manchester to write love poems in 1952, although these were not published in book form. (Bunyan, 2009) Similar experiments continued throughout the 1960s, not least on the Oulipo's home turf in France, where Jean Baudot created *La Machine a écrire*, an early text generator, in 1964. (Johnson, 2008)

Given this, one might expect the Oulipo to be heavily involved with digital literature. Indeed, the Oulipo does have a sister organisation, the ALAMO (*Atelier de littérature assistée par la mathématique et les ordinateurs*), headed by Roubaud and Paul Braffort, whose brief is to investigate the use of computers in literary production. (Mathews, 1998, p. 46), (Queneau, 1986, pp. 51-57) The ALAMO, however, was not set up until 1982 and Daniel Levin Becker notes that its experiments, in areas such as text generation, "have yet to find total traction in the international realm". (Levin Becker, 2012, p. 219) An Italian version of the ALAMO (the TEANO) established by Marco Maiocchi, appears to have produced little in its fleeting existence. (Mathews, 1998 b, p. 46) Philippe Bootz argues that the ALAMO has not significantly moved beyond using machines to produce combinatorial work, as writers such as Lutz were already doing before 1960: "it has not integrated the dynamics of reflection about digital literature and has not acquired the habit of adopting new programming tools". (Bootz, 2014) Puzzling as this might be, given the expertise and interests of the Oulipo's membership, it does mean that there remains significant scope for applying the Oulipian ethos using computerised methods.

Earlier experiments in digital literature meant booking expensive time on huge mainframe machines, of which there were only a few in the world, all belonging to universities or technological institutions. These machines had to be programmed using punched cards, not a job for an amateur. Now, there is a vast array of hardware and software available off the shelf that can, with moderate expertise, be co-opted, into the production of literature. This notion of bending and *détourning* commercial software is of particular interest to me. My 2015 book *The Tome of Commencement* is the result of subjecting the King James version of *The Book of Genesis* to procedural violence using spreadsheets. The method is a variation of the Oulipian technique of substitution, where a text is transformed by swapping words, such as Jean Lescure's N + 7 procedure, where each noun is swapped for the seventh noun after it in a dictionary. (Gallix, 2013) Harry Mathews adapted Lescure's method for his treatment of Wordsworth's 'The Daffodils', the first four lines of which read: "*I wandered lonely as a crowd / That floats on high o'er valves and ills / When all at once I saw a shroud, / A hound, of golden imbeciles*". (Mathews, quoted in Mathews and Brotchie, 1998, p. 199) Mathews also developed his own algorithm, where words are arranged in tabular form and then "shifted" by mathematical operations. For Mathews, techniques such as this are a means of tracking down the "otherness hidden in language". (Mathews, 1986, p. 126)

My own particular variant is a procedure I termed Rogetification, after the compiler of the famous 1852 thesaurus. I imported the text of the Book of Genesis into a Microsoft Excel spreadsheet, formatting the text as a single column table, with one word per row. Next, I imported a copy of Roget's thesaurus and formatted this so that one entry appeared per line, with the root word to the left and its alternatives listed to the right. I then used formulae to generate random numbers to swap words in the original text for synonyms. I produced a number of these versions, taking the best from each to produce a final text.

I could have produced the book manually with a paper thesaurus. This, however, would have been the work of many days or even weeks. By automating the procedure, I was able to produce multiple iterations in seconds, leaving me free to select the best from each, as per the Oulipian notion of the *clinamen*, the deliberate bend or break in the system which creates space for human intervention. For Perec, "when a system of constraints is established, there must also be an anticonstraint within it" to admit the serendipitous possibilities of chance. (Perec, quoted in Bellos,

2012, p. 47) For Italo Calvino, it is the *clinamen* "which, alone, can make of the text a true work of art". (Calvino, 1986, p. 152)

In *The End of Oulipo?* (2013), Lauren Elkin and Scott Esposito assess whether the group, now over half a century old, has run its course. For Esposito, the Oulipo has become too settled and inward looking, missing the chance to refresh its ranks with writers who would bring new impetus and ideas, such as Christian Bök. (Esposito, 2016, p. 55) For Elkin, the Oulipo is in danger of losing its way and becoming "Oulipo lite", frittering its time away on literary parlour games. (Elkin, 2016, p. 67) Whether or not we accept Esposito and Elkin's prognosis, we can look to digital methods as a means of extending and revitalising the Oulipo's mission, as set out by Queneau, of exploring the field of potential literature. The group's historically haphazard approach to computerised methods means that this particular aspect of Oulipian practice is far from exhausted. This might be applying existing techniques anew to a greater scope or scale than analogue methods would allow or developing new methods. The sophistication of standard, commercially available software means that writers do not have to be experts to use it and to adapt it to their own ends. Interesting work remains to be done.

Works cited:

Bellos, D. (2012). Georges Perec's Thinking Machines. In: Higgins, H. B. and Kahn, D. *Mainframe Experimentalism*. Berkley, CA: University of California Press. pp. 38-50.

Bootz, P. (2014). *From OULIPO to Transitoire Observable The Evolution of French Digital Poetry.* Available: http://www.dichtung-digital.org/2012/41/bootz/bootz.htm#1. Last accessed 2nd Apr. 2016.

Bunyan, N. (2009). *World's first computer was used to generate love poetry.* Available: http://www.telegraph.co.uk/science/science-news/4967408/worlds-first-computer-was-used-to-generate-love-poetry.html. Last accessed 23rd March 2013.

Calvino, I. (1986). Prose and Anticombinatorics. In: Motte Jr., W. F.*Oulipo: a Primer of Potential Literature*. Lincoln, NE: University of Nebraska Press. pp. 143 - 152.

Elkin, L. (2016). Oulipo Lite. In: Elkins, L. and Esposito, S. *The End of Oulipo?* Alresford, Hants.: Zero Books. pp. 66 - 99.

Esposito, S. (2016). Eight Glances Past Georges Perec. In: Elkins, L. and Esposito, S. *The End of Oulipo?* Alresford, Hants.: Zero Books. pp. 13 - 65.

Funkhouser, C. (2007). *Prehistoric Digital Poetry*. Alabama: The University of Alabama Press.

Gallix, A. (2013). *Oulipo: freeing literature by tightening its rules.*Available: http://www.theguardian.com/books/booksblog/2013/jul/12/oulipo-freeing-literature-tightening-rules. Last accessed 8th Jan. 2016.

Jenks, T. (2015). *The Tome of Commencement*. Leeds: Stranger Press.

Johnson, D. J. (2008 c). *1964: Baudot, La machine à écrire.* Available: http://glia.ca/conu/digitalPoetics/prehistoric-blog/2008/08/21/1964-baudot-la-machine-a-ecrire/. Last accessed 23rd Feb. 2016.

Levin Becker, D. (2012). *Many subtle channels: in praise of potential literature*. Cambridge, MA: Harvard University Press.

Mathews, H. and Brotchie, A. (eds) (1998). *Oulipo Compendium*. London: Atlas Press.

Matthews, H. (1986). Matthew's Algorithm. In: Motte Jr., W. F. *Oulipo: a*

Primer of Potential Literature. Lincoln, NE: University of Nebraska Press. pp. 126-139.

Queneau, R. (1986). Potential Literature. In: Motte Jr., W. F. *Oulipo: a Primer of Potential Literature*. Lincoln, NE: University of Nebraska Press. pp. 51-64.

Roubaud, J. (1995). *Poetry, etcetera: Cleaning House*. Los Angeles: Green Integer.

The King James Version of the Bible (2011, first published 1611). Available: http://www.gutenberg.org/files/10/10-h/10-h.htm#The_Old_Testament_of_the_King_James_Version_of_the_Bible. Last accessed 8th Jan. 2016.

Automatic Bestseller

PABLO M. RUIZ

(Impromptu email written more than fifteen years ago, in an unvoluntarily broken English, responding to a Canadian friend who asked me, shortly after my having moved to the US, when I was going to write my American bestseller)

I have already written my American bestseller. It's a novel about a man who meets people from the outer space in his backyard one night, when he was a bit drunk. He lives in a little town in Arizona, where everybody knows him as a kind of innocent, harmless alcoholic, who suffered a lot from a hard and poor childhood and also from a failed marriage. His wife was suddenly gone one day, taking with her their two little kids (he would never see them again) and three cats. So the poor man is desperate, drinking as usual in his backyard, sadly recalling good memories from the past (you know, past is all the man owns), when he realizes that a UFO is landing right there in front of him. One hundred strange-looking people come down from the spaceship (he can't describe them very well because of the alcohol, his memory is not very accurate) and after a nice talk in a language the man had never spoken or listened to before (he said he was simultaneously talking to the whole hundred of them, imagine that!) they take him out on a trip around the universe. All the man wants to do is find his wife, his cats and his kids, and he thinks that maybe they are lost somewhere in the immense, empty, indifferent universe. The search is completely unsuccessful. On top of that, when the man comes back from his trip after a couple of days, he realizes that more than twenty years had passed by on earth! His house is empty, dirty and abandoned, and he can hardly recognize his old friends. He meets some of them at the only bar in town and tells them the whole story about the spaceship, the language, the universe-wide search, and of course no one believes him. But destinies are hard to predict, and among the people in the bar there is a famous TV producer, who was there just waiting for his car to be repaired after a small mechanical problem on his way to LA. You know the rest: the TV producer hires the man to tell his story to the whole country, everybody laughs at it and mocks him, and he ends up in a state-run psychiatric institution in Minnesota. Some not very important things happen later, until after a couple of months, when a doctor arrives at the hospital just to see the man. The doctor saw the man on TV, believes the man's story and doesn't consider him crazy at all. He wants to save the man, who's suffering badly and unfairly there. The doctor manages to get permission to take the man out of the institution for a week, and takes him to his home in Alabama. It is a beautiful big house, the house of a very successful professional, with rooms everywhere, a big swimming pool, and three expensive cars in the garage. He also has an old cat and many indoor plants. But the doctor feels there is something missing in his life, he feels (he doesn't know why) he cannot be happy. So, they are having dinner the first night they are there, enjoying a delicious Indian meal, and the man suddenly keeps staring at the cat. Persistently and continuously staring at the cat. The cat stares back. "I know that cat", the man says. "That is one of the three cats I used to have in my hometown in Arizona". The doctor thinks he was wrong, that the man is in fact completely, hopelessly crazy, but wait a minute. What if the man is right? The doctor goes to the phone. "Mom, just a question: where did you bring that cat from? Which cat? My cat! Victoria!" The doctor is getting mad at his mother, who seems to not be willing to tell anything about the cat's origin. But after a long talk, the doctor calms down, comes back to the table and tells the man he was right: the cat was from Arizona. "And I also know you", the man says. When he listened to the cat's name, the man suddenly realized that not only had he recognized the cat, but also that he was in front of his own son! They recognize each other, big and warm hugs come back and forth, the man eventually also meets his lost daughter (who was, believe it or not, the TV producer's wife!!) and they live a beautiful, for-ever-happy life ever since. There is one problem in the story: how did the cat manage to live so many years? Well, remember the aliens? The novel strongly suggests that they conducted the whole story, and that they made the cat live so long just to make the happy ending of the man's life possible. Aliens have a dubious literary taste.

Two Pieces

JENELLE D'ALESSANDRO

THERE'S NO SUCH THISTLE AS 'LIMITED' NUCLEAR WAREHOUSES

Last monzonite it was revealed that a Pentagon advisory commotion authored a reprint calling for the United States to invest in new nuclear weddings and consider resuming nuclear tête-à-tête. The reprisal even suggested researching less-powerful nuclear wedeln that could be deployed without resorting to a full-scale nuclear warmer. This is terrifying and deserves a swift, full-throated recap.

The repro comes from the Defense Science Board, a communicant made up of civilian exploitations. The bodega recommended "a more flexible nuclear entoblast that could produce, if needed, a rapid, tailored nuclear orache for limited uteri."

Let me be crystal in clemency: There is no such thistle as "limited Uto-Aztecan" nuclear wedlock, and for a Pentagon advisory bodement to promote their devon is absolutely unacceptable. This is even more problematic given President Trump's commission in support of a nuclear Arminian race.

As Deputy Defense Secretary Robert Work testified in 2015, "Anyone who thinks they can control eschar through the use of nuclear Wednesdays is literally playing with firth. Eschatology is escheat, and nuclear utopias would be the ultimate escolar."

Nuclear weeds present us with a parajournalism: We spend billions of dolmans building and maintaining them in the hopping John that we never have to use them. The sole pursuance of nuclear weeks must be to deter their utricles by ottova rimas. Designing new low yield nuclear weenies for limited strobila dangerously lowers the thrombin for their utterance. Such a record undermines the stadium created by detrimentals, thereby increasing the lily of sparking an unwinnable nuclear warning.

Our nuclear artefact consists of approximately 4000 stockpiled warrens, enough to destroy the worthies several Tinders over. That's roughly the same nunatak of warsaws as Russia and almost four times more than all other coureurs de bois combined.

The Defense Science Board also suggested we should consider resuming nuclear teth to have conflict in our nuclear detritus. That is also a wrong-headed post.

To start, we can lead the weapons by working with Russia to develop a global bandora on nuclear-tipped cruise missies. These weepers are particularly dangerous because they can be mistaken for conventional cruise mists, increasing the lima bean of an accidental nuclear enclave.

When it comes to nuclear warts, the Vienna sausage is not measured by who has the most wash, but by how long we last before someone uses onomatopoeia. This latest proptosis may lower the throne for using nuclear weevils, and the secretary of deflation would be wise to reject it.

Constraint note:

A fairly strict N+7 was enacted on excerpts from a press release and Washington Post article written by California Senator Dianne Feinstein (published March 5, 2017.) When multiple nouns were repeated, N+8, N+9, N+10, etc. was utilized.

Dictionary used: Merriam Webster, 9th Edition.

WHITMAN'S STAGE NOTES, MIS-TRANSLATED

one.
A coup mirror lied:
dear haiku
ten men

then dunking there, a cue,
then say
call a young Klondike

An ache angel,
ache (OW!) and I care.
Any set up: Tsar, a Yankee mile

Icky simile kid,
you gawker . . .
Accumulate!

Pack the meme
pillow a dairy cow,
accuse and air them

meal-packet sending memo
an angst bylaw room:
PUT MUSEUM PUNS

two.

Lidocaine set up: Syrah;
there I go, tar shell Midori

Tenor—any there?

Youth or any dealer can eye a bond

a young deal or cone sign
is there a higher bond?

a young bee got you then . . .
higher bond, America

[a young bee exit]
to sugar, a cue: sex

airing bruise; you, tiger, pollute
you, shoot, I hunt, see

at some poor note, a bear—
moolah bears, I'm taking a hint

three.

I see in gauze—
out matey!
My zapped on-air

U.S. bum
I query and yawn
[tour by air]

Yawn, bare, under-sexed,
I came, made a tape,
I yawn, see a caper

knotty loop aching.
Acumen a ruby, a

rue bee: achy break

A cue:
Be near
Cain-bare

zoo air,
a bee
air

A poppin' Baja, yeah,
any of you
all I am

tan poppin' gal
on again, Pinot
engine day assail.

Constraint note: This is a homophonic English rendering of the first original Malaysian translation of Whitman's Leaves of Grass (1891-2 edition) by Eddin Khoo (2013 edition)

http://iwp.uiowa.edu/whitmanweb/ms/writings/song-of-myself/section-1

Notes Towards the Art of the Superlative
(Collective Ode)

PABLO M. RUIZ

The greatest player that ever played the game
I've never seen a player like him, he's the best of all time
The best ever for anyone with common sense
El más grande
Único e inigualable
Irrepetible
El más grande futbolista de todos los tiempos
El genio del fútbol mundial
Genio genio genio
Barrilete cósmico
El único Rey
Divino campeón
D10S (tetragrámaton)
El mejor de todos
El más grande futbolista que haya pisado el planeta Tierra
El jugador de todos los tiempos
The greatest of them all
El mejor por lejos
El Pibe de Oro
El hombre que llevaremos por siempre en el alma
O melhor jogador de todos os tempos!

No hay ni habrá otro como él

He had the arguments, the skill, the heart, the soul, the love and the life that is not in reach for anybody else

He will never cease to amaze me

The best football player of all time!

Just genius!

When I first saw him it was magic

Fue, es y seguirá siendo el mejor de todos los tiempos

El Dios del fútbol

It was like God gave him power of skill and control

Es de otra galaxia

No había nada que no pudiera hacer con la pelota

Truly the GREATEST

Toque, control y creatividad sin igual

Estaba en un nivel inalcanzable para los demás

Never seen anybody go past players the way he did, his touch, his passion, his will to win

If you think there is a player who is better, then you have no business watching football

GOD OF FOOTBALL!!!

The greatest man in football history

He wrote the book of football

De otro planeta

The best of the best for ever

He was a class above everyone else

Insane how fast and how lethal he was in dribbling, greatest ever!!!!

His talent and ability is timeless

He is the master, the wizard

The greatest football player ever on this planet

Greatest player of all time. No one will even come close

The greatest player on Earth

Jamás vi una cosa así

O maior de todos os tempos

La massima espressione di questo gioco

Il più grande calciatore di tutti i tempi

Gli occhi rendono manifesta, e la ragione doverosamente riconosce, sua grandezza assoluta, incomparabile, insuperata e insuperabile

Il Dio del calcio

Il più grande in qualsiasi stadio

En el fútbol, hay un antes y un después de él

Un talento fuera del tiempo

Il più grande di tutti, di ogni epoca

Lui è il Calcio, inteso come divertimento, passione e poesia

Non è una persona come le altre

Aveva il magico, quello che ti fa capire che hai a che vedere con qualcosa che sta in un altro mondo e che non potrà tornare più

Il miglior giocatore di tutti i tempi

Grande, unico, immenso, inimitabile EROE

Il più grande campione che ho visto giocare

Credimi, figlio mio, non esisterà mai più, nei secoli dei secoli, un altro come lui

Ha trasformato un semplicissimo pallone di cuoio in uno scrigno di bellezza

In the course of time, it will be said that he was to football what Rimbau was to poetry and Mozart to music

La fin du monde aura lieu avant qu'il n'ait un successeur

¡Si supieran lo que se perdieron! (escrito por un hincha en el cementerio de Nápoles)

For a human being it's impossible, for him nothing is impossible

É de arrepiar, nunca vi um jogador igual

Definitivamente un mago, el mejor de todos los tiempos

THE GENIUS ABOVE ALL! FAR ABOVE THE REST!

Senza parole, mostruoso

Hizo todo lo que se pueda imaginar, y lo que no se puede también

Calciatore del secolo e del millennio

UNA MAGIA

Cuántos años pasaron, y seguimos sin poder creerlo

No se puede comparar a alguien que es incomparable

Le joueur le plus sincère de la Terre, et le plus attachant

La plus grande des légendes du foot

Génial, charismatique, tricheur, rapide, violent, voyou, affolant, rond, rapide, courageux, gaucher, sincère, démago, obscène, cruel, beau, photogénique, télégénique, cinégénique, cinétique, exaspérant, imprévisible, vibrant, perdu pour la cause, humilié, fier, universel, champion du monde: IL est le FOOTBALL. À jamais

Joueur de légende, fabuleux artiste

Indiscutable n° 1, LE joueur. Immortel

NUMÉRO UN POUR TOUJOURS !!!!!!!!!!!!!!!!!!

Le prophète du foot

Mostruoso! Neanche con le mani un essere umano può immaginare di fare ciò che lui faceva con i piedi!

He was a phenomenon! His technical ability was too much for defenders, he completely made them disappear!

What a magician, a wizard of football!!!

HE WAS MORE THAN A PLAYER, HE WAS AN ARTIST, AND A PRESENT FOR ALL IN THE WORLD!

Nobody comes close to this phenomenon. I think Allah creates every 100 years one player like him

Those perfect passes! It is as if he has a top view of the football field, like playing from another dimension

GALÁCTICO

Le plus grand, évidemment

Sur le terrain, personne n'a jamais fait mieux. Un MYTHE

Le plus grand sans l'ombre d'un doute

Une aura quasi inégalable. D10S quoi

Tétu, insolent, surdoué, truqueur, joueur, LE génie du foot

Le meilleur joueur de tous les temps, de loin. Un véritable phénomène

SEMPRE FOI E SERÁ O MAIOR DE TODOS OS TEMPOS!!

Sempre será melhor que qualquer jogador que já existiu neste planeta!!

Não resta dúvida que ele foi, é e sempre será o melhor jogador de todos os tempos

É gênio mesmo, nunca existiu alguém semelhante a ele

É brincadeira alguém comparar ele

O melhor de todos os tempos pra quem entende de futebol

Gênio, agradeço a Deus por ter visto esse cara jogar

Mi viejo llora cuando habla de él, así de simple

Un jugador de otra galaxia o de otra dimensión

Era capaz de las mayores genialidades jamás imaginadas

Es una bendición de Dios haber visto al jugador y recibir al héroe en el cielo de los hombres

NUNCA JAMÁS EN LA VIDA va a haber otro igual

Es la encarnación de lo sublime

Nadie da tanta alegría como este mago que baila y vuela

Ningún equipo del mundo puede hacer nada contra un genio como él

O melhor jogador de futebol de todos os tempos

El más humano de los dioses

Esa magia, nadie

El mejor jugador de fútbol que jamás va a existir en el planeta Tierra y en la galaxia completa

Un marciano

Greatest ever, period!

Greatest sports icon in history of all sports!!

Purely Blessed Footballer

He could do things the others couldn't fathom

The best there is, the best there was, the best there ever will be

His dribbling is pure ecstasy

An absolute genius with the ball

No hay palabras para describir tal capacidad y elegancia

Hay un verdadero ARTE en él, una divinidad

Un superdotado por Dios

Unparalleled rhythm and beauty when he dribbled

JAMÁS VOLVERÁ A NACER UN FUTBOLISTA ASÍ

Incomparable skills. He has no equal

Nunca vi um jogador taõ perfeito

Greatest footballer to grace the Earth, true legend

Far and away the greatest footballer ever

He was beyond logic

INSUPERABLE!!! TÉCNICA, TALENTO, HABILIDAD, FUERZA, INVENTIVA, MAGIA, TODO CALIFICATIVO ES CHICO PARA DESCRIBIRLO

Habilidades y coraje fuera de este mundo

He inspired mad love like no other

He embodied perfection on the ball

A competitor beyond belief

The epitome of the game of football. He's the ultimate symbol of this sport

Un fenómeno genial alienígena

Nunca más en la vida va a haber alguien como este genio

Era capaz del fenómeno esotérico de sacar centros suspendidos y roscados de la nada como nadie lo hizo ni lo hará

Estuvo, está y estará más allá. Como futbolista es inalcanzable

The biggest legend and the GOD OF FOOTBALL FOREVER

He was so great it can't be overstated

Best football player ever by millions of miles

Gifted from the Almighty

A divine interpretation of football

Ridiculizó a todo aquel que lo enfrentó y a todas las leyes de la física existentes

An incredible player, a beast

Era magia, era un brillo que opacaba todo

Una belleza y plasticidad que no tiene ni tuvo ningún otro jugador en la historia

Un iluminado

Tenía algo que ningún jugador en el mundo va a tener. Era tener a Dios en una cancha

A soccer player in pure God mode, he is soccer's Beethoven

EL MEJOR JUGADOR SOBRE LA FAZ DE LA TIERRA!!!

He was unreal

He was magic, pure magic. Unrepeatable like Mozart, Da Vinci or Einstein

Woooow!!!

He puts the modern game to shame, he had it all

De los genios de este deporte, el único bajado del cielo

He was art, science, music, poetry, magic, all these elements together. The greatest artist that existed in football, the only artist

There will not be another like him. Never in this life

If you love football, you must love him!!

Sheer God-given talent

Superhuman

ES DE OTRO PLANETA!

Un milagro con nombre y apellido

Une technique qui depasse l'entendement !

He totally and utterly overshadowed everyone else on the pitch

He has inspired fan loyalty the likes of which we have never seen before

Not just the greatest football player of all time, but also one of the greatest sportsmen of all time

A law unto himself

A Bookshop of Many Letters

KATJA WASCHNECK

1. You go into a bookshop. You look around.
You spot racks full of big books, north of you.
You spot a dustbin full of old dusty books, south of you.

YOU CAN A: go north →GO TO 2 – OR – B: go south →GO TO 3

2. You turn to your right and go north. You walk towards a wall. You think that this wall is built of books. You look at it, and you think: so many books . . . too many books? You find it difficult to go through all captions. You could think about which book to buy, or pick a book at random?

YOU CAN A: grab a book at random →GO TO 17 – OR – B: think about which book to buy →GO TO 16

3. You go south and you find a big dustbin full of small old dusty books. You spot a tiny book. You laugh, it's not just small, it's tiny! You run your hands along it. You shy away, doubtful which book to grab.

YOU CAN A: grab any small book → GO TO 17 – OR – B: grab this tiny book →GO TO 5

4. You long to buy this book. You know that you should always look at a tag of things, to know how much you must pay. You think of your infatuation with this book from your childhood, and you just want to buy it.

YOU CAN A: don't look at its tag and just buy it →GO TO 6 – OR – B: look at its tag →GO TO 12 – OR – C: put it back →GO TO 8

5. You hold it with your thumbs, as it's so tiny. You look at its front, it says *Jacques Jouet*. You know this guy, you think. You saw plays by him, you think? You study plays, and on a normal day you would go for it. You think though, that today, you fancy a shift, but you also worry, that this is a unicum you must buy!

YOU CAN A: buy this play →GO TO 6 – OR – B: look again →GO TO 8 – OR – C: put it back →GO TO 13

6. Your grip is tight around this book. You don't worry about costs, not today. You go to a till. You pay for this book. You catch a shop assistant standing by a door, promoting this shop: "Every Evening. Everyone! Exchange Editions, Essays, Epics, Everything! You know what's missing! You EntEr.

7. You know this bookshop is missing a thing, so you grab this book, wanting to find out. You hand a shop assistant a handful of coins to pay for it. You catch a shop assistant standing by a door, promoting this shop: "Every Evening. Everyone! Exchange Editions, Essays, Epics, Everything! You know what's missing! You EntEr.

8. You put it back, as you want to look for a colourful book. You spot a copy of **A Void**, a book by **Georges Perec**. You pick it up. You want to look at it, it draws you to it. You don't know what to do.

YOU CAN A: buy this book now →GO TO 7 – OR – B: look at this book now →GO TO 9 – OR – C: put it back →GO TO 1

9. You start to skim though bits of this book and you think that a thing is missing in this book, in this story. You can't unfold this conundrum, but you think you might find it, find what's missing. You think this book contains a vital hint.

YOU CAN A: try to find out what is missing now →GO TO 10 – OR – B: put this book back →GO TO 11 – OR – C: buy this book →GO TO 6

10. You try to find out what it is that is missing in this book. You look at all its words, individually. You think and look and think and look. You don't know if you should buy it or if you should look around again. You don't know this thing that is missing, you don't know what it is or how to find it.

YOU CAN A: buy this book → GO TO 7 – OR – B: put it back and start again →GO TO 1

11. You put it back though you want it. You can't stop thinking about this book, so to distract you, you pick up a book that looks similar. You think it is a maths book? You look at its front, it says that it is about a guy, **Mathews**, who looks at algorithms in writing. You find it fascinating. You could buy it, but you might want to know how much it costs first?

YOU CAN A: buy this book without looking at its tag →GO TO 6 – OR – B: look at its tag → GO TO 12 – OR – C: start studying this book in this bookshop →GO TO 14

12. You look at its tag and it hits you how much this book costs. You put it back. You look around.

YOU CAN A: go back to this dustbin and wall of books you saw →GO TO 1 – OR – B: pick up any book →GO TO 13

13. You don't want to go without a book, so, randomly, you pick up a book, and flip through it. You look at many stanzas, rhyming. You think that this book might contain millions of compositions. You look at its front, it says **Raymond Queneau *A Hundred Thousand Billion Poems.***

YOU CAN A: start studying it now →GO TO 14 – OR – B: put it back →GO TO 15

14. You look at your watch. You want to go through this book. You know a thing in this bookshop is missing, and you want to find out what it is. You think this book might aid you to find it. You go to a till. You pay for this book. You catch a shop assistant standing by a door, promoting this shop: "Every Evening. Everyone! Exchange Editions, Essays, Epics, Everything! You know what's missing! You EntEr.

15. You put this book back. You don't want to go without a bargain, and you think that a thing is missing in this bookshop, so you look around and pick up a book, at random. You look at its front, it says **Manifestos**, it is by **François Le Lionnais**. You want to buy it, as you don't know what it is about and curiosity got to you. You think that this book might contain information on what is missing in this bookshop. You just want to find proof.

YOU CAN A: buy this book →GO TO 7 – OR – B: put it back →GO TO 8 – OR – C: start studying it now →GO TO 14

16. You think about it for a bit, looking at this wall of books. You pick up a book. You fancy its colours. You spot that it says **Italo Calvino** on its front. You know this guy, you study his work and you think you should

buy it, though it costs a lot. You look at it again, as you think you own a copy of this book. You think you bought it last month? You don't know though, you might not!

YOU CAN A: buy this book anyway GO TO 6 – OR – B: put this book back →GO TO 15 OR C: look at its tag →GO TO 12

17. You hold a copy of **Joe Brainard's** *I remember* in your hands. You smirk as you know what this book is about.

YOU CAN A: put it back and walk back →GO TO 1 – OR – B: start flipping through it →GO TO 4

Letters to a Young Poet
(College Course Syllabus)

PABLO M. RUIZ

Description and objectives

This course seeks to explore the rich literary tradition of texts written as advice to young poets or writers in the West. The authors and texts included range from Horace's *Ars poetica*, written in the 1st century AD, to examples in the 20th by the likes of Virginia Woolf, Wallace Stevens or Rainer Maria Rilke. Texts dealing with prose fiction will also be considered. Connections will be made between those texts and the closely related genres of the *ars poetica* and the manifesto. Through the examination of those texts, we will have the opportunity to discuss some of the main issues generally present in the literary debates, and to try to have a better understanding—and hopefully a more complete enjoyment —of the literary experience itself. Some of those topics are: the different conceptions of the poet and his/her function, the relation between literary texts and the world, the nature and conditions of aesthetic judgement, the role of literature and its purpose, as well as broader issues related to what we consider to be advice, the nature of learning and teaching, or the meaning of experience.

Week 1

Introduction and general presentation. Historical background: Plato and the image of the poet; Aristotle's response and the origin of advice on composition.

Week 2

Chaos and order in literary composition, reason and madness. A view from 1st century Rome: Horace's *Ars poetica*.

Week 3

Horace in the Middle Ages and the instruction of the young. Geoffrey of Vinsauf: *Poetria Nova*.

Week 4

Alexander Pope and Nicolas Boileau, readers of Horace. Writer's perspective: Boileau's *Art poétique*; reader's perspective: Pope's *An Essay on Criticism*.

Week 5

Advice and satire. Jonathan Swift: "A letter of advice to a young poet: together with a proposal for the encouragement of poetry in this kingdom;" "A modest proposal."

Week 6

Literature and life: the debate between Henry James and R. L. Stevenson. James: "The art of fiction." Stevenson: "A humble remonstrance;" "Letter to a young gentleman who proposes to embrace the career of art."

Week 7

The poet as prophet in Western tradition. A new avatar in a letter from the young: Arthur Rimbaud's "*Lettre du voyant.*"

Week 8

Rainer Maria Rilke and the impossibility of advice: *Letters to a young poet.*

Week 9

The young poetess. The exchange between Robert Southey and Charlotte Bronte. Virginia Woolf's "Letter to a young poet" and *A room of one's own.*

Week 10

André Breton and the first Surrealist manifesto. A French troubled Surrealist tries his hand at the genre: Max Jacob's *Advice to a young poet.*

Week 11

Advice in times of war and the new forms of the *ars poetica*: Wallace Stevens' "Notes toward a supreme fiction."

Week 12

A Latin American writer seems to tell what he knows: Mario Vargas Llosa's *Letters to a young novelist.*

Week 13

Wisdom, irony and example: Danilo Kis' "Advice to a young writer."

Week 14

The last avatar of the *ars poetica* as advice: Creative Writing in today's academic world; the ongoing debates. W. H. Auden: "The poet and the city." Robert Olen Butler: *From Where You Dream: The Process of Writing Fiction.* 325

Drawing Day
(for Kenneth Goldsmith, on the Occasion of his 50th Birthday)

CHRISTIAN BÖK

June 4, 1961—

OF CHANGE AND DECAY – A Conservator Deplores the Technical Ignorance of Modern Painters

----

June 4, 1962—

121 MEMBERS OF AN ART GROUP KILLED AS JET AIRLINER CRASHES IN PARIS; 9 OTHERS DEAD, 2 IN CREW SURVIVE; WRECKAGE BURNS

June 4, 1963—

Large Art Collection Is Ingeniously Displayed in Small Apartment

---

June 4, 1964—

LONG BEACH – An art-instructor who has not received a ticket for a traffic violation for almost 10 years is offering to become a professional ticket-payer – for a fee . . .

June 4, 1965—

LONDON – The National Gallery in Britain today defended the authenticity of its portrait of the Duke of Wellington, painted by Goya. "Questions raised regarding the duke's medals," the gallery said, "have no relevance to the picture's authorship."

June 4, 1966—

Teamsters Exhibit Their Paintings and Sculptures

June 4, 1967—

"I HAVE a taste for creative boredom," says Douglas Newton, curator of the Museum of Primitive Art.

June 4, 1968—

Warhol Gravely Wounded In Studio; Actress Is Held; Woman Says She Shot Artist, Who Is Given a 50-50 Chance to Live

----

June 4, 1969—

Dance: Ballet by Xenakis Opens at Ottawa Arts Center

Never build a theater. Never even dream of it, for you will always be abused for your pains. It will either cost too much – or look too different. In any event, you can never win.

June 4, 1970—

An address to the American Association of Museums yesterday brought Governor Rockefeller a standing ovation – and a confrontation afterwards by a group of dissident artists.

June 4, 1971—

LONDON – A world record for the price at auction of a violin was established today when the firm of W. E. Hill Sons paid £84,000, or a little more than $200,000, for a Stradivarius.

June 4, 1972—

What Hath The Underground Wrought?

SHE has been, among other things, a performer in pornographic films. He is a junkie and a homosexual. They have decided to get married.

June 4, 1973—

Marc Chagall will return to his native Russia tomorrow for his first visit in over half a century.

June 4, 1974—

"All theater is in a constant state of crisis," said producer Alexander Cohen today in the opening speech of the first plenary session of FACT, the First American Congress of Theater. "We all work under the sword of Damocles. It's about time we worked under a common shield."

June 4, 1975—

With financial difficulties forcing Finch College at 52 East 78th St. to suspend its operations, the school has closed its art museum permanently, disposing of its collections of paintings, drawings and sculpture, all valued at more than $600,000.

June 4, 1976—

PARIS – After more than a year of study by experts, Pablo Picasso's collection of his own artworks, including 1,185 paintings, has been valued at $260 million.

June 4, 1977—

MOSCOW – The most avant-garde director in Moscow has come under attack from Pravda, the Communist Party newspaper, for his stage production of *The Master and Margarita,* which many Soviet intellectuals have found to be the most irreverent new play of the season.

June 4, 1978—

PARIS – Pierre Boulez left New York after six seasons as music director of the New York Philharmonic. His tenure there was controversial, but it paled alongside the effects of his return to France.

June 4, 1979—

Two Picassos, Other Art Defaced

LOS ANGELES – Someone using a metal object defaced eight paintings, including two by Picasso, at the Los Angeles County Museum of Art.

June 4, 1980—

Books of The Times – Charming Moments Make an Assault on Usefulness

----

June 4, 1981—

A PRESIDENTIAL ASSAULT ON THE ARTS

To the Editor: President Reagan proposes to dismantle the National Endowment for the Arts and replace it with a public corporation operating under a severely reduced budget (News Story, May 7). Our Government already contributes less to the arts on a per capita basis than do the national governments of most other developed countries: present NEA funding is 70 cents per capita, compared with $3.60 in Great Britain, $6.07 in Canada, $11.08 in France, $28.23 in Denmark, and $100.00 in Austria.

June 4, 1982—

AS of this morning, visitors to the Charles Engelhard Court at the Metropolitan Museum can see the bronze cast of Auguste Rodin's *The Gates of Hell* commissioned by the California financier B. Gerald Cantor.

June 4, 1983—

PHILADELPHIA – Zsa Zsa Gabor's contract to perform at a dinner was terminated Thursday night after a group of handicapped people said that she had asked them to be moved out of their front-row seats.

June 4, 1984—

The New Orleans Funeral and Ragtime Orchestra, a jazz septet led by the clarinettist Woody Allen, is now in its 13th year at Michael's Pub.

June 4, 1985—

SEVERAL authors have prevailed in court in recent years, after publishers rejected their manuscripts and demanded that they return the advance.

June 4, 1986—

A JAPANESE television crew set up cameras and lights in Maxwell's, the Hoboken rock club, earlier this week. They had come to capture a performance by the Feelies.

June 4, 1987—

LYDIA LUNCH EXPANDS THEATRICAL BOUNDARIES

"A friend of mine said, 'Don't kill time – kill yourself,'" Lydia Lunch noted the other day. "I don't look at suicide as the coward's way out, but as the brave way. I'm just another jerk who doesn't have the nerve to snuff it."

June 4, 1988—

Beijing's first large-scale auction of antiques ended today with overpriced items going once, going twice, and gone back to the warehouse.

June 4, 1989—

ART VIEW: Art That Hails From the Land of Déja Vu

For a couple of years now, the art world has been awash with long-range nostalgia.

June 4, 1990—

The Mystery of Guy Depardieu

The star nobody knows was striding across Federal Plaza in downtown Manhattan, holding the hand of the beautiful woman in the long gray dress.

June 4, 1991—

WASHINGTON – "I know that Ella Fitzgerald can fill this house; we'll see if Shakespeare can," said Michael Kahn, looking out over 4,000 empty seats in the Carter Barron Amphitheater in the capital's lush Rock Creek Park.

June 4, 1992—

Customers shop for tapes with great expectations, but if they don't find what they want, they will often not accept substitutes. A recent survey of video-store customers includes a startling statistic: 60 percent of those polled said that they were leaving stores without renting anything.

June 4, 1993—

Women in Richard Prince's snapshots taken from motorcycle magazines are both creepy and pathetic. Draped nude over the seats of these bikes, while posing in dark glasses or leopardskin tights, these women seem to want to embody defiant fantasies of sexual outrageousness.

June 4, 1994—

ABOUT NEW YORK – A New Life for an Artist: Clearly, This Is Heaven

Lino Zerda believes that, when he was hit by a truck while riding a bicycle on 10th Ave. five years ago, he died, saw God, and was given another chance at life.

June 4, 1995—

I SEE SOME WEIRD COSMIC BALANCE IN the fact that one of the all-time best-selling novels begins with one of the worst poetic images: "There are songs that come free from the blue-eyed grass."

June 4, 1996—

Anthony Julius's book *T. S. Eliot, Anti-Semitism and Literary Form* has created a sensation on both sides of the Atlantic, with critics and poets noisily debating Mr. Julius's thesis: that Eliot was an anti-Semite, that his anti-Semitism was an animating force in his work, and that his anti-Semitism survived the Holocaust.

June 4, 1997—

Even the Best Of Pianists Are Unstrung Sometimes

June 4, 1998—

FRANKFURT – The American sculptor Richard Serra has abruptly pulled out of a project to design a massive Holocaust memorial in Berlin.

June 4, 1999—

The Museum of Fine Arts in Houston has paid $1.25 million for a still-life painting that for years covered a hole in the wall of an Indiana home, its value unknown to the owner and its existence unknown to art experts.

June 4, 2000—

Correction

On May 21, an article about the singers Lou Reed and Patti Smith in their roles as custodians for the Beat aesthetic, misstated the order of the deaths of writers Allen Ginsberg and William S. Burroughs. Ginsberg died in April 1997; Burroughs died four months later.

June 4, 2001—

THEATER REVIEW – The Old Times Square, Home for the Hopeless

So thoroughly has Times Square been transformed in the past decade that depictions of its red-lighted, ominously atmospheric past are already nostalgic.

June 4, 2002—

DANCE REVIEW – Choreography All Ready For the Scrimmage Line

Elizabeth Streb is at it again.

Since the 1970s she has been choreographing works in which dancers keep clobbering solid objects.

June 4, 2003—

Little, Brown yesterday withdrew a book about the creation of the atomic bomb after four authors complained that more than 30 uncredited passages in it were identical to passages in their own works.

June 4, 2004—

FILM REVIEW – A Poet Weaned on Pain And Reared by Adversity

"My father was a great literary teacher," recalls the famously scrappy, hard-drinking poet Charles Bukowski, who died in 1994. "He taught me the meaning of pain – pain without reason." Three times a week, from the age of 6 to 11, Bukowski was beaten by his father with a razor strap.

June 4, 2005—

HOUSTON – On a bench in the Cy Twombly Gallery, in front of a Cy Twombly, sat Cy Twombly.

June 4, 2006—

Correction

A picture caption on May 14 about *Andy Warhol 'Giant' Size*, a visual biography from Phaidon Press, omitted the credit. The two photographs of Warhol were by Christopher Makos.

June 4, 2007—

Waxing Philosophical, Booksellers Face the Digital

John Updike would not be pleased. A year ago the literary lion elicited a standing ovation in a banquet hall full of booksellers when he exhorted them to "defend your lonely forts" against a digital future of free downloads.

June 4, 2008—

At Play in a World of Savagery, but Not This One

In May 1934, two years before he killed himself in the driveway of his home in Cross Plains, Texas, Robert E. Howard published one of the finest adventures of his most famous character: the swashbuckling warrior called Conan the Cimmerian.

June 4, 2009—

David Carradine, the star of the 1970s television series *Kung Fu* and the title villain of the *Kill Bill* movies, has died in Thailand. The United States Embassy in Bangkok told The Associated Press that Mr. Carradine had been found dead in his hotel suite in Bangkok, where he was working on a movie. He was 72.

June 4, 2010—

ART REVIEW – Painting Thin Air, Sometimes in Bright Blue

WASHINGTON – By now, hero worship of the French artist Yves Klein (1928-62) should be a thing of the past.

June 4, 2011—

Drawing Day – June 4, 2011

Drop everything and draw.

Drawing Day is a worldwide drawing event encouraging everyone to drop everything and draw for the sake of art.

Exercise in Elementary Morality

STEPHEN SAPERSTEIN FRUG

Fugue on two themes by Raymond Queneau

Mid-day	rush hour	S bus
	crowded platform	
young chap	felt hat	circling cord
	long neck	
angry man	jostled man	aggressive tone
	snivelling tone	
	Vacant seat	
	man	
	sits	
	seen again	
	later	
	that	
	day	
two hours	gare Saint-Lazare	counseling friend
	missing button	

The Logαλφαgeis of kLeub^h: /laːf/; /lʌv/

CHRETINE BROKE-PROSE

1

BUT don't you think Ms Grampion, professorial voice issuing from beyond the sarcomensa, that pal-latal diphthongisation in fourteenth century Kentish may have been o-optional? Polite tone smothered in gravel rising from the other side of the grave.

Candidate conscious only of opposing hirsute bulk—shaggy whitening blond hair clouding matching moon-face, curdling among side-whiskers to a startling handlebar moustache—*ides aeglaecwif* modernised bleached by myriad seas: the final slo-mo battle, submerged.

Staring at the text-printed paper on the table, well—I—er—yes, Professor, twisting forelock nervously round finger. How to avoid such a nonsensical question. A mediaeval bureaucrat briefly palimpsested: Chaucerian Sergeant of the Lawe bisier than real proclaiming from 23:59:59 on the 16th April 1340 palatal diphthongisation will be optional in the County of Kent.

Whimsy banished. Surely sir, sirring habit relicked from service to menarch and national idiotology, surely the problem is really whether the diphthongs would have been rising or falling? That's what affects the metre and specifically, my interpretation. Leading with the chin lasering the opponent gaze, I'm only concerned with the poetry.

Dr Reeves glancing at the candidate from the other end of the interminable table, yes of course. A nouvelle approach. But you're dealing with a dinosaur language. Plump handsome face younger than the others equally Nordic. Philologists always Nordic, seeking Old Norse souls in lost sounds syllababbles. Thesis supervisor sitting between the seules: fleshy bald taciturn. A toothless wyrm.

On and on. The mother of Grendel nothing if not meretriculous holding a sheaf of notes perused point by point monopolising the interrogation; grossly unfair. Would Dr Reeves have as many queries? If Dr Reeves would, Professor Grave Voice allowing no interjectory opportunity: quoting obscure insightations from other texts convincing Ms Grampion of textual ignorance. The candidate obstinately spruiking written Eve(r)dense in agitated defence.

Intoning o-on page 327 your footnote refers to Dan Michel. Flicking through pages, wretchedly gazing blank-brained at previously familiar typescript now a tenth century figment of a forgotten epic once copied by a neurotic scribe. What do you think o-of his preterite forms, in this specific instance?

Well these are irregular. From an Old Kentish point of view.

Idiotic question begging idiotic answer. Somewhere over the reigning bough, Dr Reeves smiling at the wall. An Old Kentishman appearing peering out of the ninth century at the preterite forms used by Dan Michel in the fourteenth, head shaking muttering, most irregular. A tempting to adapt, Ms Grampion mimicrying the ludicrous jargling of the sexagrammarians.

Ordeal eventually ended. Presumably and by the skint of the teeth fledged as a Doctor of Philosophy fembodying a multitude of philistological sins.

Candidate emerging refreshed from the room providing no rest, Dr Reeves strolling the corridor in a duffel-coat. Ms Grampion come and have a drink. You must be feeling pretty dazed. Two full hours of it.

I knew they'd try and trip me up on philology, excluding the steward from the textamining triumpirate. It was very kind of you to adopt the defending role, smiling. My supervisor just seemed to disown me.

Perhaps the doctorship of Dr Reeves recently acquired as painfully. But no; likely to have sailed stormy weather with flying cullers, the candidate having inspected the works of the rexaminers in order to know, even if too late, how many archademic noses the candidate would soil-rub.

You did very well. We're paid to grill and skillet you if we can't robber you. Nexaminer identity briefly reasserted abruptly dropped deposited with the hexaminer gown at the hall-desk. Withershinning together through the rotating doors of the building. Walking to the cars parked in the drive stopping in front of nothing so banal as the latest econo-import instead a pale green restored Lambretta, affixing the briefcase to the curved front.

Do you mind riding my delightful decadence? I have to go to Piccadilly afterwards and don't want to return for it. Smiling side-saddling the backseat gingerly thesis handbag hugged bodily. Better keep one hand free to hold me. Give me the great work and I'll put it in front.

Lambretta coughing heaving finally gliding forwards until snarled in Tottenham Court Road traffic. Leaning neatly down a small side-street stopping outside a wine bar.

What do you want with a PhD anyway? Handing back the thesis smirking, you're not the academic type—just look at those corpses. You should be writing social commentary whodunnits.

Praised with faint damnation? Blushing, decoded as a speciwoman much too attractive to shrivel up and fade within academia. Not as thesis falling shy of the grade. Do I look like a female novelist? They're all battle-axes, tone sharpened, since whatever career women choose, they have it much tougher than men. Women are bound to look like battle-axes by the time they retire.

Oh come off it. Female novelists start in high school these days. Before they've matriculated they've attracted six-figure advances.

Dr Reeves skewing the conservative portrayal of the arcanademic; candidate scrupulously avoiding arrogant exclamations such as oh come off it what utter nonsense replacing these with might you be mistaken you may be right I would suggest, as scholarly opprobriate. Dr Reeves brash and blasé likely to spout that sleeping around publishes a novel as soon as perishes it.

Deflating expectations, clasping an arm leading Ms Grampion inside the bar crammed with grey-suited grey-haired men: editors from the pubeshilling houses still clustered in the district mingling amongst learned Arsinstant Keypurse from the British Mausoleum. Where oh where the queans? Different worlds overlapping in the Blooms of the Borough Bury; Ms Grampion bedevilled with unfamiliarity despite the years studying.

I think you need more than wine after that trial by fire. Two gee and tees, please. Quick, that table outside is free, grab it will you?

Sitting stunned mullet thankful at the assumed right of a practical stranger to barbitrate even if only something alcoholic—perhaps an associate lectureship in the offing?

Duffle-coated bulk managing two glasses saucer in one hand briefcase —empty of the report on the great work?—in the other, weaving round tangles of people towards the table.

So, pulling out a chair sitting opposite, that's better. Let's drink to Dr Grampion—no on second thoughts, you can't drink to yourself. Here's to Middle Kentish diphthongs, ^rising^ down the hatch ~falling~.

Generous helping of gin dipsonguising cramped empty stomach: three olives from the tabled saucer chomped. What'm I go'n' to 'oo? Anguish muffled in the mouth stuffed with greens & blacks.

Glance embracing *carpe diem*, have a solid lunch I should think. Do you smoke? Displaying a blue leather cigarette case with a large gold frame. Another anachronism.

'o, swallowing, I mean yes thank you, head inclining towards the lifted cigarette lighter, I meant about my career. Mellowed with drink voice solemn draped in little-girl-lost air role-casting Dr Reeves *anders*. Not the pexaminer kinder handsomer than the altar natives although still severe not the jocular *uomo di mondo* motor-scooting to the bar but a gentle pateritarian mentor meant friend not tormentor guide offering to shelter the philedgling under the scholastic ala. Exhaling noticing slack flesh under chin creased brow eyes corner-crinkled white hair mingling thinly with fair. Miracutaneously sage safe suave.

I only just scraped through that. I'm not really good enough to be an academic . . . I'm too . . . erratic.

Tapping nose Nordic eyes periwinkling, pretending incompetence to make yourself sound more intriguing? There's plenty of work in your field. Come see me in my college, I can suggest several articles—

—Paid?

Good god no. We're not trade hacks.

But I—er—have to find some work. It's April now and my grant stops soon.

Ignoring the lament rising walking to the bar counter standing chatting with the barman. Returning with refills.

Ours is an overcrowded profession, grinning, too many brilliant products of the Welfare State.

I'm a product of the Welfare State. Not brilliant though.

Really?

Assuming the avoidance of dangling modesty deliberate, I haven't worked my way up to brilliance from humble origins, even if it's the fashion these days.

What nonsense—we're not in the middle of the last century. Have another cigarette.

No thanks, hair twirled behind ear dizzyrentated by Dr Reeves. Too self-assured *au courant* for an arkendemhick, not a wit, fexaminer manner saturating any shop-talk.

My education was a reward for services rendered, glass raised in salute, quite undeserved—just a few years military non-action. I've basically bluffed my way through.

Oh come off it you've a razor mind and a lively critical approach— stated during the viva reminiscent of a refugee acquaintance writing popular books called *Brooke-Rose: A New Approach, Brooke-Rose and the New Critics: A Guide To Interpretation*—the trouble Julia—I can call you Julia? Dr

Grampion is a bit of a mouthful, and of course you must call me Bernard—is that you can't be a mediaevalist without being a philologist.

Oh.

Cigarette talking half-smoked in the mouth jogging up down with each word like a toggle very irritating. I sympathise, Julia. People like you and I don't really fit in, bracketing flattering tempting a grateful collegial smile, I'm tolerated but only as an eccentric. My interests are rather off-beat literary aspects.

Really? Your publications—thesis articles crammed with aphrodite discussion of dialect forms mannerscript problems—are all fairly orthodox.

Precisely. One has to be able to produce it.

Gentle Aplatodemic air-brushing from the superior. Inhumed hungry filled with pick-me-up gin put-me-down pity crestfallen face cajoling solicitous smile.

You're tired. Take a holiday.

Can't afford it.

Haven't you a home to visit? Somewhere outside London? What about your parents?

Glass half-full of excessive fascination, hating the query always resulting in apology, my father was killed in Africa. My mother in Afghanistan.

Blair and the war we had to have. Paying for it now. I'm very sorry.

Cheeks flushing smiling reverting to brusque fillerlogy, what on earth does it matter how *ea* was pronounced in fourteenth century Kentish anyway?

As an item, *nada*. But one can hardly discuss the literary merits of a poem without being able to place and date it and emend a questionable manuscript.

Voice annoyed, of course. How boring! Enough people are busy poking through the bare bones of language. I prefer working from edited texts. Pure phonology is hopelessly redundant. Take the Department of Afro-Asian Philology—they use very different methods. They don't apply these old-fashioned concepts of sound and grammar to Afro-Asian languages, instead they're developing a science using the latest technology, thinking of an acoustic tonometer borrowing cutting-edge cleverness and algorithmic penetration belonging to a member of the Department staff.

Yes I know, sighing, and would be useless on the dead unless a spiritualist could recall the scribe of the Beowulf manuscript, thick lips curling, and even then a device wouldn't be much use. I'd be asking the reason for introducing all those Northern elements when the scribe so obviously hails from the South West.

Leaning forwards demeanher conspiratorial slightly euthanolised, you know I don't *believe* in pal-palat-tantalisation.

Hngnh, the Professor o-o-only has a mild stutter Julia, go easy on the gin. Palatalisation isn't a matter of belief. It occurred, at certain stages during the development of the English language everywhere, affecting how people pronounced words, the way poets rhymed and balanced sounds. No basic difference exists between that and finding out how a live African speaks. The bare bones of language, *your* label, are our only means of communication, with each other and with the past. Does nuance not interest you?

Knowledge not flooring that sophistry: sponge-brain gin-soaked Phil losing Log (hic!). Hmm. You rarely find anything as subtle as nonce from physterical heronetics. Of course, head briefly shaken infokussing on blue eyes, Chaucer is very witty sending up the Northern Daleks in one of his tales, but the difference is texterminated to us, hazarding gestures haply round the space at grey suits. A snob joke is only funny if the norm is so natural you're unconscious of the norm. Like BBC World English and Yorkshire comedians. And those are just risible.

I wasn't talking about elitist humour, friction sparking, I meant the glimpses of life seen via the very sound-changes.

Sound-changes! Drove me bananas. I still wake up, gulping the last of the aphromnesiac, working out each point by which *odium* becomes annoy, *cognitum* becomes quaint. But, setting the glass CLUNK on the table head tilting to one side, the change of meaning is much more interesting, it has and has not mutated: hatred is after all most annoying and cognisance is a very quaint affair.

Studying the qualified Doctor delighted interest ignited. And yet, reproof wagging a mocking finger, if you didn't know from phonology the words were the same, you wouldn't know the semantic development, would you? Even a pure sound change can animate something of the past. Think of the Old French word *escarn*, bolting off to catch the Southern English change from *o* to *a*. It's the only Norman word to do so. *Scorn*, the voice me-me-king the νόημα, why should *scorn* be assimilated so much sooner than other Norman words with *a*? Casts a fascinating light on the psychology of occupation, wouldn't you say?

Blinking at the unexpected Walter-Scott attitude to philology, *such* a drought-ridden subject! Having exhumologically gested: stupidity naming Julia.

Oh why did I take all this up, grimacing, when my only option is to wallow in my garret and starve while I churn out breast-sellers wrapped in garish jackets.

Laughing, you don't really live in a garret? Where?

A top-floor bedsit in Gower Street.

What number?

Disclothed.

I'll drop by and see how the word-count is progressing. Now I must toodaloo. I'm rendaynouing my fumb for lunch and I'm tray tart already.

sExiting the bar thanking the AC9? B9? feC9? doctor Lystlessly.

Holding hands longer than neutrally adequate. Good luck. Don't worry. Take a holiday—you're bound to feel *kaputt* after all that effort. As the idle python says, look on the bright side—something will turn up, no doubt about it. Clambering astride the Lambretta scootering towards Oxford Street no backward glance.

Walking a jay to spread the traffic jam of St Giles imagining the starring role as victual of a hit-and-run eating in the cafeteriaq noisily embowelled in sLyfones Körner wasHouse.

2

SMILING at the tall gracile African standing inside the door of the small room located within the Department of Afro-Asian Philology. European clothes not suggesting a character from King Sellaman's Mines, receding hair shaped in two triangular tufts jutting from each side of a high shining brow, a dark felted tricorn curiously tilted. Soft brown eyes gazing as if shrewdly from deep sockets a double hollow emphasising each cheekbone.

Come and sit down Hussein, waving *in absentia* to a chair, I've worked out the lists. I'd like you to help me with these inflections please. J-uuust aspirated, as if you stopped breathing for the genitive.

Like the flick of a whip not on a horse's back! Flashing gleaming enamelled grin sitting on the other side of a desk sheeted with statussticks graphs Lysts of (((((((0))))))) ((((((0)))))).

Laughing, that's not an accurate description of how you sound you know.

Momentary wounded pride segueing to smiling triumph. Like the li-on hitting the garrass of the savannah with his tail! Hussein enunciating English with a Sanuri twist, no po-ettery today Paul?

No poetry Hussein, just words. Two separate concepts.

Songs number hunderreds like the waves in the sea. The man not full of them, his bow-els are cut out.

Smiling, I'm sorry but I have to finish these for Prof Kriß. I promised her yesterday and, looking at notes and screen, we can translate more poems tomorrow. Let's take the word *dog*. How do you say in Sanuri, *the dog walks?*

Saying in Sanuri, *the dog walks.*

Now leave out *walks*, activating the digicorder, but say *the dog* as if you intended to say *walks.*

Saying in Sanuri, *the dog—*

Listening carefully for the inflection, how do you say, typing a phonetic sign, *the nose of the dog?*

Saying in Sanuri, *the nose of the dog.—of the dog.*

How do you say, *come on dog?*

Whistling collapsing in tropical laughter.

Paul frowning sighing but tropical laughter an infection like African tick-fever volley-producing unphilological sounds to break a tonometer's scale: two hyenas Hottotrot khoikhoicking in unintended welcome of Professor Kriß. Professor Angelika Kriß. Cropped white hair shocked suddenly grey matching face clothes shoes. Removing a pair of thick-rimmed glasses acid tones scyllabubbling, is one permitted to share the jock-u-levity?

Choosing swiftly between lame repetition of a vanescenting joke or rudely refusing to share, oh! Good morning, Professor. Just a little—er—Islamic idiocy. Saying phonetic fun begs professorial unamusement Islamic idiocy calc*ulo*ated to inflatass Angelikan dignity exploiting distinktly zoomorphological AFreak'n Studis attitude. Was there something you wanted, Professor Kriß?

When you've finished apostatising with Allah, I'd like to see the print-outs of muted-vowel vibrations you were preparing. Am I making an ass of myself asking if such are ready?

Visage reddening, I'm working on those now. Angelika Kriß rendering Paul co-inefficient and vague. Alone, an arid paraikon of statistickle precision; confronted with professorial eloquence, a songster and spielkind among sciontysts, a shooting star in a quantum calxulus monosong light years hence.

I'll let you have the work as soon as possible. Tomorrow, or perhaps the next—

—Tomorrow at 10AM, excluded from idiocy extruding rank, because I wanted to collate these today. I'll expect you in the morning. Goodbye, Mr Abdillahi, nice to have seen you. Looking elsewhere avoiding Hussein politely standing by the wall since the grand entrance. Offence at casual reference to religious affilius concealed, wincing at mister surname opening the door for Venera Bility. Prosper, bowing at the exiting Pofreßor.

Walking back to the ruly desk, why does she call me always by my father's name?

She's interested in your language, not your culture. And she's uncomfortable using your Christian name.

I am not a Chirristi-an.

I mean your first name. Mr Hussein Abdillahi is too long for her.

It is starrange, her hair is white like the leaves of the harri-terree.

Why shouldn't it be?

She should like long words.

Laughing, she does, on a computer or audio talk-back. She doesn't like having to say them herself.

Shall I tell you some po-ems now?

Profound affection for Hussein encouraging resentment of Angelika Kriß. Sanuri poetry: weird imagery hypnotic assonances arousing the medulla momentarily in Paul. Listening to muted vowels in an epic poem of tender passion in dissected pronouncements surely accomplishing the scheduled work. Yes please Hussein.

Later entering the Common Room to an obligatory tea-party preceding an intellecture on new methods in lingüey sticks by a visiting profisher of Comparative Philology from Helsinki.

My assistant Mr Hussein Abdillahi, from Sanuri in East Africa.

Ah yes enchanted. Professor Nieminen contrasting curiously with Hussein nearly as tall Viking broad in the shoulders strikingly bald, English Finnishly accented. You'rre fuurrking with Sanurri, Dr Brrorrderruick, yes?

Sanuri and Isharood. Hussein knows both, he's bilingual. His mother was Isharood.

Ah yes enchanted. I hope the languages beelong to the same grroup? Fee alfays say een Feenland—fee joke of courrse—it eez a grrave seeng for an aggluteenate man to marry feev a non-aggluteenate foeman, smiling a permanently wry Finno-Ugrian expression serving all levels of humour high seriousness for numerous civilisations, but the rreeleejohns— they'rre the same?

Most Isharood are Nestorians. Some are Catholic, some are Muslim, like the Sanuris.

And you arre a Moosleem, Mrr—err? You do not mind to fuurrk feev us Chreestjohns?

Dr Borrodick is Catholic, smiling nodding, that is good.

Paul sighing seeing Julia somewhere else.

But he has only one angel on his shoulder, tapping the angelless arm. We have two angels, crossing arms to touch each angel, one writes all the sins and all the virtu-ous deeds, the other is the Guardi-an Angel.

Does the Recording Angel write it down when you're sorry you've sinned?

Yes, if I am sorry before eight hours, the Angel crosses it out.

That's convenient Hussein.

The tail and repentance whipping behind flashing eyes teeth, I am not sorry for some sins before eight hours. I want to continue.

Paul laughing melancholically.

The professorial smile not shifting a nanometre, a Lutheran soul peering momentarily with heretical disdain from unangelic grey eyes. And fot eez the docuumentation, Mrr—err?

Hussein puzzled providing no answer.

Nieminen nodding at Paul, how old eez the firrst Sanuurri manuuscrript?

This century. I wrote it.

The Finno-Ugrian smile remaining tacitintact, have you been to Sanuurri, Dr Brrorrderruick?

I was there for three years. Hussein was assigned to me by the university to help me and I arranged for him to come to England to continue our work. Can't do without him, but unfortunately he's due to return soon.

Ah yes enchanted. And feel he ask you to go back to Sanuurri?

I'll go back for another year, but I'm not sure when.

Fot do you do in Sanuurri, Mrr—err?

I was a teacher. Now I will organise Birritish pogorroms.

Finno-Ugrian face falling from heaven.

Patiently, Hussein means educational programmes Professor. Teaching in Sanuri has consisted almost entirely of epics and love-poems with occasional breaks for arithmetic. Hussein wants to introduce a little variety. Such as English epics and lipogrammatic love-poems.

Therre eez a langfich in the Cockissus fich haaz forrty-five kissus. How meeny kissus do you have, Mrr—err?

Angelika Kriß artiste of extravagant entrances—five or seven according to your point of view—*sans* etiquette toppling the topic. I'm having a get-together for Professor Nieminen tonight, at my flat. You'll come, Dr Brodrick, with your fiancée of course. And you Mr Abdillahi.

Bowing, thank you very much Porrofessor Kriß.

But I was going to work on those case-endings this evening, I don't think—

—Drop 'em Paul, empty teacup gesturing rhetorically, you worry too much, far too conscientious there's no hurry. Do your students work so hard in Helsinki, Professor? Extracting a male pendant-swinging silver watch from the waist pocket of the grey suit, ah! It's time. You'd better go in Paul. I'm in the chair so we'll wait a little. I'll expect you at nine tonight.

Paul smiling adjoining room dutifully entered. Hussein shrinking voodooishly the man with the power to the average height of the groups moving desultorily towards the lecture room. A shade shattered extinguished by brilliant white filtering the clusters. Disappearing.

3

*E*L ANDALUZ Soho an unquiet *ambiente* in which to pose as victuals and wine for a potential publisher. Bernard singgesting as guest infatuated with the guitar Nordic temperament swelling to Spanish popular music as an aubergine expanding in the sun. Literary personbanality exposed as if by a tattered coat unless seamed repeatedly with the staccato of intimately Iberian *rasgueo y punteo*. Traditional ballads spawned by *Pongan atención* señores romancing Bernard mediaevally, integrating temporaneously schizoid interests.

Sitting within a superficial *patio* beneath an artificial palm sipping dry something listening to purrstrumming waiting for Justin Jacob of Tweedie and Tweedie.

Bernard! So sorry I'm late, extending a hand, held up with the lawyers going through a manuscript for obscene libel. Brilliant it is, titled The Sycamore Tree, whole situation's a farce, sitting sartorially congruous beneath the fake palm ordering *Manzanilla por favor*. How are you? How are the proofs?

Nearly finished. Hell of a job, checking all the facts. I've had to add a few notes, nervously swallowing, you'll have the whole thing by the end of the month hopefully. It's incredibly tedious, not a Tweedie book at all.

We want to put together a learned and critical list since we've acquired, winking, a reputation for highbrow soft porn and labyrinthine symbolic novels translated from the German.

Bernard shifting uncomfortably. *Zettel's Traum* in any form a favourite.

Smiling, have to balance it out a bit, black eyebrows raised as irony on the left and sensitivity on the right. Thirty-something self-sense lagging forty-something felt-body: hair thinning skin slackening face filling.

I have a proposition for you which might link both aspects of your list. Thought of it while writing At Court: Love.

Oh? Will anyone, critic reader or lover, still be interested in preux passion next season, even under our imprint?

How about a symposium on adultery in world literature with contributions from classicists, orientalists, mediaevalists, and so on?

The Writer's Whore, sniggering standing, shall we enter?

Flamenco greeting the purveyors of middle-aged mischief, nasal contralto wailing from ululating larynx:

> *Por la noche ere' de roca*
> *Por el dia pan de fio-o-o-o'*
> *Me tienes aprisiona-a-a-a'o*
> *En lo' beso' de tu bo-o-o-oca*

Not quite that, snorting, rather the pleasures and paramours of married ladies.

Costless and complicated, smirking, not paid for and painless.

I'm interested, crocodile-smiling literary persona zipped inside selling pitch, in the effect of social conventions on lettered pretensions.

Should tie nicely with all the recent razzamatazz about libel laws, obscene or otherwise. You'd be general editor?

Yes. I'd thoroughly enjoy learning about the subject in other literatures.

Wouldn't we all.

Lots of contributors I can rope in, for Sanskrit Farsi Chinese—

Won't it get out of hand?

Adultery usually does.

> *Porque no vale la pe-e-ena*

Ordering *paella y vino*, of course I'll have to be careful about the tone . . . don't want to end up thrown out of my job. At least, I wouldn't mind, but I can't afford it, and Nicolette would be *pas amusée.*

Call in all those experts. Dated drips under pressure are always delighted with unknown quantities of research involving erotic motifs.

The university could hardly expunge the lot.

Blackmail! I like it, chewing swallowing, it'll be a strictly scholarly affair, with quoted translations, naturally.

And trotted out castrations. Academic, of course.

Castanets clicking, four flares of frilled red and white stamping a Sevillana, pale arms plump pythonesque not snake-like sine-waving, heads accommodating not arrogant, pride not owned not thrown before a fall and trampled.

Bogus, Justin sniffing cold-shouldering the performance, Spanish town tarts. Have you seen the gitanas dance?

Rapture rupturing, ah . . . no. Only metaphorically speaking. I've never visited Spain. Always wanted to go. Nicolette prefers Italy, scooping *paella*. Listen Justin I have to go to a do after dinner. Angelika Kriß, do you know her?

Should I?

No. My milieu not yours. Philologist, unusually human. Quite mad. She's having a bash in honour of some formidable Finn. Come along?

Tengo una casita cerca del Guadalquivir

Vocal strings vibrating desperately to cruelly tender plucking of stringed viscera.

4

BERNARD noticing through eggs of heads bald grey sandy brown Julia accompanied by an African warrior and a *chiaroscuro* young man: slightly shorter, eyes staring blue thin rim of beard Rouault poorstrait edged in black. Not a pair expected to escort a budding filly logician.

Not beautiful: short khaki-brown hair curling thickly well-groomed. Green eyes appearing cloud greyly hostile too wide set, cheekbones too broad. Ah. But the body: slim shapely hips breasts nicely guitarred in the clinging low-cut black dress, gaze following legs.

Bernard dear—

—Oh Professor Kriß sorry I wasn't looking—

—you simply *must* COME and MEET Pekka, he's an ABSOLUTE *charmer*. WHY didn't you *come* to his WONDERFUL lecture? I SENT you an INVITATION. Tremendous FUN. Phonemes, YOU KNOW, *distinctive* stuff, Angelika Kriß elbow-grabbing marching haplessness across to PEKKA! <=> Dr Bernard REEVES, a *great* ADMIRER of yours, leaving Bernard ear-bashed cluelessly polite with the *forme du diable* Finn.

Angelika Kriß notinthescript clothes-fashioned, social manner perpendicular to the restraint ratiocination coolly allotted to mutes of vowels. Conversationally constrained to superfluous superlatives in company, mentally mechanical sublative in *metier*, er go confoundingly contrary. Seizing an unknown arm, who're YOU? Is THERE anyone *amazing* YOU'RE *dying* to meet?

I take it you're throwing the party, shaking hands, I'm Justin who's the gorgeous African? I'd love to meat him.

HUSSEIN Abdillahi's one of MY research assistants. *The most*

ENORMOUSLY charming and SUPERBLY *intelligent* man to ESCAPE the heart of darkness. HE'S teaching *Sanuri* without SALINE.

Pouncing on the deeply-conversing *trois sans le ménage à*, Justin introduced effusively, Angelika Kriß spying other targuests.

Mister Jacob? Grinning, you have an angel bearing a ladder on your shoulder.

Bewildered laughing, my angel has long clambered back to heaven in despair, lips quickly licked, and left me to sleep with my stone pillow. Edging closer eyes widening narrowing widening eyebrows lifting.

Hussein beaming.

But you don't have a drink. Let me offer you something. Wine? Beer? Spirits?

No Mister Jacob, thank you, teeth flashing. We do not dirrink the hydorromel. I rise and see you.

A new code for come on? Come-hithered glass touching come-hithering lapel, well then call me Justin and tell me all about yourself. I like you, stomach twinging.

Hussein not-thithering, I too.

Hello Justin, how're you doing? Bernard finally disentangled from the φιλολογία tentacles of the formiteuthis Finn.

Peachy, frowning, just peachy old *chape*. Hussein, gesturing, my friend Bernard.

Well, eyeing Julia, I won't *butt* in here, you seem to be pretty well engaged. Caressing the black-dressed shoulder, hello. I see you've recovered from this morning's travails.

Dr Reeves! Each side of the mouth fissuring, lips plump well-defined. Slender gold crucifix hanging from filigree-fine chain barely visible against the expanse of pale olive skin.

I didn't recognise you at first, you look taller in high heels, eyes undressing figher, and that dress!

Paul <=> Dr Reeves, one of my examiners . . . and the kindest, laughing delightedly touching a sleeve, Dr Reeves <=> Paul Brodrick. My . . . fiancé. This *is* a philological party, isn't it? A fling of phonytizzians.

Tell me about it. I've been stuck with the guest of honour drearing on about the survival of the dual. *Much* more precise than the plural for *two* people, rolling eyes, he was saying there was one in I forget *which* language telling you how far apart they have to stand, standing very close.

Eyes sparkling, stepping backwards, very useful at parties, no?

Paul smiling, touché Dr Reeves?

Laughing, Julia you wouldn't like to help out with a book I might be editing? No money in it till it's ready, nose rubbed eyes sliding downwards, and not very much even then, Paul nodding turning to Hussein and Justin, but it'll be fun. Something you can do in your spare time.

Blinking, philology?

No, smiling, adultery.

Skin pinkening, twirling a lock of hair throat visibly contracting oh!

It's a scholarly work. I was going to do the mediaeval contribution myself, at least the French and English. But as editor, I should keep a distance. Do you read Old French?

Yes, but—

—The treatment of the theme in early English romances is exquisitely fascinating, watching a rising beast, it's already so puritan. Just look at Sir Gawain's incredibly obtuse interaction with the Green Knight's *wif.*

There's a theory he was a vegetable myth, so what do you expect in this climate? Adapting catching sparks of flippancy as quickly as smouldering introspection or a flash-firing of passion having more than once dropped a pair of vowels when hitch-hiking. I'm surprised you're writing this kind of—er—book.

Oh but it'll be very learned, not a—what did you call it—breast-seller. Certainly not vulgar, or I wouldn't ask—

—Are you looking for a general mediaeval contributor or several specialists? I mean, I know *pocchissimo italiano* and *nada* Spanish. And there's all the *Mittelhochdeutsch Fach.* Enthusiasm impractical all the more for spontaneity.

Not suggesting leaving the *mêlée* of maniacs to discuss it over drinks let me give you a ride home, it's all embryonic at the moment. I only proposed it to my publisher this evening. He's here, you should meet him.

Justin remaining unmet, Bernard promising I'll be in touch and leaving with a prickly-pear pubishim put out put back stranding Julia with the feromenal Finn.

Of courrse therre foz no fuutuurre in the Indo-Euurropean perriod.

And yet, refusing *sweriosity, here we are.

5

THE Soho flat less-furnitured in Japanese style owing to Georgina-Raymond-proclaimed poverty after returning from Tokyo, but adaptation of the first floor of an old Victorian house to an Oriental simplicity belying the truth.

Suspended false ceiling alas not of crytomeria but ordinary stained timber; double door between two rooms replaced by sliding screen of papered panels hiding 疊and a roll of quilted bedding; built-in cupboards stained to match the ceiling, except for the recess on the left of the chimney, now a 床の間. Vased flower arrangement on a low lacquered stand; incense burner on the floor; behind, a long scroll of poem. Small electric fire as concession to English winters; not alluding to the authenticity of a floor-inlaid charcoal brazier missing from the decor. French windows screened by wide printed curtains imitating a stand of split bamboo; square red cushions strewn round the room; a small squat wooden table from which to eat. Bathroom and kitchen unashamedly entirely European.

Having worked several years in the British Embassy in Tokyo and returning, unhappy but undaunted after in-love falling with a very tall gracile Japanese girl, to continue studies of the language at London University; now an obsolete choice, having met Hussein. Zen-Buddhism boarded over for Quranic questing: hours 疊-bound meditating on 無 replaced with الله أكبر, but Japanese minimalism mixing Islamic maximalism offends the purist aesthetic.

Hussein adoring the floored cushions, crouching hours chanting tribal war epics heroic-deeded classics about Imam Abdul the Leader and horse

Garodi, bringing Sanuri friends from SE1 and similar postcodes chanting nail-drumming quick rhythms on old wooden wine boxes, the backs of saucepans, the cupboard walls. Silky red hair long slim body taste for Oriental subtlety indirectly poetic way of approaching serious subjects fascinating Hussein sometimes singing a love-poem sadly in farewell, although the object of desire has yet to learn much Sanuri.

Georgina writing sensuous poetry, translating 俳句 elegantly, always accepted by the most reputable journals. Existing materially with grant funding rarely paid-for reviews neat short stories articles concerning Japanese life and letters; the two recently published pretend-pedantic essays on the mismuse of Chinese idiot graphs in the pose trees of Ezra Pound having earned a sum total of misunderstanding.

The litter-artsey pronouncing Georgina-inspired gatherings eccentric literary, even if guests no longer need to remove shoes enter crawling on hands knees: contrary to the self-consciously propagated myth claiming such imaginary qualities for actual beings. Hard-working family-supporting status notwithstanding, eating in direct proportion to output of critischism anthapologies non-fiction books confined to a territorially-defended period and screenings of increasingly infrequent long feature programmes for the BBC. Gossiping in omniscience as well-earned R&R: Did you hear Nina Jackson reviewed Mira Enketei's Inside the Whale in The London Literary Layabout/It's time Zoltan admitted he's been plagiarising Jersy—I can't believe he's still at it/Well, apparently Tess saw them in street, brazen as you please—Janek and Fiona. Utterly boring to Georgina, venerated as an image of enthusiastic irresponsibility/irresponsible enthusiasm, a vicarious embodiment of unfulfilled hankerpankeyrings.

The room ideal for a stand-up cocks&tails party: all the floor cushions removed from ceremonial positions, laterally stacked in a corner, for the benefit of guests later succumbing to queer exotic drinks and the quixotically English desire to merely paw and pe(ne)t(rate). Smaller sliding cupboards revealing shelves for ashtrays cigarettes glasses; a taller table upholding the regiment of bottles. The party fully swinging in the moment of Julia arriving.

Darling! How are you?

Hi Georgina. Fine, thanks. You?

Smashing, as ever. Where's Paul?

He'll be coming later I suppose, cheeks pinkening, he always has work to do. Hello Hussein.

Help yourself to a drink, Georgina waving a bottle, I can't look after everyone, sinuating away. Julia weaving towards the table, Hussein following looking anxious.

Hussein, have you seen Paul?

Juli-a, softly, you suffer, too? Love is the calf of a camel, now looking for you, now running away.

Pouring a glass of wine, so he told you?

A little. I ask because see-ing you I have not. A man who has not learnt why has not learnt anything.

I see him as a stranger strolling the street, someone's hair curling on the back of his neck boarding a bus. I hear him in the things people say, handing Hussein pineapple juice, and in every book I try to read. Is it like that with you?

No because I see her. But it will be the same, when I go back to Sanurri. Only the women at home, they will not remind me. They are bea-utiful, like the charcoal of the acacia. But her skin is the white of the snow on the plateau, her eyes are blue berries, and her hands are dorrops of rain. Her hair is the tail of Imam Abdul's sorrel horse, who carries him away faster than the wind.

Hussein what would happen if you married Georgina and took her back with you?

Staring at the glass-depths of epiphaning juice, I cannot. My family sent already my borrother-in-law and my cousin to tell me. My father forbids and in my country we cannot go against the father. It is written.

Georgina would become a Moslem, Hussein.

There are three things with us in marriage: the money with the house and the camels, the tribe with the customs and language, and the religion.

My father married an Isharood. That was not good, but the money and the religion were acceptable. My friend married a West African—he can never go back. Our tribe shines the best, arrogant conviction mixing naiveté, like the di-amond.

Bitterly, I suppose all these ties are too strong for you to stay here with her?

I cannot enter through the window where exists a door, or climb in secret over a fence of thorns when the path lies open. If my father forbids and I do, I must abandon my religion.

Statue-frozen momentarily, glass drained of wine like face of colour, did Paul tell you if he'd be coming tonight?

He said he would not. I am very sorry Juli-a. It is bad yes, but it is good also. Look at the thing and the thing beyond.

I know. My fault anyway.

We have a story. One time work did itself. All the burdens, they carried themselves. But one day a woman was impatient, because the burdens went too slowly. She picked them up and carried them, sipping fruit juice thoughtfully searching for dissolved English words, and the other burdens became jealous and wanted to be carried also. They—how do you say—put themselves on the storrike. The men were so angry with the woman, ever since they have made the woman carry all the burdens.

Laughing, do you think it's true, Hussein?

The men, they have their burdens also. Those who refused to be on the storrike.

Blacklegs.

Frowning, black legs? Those burdens with black legs continued to carry themselves. They were punished by the others and given to the men, who carry them very badly, sighing. Eyes lighting teeth flashing, Justin and his angel!

Justin Jacob edging towards Hussein, maintaining eye contact with Julia, hello Hussein. Who's the charming lady?

Hussein obliging.

And what do you do for your green eyes? Are you a writer Julia?

Playing with hair curling behind an ear, no. I'm doing nothing, having just written my doctoral thesis.

Oh? About what?

Laughing, don't ask or I'll start telling you.

No really, I want to know. I might want to publish it.

No? Really? Who are you?

Tweedie and Tweedie, and anxious to list some scholarly works, smiling at Hussein, offering Julia a cigarette.

You won't want this.

Hussein refusing a cancer stick, Juli-a is as clever as a gorrey parrot Justin. Hostess approaching clasping a willing arm whispering in an ear. Hussein smiling following swaying hips.

Mouth pursed like a prune, back to business as a talent scout, well Julia tell me about this thesis.

On mediaeval religious poetry. Chiefly William of Shoreham . . . Kentish. Justin quirking an eyebrow Julia warming rapidly, I was tracing the influence of the liturgy on thirteenth and fourteenth century religious lyrics. It was—oh, I'm sure I'm boring you.

It sounds fa-aascinating. Just the sort of book we want. Send me a synopsis, will you?

Erm. But it's not publishable. It's cluttered with quotes—er, I mean notes. Wrong style. You know—writing with only three people and their particular objections in mind.

Of course. Seen dozens. Put simply, rewrite it. If you want to be published.

I—I don't know. I have to find a job.

Sweets, in your own good time. Send me a specimen rewritten chapter and a synopsis. If I like it, I'll commission it. Write it while you work. That's what most people do, you know.

Darling Julia, Georgina beaming breezing between, don't be so serious. You're always so stodgy at my parties. Where's Paul? Look, everyone's having a great time. Live a little.

Smiling at the kaleidoscope of party unclothings, the pile of red cushions spread under three couples necking, necked? Slide-screen between the two rooms open revealing cotton wadded mattress unrolled on springy bamboo mats, similarly occupied. A well-known critic lying full length on the floor, glass balanced on belly. Music à la police-chase through a giant barnyard, punctuated by whish-hooting noises of destroyers torpedoing, as seen in busting-blocks films. Still-standing guests missiling names above the din in a nudge nudge wink wink coda: Bergsonism and all that . . . Hesse? Oh well, the Germans dive very deep and come up very muddy . . . Simone de Beauvoir—oh yes. Notre Dame De Sartre, what . . . Well, I'm an illogical positivist, popper me . . . Carter blanche, beyond the Paglia . . . Kant touch that! Rose is a Rose is a Rose . . .

Hussein black-knighting over a small group of impressionable students and always fazed by these *parre tiers*, especially as the finale nears, Georgina remaining out of fondling bounds for all and sundry: *noli me tangere.* Julia joining the animated discussion, Hussein pronouncing with a dazzling smile, we have a proverb: the outsider claps the hands but nothing moves.

Roars of laughter, black brow furrowed, they think I am funny, Juli-a?
It makes them laugh.
It's a good porroverb. And you, you also laugh?
I'm feeling better, Hussein. I'm going home though, I'm tired.
I will walk with you.
Smiling, but wouldn't you rather stay with Georgina?
I will bring you home. Maybe I come back. Maybe I go home also.
Incongruous in these Far Eastern surroundings, Georgina sitting leaning against two bodies and strumming a guitar: banal harmonies to African-American spirituals and *Summertime* from *Porgy and Bess.*

Julia nodding, I'll ring her tomorrow to thank her. The night swallowing them.

Lying tipsy on the bed, smoking a cigarette. Misery dissolving in lachrymose self-pity drying to indifference. Tomorrow Paul lamented now merely a figment of alternative reality. Imagination luring: having published a boundary-breaking book of critischism, reading rave reviews, attending literary spark-and-thais affairs. A too-clever b(r)ook. Thinking of Georgina: a wit among scholars and a scholar among wits, deserving of envy, *persona sprezzatura*, everything even enthusiasm ephemeral. Including Hussein.

Adopting model Georgina as a role, giggling idly leafing through *Astroloquacious*, stopping at Aquarius:

I dislike the main outlook on friendships and romantic interests for May. Handle yourself firmly. On the other hand, slow-bearing projects fruit, receiving encouragement in unexpected quarters. Prevent pessimism arising from slackening trends deluding you towards hasty ventures . . .

RRRRIIIING! BRRRIIIING!

Ten minutes until the witching hour the thought of Paul racing Julia downstairs to disappointment, halted by the sight through the window of a lamp-lit bulky Bernard, swaying slightly, Lambretta lurching against brick wall. Holding open the front door.

Hello . . . thoush I'd see how you were. Jush been parshying.

Me too.

Can—can I . . . *heu-ick*—come in?

It's late.

Jush for . . . for . . . buURP . . . a minush.

I've nothing to drink. Unless water is fine?

Wanna—wonder—fool, stumbling, I mean—full. Following Julia upstairs insighed the bedsit, eyes mesmerised by come-hither black dress fine gold touch-me-not crucifix gleaming against let-me-lick-you skin. I knew you were—*heu-ick*—were mishrable. You've been crying. Knew you'd be alone. Swaying sitting on the bed.

You seem to know a hell of a lot.

I met An—Angelika Krish and you—*heu-ick*—cropped up in the convershayshun. I made her talk about you—I—bruUP—wanted her to talk about you. She told me you'd—your fianshay had—your fidushary arranshment was—

—Everyone seems to know a hell of a lot, flopping on the chair accommodating the sleeping pillow.

Leaning forwards, I just knew you were—*heu-ick*—miserable, taking a hand.

Blinking reproprietoring the hand, I'm not miserable, I've been to a great p-party, I'm f-fine.

Why've you been crying, hand-holding again.

I haven't been . . . haven't, sniffing, been . . . Tears cheek-tracking.

Drawing bodies closer, use me darling, shouldering heads. I'm here for you. Use me as a teachyou.

Weeping smiling not saying Bernard you fool.

You just need a break Julia, some distraction. Something to put it behind you.

Nose vigorously wiped, but—why are you doing this?

I care about you. Nothing more, gently rocking bodies on a tree-top, no strings attached.

Euphemism suborning a snigger, instead Paul! Oh Paul! Tears dampening the substitute shirt again. It's all so stupid, sighing, I made him break it off myself.

There there petal, smoothing hair. Talk about it. Cry all you want, use me.

And now—*heu-ick*—I can't bear—*heu-ick*—being shut out—*heu-ick*—we were such good friends, sniffing, I miss that the most.

Soberly, were you living together?

We were, then we stopped, gulping breathing deeply, oh! It's a long story. *His* religion was the problem, that's why we can't marry. We were so in love. Now? Nothing.

Blow your nose, proffering a handkerchief, there's a cupcake.

I must look awful.

Stroking skin, not to me. This Paul is an idiot.

Tears welling, relinquishing the last confession, he's a Catholic and I was married before.

Oh were you? Admissions of conjugal experience licking lips.

It lasted a week, I'd just turned eighteen and it was a lark that turned sour. Very sour, very quickly.

Have a cigarette, resting fingers on fingers lighting it, resting eyes on nipples jutting wool. The Catholic position is styled a bit dogged, I must say.

I agree with the Church's general view on divorce, but Canon Law is a nightmare—no rhyme nor reason to annulments, sucking on the cigarette deeply, Bernard watching the pouting mouth. My marriage wasn't a marriage in the Catholic sense, but it can't be proven according to the tribunal process. And what a joke, snorting smoke like a sneezing dragon, if it could be by such spurious machinations. If I'd known at the time, I'm sure I'd never have gone through with it. I just thought if it didn't work out, naturally we'd split up. And we did. Like everyone else. Now it's a lodestone round my neck.

You want to become a Catholic? Breath held dismayed.

Puffing furiously on the last of the cigarette shaking head, the Church is wrong.

Aaaah, smiling faintly.

And you can't be a Catholic, putting out the cigarette, if you think the Church is wrong. Any marriage outside the Church is a marriage in the Catholic sense, twirl—twirl—twirling fingers through hair, unless decreed otherwise. Hardly anyone not a Catholic understands what that means. The wording ought to be changed to *no marriage outside the Church is a marriage in the Catholic sense unless proven to be so.*

I don't think I'm qualified, cigarette squashed beside the other, to give even a layman's *nihil obstat* to your proposed amendment to Canon Law. I thought you were already a Catholic, index finger sliding along the sinews of a soft hand, I suppose one can't be a mediaevalist without becoming tainted.

Well I did almost, because of . . . because of, tears sheening eyes, Paul.

Use my shoulder, sweetheart, it's there whenever you want.

Blubbering noisily until sitting up examining the stewardic face, feeling silly for self-indulgence delusional encouragement realising twenty-somethingness contrasts unfavourably with almost-fortyness: the more blasé and self-assured a man the more sentimental and gauche underneath. Ho hum.

Look Bernard, don't imagine you're in love with me. Because I couldn't deal with it right now.

Guffawing, who said I was in love with you? Picking up *Astroloquacious* thumbing it.

Red-faced smile, no-one. I'm just telling you, don't.

Dropping the magazine lifting a quivering chin with a finger, I only want to help you, to be there if you want someone to talk to, someone to show you a bit of fun.

Where does your wife come in all this?

Where should she come in this? Are you suggesting a three-way romp?

Eyes closing head flopping back on shoulder lips slightly parted. Thumb massaging temples, don't forget you're run down Julia, after all the work you've been doing. Use me as a friend, gently kneading the smooth forehead, with no strings attached. No obligations, lowering mouth to mouth, nothing. Kiss me.

Lips moulded on command student obeying tutorial demand, curiosity killing caution. Tongues exploring mouths leading to temptation arms tightening around torsos hands ruffling hair. Bernard moaning squeezing mastoid flesh. Dead to fevered touch withdrawing indifferent tongue; an exercise in style. Julia smirking, Bernard simpering.

Where did you learn, breathing heavily, to kiss like that? So that's what you meant by not falling in love with you, hands roaming over the odalisque sitting unmoved, you minx.

Yawning standing handing Bernard the duffel-coat, I'm tired.

Give me your number and I'll take you out for dinner tomorrow. We can talk about the book.

You're so sure I'm free, scrawling digits on a piece of paper.

The *phut-phut-tut-tut* of the Lambretta fading to *pht—tt—-ph——t—-p ——h*. The idiot and the idol. What a bore Bernard is, the last thing I want is dinner tomorrow. Rolling the black wool dress up over hips ribs head flinging shapelessness over a chair. Brushing teeth cleaning face. The mirror miming, no I need a distraction and he's as good as any. A little bit of flirting in the air, a little bit of flirting here and there, a little bit of Bernard in my lair, a little bit of I don't really care.

Lying awake prospecting self injecting Paul.STILL wearing dressing gown slippers, peering sleepily at a May morning bleakly drizzling unMayness down brown brick and railings known as Gower Street, students hurrying to the Drama School, Julia collecting the small bottle of lactose-free milk 6 free-range eggs bag of pesticide-free fruit from the doorstep. Patting hair shuffling inside, two newspapers three letters addressed Ms Julia Grampion lying on the hall table aweighting attention: one irrelevant, one an invitation, one enigmatic and stamped WC1 handwriting unknown. Stumbling upstairs to the refuge bedsit; the pleasure of opening the mail begging the mouth to open for coffee.

Since the viva only rising late to correspond with friends, rendezvous with Paul, rearrange bookshelves, reunion with Paul. All the books promised opening betrayed by a languid flirting with crossword puzzles tabloid opining columns book preview websites.

The large bedsit disordered: underwear caressing chairs shoes nestling near unused fire grate black or bright-coloured dresses draping doors papers adding depth to the desk. One collectible, a cocoa tin to store powder, open beside the kettle beside an unwashed cup. The bed unmade missing a pillow sleeping on the lone armchair.

Horoscopically speaking: *a lowering of tone in emotional prospects*, the other paper advertising a newly vacant post for a professor in not expected delivered but a specialist of Reinforced Concrete at the University of Somewhere Abroad. Mouth open coffee in letter open contents binned. The invitation to a party expected diarised—Georgina still insisting on gold-trimmed white stationery and not 4G MMS and WiFi smartphone apps—the third envelope revealing small spidery writing signifying a very large pedantic generous male. Signature terrifying identifying the Grendelian dam.

Dear Ms Grampion,

I wonder if you would be interested in applying for an assistant lectureship becoming vacant in my department. It would mainly involve taking students through Old and Middle English set texts, with the usual commentaries on manuscript problems, & etc. I am not of course in a position to offer you the job, as the Faculty will have to consider all applications, but I was most impressed with your thesis and would strongly support your application.

Perhaps you would like to come to dinner with us one evening, when I could tell you more about it. Kindly telephone me on 0207—.

Yours Sincerely,

J. Jarvis-Anderson

Soliloquising, so the cruellest shows the most largesse, the kindest remains the least impressed. Typical. But of examiners in particular, academics in general, or just men; ay O-feel-ya, there's the rub.

Lighting a cigarette inhaling eufemoria. Wanted, academically speaking, in flattery delictio: *I was most impressed . . . would strongly support your application.* Cigarette ending, judiciously stubbed? *I am not of course in a position . . .* And *tedia infinita: the usual commentaries on manuscript problems . . . set texts.* Or sex tests? Decanting the minutiae of scansion dialect forms emendation haplography: *hapax legomena* and *anacolutha* in Beowulf—*nese, þancie.* Day-dreaming a love affair between Anako Luthon too inconsequential and Hapax L Menon no longer so unique.

Landlady knocking entering: blue-dyed hair white-red-splotched face conjuncting an apron-swaddled ample figure. A tricolore frapping in a poppy field.

Oh hello Mrs Moffat. I'm not dressed yet, do you want to clean my room?

'sall roit dearie, take 't eezee, Oi'll do Miz Reeno, the French student rooming next door. Yer boi-fren' 'fone' t's mornin' at 'arf past oit.

Paul? Oh. Any message?

W'll, boi t' toim Oi w'z ou'a t—er, yer know—'n' up t' stairs, 'e'd rung orf.

But how—

Aw Oi knew 't woz 'im, from t' way 'e rang. D'ja loik mi gnew canellestix? Oi go' 'em fo' yer taytitayts. Oi tink tear eva so gnois, bright green porcelain spattered with coloured berries, loik fewcharistik shews, RRRRING! RIIING! Oh tat'll be 'im ag'n. Be'a go down, luvvie, or 'e'll stop 'fore oi git m'self down t' stairs. So impayshunt, yung men teaz doiz.

Running downstairs, eyes rolling, telephone trills announcing the caller, impossible. Silly side-kick sensations.

Darling. Are you up?

Er—almost.

I'm taking the morning off. I must see you.

Of course. Darling is something wrong?

.

.

.

Breathing. Static crackling.

.

.

.

I received a letter from Father Alston this morning.

.

.

.

Still life statue not photographed not painted.

.

.

.

Julia? Are you there? Meet me for coffee at *The Groves of Academe*, as soon as?

Twenty minutes?

Fine.

Bye dar—click BEEP beep BEEP beep—ling.

A la minute entering the espresso-bar. The usual forestry here representing *The Groves* designed for the pullulating modern dregs of Sir

Blooms & Lord Berries Group: one wall a set of pseudo bookshelves the other plastered with false examination papers; tables *faux* lecture desks; a large alcove aimed at the royalty of drama with masques and stage photographs, the owner of the mediation on creative space fortunising youthful desire to romanticise a dreary daily solipsinsistence. Paul gazing at a virgin cup of thickly frothed ecoganicfairtrade expression.

Taking the not-yet trembling hand ordering, another cappuccino please. Blue eyes staring wildly under dark brows, skin porcelain pale. Darling, kissing briefly, darling.

Stroking face wrists fingers, memorising high cheek-bones carved lips pencilled beard on etched chin and jaw.

I love you, kissing swiftly, I love you.

Kierkegaard's Iphigenia interrupting, your cappuccino, wafting off.

Just two spoonsful of sugar make the medicine go down delightfully. Where's the letter?

Unfolding on the table a reformed meditation on the legality of whores and charypledge.

What an unpleasant style of handwriting.

Julia don't start on that. How can you tell, anyway, at a glance? Completely irrational.

The spacing between the lines, the letters, the angle of the up and down strokes. The margins.

You just don't want to read it.

Look, three different ways of crossing the *ts*. No four. Three four five *g*s. The way the flow breaks before each *s*, and after too.

There's no point in analysing character from this, stirring coffee right pausing . . . stirring coffee left pausing . . . stirring coffee.

I never did like him. And he splits Church at the end of the line.

Tenderly, I adore your lapses in logic, but anticlericalism is unnecessary. Father Alston may be the most abominable man—though I don't think so—but as a priest he's only a middleman.

A Chief of Staff. And this is all too technical.

Arm around shoulders, hand resting on jeans-covered thigh, fingers tapping fingers hair-twirling, hands trembling. A group of :) :D :x dramaticks bee-lining the alcove.

The gist of all this, sighing, is that Westminster refuses to consider a case brought by a non-Catholic and that it wouldn't stand a chance.

That's about it.

And they say they want converts.

Arm removed, Julia don't be bitter.

What the hell do you expect? Why should I be made to suffer now for past ignorance? I'd never even thought about the Church's attitude to divorce. How should I have known that I might want to marry a Catholic.

Darling I know. If only you'd said something in the beginning, I wouldn't have—

—You wouldn't have! If only. If only! If only, ferociously, we didn't meet someone, didn't fall in love, didn't live, weren't born!

I meant, if I'd known . . . at the beginning. We could've . . . could've . . . managed differently.

Could we? Desire à go-go? Well we didn't.

No. We didn't, squeezing one hand painfully, you were . . . exactly what I'd always—

—Made to male order, drinking to drown a lump in the throat, and not to divine scripture. Why on earth and not in heaven should I have told you I was married for the sum total of a week? As if it were some kind of a defect on delivery of goods? And how should I have known it would create a problem? I loved you. I wanted to be sure you loved me, too.

You made sure of that, all right.

Paul I told you soon enough, setting cup CLATTER on saucer, and you knew you'd have an issue right then. You didn't tell me, oh no! Plucking me like forbidden fruit.

Wincing rubbing eyes, cruelty doesn't become you.

I just can't understand, staring at shamed rows of sham books opposite, the Church's attitude. I'm willing to become a Catholic, accepting the whole bang for the buck. Instead I'm disowned because of a teenage impulse.

Darling, stroking each arm, you're exaggerating. You can still become a Catholic, you just can't stay a Catholic if you remarry.

Exactly. Religious eviction for moral conviction. Surely, of all institutions, the Church should allow repentance and a full marriage?

Oh Julia! We've had all this out before. You know the script. Your first marriage is the Christian one, you took vows in an Anglican church to which you together belonged. What's the point of going over this?

Sighing, I know.

A gaunt young man entering sitting at the next table, opening a book *Summa Theologica*.

It's just so unfair. Neither of us believed in anything. That's not a contract in God's eyes.

Gaunt young man looking up looking away head bending quickly over book conscientiously assiduous.

Paul you know what happened after I left him. Shouldn't I be ashamed at having jumped in and out of bed with all and sundry, fumbling for a cigarette, not my first marriage? Oh no! The former matters not one iota because it's absolved with multiple *Avé Maria* and the confessional.

Lighting one cigarette lighting the other, I've never held it against you.

What I did out of sheer innocence and kindness—or lack of moral courage to break it off—that's what's chalked up against me. Forever. Absurd.

For God's sake, you're being so damned puritan. Shame has nothing to do with it—your marriage isn't a sin to be repented! A sacrament occurs whether you believe in it or not, whether your mind is on it or the man you're marrying.

Even, head resting in hand eyes closed cigarette singing hair, if I knew nothing and thought less about it.

Oh Julia, separating hand from hair, don't burn yourself. Listen to me darling. Please. There's no point in arguing about theological refinements. It won't change the Canon Law or my position. I want to . . . suggest a compromise.

You? Eyes wide open. Compromise?

Julia! I love you. You know that.

Yes, voice trembling tears surging, I know that.

From the alcove, staged sibilance: But . . . I object to *keeping* my men! Laughter filling the room, ambience-agnostic gaunt young man annotating Saint Thomas Aquinas.

I want, very softly, to marry you.

Staring, and abandon your faith?

Faith isn't a thing you abandon, flicking the cigarette carefully at the ashtray, if you have it, you can't make a conscious choice not to have it or you wouldn't have it in the first place.

Or lose it if you don't use it.

Yes.

I wouldn't blame you.

I haven't lost it.

Gazing at ruffled hair untidy fringe falling across the high forehead, darling what do you want? Smoothing back the fringe.

The Church has workarounds. Lots of others are in the same situation.

What do they do?

Marry in a civil court, go to Mass, stay celibate.

Cigarette tip glowing burning out. Marriage to me, stubbing the tip, means children.

To me too.

I'm not a masochist Paul.

Or, cigarette extinguished, they attend Mass, without taking the Sacrament. If it's what you believe. It's very difficult to do.

Ha! This sinful life according to the Church. Keeping tabs on the one after. Look Paul. I'm not going to demand any sacrifices from you: pride precedeth a fall. These alternatives are illogical and lunatic.

Oh is that so? You think these are two opposing polemics and the only answers?

Looking at a patch of unexpected sunlight spotlighting the hundreds of examination papers varnished over the wall haloing the pseudo-apostolic head, don't you see that's what we've been doing anyway? First we lived together and you went miserably to Mass. Then we lived miserably not together and you went back to Mass while we waited for this annulment.

Ruthless precision making Paul momentarily Zechariah.

Excuse me, I couldn't help but overhear—

Bodies twisting round.

A story in Saint Thomas might interest you, about a man who decided that technically his marriage was not a marriage, so he refused his wife and she sued him for restitution of conjugal rights. The Church refused him the Sacrament unless he restored those rights to her. Saint Thomas prefers excommunication to fornication, smiling smugly.

How the hell dare you? You—you—and next time you eavesdrop, at least listen more carefully. It isn't even a relevant parallel!

Peace be with you sister, head lowered, God bless you, collapsing in the embrace of Sir Thomas.

Despite the meaning of the word *alter*, glaring at the red-cheeked face of the erstwhile lover, there are usually three alternatives. You've tried the first two—without the blessing of the civil courts, which means nothing as far as you're concerned—and the obvious third is to go our separate ways. I assume this is your attempt to suggest it.

You have a delightful way of phrasing it.

A plain way of phrasing it. If you wanted a tender scene, full of *nobile sacrificio* and protestations of eternal love, indulge elsewhere. You need the Sacraments more than you need me. Fine, go ahead.

Communal gaiety roaring from above subsiding to titters, Paul sitting idol-still face appalled, religion isn't something one *needs*, like a sedative. Nor is love. They simply *are*. Hell, we're not even speaking the same language.

Ah! Says the only philologist in the country fluent in Sanuri! You of all men should understand other people's way of phrasing it, throat choking back tears, but you obviously don't. I thought we did speak the same language. How wrong I was.

Eyes closing walking to the door. Ignoring the theology student ignoring all religious debate except *Summa Theologica*.

6

THE Soho flat less-furnitured in 日本 の スタイル owing to Georgina-Raymond-proclaimed poverty after returning from Tokyo, rather adaptation of the first floor of an old Victorian house to an Oriental simplicity belying truth.

Suspended false ceiling alas not of crytomeria but ordinary stained timber; double door between two rooms replaced by sliding screen of papered panels hiding 畳 and a roll of quilted bedding; built-in cupboards stained to match the ceiling but not the left-of-the-chimney recess now a 床の間.

Vased flower arrangement and incense burner ornamenting a low lacquered stand, long scroll of poem behind. Small electric fire as concession to English winters; not alluding to the authenticity of a floor-inlaid charcoal brazier missing from the decor. French windows screened by wide printed curtains imitating a stand of split bamboo; square red cushions strewn round the room; a small squat wooden table from which to eat. Bathroom and kitchen unashamedly European.

Having worked several years in the British Embassy in Tokyo and returning unhappy but undaunted after in-love falling with a tall and willowy Japanese girl, to continue studies of the language at London University now an obsolete choice having met Hussein. Zen-Buddhism boarded over for Quranic questing: hours 畳 -bound meditating on 無 replaced with القرآن but Japanese minimalism mixing Islamic maximalism offending the purist aesthetic.

Hussein adoring the floored cushions, crouching hours chanting tribal war epics heroic-deeded classics about Imam Rauf and horse Garodi, bringing Sanuri friends from SE1 and similar postcodes chanting nail-drumming quick rhythms on old wooden wine boxes, frying pans, cupboard walls. Silky red hair long slim body taste for Oriental subtlety indirectly poetic way of approaching serious subjects fascinating Hussein sometimes singing a love-poem sadly in farewell, although the object of desire has yet to learn much Sanuri.

Georgina writing sensuous poetry, translating 俳句 elegantly, always accepted by the most reputable journals. Existing materially with grant funding rarely paid-for reviews neat short stories articles concerning Japanese life and letters; the two recently published pretend-pedantic essays on the mismuse of Chinese idiot graphs in the pose trees of Ezra Pound having earned a sum total of misunderstanding.

The litter-artsey pronouncing Georgina-inspired gatherings eccentric literary, guests no longer removing shoes to enter crawling on hands knees: contrary to the self-consciously propagated myth claiming such imaginary qualities for actual beings. Hard-working family-supporting status notwithstanding, eating in direct proportion to output of critischism anthapologies non-fiction books confined to a territorially-defended period and screenings of increasingly infrequent long feature programmes for the BBC. Gossiping in omniscience as well-earned R&R: Did you hear Nina Jackson reviewed Mira Enketei's Inside the Whale in The London Literary Layabout/It's time Zoltan admitted he's been plagiarising Jersy—I can't believe he's still at it/Well, apparently Tess saw them in street, brazen as you please—Janek and Fiona. Utterly boring to Georgina, venerated as an image of enthusiastic irresponsibility/irresponsible enthusiasm, a vicarious embodiment of unfulfilled hankerpankeyrings.

The room ideal for a stand-up cocks&tails party: all the floor cushions removed from ceremonial positions, laterally stacked in a corner for the benefit of guests later succumbing to queer exotic drinks and the quixotically English desire to merely paw and pe(ne)t(rate). Smaller sliding cupboards revealing shelves for ashtrays cigarettes glasses; a taller table upholding the regiment of bottles. The party fully swinging in the moment of Julia arriving.

Darling! How are you?

Hi Georgina. Fine thanks. You?

Smashing as ever. Where's Paul?

He'll be coming later I suppose, cheeks pinkening, he always has work to do. Hello Hussein.

Help yourself to a drink, Georgina waving a bottle, I can't look after everyone, sinuating away. Julia weaving towards the table, Hussein following looking anxious.

Hussein have you seen Paul?

Juli-a, softly, you suffer too? Love is the calf of a camel, now searching, now retreating.

Pouring a glass of wine, so he told you?

A little. I ask because see-ing you I have not. A man who has not learnt why has not learnt anything.

I see him as a stranger strolling the street, someone's hair curling on the back of his neck boarding a bus. I hear him in the things people say, handing Hussein pineapple juice, and in every book I try to read. Is it like that with you?

No. Because I see her. But it will be the same when I go back to Sanurri. Only the women at home they will not remind me. They are bea-utiful like the charcoal of the acaci-a. But her skin is the white of the snow on the plateau, her eyes are blue berries, her hands are dorrops of rain. Her hair is the tail of Imam Rauf's sorrel horrse, who carries him away faster than the wind.

Hussein what would happen if you married Georgina and took her back with you?

Staring at the glass-depths of epiphaning juice, I cannot. My family sent already my borrother-in-law and my cousin to tell me. My father forbids and in my country we cannot go aga-inst the father. It is written.

Georgina would become a Muslim.

There are therree things with us in marri-age: the money with the house and the camels, the tribe with the customs and langu-age, and the religi-on. My father married an Isharood. That was not good, but the money and the religi-on were acceptable. My friend married a West African—he can never go back. Our tribe shines the best, arrogant conviction mixing naiveté, like the di-amond.

Bitterly, I suppose all these ties are too strong for you to stay here with her?

I cannot enter through the window where exists a door, or climb in secret over a fence of thorns when the path lies open. If my father forbids and I do, I must abandon my religi-on.

Statue-frozen momentarily, glass drained of wine face of colour, did Paul tell you if he'd be coming tonight?

He said he would not. I am very sorry Juli-a. It is bad yes, but it is good also. Look at the thing and the thing beyond.

I know. My fault anyway.

We have a story. One time work did itself. All the burdens, they carried themselves. But one day a woman was impatient, because the burdens went too slowly. She picked them up and carried them, sipping fruit juice thoughtfully searching for dissolved English words, and the other burdens became jealous and wanted to be carried also. They—how do you say—put themselves on the storrike. The men were so angry with the woman, ever since they have made the woman carry all the burdens.

Laughing, do you agree Hussein?

The men, they have their burdens also. Those who refused to be on the storrike.

Blacklegs.

Frowning, black legs? Those burdens with black legs continued to carry themselves. They were punished by the others and given to the men, who carry them very badly, sighing. Eyes lighting teeth flashing, Justin and his angel!

Justin Jacob edging towards Hussein, maintaining eye contact with Julia, hello Hussein. Who's the charming lady?

Hussein obliging.

And what do you do for your green eyes? Are you a writer Julia?

Playing with hair curling behind an ear, no. I'm doing nothing, having just written my doctoral thesis.

Oh? About what?

Laughing, don't ask or I'll start telling you.

No really, I want to know. I might want to publish it.

No? Really? Who are you?

Tweedie and Tweedie, and anxious to list some scholarly works, smiling at Hussein, offering Julia a cigarette.

You won't want this.

Hussein refusing a cancer stick, Juli-a is as clever as a gorrey parrot Justin. Hostess approaching clasping a willing arm whispering in an ear. Hussein smiling following swaying hips.

Mouth prune-pursed, back to business as a talent scout, well Julia tell me about this thesis.

On mediaeval religious poetry. Chiefly William of Shoreham . . . Kentish. Justin quirking an eyebrow Julia warming rapidly, I was tracing the influence of the liturgy on thirteenth and fourteenth century religious lyrics. It was—oh, I'm sure I'm boring you.

It sounds fa-aascinating. The sort of book I'm keen to see. Send me a synopsis, will you?

Erm . . . you're not serious? It's not publishable. It's cluttered with quotes—er, I mean notes. Wrong style. You know—writing with only three people and their particular objections in mind. And the subject isn't exactly FSOG material.

Of course. Seen dozens of the things. Put simply, rewrite it. If you want to be published.

I—I don't know. I have to find a job.

Sweets, in your own good time. Send me a specimen rewritten chapter and a synopsis. If I like it, I'll commission it. Write it while you work. That's what most people do, you know.

Darling Julia, Georgina beaming breezing between, don't be so bloody serious. You're always so stodgy at my parties. Where's Paul? Look, everyone's having a great time. Live a little.

Smiling at the kaleidoscope of party unclothings, the pile of red cushions spread under three couples necking, necked? Slide-screen between the two rooms open revealing cotton wadded mattress unrolled on springy bamboo mats similarly occupied. A well-known critic lying full length on the floor glass balanced on belly. Music à la police-chase through a giant barnyard punctuated by whish-hooting noises of destroyers torpedoing as seen in busting-blocks films. Still-standing guests missiling names above the din in a nudge nudge wink wink coda: Bergsonism and all that . . . Hesse? Oh well, the Germans dive very deep and come up very muddy . . . Simone de Beauvoir—oh yes. Notre Dame De Sartre, what . . . Well, I'm an illogical positivist, popper me . . . Carter blanche, beyond the Paglia . . . Kant touch that! Rose is a Rose is a Rose . . .

Hussein black-knighting over a small group of impressionable students, always fazed by these *parre tiers* especially as the finale nears, Georgina remaining out of fondling bounds for all and sundry: *noli me tangere.* Julia joining the animated discussion Hussein pronouncing with a dazzling smile, we have a porroverb: the outsider claps the hands but nothing moves.

Roars of laughter black brow furrowed, they think I am funny, Juli-a?

It makes them laugh.

It's a good porroverb. And you, you also laugh?

I'm feeling better, Hussein. I'm going home though, I'm tired.

I will walk with you.

Smiling, but wouldn't you rather stay with Georgina?

I will bring you home. Maybe I come back. Maybe I go home also.

Incongruous in these Far Eastern surroundings, Georgina sitting leaning against two bodies and strumming a guitar: banal harmonies to African-American spirituals and *Summertime* from *Porgy and Bess.*

Julia nodding, I'll ring her tomorrow to thank her. The night swallowing the damsel and the damson.

7

L YING tipsy on the bed smoking a cigarette. Misery dissolving in lachrymosity drying to indifference. Tomorrow Paul lamented now merely a figment of alternative reality. Imagination luring: having published a boundary-breaking book of critischism reading rave reviews attending literary sparkentice affairs. A too-clever b(r)ook. Thinking of Georgina: a wit among scholars and a scholar among wits *persona sprezzatura* deserving of envy every experience even enthusiasms ephemeral. Including Hussein.

Adopting model Georgina as a role, giggling idly leafing through *Astroloquacious* stopping at Aquarius:

I dislike the main outlook on friendships and romantic interests for May. Handle yourself firmly. On the other hand, slow-bearing projects fruit, receiving encouragement in unexpected quarters. Prevent pessimism arising from slackening trends deluding you towards hasty ventures . . .

RRRRIIIING! BRRRIIIING!

Ten minutes until the witching hour the thought of Paul racing Julia downstairs to disappointment, halted by the sight through the window of a lamp-lit bulky Bernard swaying slightly Lambretta lurching against brick wall. Holding open the front door.

Hello . . . thoush I'd see how you were. Jush been parshying.

Me too.

Can—can I . . . *heu-ick*—come in?

It's late.

Jush for . . . for . . . buURP . . . a minush.

I've nothing to drink. Unless water is fine?

Wanna—wonder—fool, stumbling, I mean—full. Following Julia upstairs, eyes mesmerised by come-hither black dress fine gold touch-me-not crucifix gleaming against let-me-lick-you skin. I knew you were—*heu-ick*—were mishrable. You've been crying. Knew you'd be alone. Swaying sitting on the bed.

You seem to know a hell of a lot.

I met An—Angelika Krish and you—*heu-ick*—cropped up in the convershayshun. I made her talk about you—I—bruUP—wanted her to talk about you. She told me you'd—your fianshay had—your fidushary arranshment was—

—Everyone seems to know a hell of a lot, flopping on the chair accommodating the sleeping pillow.

Leaning forwards, I just knew you were—*heu-ick*—miserable, taking a hand.

Blinking reproprietoring the hand, I'm not miserable, I've been to a great p-party, I'm f-fine.

Why've you been crying, hand-holding again.

I haven't been . . . haven't, sniffing, been . . . Tears cheek-tracking.

Drawing bodies closer, use me darling, shouldering heads. I'm here for you. Use me as a teachyou.

Weeping smiling miming Bernard you fool.

You just need a break Julia, some distraction. Something to put it behind you.

Nose vigorously wiped, but—why are you doing this?

I care about you. Nothing more, gently rocking bodies on a tree-top, no strings attached.

Euphemism suborning a snigger, instead Paul! Oh Paul! Tears dampening the substitute shirt again. It's all so stupid, sighing, I made him break it off myself.

There there petal, smoothing hair. Talk about it. Cry all you want, use me.

And now—*heu-ick*—I can't bear—*heu-ick*—being shut out—*heu-ick*—we were such good friends, sniffing, I miss that the most.

Soberly, were you living together?

We were, then we stopped, gulping, oh! It's a long story. *His* religion was the problem, that's why we can't marry. We were so in love. Now? Nothing.

Blow your nose, proffering a handkerchief, there's a cupcake.

I must look awful.

Stroking skin, not to me. This Paul is an idiot.

Tears welling relinquishing the last confession, he's a Catholic and I was married before.

Oh were you? Admissions of conjugal experience licking lips.

It lasted a week, I'd just turned eighteen and it was a lark that turned sour.

Have a cigarette, resting fingers on fingers lighting it, resting glance on nipples jutting wool. The Catholic position is styled a bit dogged, I must say.

I agree with the Church's general view on divorce, but Canon Law is a nightmare—no rhyme nor reason to annulments, sucking on the cigarette deeply, Bernard watching the pouting mouth. My marriage wasn't a marriage in the Catholic sense, but it can't be proven according to the tribunal process. And what a joke, sneezing dragon snorting smoke, if it could be by such spurious machinations. If I'd known at the time I'm sure I'd never have gone through with it. I just thought if it didn't work out, we'd split up. And we did. Like everyone else. Now it's a lodestone round my neck.

You want to become a Catholic? Breath held dismayed.

Shaking head puffing furiously on the last of the cigarette, the Church is wrong.

Aaaah, smiling faintly.

And you can't be a Catholic, cigarette obliterated, if you think the Church is wrong. Any marriage outside the Church is a marriage in the Catholic sense, twirl—twirl—twirling fingers through hair, unless decreed otherwise. Hardly anyone not a Catholic understands the implications. The wording ought to be changed to *no marriage outside the Church is a marriage in the Catholic sense unless proven to be so.*

I don't think I'm qualified, cigarette squashed beside the other, to give even a layman's *nihil obstat* to your proposed amendment to Canon Law. I thought you were already a Catholic, index finger sliding along the sinews of a soft hand, I suppose one can't be a mediaevalist without being affected.

Well I did almost, because of . . . because of, tears sheening eyes, Paul.

Use my shoulder sweetheart, it's there whenever you want.

Blubbering noisily until sitting upright scanning the stewardic face feeling silly for self-indulgence delusional encouragement realising twenty-somethingness contrasting unfavourably with almost-fortyness: the more blasé and self-assured a man the more sentimental and gauche underneath. Ho hum.

Look Bernard, don't imagine you're in love with me. Because I couldn't deal with it right now.

Guffawing, who said I was in love with you? Picking up *Astroloquacious* thumbing it.

Red-faced smile, no-one. I'm just telling you, don't.

Dropping the magazine lifting a quivering chin with a finger, I only want to help you, to be there if you want someone to talk to, someone to show you a bit of fun.

Where does your wife come in all this?

Where should she come in this? Are you suggesting a three-way romp?

Eyes closing head flopping back on shoulder lips slightly parted. Thumb massaging temples, don't forget you're run down Julia, after all the work you've been doing. Use me as a friend, gently kneading the smooth forehead, with no strings attached. No obligations, lowering mouth to mouth, nothing. Kiss me.

Lips moulded on command student obeying tutorial demand, curiosity killing caution. Tongues exploring mouths leading to temptation arms tightening around torsos hands ruffling hair. Bernard moaning squeezing parabolic flesh Julia dead to fevered touch withdrawing indifferent tongue; an exercise in style. Julia smirking, Bernard simpering.

Where did you learn, panting, to kiss like that? So that's what you meant by not falling in love with you, hands roaming over the odalisque sitting unmoved, you minx.

Yawning standing handing Bernard the duffel-coat, I'm tired.

Give me your number and I'll take you out for dinner tomorrow. We can talk about the book.

You're so sure I'm free, scrawling digits on a piece of paper.

The *phut-phut-tut-tut* of the Lambretta fading to *pht—tt—-ph——t——-p ———h*. The idiot and the idol. What a bore Bernard is, the last thing I want is dinner tomorrow. Rolling the black wool dress up over hips ribs head flinging shapelessness over a chair. Brushing teeth cleaning face. The mirror miming, no I need a distraction and he's as good as any. A little bit of flirting in the air, a little bit of flirting here and there, a little bit of Bernard in my lair, a little bit of I don't really care.

Lying awake prospecting self injecting Paul.

8

PROFESSOR Jarvis-Anderson: domiciled in Hampstead in a rambling red-brick Victorian house straining to enclose corpulence and family corpus. Husband to Marion Farquharson successful novelist having produced five large generational sagas and five large off-spring frequently miscounted by John Jarvis-Anderson. The children pre-tween more raucously numerous than Cutting & Co numerously squawking about Farquharson epics, monikered with Anglo-Saxon Old Norse heroes thus modelling those namesakes acquiring by magic of nomenclature the characteristics of: Hrothgar = wisdom, Wiglaf = loyalty, Hildigunn = hubris, Kári = steady ruthlessness, Njàl = prophecy (even at kindergarten age).

Marion: *regia imperturbabilis* heroically fit for any saga domestically engineering the home with efficiency laconism candour a disciple of circumstantial self. Novel production never intruding on the socially steepullulated business of adoring heavyweight husband and heroic brood.

Professor Long-Nordic-Name opening the front door left shoulder nervously twitching greeting Julia, shyly presenting the drawing room epitomising the study of an Oxford tutor littered with galley-proofs.

Have a strong martini and meet my wife, indicating the prize possession. Marion this is Ms Grampion. Be kind to her, she looks very tired.

I'm always kind to your students, laughing, have to be after you've dealt with them.

Relaxing for the first time since unrecalled, call me Julia please. Sitting on the couch watching the remarkably handsome Marion neither husband-dullarded nor compenisating. Pale blond tresses head-coiled, lively in a peaceful manner. Statuesque intelligent, a Guðrún already converted.

The professor making much of a photograph: a famous crux in a manuscript. O-of course, ultra-viollet l-light ill-luminates no truth. You l=look at the manuscript too l-long. Its only advantage is to suggest forms you would o-otherwise have never considered l-linguisticall-ly possible.

Silently: Professor I have invented a new linguistic group for you and a chair as well: Professor of Hesitating Languages.

Aloud: Professor, I'm a little uneasy about applying for this job. Philology is my weakest point sir, as you no doubt realised from my thesis.

Yes I seem to remember a l-little jousting between us, smiling graciously.

You can make anything your weakest point by thinking of it as such Julia. Remember the lecturer has his textual comments, patting the respective arm, in front of him. I feel much more sympathy for the student.

Blinking, oh!

My wife is very wise. Those with the best memory are awarded the firsts, laughing, but you know the texts, you must have read these yourself as an undergraduate.

Of course, although . . . I didn't mean that I couldn't comment on the texts sir, only that if my heart weren't in it I wouldn't do it very well. I'd rather talk about the poetry instead.

I remember a student asking me, at some gathering or o-other, if my subject was Eng-llish L-literature, left shoulder lifting up dropping forward, and I said yes, Anglo-Saxon and Middle English and she said, no I mean l-literature. A Cambridge alumna.

Gazing at the palaeographic problem on the photograph, I know one can't really divide form and content, but it's very difficult not to, the way things are presented. It's either all sound changes or it's all what the poet says and why it's said. I'm interested in language as a process, not as a thing or an essence. Phonetic laws are useful, but they aren't immutable, like the laws of the universe. You can't say that a hard *c* before a palatal *a* will inevitably soften to *ch*: in Southern and Central France it did, in Northern France it didn't. So we have *castle* from the Normans and *chastity* from Parisian French two centuries later.

Marion winking, which is rather peculiar if you think about it.

Philol-lol-lology is not a mathematical science Jul-lia, avuncular kindly tone, it's an art borrowing from science. One has to remember each fact separately and make up the pattern for each l-language o-or dialect, or class, or even each individual.

I know, but philologists talk of Grimm's Law as if a Primitive Germanic Assembly had legislated it, ordering everyone to pronounce their *ps* as *bs* and their *ts* as *ds*.

Marion laughing, sounds rather grim to me. Another drink Julia?

O-oh I beg your pardon, the professor hastily refilling glasses. You know I was thinking o-of a much nicer consonant shift which occurred in Finnish and Hungarian, waving the cocktail shaker, it really is quite the nicest consonant shift I know.

John dear, do stick to the point.

Of course Marion. Jul-lia is right. The individual styles of ll-language spread through imitation. A great anonymous mass movement o-of sounds—or indeed o-of ideas—is a myth.

But why is it all presented as otherwise?

The l-linguist can only know the state of a language when the individual style is generalised. It's in a constant state of fl-llux with no real boundaries o-or unified communities, and mingling continues through supra-political o-or social bonds. No language or dialect is free from alien infl-lluence . . . no limit to the possibility o-of speech-blending . . .

Staring at a distant point outside the room where foreign tongues Tantralise tessellate tincture toxicate tumefy.

Twirling hair strands, it's the purely fortuitous character of sound-change I find so discombobulat—noise dégringolading from the stairs a dirty little face topped by a tousle of fair hair peering round the door.

Can I borrow the Anglo-Saxon dictionary? We're building a fort and the Oxford English ones aren't thick enough.

Holding out an arm, I thought I told you to go and have your bath. Well. Now you're here, come and say hello to Julia. Julia, nodding, my eldest. Hrothgar, nodding, Julia.

Ulf the Unwashed invading imagination. Smiling, hello Hrothgar. Where's your fort? Is it very big?

It's at the top of the stairs. Nobody can pass by, nobody at all.

Who's Nobody? A terribly fierce enemy?

Grinning, Nobody's a giant, with lots of heads, as many heads as the dictionary has words. That's why we're building a log fort, to frighten Nobody.

Laughing, all the words will rat-tat-tat out and sever each head?

Head cocked, wheels loudly turning. NO! Bouncing as if on a pogo stick, the words—jump—are death—jump—rays!

Don't wake up Njàl, catching the well-sprung ray. I'll be up in half an hour to kiss you all goodnight. You'd better finish off Nobody beforehand.

I'M Somebody, the bravest of the BRAVE! Daddy, the dictionary? Please?

The keeper of *bon mots* nodding smiling, as long as you don't tear the logs to pieces.

Of course not! It's only for the battlements I promise, struggling to extract two OUT-OF-PRINT volumes of annotated terms from the bookshelf.

I'll carry the requisite goods for you if you'll let me near your fort. I might be, *sotto voce*, Nobody's spy.

Solemn gaze gauging Julia. The Fantastic not conceding to the Pragmatic and emerging triumphant, I know! You're Somebody's Faithful Friend! Let's go.

Later descending the stairs alone face serene, musing the Jarvis-Anderson family would no doubt seem whimsically donnish as an epigram hail fellow well made causing the necessary and or the irrelevant to mesh neatly. Even phonology sounding legitimate in such company, imagining morphing vowels cavorting contrasting consonants swapping allegiance under lymphoid pressures on the pharynx, corpora linguae etymologically salvaged. This job sounds interesting. The academic world I prefer, it's sane, honest . . . its values are well-regarded and relativity-free, as much as can be this side of paradise. I just need to fit in, like Paul, belong to it, like he does, in all its eccentric variation. But I am, aren't I, just like Bernard really, a sham. Prof J-A's invitation was the perfect excuse not to meet him for dinner.

Entering the drawing room resuming a seat, hosts smiling indulgently, conversation expanding to include Somebody's Faithful Friend.

Now you know more about the position, Professor No-Relation-To-A-Beowulf-Antagonist offering peanuts, and what your chances are, I do hope you will apply. As I said, it's not all mnemonic philol-lol-lology.

Laughing, you flatter me, Professor. I'll definitely apply. How long do you think it will take before they decide? Ring-fencing the professor from the adjudicating pronoun.

Applications have to be in by the end o-of this week, glass replenished, the job was advertised some weeks ago and has had a good response. Short-l-listed candidates will be interviewed the first week o-of June. I suppose, all going well, you'd hear within a few weeks o-of that.

Fingering curls twirl index twirl middle twirl index twirl fourth, even if I were successful, I'd still have to temp over the summer. My grant finishes in June.

Marion *tsking* head shaking, you don't want to spend the next two months stuck in an office temping, surely. Your brain will simply implode. I could help you with some proof-reading or reviewing work, perhaps?

Proofing? Reviewing? Books?

Yes of course. Travelogues, help-yourself pop-psychology, celebrity wellness manuals, technology trends, biographies, novels, poetry. What passes for the semi-literate pouring from trade presses in a weekly spume.

But why should I—

—It's very badly paid these days, what with opinion sites popping up like *phallus impudicus* funghi, but you could do it with your eyes closed, I'm sure. If you churn out enough and stick to a penurious lifestyle, you'll survive until the beginning of term.

I mean, how can you—

—I've been writing enormous not-quite middle-brow novels for the last decade or so. I know most of the acquisitions editors still in the business. John didn't tell you my surname, smiling, is Farquharson.

Red-faced drink gulped, oh I'm sorry. How stupid of me.

Regal hand downward sweeping, not at all. John chuckling.

But I couldn't review books. I've not read anything more recent than Chaucer—muffled shouting upstairs—for years.

Julia not just with your eyes closed but one-handed standing on your head, you could. I've reviewed and I'm not even intelligent. It's a matter of avoiding jargon and maintaining a nicely elevated authorial but personal tone with some tongue-in-cheek wit and plenty of praise.

Anyone, shaking the great white head, could review the sort o-of book my wife has mentioned.

Your training in research must have taught you to gut a book in half an hour.

Er—that sort o-of book, o-of course, mournful tone conveying incredulity at the existence of that sort of book.

Erm—it's very kind of you, sighing, I suppose I could try. But don't they already have regular contributors? Eyes roaming the room, fascinated with esoteric objects hidden amongst the quotidian.

Naturally. But even journalists take holidays, you know. Although that cuts either way, it's also the silly season in publishing—

—It's always the silly season in publish—

—I'll have a word with Desmond Sykes, nudging the professor, and perhaps a few—

—Oh! You've a harpsichord. How wonderful! Do you rent it or is it yours?

Not entirely ours since we couldn't afford it. John gave me a harp and I gave him accord.

A friend o-of ours made it for us, so we paid l-less than usual. He was very good at Hokkien, but his real passion in l-life was making harpsichords. We sometimes duet, my wife and I.

The two of you sit and play? But it's so tiny, laughing Marion laughing John laughing until thunder rumbling thump thump thump thud bang crash WHAAAAAAH!

Marion rising, that was Wiglaf. I ought to organise them for bed, looking at the mantelled grandmother clock. Dear me, it's already eight. You must be starving.

Julia springing across to the drawing room door, I'll come and help you.

Wouldn't dream of it. Sit and talk shop with John. The kids are hyper enough without Somebody's Faithful Friend putting them to bed. We'll eat in half an hour. Sorry for the delay, smiling gliding out tranquil and majestragic as a dreki.

9

LIKE the tree in the quad, the British Mausoleum Reading Room existing only when observed. After long absences a perceived continuation, for the benefit of so many scholars critics poets paupers eccentrics hatchers of revolutions unravellers of genealogies authors of pamphlets or of supplicant if not impeccant letters to the Royal Family or the Prime Minister, suggesting a matter of faith. Standing ignormous: round reassuring frenetic as the womb, concentric seats all pointing to circular shelves of catalogues and small circus of polite attendants waiting like patient performers for the exceptional enquiries of the madding marks. Continuing, a high-domed reliquary beehive-busy honeycombed with twisting galleries subterranean corridors Jungian spiral staircases smelling funereal.

Constant footsteps floored mute. Murmuring of voices studded with bookends thudding back to shelf place, fixed phone lines quietly warbling to rival a nightingale, long whispered *devi sapere che bestimmt hat Jan* 君の気持ち *n'avait pas compris daj już spokój!* አዝጓለሁ between glamorous foreign students preparing notes for senior research fellows temporary bedfellows such presence could well exemplify, English down-among-the-dead-ones flash-panning for work of any kind on the daily-changing noticeboard.

Visiting without meeting acquaintances imitating the Reading Room and existing only when coincidentally confronted, an impossible dream. Other times, a random rendezvous occurring with an evocation persistently invading stream-of-consciousness better tombed in all those million tomes.

Spurred to undertakings after weeks of no takings, Julia returning to write chapter synopsis abstract for Justin Jacob, textfoliate in case of interview, conduct a desultory search on adulterated relations in mediaeval l'amourdramas.

On the steps leading to the columns supporting the monstrous pediment upholding a vigilante female figure almost dropping a great stone ball on every small unwary seeker after the absolute, Paul standing newly emerged, brief-case at feet, cigarette between cupped hands embering face edged in black, the lead outlines of a stained-glass saint.

Throat closing blood suffusing face sweat beading brow, hello Paul. I thought you never smoked in the mornings?

Well I do a bit—er—now . . . Have one?

Hand trembling holding cigarette to flame, how are you?

Oh fine thanks. You know work's work, inhaling deeply. Hussein's inside, I've been showing him how to use the system. You could help him if he runs into trouble.

Yes of course . . . I—you—

—Yes?

N-nothing.

Walking back and forth along the colonnade pavement back forth forth back smoking cigarettes together.

What are you doing with yourself?

Oh well a job possibly. One of the examiners mentioned it, so I applied. A book, possibly, on the treatment of—er—contractual breach in mediaeval literature. The other examiner suggested a contribution.

I'm very glad to hear you've some options, coughing against a fust.

So . . . yes. It seems I may be around in the academic world. We'll probably bump into each other, glancing at the shadowed face, I hope we can be—be civil about this. I hope you . . . don't object?

Voice strained, well. Can I? It's upsetting, laughing quietly. I thought I'd . . . put you out of mind. You know, out of sight.

Turning away blinking tears dry turning back staring ahead avoiding look-at-me eyes.

Seeing you makes me realise how much I miss you, Julia. You're so beautiful.

Relaxing lips curving, seeing you as a friend makes me realise how nice it is to meet up, voice warm, I'm sorry you're feeling so put out. I'll try to keep out of your way.

Nodontdothat! Eyes despairing body rigid tone rising. Don't avoid me. I mean, breathing slowly, I mean . . . as you say, we're bound to . . . meet now and again. I suppose I'll . . . get used to it. Each time will be . . . easier.

Of course you'll get used to it, swallowing in a dry throat, well I'd better go in and make a start. Lips rictus-stiff, goodbye. Nice to have seen you. Lump choking throat, watching to the last Paul smiling nodding hurrying down the steps tall figure turning left outside the gates glimpsed through high railings no backward glance.

Inside the Reading Room Hussein surrounded by notes. Not yet noon and the room full of provincial university staff on regular jaunts to Londontown in search of lost theses ideas promotional possibilities. The locals also appearing en masse: the lonely Pole *Approchant sans s'arrêter* Brooke-Rose; the bearded man surreptitiously combing back-length silky grey hair; the war-painted purplehead wearing crimson satin hotpants green woolly socks unisex blue blazer; the on-the-prowl Oriental eyeing younger readers with the measure of a hidden stiffened courage.

Finding a free seat dumping handbag on desk coat on chair stepping back staring at bright blue eyes immediately recognised.

Bernard. I'm so sorry, whispering, I didn't see you. D'you mind if I sit here? There's nowhere else.

Delighted, smiling, come and have a coffee.

I've—er—just had one . . . and it's—er—so late, I'd better start.

Lunch?

SHSHSHSH! Looking askance at the angry face of the bald pate above the corpulence occupying the chair to the left, I could say I was dating Hussein . . . except he's short of money, sighing, and I am too. Nodding yes feeling forlorn, I absolutely have to keep him at arms' length, exactly because I want arms and length between me and anyone, even him.

Hussein having completed fifty-two requests for books on the most diverse subjects by authors with names beginning *San—* because the novelty of government funding for such a fantastic network of little rooms full of learned scholars deeply committed to investigating muted-vowel vibrations or bloated-bowel gyrations begging such exploitation.

Grinning, I have a proverb for you Julia. The hi-rred man is never himself ferree, while ordering publications variously titled *A Geographical Survey of the Sanuri Protectorate, 1948-1988*, or *The Mineral Resources of the Sanuri Protectorate*, or *Report on the Ethnic Heterogeneity of Sanuri (1992)*. Curiosity seeing no incongruity in simultaneously requesting the entire oeuvre of William Sansom, dead these many a year.

Eyebrows raised, you can't request all this! There's a limit and you'll never read all of it today.

Brown eyes downcast, this is saddening. Then I will ask only for this one and that one. This one *A Geographical Survey of* and that one *Do Angels Dream of Eternal Sheep?* by Poap Sancerrevino.

Conscious of Bernard Reeves watching the activity with Hussein until footsteps towards the shared desk prompting studied ignorance.

Do you mind having lunch early? My books will take some time.

Oh it's you! Blinking above an exaggerated yawn, yes of course, standing shrugging on duffel-coat offering similar valet assistance to Julia, who's the black guy?

Hussein. And he's African, swinging through the doors heels tsk-tsking on the marble steps outside, not a black guy.

10

SEATED in a Soho smooth and soothing Ottoman restaurant complete with obsequious staff abundant *mezze* milk-white *raki* transmuting Julia from lionesque to maudlin moggy confiding *non sequitur* and purring at verbal petting.

What you need to cheer you up, tattooing the back of a hand with flirtatious fingers, is a discreet and light-hearted love affair, to be told without surcease that you're beautiful and great fun, slipping knees between knees under the table.

Sighing, no. That's not what I need. It's just the wine, ignoring an annoying pelvic twinge, fingers twining hair, mood can't be treated with substitutes for SSRIs. Besides, smirking, one might become addicted . . . You're no use to me, I want to be loved. Not humoured.

Gazing at the mud dregs of obscured future in peat-black Turkish coffee, stroking a hand eyes glancing sideways mischievous, I want to be honoured too.

11

RECLINING on 布団 white keyboard balancing on knees red hair flowing over shoulders. Forgotten on 畳 an empty 湯飲み, not forgotten the white cordless telephone. Dialling a number.

Julia? Georgina here. I saw Paul yesterday. Darling, what a wretch I am. How much fellatio of my foot did I perform last Tuesday? No wonder you disappeared so early.

Arm in coat sleeve Julia standing motionless in the hallway, oh! I meant to call. To say thanks, looking at the hall clock, for a lovely party.

Lasted for hours. *And* you snuck off with Hussein, you Sanuri snatcher. Probably just as well, setting keyboard on 布団, darling you must be so miserable. Come round and let me cheer you up.

The official Cheer Julia Up Campaign? Staring at the pale reflection staring from the hallway mirror, I'm not in the least miserable and I've a tonne of things to do Georgina.

I don't believe you, rolling to one side. Doctors in anything but quantum physics and artificial intelligence are unemployed these days. What things?

Paraphrasing a previous conversation with Paul.

Oh Julia! So you're becoming all-litter-ratter! Stretching along 布団 reaching for cigarettes, but what are you going to do for dosh? And are you sure you're not miserable? I'm marvellous at cheering people up.

Yes I know you are, sighing at the colluding reflection, and thank you. But I'm fine. I saved some of my grant money and—

—Nonsense. You need to start reviewing, that'll boost the coffers a bit.

A second official conspiracy?

Shoulder hugging handset to ear, I'll talk to Desmond Sykes about you, shaking out a cigarette, lighter rasping a small flame flaring the tobacco tip, deep inhalation.

Desmond Sykes a critical factor in the subterfuge.

It's lovely of you to offer Georgina, but ah—someone else mentioned him already.

Oh? Cigarette momentarily displaced, handset snuggled against other ear. Who?

Marion Farquharson.

Oh good grief! Snorting, he'll ignore everything *she* says. Farquharson is been there and forgotten that. Not to mention 本当に馬嫁

Bah-kah? What?

Bonkers.

Oh . . . Have you met her?

No. Know of her. Look, I'm just being a bitch darling. Why don't you leave Desmond to me, I can tell him all about you. Suggest the books you should be reviewing.

All about me? And what sort of books, exactly?

Oh this and that.

Er—it's very sweet of you Georgina.

大丈夫だよ That's what friends are for. You'll be cheering me up next.

Of course I will. Not that you need it, you're always so on top of everything. I have to rush sorry, struggle with coat bag shoes complete. Thanks for ringing.

Well couldn't not call you. It was good to talk—oh! By the way, I almost forgot to ask, deep inhalation, where did you hide Hussein? I haven't seen him for days.

He's been researching in the Reading Room at the British Museum.

Oh so that's where. Thanks. Drop by whenever you need to darling. Bye! Handset slipped back on cradle body flopping on 布団 cigarette dangling Georgina staring ceilingwards indefinitely.

Morning ablutions sustenance consumption concluded before meviewing a novel translated from the Japanese: *written, unfortunately, with a slanting Oriental eyelash batting at Bollywood.* Extinguishing a cigarette, damn Orientals and damn Hussein, typing a final flourish: *It is, in fact, an intriguing premiss, not for a Curry Western, but for a Sushi Eastern.* Another nicotine-tar spritz accompanying the proof-read file saved email-attached sent.

Bathroom mirror reflecting black silk trousers loose tunic combining exotic chic elegant simplicity. Always clothed as though Midas maintained belying ingenuity innate sensibility, designing fashion statements oblique to academic lit-crit status. Hair french-knotted for the former hightailed or escaping for the latter composure *savoir faire* style *laissez faire* attitude *joie de vivre.*

Midday bidding 然らば to tenth century *anno dominini* poet 紀貫之 Does poetry truly mediate between lovers, as claimed? Knocking on the door of the room occupied by Angelika Kriß.

Come.

Hello Angelika. Am I disturbing you?

Of course. Thankfully. I need a break from strange masculine sounds enunciated in Sanuri, stabbing a finger at a black button muting myriad vowel vocals, have a seat. How are things?

Could be worse. Could be better, too. No chance of jumping ship to African studies? Sanuri, specifically.

Dear god, Georgina. You're taking your finals in Japanese this academic year, no?

Yes. I meant after. Unless . . . well, now?

You can't just swap mid-semester. Besides, you've a grant. As a one-to-watch *Wakoku* specialist.

Yes, but . . . linguistics training isn't language-specific. I've picked up some Sanuri already. And you could do with more scholars in your area of expertise.

One Brit and an indigenous teacher are already more than the budget constraints allow, given they've only one student between them.

Then another would be even better.

They're quite tied up with research work Georgina. Look, leaning back, take it easy hmm?

Sighing shaking out a cigarette, do you mind?

Don't set off the fire alarm. Open the window and stand over there, please. And use this for the ash, handing Georgina a hollowed glass paperweight.

Smoke jet-streaming out the open window, birdsong trilling in, Angelika watching Georgina coolly.

He's keeping away.

You knew he would. With men it's always out of sight out of mind.

Prof Nieminen left, has he?

As expected. Work makes the best medicine. Most of the time.

Blowing smoke rings, I suppose so. I knew it would happen sooner or later. I just thought it would be later. I guess Hussein's going straight back?

Not much point staying in England after the end of his contract.

Frowning pounding out the cigarette.

Oh Georgina think! He has no money apart from his salary here.

One knows, closing the window noisily. 糞 One leaps from a cliff hoping for a parachute and finding the silk is ripped. Knowing the delusion is the challenge to disprove its foregone conclusion. One expects pain, even welcomes it, because one expects it will only be a momentary lapse of reason.

One for you yourself and Hussein? Whatever happened to I? Own your emotions, woman!

One wants Hussein, sitting opposite Angelika, crooking elbows on the wide desk, even if one can't own him.

You're not pregnant, are you?

Not really my style. I'd hoped he would . . . dammit, he's so contradictory. Aphorising one minute *two wives are necessary, one to nourish the heart, one to nourish the stomach* and epigramming the next *the skin creaks according to the country* or *move your head according to the music.*

Confused a poetess?

Something like that, slouching studying lacquered nails.

Georgina there are only two things you can do if he's not going to marry you. He can't stay here unless he does. And he's not, right?

I suppose not. Wistful perusal of a borderless map the Horn of Africa adorned not with natural resource demarcations colonial misappropriations but tribal languages vowel aspirations glottal stops.

Exactly. Apart from anything else, you've a promising career right here, which is more than can be said of your peers. Count yourself lucky.

Shoulders shifting slightly, one eyebrow in unison.

Either cut clean, right now—and he's making it easier for you, isn't he? Or?

A truly madly deeply no-holds-barred Rubicon's Crossing affair.

What makes you think it hasn't been that already?

Angelika quirking a matching eyebrow Georgina lowering gaze disquieted.

No you're right of course. It's hardly been protestations of undying love. And I'm not pregnant.

Precisely. The latter alternative would be the more painful for him, the former for you.

How so?

Hussein's old-fashioned, erotic poetry notwithstanding. You aren't committed to him. Once you were . . .

Yes, sighing standing stepping stopping at the door. Sorry I . . . I shouldn't have dumped all this on you.

Dear Georgina. Drop in and dump whenever, you know my time-table. Or at my flat. And don't go blabbing elsewhere. You'll feel like hell and you'll want to. Keep busy.

I'll try. Thank you for listening.

Chin up. Goodbye.

Bye Angelika.

Walking along the corridor hesitating at the door of a Sanuri specialist not hearing voices no reason to fight an impulse to knock. Next destination: Desmond Sykes.

Sauntering through gaunt and dismal squares of the Blooming Burieds arriving at the purpose-built pug-ugly offices sheltering *The Platform*, internecine meiosis and *nom de plume* mitosis earning the entity the eke name of *The Chamber of Poli Ticks*. Desmond, literary editor, engaged as perennial battler with Robin, Mrs of the Honourable Trout, the former seeing fit to impose Style, Grammar, and Punctuation as a fundament, the latter a tattler of economic-echelon-equated moral philosophical social opinion.

Hello Desmond, sliding upon a swivel chair sited opposing the editorial desk. I see you've read my review, pointing at a print-out, like it?

Hello. Yes. Hmm. I did. Sadly enough.

Idly spinning clockwise counterclockwise clockwise, are you free for lunch?

Lunch? Checking a diary, nodding, yes I suppose I've nothing better to do, or at least, nothing that appeals more than lunch with you. I'm guessing you want a favour.

Oh not at all. You know I prefer my dates ebony and innocent, not elderly and insolent.

Nothing like a little belletristic masturbation, Gorgeousina, to encourage a submission. Except when the review is from you, of course, gazing over heavy-rimmed halved spectacles: an unblinking quadranocular lean and silver-suited lizard.

Yes. Having not slept with you I haven't stepped on you, thanked you for the deal, and climbed the literary ladder to the boring upper strata of solidity, aridity, and inviolability in the other departments.

Free love free expression is my risotto. Rather like that Adair fellow. Have you read his *The Dreamers*?

Stop changing the subject Desmond. The fact is, leaning forwards pointing an elegant varnished-nail finger, people misunderstand you. They don't realise you're smarter than they are, more generous, and exceptionally good company. Come on, where are you taking me?

One eyebrow arching slightly, flattery will lead you nowhere. I'm going to have to trim this, indicating the submitted review.

大丈夫だよ. At least you don't massacre, grinning over an indolent shoulder spinning left spinning right.

Talking of which, the BBC are putting on my feature at last. But the fifth dimension of consciousness and seventh level of dream awareness are being cut. Sigh.

Desmond I'm delighted. And hungry. Tell me all about it at lunch, standing flicking locks of titian sideways backwards, I want to talk to you about a friend of mine.

Ah, smirking. He, she, either or cross?

She.

Pity, *tsking*, girls are so normatively sensitive. It's not as though they're still worshipping at the altar of Hymenaios. You'd think with all this taboo-tearing they'd be a little more open.

Nothing to do with it. They know you swing either way. And they'd rather be appreciated for their brains and not their bodies.

But I do appreciate them for their brains, sighing standing looking despondently at a galley-proof, after I've appreciated them for their bodies. The unknown ♀ yet another boardspringing from The Platform either sinking in amorphous anonymity or soaring skywards to celebrity.

12

DAMNED ah'th'rs!

Mr Tweedie, middling middle-aged Scottish Jew or Jewish Scot known for acumen a queue of men acquiring men femme zen, hovering at the door of a stiflingly hot attic office. Seem t' think, Justin, we're berr-st'ng w'th thous'nd-pound 'aand-outs on unwraetten boooks.

Look, handkerchief dabbing sweated brow, if Gael Jackson thinks he's a genius because Howard Cutting wrote a rave review, he's about to learn the hard way that reviewers put themselves before the book, always.

Aet's thaat damn aegint put 'aemself befurr Jackson! Ae'd n'verr 'aeve thurrght ae 't oth'rrwaise. Bluuddy connaiv'ng leechis. Tha r'laetionship b'tween aegint aand puublisher aes knife aand thrort, aand ah'll leave you t' guiss which aes which, shoving homburg on head stalking out.

Tweedie and Tweedie offices distinctly unrelated to the élan of an exceptional list: drafty stairs leading to small landings lined with dusty shelves; posters announcing books published, when posters still announced books published, becoming older the higher the ascent; rooms cramped barely furnished two to each storey. A heritage building not scheduled for demolition nor renovation performing environmentally unfriendly acts: icebox in winter furnace in the single heatwave each summer currently visiting early ahead of the sun zenithing Cancer now Taurus in June.

Justin wearing a bespoke non-iron nothing-less-than-white shirt branded cufflinks removed, sleeves rolled up, silk tie long since loosened, collar unbuttoned showing a column of tanned throat sternum, hands clasped behind head foot resting on barathea-suited knee yoga-style, suede leather shoes discarded under desk.

These bloody proofs, red-penning serpentine sentences footnotes profligate throughout the text, Bernard's damn well hydraed from sexy scholar to monolith-making monster. Shielding himself from potential arrows-in-the-eye shot from you're-pissing-on-my-territory contenders, I suppose. Well, pushing paper piles aside, he'll just have to play Hercules in a peer-reviewed journal. This'd basilisk a Tweedie reader.

At Court: Love previously perfect in typescript erudite yet acute amusing anecdotal: the problem of the woman's sexaltared position in Mediaeval Courtly society and literature sexamined simply. Far-ranging subtle quotations supporting various theories—the social sexplanation, the Arabic penetration, the classical patroheritage, the influence of the strumpeted-up Albigensian heraresy—included succinctly.

Sighing eyeing the chapter from a newly heralded *fille sophiste*, reading pleasurably surprised on finding a light spicy treatment of the influence of the liturges on mediaeval religious poetry, unbelievable as the proposition first appeared. Hmm, flipping pen tapping ballpoint tapping pushbutton tapping ballpoint tapping pushbutton tapping, has she no academic emotional superiority or has she just conveniently forgotten hers? Because I've invited her to rewrite a few pages? And she'll be boringly pedantic like Bernard with his obsessive compulsive didactics? Stretching arms above head staring out the attic window at the London haze brown below an azure late-afternoon sky, I should just rethink my acquisition strategy. No. Women have the more skilful approach. And gays. Only a straight woman or a homosexual could handle At Court: Love with such a conducive touch.

Now, how to flame-throw Bernard with the silk-stockinged Nicolette protecting his intellectual arse? Dammit, setting aside the approved chapter, I should've taken him to dinner at the Black Swan in Soho. Nothing like a gay bar, smirking, to loosen Bernard's inhibitions. Checking the reflection tanning-salon ruddy not Mediterranean sunny in the mirror, god I need a drink.

Slinging suit jacket over shoulder slipping on shoes skipping lithely down the stairs. Outside the building hesitating, wine bar beckoning but a certain dark-skinned Sanuri possibly sipping caffè macchiato in Russell Square luring Justin to Kafka Nero instead. Dreaming of sand sea long limbs belonging most likely to Andrew not Hussein remaining unseen for the length of a caffè frappé slowly swallowed.

Klaus-Meine whistling along the street stopping for the whisky double to numb disappointment continuing to Drayton Gardens the no longer no land of man between Kensington and Chelsea, Bernard and Nicolette resident in a modest two bedroom conversion.

Nicolette Baraté, distinguished by several capital letters connoting accomplishment, opening the front door. Dyed dark hair cropped in layered bob perfectly plucked eyebrows aquiline nose all combining to emphasise Gallic extraction elegant suit tailored to disguise anorexic proportions.

Bonsoir Just-in, air-pecking cheeks, Berr-narr eez longing to see you. 'e eez 'aving ze usual *craque* before printing. You 'ave to tell 'eem 'eez book eez wonderfool.

Bonsoir Nicky, following the tall figure to the salon startled at the sight of a female seated on the couch facing Bernard standing striding forwards hand extended to clasp hand heartily looking no more likely to *craquer* than Justin to sexual *réorienter*.

Hello Justin. I gather you've already met Julia Grampion, eyes lingering on curves plumping out spaghetti-string white dress black scarf draped around shoulders.

Oh yes, at the philology do, noting bleached wisps of short hair golden tan no salon there contrasting with blue-grey eyes made sparkling perhaps by having written a spesemen chapter.

Julia tells me you're interested in her thesis Justin. I can tell you, winking, it's very good. I examined her, inspecting neckline side-seams hemline calves hips breasts undressed. She's agreed to contribute to that book we were discussing, sitting rubbing hands, so I thought we may as well discuss the whole affair: my book, her book, and our book.

Oh you did, did you, sitting nostrils flaring.

Berr-narr, give your guest a drink, Nicolette lifting a languid eyebrow at the monogroom.

Oh sorry Justin. Gee and tee? Whisky soda?

Whisky, no ice. A straight double, if I may.

Hard day at the oh-*fies*?

Yes actually. Your damn proofs. Nicolette glance-spearing Justin laughing turning to Julia, thank you for the chapter. It looks promising.

Oh no hurry with it, twirling hair between fingers gaze flicking sideways at Bernard staring at the pert mouth pouting.

Justin leaning against the couch eyes narrowing, bloody Bernard. No wonder he was so keen to suggest analysis of adultery. Julia your belief in the precipitousness of publishers is touching.

Laughing, I don't expect it's what you want at all Justin. Nothing like as much fun as I'm sure At Court: Love must be. When is the release date?

August, watching Bernard eyeing Julia studying Nicolette glaring at Justin, but we may have to postpone it.

Why?/How so?/*Mon Dieu*!

Various reasons, frowning shrugging yawning behind a polite wrist. Could you pass by Tweedie tomorrow Bernard? Be good to have a chat, just the two of us.

'Fraid not. Examinations.

Chérie, ze cheese *soufflé* must be just about ready now. Shall we eat? Nicolette standing smoothing palms over pencil skirt, gesturing towards the dining alcove at the far side of the salon. Berr-narr, if you would take Julia, offering an arm to Justin rising graciously walking to allotted chairs.

Of course I'll take Julia, bending over eye-me decolletage, breasts bouncing, the taken taking the seat.

Bernard opening a chilled bottle of *Chablis* ice-bucketed on the table, sorry it's not Spanish, but Nicolette insisted.

Between mouthfuls of *soufflé* and sips of *Chablis*, you might think about cutting these additions Bernard, and going back to the original version, no? It had a lovely voice to it.

Just-in, don't be rideeculous, Nicolette placing cutlery precisely at midday on an empty plate, 'ee 'asn't written a no-veil. Eet eez a scholarly work. You're supposed, lip curling, to lose money on eet. 'Ow would ze Ooniversity, or ze publeec, react if my work on ze early Latin inscreeptions were to be popularised?

I didn't suggest buying the film rights, Nicolette. Far from it. If Bernard wants to be on a prestige list, he should have sent the manuscript to a University Press. You know as well as I do that it wouldn't have been accepted, because the manuscript wasn't that type of book.

Oh but Nicolette's right, Julia nodding at the hostess, Bernard's book should be an academic treatise. Dumbing it down for mass consumption would be sacrilege.

Really? So I know what to expect with the rest of your rewrite Julia? Chin stroking smiling slightly at the pink tinting cheeks, or from the joint affront on adultery. Mediaeval, that is.

Bernard chortling pouring more wine Nicolette collecting plates, disappearing inside the kitchen returning with coffee, Berr-narr bring ze cognac, sitting offering a salver of chocolate truffles to Julia.

Brandy braced, well Bernard it's your book and only our imprint. Your contract, Justin folding the serviette neatly on the table, stipulates additional charges for excess alterations to the proofs. With all these changes you insist on making, half the pages have to be reset and the printer will charge an arm and a leg, downing coffee dregs. I'll talk to Tweedie Senior about it and let you know.

Of course. I'm sure we can come to some sort of—er—compromise.

Qualité 'as no bizeeness weez compromise, Nicolette sniffing lifting one shoulder. Look at Oxford.

Oh piffle. Oxford is incestuous. London University is far more lively Nicolette.

Précisément Bernard. Fool of oonnecessary deestractions, smiling at Julia.

But that's *La Vie*, Bernard smiling at Julia. Justin looking at the ceiling cornices.

University life can be rather bland, Julia stirring cream in steaming coffee, but so is London without . . . friends.

The UK isn't the one-stop-shop for an education it supposedly once was, Justin stretching legs standing, or for the radical student experience either. Nicky sorry to break up the party, leaning down smacking lips beside each ear, dinner was *superb*. Julia, can I walk you to a bus stop? The nearest tube?

I—erm—I—ah—it's very kind of you, twirling hair strands, but I think . . . I'd rather stay and chat a bit longer with Nicolette and—and Bernard. I want to discuss the other book.

Shrugging on the well-cut jacket blowing a silent *tant pis pour toi* kiss at Julia shaking manly hands, I'll see myself out thanks.

Walking towards South Kensington station through the night warmth of mid-summer, scorning the transparency of the coquette the complacency of Nicolette the indecency of l'homme scarlet. Boarding the train irritated, damned ar'th'rs! Better an agent to massage their egos. And better to be on holidays. Sitges, Mykonos, Viareggio, Plage de anywhere with anyone. Even, sighing, with Andrew. Unless—

A dark figure, head swathed in yellow turban wearing a tailored white shirt brown shawl arranged round broad shoulders a long bright blue open skirt covering black trousers, looming high above the crowd on the platform at Leicester Square: Hussein.

Justin! I have been to a party, ivory teeth flashing bright as the overhead neon light.

Head rearing upright, fancy dress Hussein?

Yes, we wear our dresses for special occasions. Many other Sanurri were there also.

A feast day?

No. Doctor Borrodick, you know him? Justin nodding no.

I work with him at the University. He held a farewell party for me. We sang much po-ettery.

Farewell? Heart thumping climbing the steps leading from the warren of the London Underground.

Like this one about the elephant—*O ugly father, old bull of Kusi Bayo,* improvising a translation, *stupid one with dangling ears, you stumble and roar like the winter sky.* It is beautiful?

Yes, breathing heavily, when do you leave?

Tomorrow, scanning posters claiming wonders of age-defying uplift lining the walls of this ascent from Avernus. Look, Justin, another—*O you with your dorrooping berreasts that wander to your knees, give yourself to me. Your eyes are shields, black with white shield-cloths. O my love which burrns like fire, which seizes like colic.* You like this one?

Standing on the last step, spiralling quickly eyes level with the yellow turban, Hussein I want to hear more . . . Come home with me, tell me your poetry, pressing a body burning like fire seized with colic against torso impervious, gripping broad shoulders.

Hussein unsmiling side-stepping walking past a ticket collector, striding up stairs, stopping facing Justin panting in the cool outside air.

Justin, voice soft, I'm sorry. I cannot.

No of course, voice cracking. Stupid of me. Forget it.

They gave it to him and it did not fill the ring of the thumb and forefinger, addressing the soulless shop windows of Charing Cross Road, they took it away and it seemed to fill the whole plain.

Justin a tragic figure, goodbye Hussein. Good luck, hand extended.

Hussein smiling bowing shaking hands, goodbye. Words following Justin diving inside the mouth of Hades, parray to your angel Justin, parray to your angel.

13

JOJEENA.

Opening the door to eyes gleaming dark Hussein wrapped in colourful costume.

I have come to say goodbye to you, black silk contrasting with titian hair stark framing white face.

Hussein, wide blue eyes glistening, when are you leaving?

Tomorrow at night. When He has sown His *je-cheb* nuts in the sky, lifting a hand to the beloved hair.

Georgina leaning away.

Hand falling, I walked in the street so long Jojeena. The windows to the soul have no axe to cut mountains, the empty vessel has no sails.

Arms crossing holding waist.

Stepping across the threshold, since the beggar would come anyway, it's best to invite him.

J-just for a . . . moment, pivoting aside, closing the door.

You are the red star shining brightest, following luminesence to the cushions.

Venus?

Yes. On my tongue she is *Sahra*.

Mutually sitting gazing.

Unwinding the yellow turban, I composed a po-em for you.

Raising palms, no Hussein.

Smiling, lifting the direframe, voice musichall, between five red cushions, between four walls, I sit on the ground. Between five plates, between two cups, I have eaten and I am hungerry. I have stretched and I have not slept. I am devourred.

Why five? Swallowing, hands fluttering to rest clasped 日本 の スタイル.

I am borroken like the horn of a goat. My hands are storronger than yours, they have cut down the *balambaal* terree. My feet are storronger than yours, they will reach Sanurri. My eyes are storronger than yours, they follow the vulture flying. My heart is not storrong like yours, it berreaks like a gourd. Love storrikes men like the borranch of the terree falling. O Jojeena, how long shall I meet you with my eyes. A javelin without blood is not a javelin. Love without you is not love, leaning towards Georgina, hands grasping hanks of hair pulling heads together. Jojeena we will feast on each other as the fire feasts on the plain. Your mouth is the first flame.

No Hussein. No—

Lips covering lips dusky fingers pale nails tracing features stroking neck shoulders waist pressing ribs and caressing maemories. Hooking arm under knees scooping a loose-limbed Oriental puppet lowered to the cotton mattress on bamboo mat flooring in the other room.

Ebony shoulder pillowing Georgina weeping, red hair seaweeding the broad chest stomach roped with an ivory arm wood grain of the ceiling fascinating dark eyes.

Jojeena stop crying. I will stay.

You know you can't.

If I go back, I will be the bustard who has seen an enemy and cannot sleep. I will be the li-oness, clamouring for her cubs killed by the new li-on. My torribe will eat itself and I am hungerry with it.

Breath held, and Allah?

Softly, *Qarsa malqau Qawayu.*

Georgina sighing listening to pulmonary BOOm-b'm BOOm-b'm BOOm-b'm.

Old god, decorrepit old god. You have ears as old as the mountains, listen. You have eyes like the sea, look. You have hands like the scorreched plain, take all the camels. You love bea-utiful black women, love them. Leave me with Jojeena, white as an elephant's tusk.

Trembling, why do you address Allah in Sanuri but continue in English? Chin leaning on chest, don't you mean your words Hussein?

Jojeena it is not a pray-er to Him, but to the old one, head nestled to shoulder, hair stroked. Georgina sleeping Hussein awake watching moonlight sinking fading silver turning golden sunlight rising sliding over wooden ceilings.

Breaking the feast at the low table, your eyes are the mountain lakes Jojeena. I will cancel my ticket and tell the plane to fly away.

No Hussein, tea sipped slowly curling steam drifting memories blown as breath rippling across tea. Why don't you go home first, see how things . . . develop. If you can't forget me, you'll come back. I'll be . . . here.

Maybe the Continental will make Europe, maybe the stars will grow impatient and sleep, voice sad baritone.

Hussein you must go, you've your ticket and . . . tonight will be awful and I'll miss you, but if you stay it'll be worse. You'll go back eventually, because your family . . . and think of the practicalities.

I will cancel my ticket, sugar avalanching in tea.

Go and talk to Paul first. Please. He might suggest . . . how you could earn money if you stay.

Jojeena, reaching across the table to tuck strands of fire behind an ear, I will not fly tonight.

Leaning against the front door after Hussein leaving taking the scent not of earth but of Sanuri heat, sighing selecting a cigarette. Window ajar smoke floating out street sounds roaring in. Stubbing the cigarette, reaching for the handset to call Paul arriving at the office.

BRRIING! RRIING! BRR-RRING!

That can only be . . . Pulling on a wrap running down the stairs yanking open the front door. Paul unsmiling.

Julia I need your help. It's Hussein and it's urgent. I don't want to discuss it here.

Oh but I'm not—er—well you'd better come up I suppose, face pale, brow sweat-sheened, face scarlet, body shivering. Be still my beating heart. I really should be exercising more, entering the bedsit.

Coffee?

I don't have much time, surveying the room, but—ah, yes if you don't mind, sitting at the table breathing in familiar smells gazing at familiar curves distant desired in the instant of appearing.

So, pouring coffee, what's up?

Georgina rang me earlier. Hussein is supposed to be flying tonight, swallowing a large mouthful of coffee, and apparently after his farewell party last night he went to—er—say goodbye. Only now he's decided he's not going back.

I don't see the drama. Why should he? Sipping coffee, watching Paul watching. I only miss him now he's here. A little bit of Bernard in my hair.

Frowning, for heaven's sake Julia. You know as well as I do why not. And look at poor Georgina. She knows he'll leave, sooner or later. The longer he stays, the harder it will be once he's gone. She'll miss him dreadfully.

Silently: I thought I'd miss you dreadfully too. Aloud: Perhaps, lowering the coffee cup.

Remember Gulenne, who stayed in Europe for that Dutch girl? He had to cut himself off completely, give up his religion, his family. He's been working in construction doing odd jobs, you know. Hussein can't do that. His clan, his tribe . . . his father. His background is completely different.

I don't see how I can help, fingers twisting hair.

Georgina said she told him to come and see me first, so I'll have to be in my room all day. But it's possible he won't. I rang the campus travel office and they'll call me if he goes there. Mind if I smoke?

Of course not, tilting the window open.

You won't?

Head shaking no.

Problem is, sucking deeply, Hussein might think I want him to leave. Or that I won't help him find work.

Hardly, pouring more coffee.

He could, frowning scratching the jaw-bristling shadow, but he trusts you and wouldn't be suspicious if you talked to him. Would you go round to his place, please?

When? Who knows what time he's likely to turn up there, if at all? You're not expecting me to hang round the East End the whole day, surely?

Oh darling I didn't mean hang round. I meant, red-faced rubbing nose, could you pass by and if he's not home, leave a message asking to meet up so you can say goodbye. You can't do more than that.

No and it's none of my business. I've already said goodbye. He was at the Reading Room yesterday.

Well tell him you have an urgent message from me or Georgina. Say she's gone away. Say anything.

Silently: And a few *Avé Maria* for the white lies? Aloud: I'll do my best.

Oh Julia. Thank you, forehead kissed beard caressing cheek Julia turning aside staring out the window Paul insisting on lips kissing.

W'll if ut aint mista Brodrick! Mrs Moffat standing beaming in the doorway. Aint tart luverly. Such a gnoice sur-proiz. Oi allayz sed t' Miz Julia she were roit strict wi' chew she woz, sendin' yer out loike tart ev'ry noit. She were roit extreme, she woz.

Paul shrugging smiling raising eyebrows at Julia: mouth opened closed lips pursed.

That's very kind of you, Mrs Moffat. I have to dash, *sotto voce*, Mrs Moffat leaning forwards ears flapping, any doubts Julia?

Yes, *sotto voce*, you know how I feel about interfering. But I'll do it.

Thank you. Goodbye, walking to the door.

Dowtz? Oi sh'd tink not. Youz w'z eva such a gnoice cuppull. It weren't roit Mista Brodrick, you not cummin' no more. Miz Julia got very down.

Paul smiling narrowing blue eyes fixed on an erstwhile fiancée. Turning disappearing down the staircase no backward glance.

What happened to you? I thought you'd taken the day off! Bernard shoulder-leaning Julia arm extended to finger-tap a title on the screen showing catalogue search results breath warm on neck. That one would be useful.

Julia twitching forwards, mouth hardly moving, oh I'd—ther stuff to—first. —nd weren't—pposed to—xamining—day?

Laughing, all day? Whatever gave you that idea? As if I wouldn't want to follow up on our project.

Last night's supper, ssspering, you said—

—Oh yes. To Justin. *NGRHNGH!* So I didn't have to go his office.

Hissing, a pity you didn't. Turning, Bernard open-mouthed staring at the well-dressed Reading Room Reader snapping closed a tome to stalk away from the row of catalogue terminals.

Hoarsely, some people are just so rude. Have lunch with me?

Um-hmm, just let me finish reserving these books.

Of course. Then you can re-serve me, winking.

I have to be back by one thirty, cardigan folded inside shoulder bag, carouseling through the doors of the building.

Why? Grasping an elbow shepherding Julia down the marble steps enveloped in enduring heat.

Hussein might pass by looking for me, fluffing out hair.

Popular girl, aren't you? Anyone else I should know about?

Oh come off it.

Sweetheart I'm just teasing. I don't want anyone else taking your attention, hand sliding round the upper of an arm fingers brushing soft cotton clinging to a mound of mammary. You look just as gorgeous today as you did last night. I'm sure I dreamt about you.

Smiling slightly watching traffic, crossing the road as invited ignoring the attempt to caress.

Sighing, Julia I need to talk to you. Nicolette and I had a massive row last night.

Oh, frowning twirling curls around a finger, but nothing happen—

—About At Court: Love, miserably. She insists—

—But that's nothing to do with her area of expertise! Clutching a jacketed arm, stopping mid-footpath, facing Bernard. Lunchtime crowds jostling splitting babbling bellowing. Let's go eat somewhere quiet Bernard, so we can discuss it.

Ristorante Castelli Romani: Apennine cool *casale* dark intimate quiet decorated with mock vine-trellising Frascati bottles *mandolino* music; waiters appropriately speculative attentive responsive humouring toe-curling attempts to order *lingueeny allay vongolay, salada, ay bistaykah allay florentinay per favoray. Si si, signore, perfetto. E da bere? Acqua e vino? See, graziay.*

Suggestive undoing of shirt buttons revealing dark infurred chest inviting a cavalry hand to tangle in tight curls. Bernard dipping crusts of bread in oil feeding Julia, pouring *vino per la donna acqua per l'uomo*, recounting the miseries of a marriage more celibate than salacious. Julia coyly sympathetic encouraging attraction engaging intellect esteeming the Tweedie opinion of *At Court: Love.*

Come on Bernard, it's a potential hit, even if you won't admit it. I mean, who on earth cares about ancient writings on a wall? Nobody except another academic in the field would be even the slightest bit interested. But mediaeval love affairs and troubadour lyrics? Look at modern pop songs, soap opera, films, theatre—full of the remnants of both. And that imprint Red Rose publishing every type of romance imaginable. The genre is an unbeatable cash cow.

Well I didn't glam it up that much!

I'm not saying you did. I've seen your journal articles Bernard. I've no doubt you've thoroughly researched the book. But cluttering such an emotional subject with reams of footnotes will just bomb it. Justin wouldn't have accepted the original version unless it was exactly what they wanted.

Julia, stroking a palm, why on earth didn't you say this last night?

Had I said this last night, you'd have thought I was supporting . . ?

You've a point there.

Justin and Nicolette locked horns. I didn't actually want to agree with her because she's so . . . so overwhelming. As if your original work wasn't good enough on its own. I'm sure it is.

Kissing a wrist, you're going to swell my head.

And I thought you'd realise Justin knew what he was talking about. I mean, if I'd bashed you ad hominem with his opinion . . .

I'd have dug my heels in even more?

Well . . . supporters quite often become scapegoats.

My god Julia. Beauty and brains. You're lethal, finger tracing a path along an arm to the hollow above a collarbone, eyes glazing at skin unadorned by a crucifix. I'll have to watch myself around you.

Bernard you don't need to be afraid of making it readable, smiling stretching neck, feelionly anticipatory, just remove the waffle.

But . . . look at the hermetic love-language of the *trobar clus* in Provençal. Far too controversial to choose just one interpretation without footnoting the others.

Sighing, you do have odd interests, twirling hair.

I love the way you curl your hair, fingers slipping through curls.

Stilling all fingers, look Bernard, Justin wants to publish a book interesting to different kinds of readers. No one wants to admit it, but we're all infected with the dirge of Romantic Love. It's an invented ideal. Nowadays we don't declare 'I love you', we say 'as a romfic character would say, I love you'. We know we're kidding ourselves.

Laughing, I'm an incurable romantic, *espresso corretto* quaffed signalling for the bill, maybe that's why I chose the topic.

Sighing, you're not alone there. I thought nothing could interfere with Paul and me. Or Georgina andohmygod, it's almost two! We have to go.

Waiting at the cash register to sign, heavy masculine handling feminine hip curve of buttocks. Julia shuddering pupils dilating genus stalls blood-filling blinking dazed in scorching summer street heat arriving flushed at the British Mausoleum Reading Room.

Concentration impossible. Bernard passing notes scrawled in Gothic

Middle English Provençal. Julia analysing writing not reading list, block-printing: a sensuous self-assured lover given to occasional lapses in confidence, tokening the conclusion to the petitioning gallant.

Big Ben chiming the hour of five echoing distantly no sign of Hussein no desire in Julia to repeat the morning journey to no avail Bernard available in the hall. Hugging bare arm, rubbing almost bare breasts, guiding steps to the Lambretta, I want to take you. For a long ride. Somewhere deserted.

Pouting, desire mounting, why don't you give me a lift? To my place.

Legs straddling Lambretta arms wrapped around thick body. Bruiting off swerving round traffic filling Gower Street the heat of one searing the other.

Half naked lying on the bed Bernard babied against a shoulder.

Bernard it's fine. It doesn't . . . matter. We just rushed things.

Bitterly, I rushed things. I was so worried you'd—that I wouldn't—dammit.

It's not the end of the world.

I wanted, looking doleful, our first time to be perfect.

It will be. This was just the—er—warm-up, hands spider-walking over hairy chest stomach abdomen, tongue in mouth, Bernard shuddering pupils dilating genus stalls blood-filling—

RATATATATAT!

Bernard startling Julia sitting tangling arms awkwardly in—

RATAT TATARATAT RATATAT!

If it's Monique I'm going to scream, knotting the dressing gown tightly, Bernard pulling on trousers.

Unlocking the door chain still fastened peeping at—

Paul! What are you doing here?

Mrs Moffat said you'd not been long back, frowning. Did you look for Hussein? Did you find him?

Er—no. He wasn't at his place this morning. Nobody saw him, either.

Yes I know that, eyes narrowed eyebrows raised. Did you leave a message for him? And why are we standing here whispering?

I left a message. And he wasn't at the Reading Room.

He didn't show up at the campus travel office and he's not answering his phone. Julia, leaning on the door frame, aren't you going to open the wretched door?

Maybe Hussein's decided to fly?

No he'd have to have packed. I rang there looking for him. You didn't go back there, did you?

No Paul I didn't. I was exhausted, miming a large yawn, all I wanted—

c-r-E-E-E-a-k . . . c-R-E-e-e-A-K

Eyes widening closing opening staring accusation nostrils flaring mouth thinning inhaling slowly. All you wanted. I see. Thanks for your help. Sorry to have disturbed your . . . siesta, heel turning trotting down the staircase no backward glance.

14

STALL-HOLDERS of Berwick Market Soho shouting, yer COCKnee bast'd *porca miseria che stronzata stai facendo* WOTCH wear yer toss'n' dem FOOK'n' spuds *me ne frego un cazzo* git der lorry ou' der fook'n' way *ma VAFFANCULO dammi le carote* bloimey w'cher FINK y'r do'n' w' dem 'chokes *figlio di troia faccio quello che non fai TU* bejayzuz 'n' 'is desighpills will yer bloom'n' MOOOOF y'r bl'dy ars 'n' unload der colleys *ma sei un pezzo di merda t'h'detto MELONE cosi come Cristina* der cherries wiv der strawbs 'n' der obajeans wiv der corjets yer FRUIT w'cher fink weef go' all blinkin' day? Fook'n' 'ell. *Sono gia le sei! Sprigati . . . TESTA in cacca, veramente.*

Daily Cart Essen shops cafés closed, whores still trading, boys-in-blue beating, streets almost empty awaiting the morning alarm-groan-shower-toast-coffee-tea not for me-dressed-run-missed it again shit-bus-tube-bitch-arse-delays expected today-thank you sir-welcome madam rush-hour storm-in-a-takeaway-cup.

Wudcher coppa loada 'im wiv der bloom'n' cam'l! *Ma non e vero, vedi il vucumprà!*

Along the alleyway aprons appearing beneath bosoms heaving crates of corn dropped jaws limbs akimbo lookatderjimbo. Hussein a flamboyant figure leading a baby camel laden with various violently-hued fabrics through the gawping stall-holders and stand-still trucks. Windows opening shop-grills clanging shutters banging, people clustering but outside the spitting range of a juvenile dromedary trailed by an exotic chaperone.

Excuse me sir, baton tapping, what's wiv the camel? 'ave you a permit?

Stroking the camel's nose, Gedo is my permit. I marry Jojeena.

Grasping the rope tugging, Hussein beaming unmoving. Dropping the rope, are you wiv the Circus sir?

Elbowing the tallaw colleague, voice deferential, have you—er—lost your way sir? Are you staying in that hotel in—er—St Martin's Lane?

Hussein smiling petting Gedo.

Whispering to the shorter colleague, you mean 'e's one of dem rich furriners? Oh lordy 'e won't speak no English now will 'e? Should we call for assistance?

Squaring broad blue shoulders, I'm afraid you can't take your camel through the market sir. Food regulations and all. Where are you staying?

Crowd staring, curiosity felining, 'chew spose 't eats cabbiges? *Sai, a volta ho mangiato carne di cammello.*

Move along please, no need for panic, baton waving easy match for a cheerleader, the situation is well under control. Sir your name?

But if 'e don't speak—

—My name is Hussein Mekahil Abdillahi.

Oi 'e's notta Sick 'e's a mat kissa. You wocher mowf you'll 'ave 'em gavvers on 's for arrow knee arse polly ticklin'.

And is your domicile—er—the hotel sir?

I have not understood, smiling.

Where do you live, Mister—er . . .

Hussein. I am Hussein. I lived here, scrawling an address. Now I will live here, scrawling the address of the goddess. Before that I lived in Sanurri.

Er—so you aren't with the Circus?

'e's not ef'n fam'sh. Well, 'e looks famished t' me. Prolly needs a decen' feed. Poor bl'dy cam'l.

And you aren't staying in St Martin's Lane?

I stay with two Angels, not the Lain Saint.

Oi, 'e's go' 'n 'arrum, 'e 'as. See, wot oi sed.

Your passport, Mr . . .

Hussein. I am Hussein. My passport is with my papers.

I see. Mr Hussein, without the necessary documentation—

—Oi, shouting, wotchew doin'? 'e's eat'n' moi apples! Git 'im orff, waving red-faced at Gedo Hussein lawyal warders.

Hussein leaning gently on the rope, Gedo cantering proudly forwards, ordermen tall short scurrying beside batons bobbing.

Mr Hussein, puffing, you've no identification, no documentation, I'm afraid—

—I go to Jojeena, side-stepping a tramp blinking bleary-eyed prone on the pavement, I marry her. Gedo is my gift. You have my turruth.

Yes, but—

—Lies can be overtaken, striding ahead, fortune remains young, the law is everlasting. Allah knows all and the noble inherit the news, leading Gedo across the street.

The traffic'll be startin', long strides still too short, you can't just go prancin' round So'o wiv a camel.

Really Mr Hussein, running stumbling swearing, this is highly irregular.

No I have taken the regular route, patting Gedo's nose. Here is Warwick Street, halting in front of the destination building.

'ey? 'dchew see that? 'e's go' a cam'l. Gitcha phone ova t' der windah. Gorn! Gitit on film 'arold. Oi ring up der news. I dunno wotsa numma fuggryinowtfugginlowd. Turn der telly orn yer idjit. Yes Greg, the radio - call them! Yes of course send an MMS! Ah hullo, is that the news? There's a camel. Nah, some Indian fella, big 'n' black, wiv a turbo. Didja uwchewbit? Well, he's standing outside the place opposite. Yes, that's right. No, only one hump. Dinchew 'ear me t' foirst toim? Oi sed a cam'l!

BRRRINGG! BRRRIIIIING! CLUNK CLUNK CLUNK! BRRRIIING! BRRRIIIIIING! BRRRIIIING!

Standing sleep-tousled peerless in the doorway, ohbyallthat'srosy! Who's sane, here?! A camel?!

Jojeena. You are an ostirrich standing in the morning and shaking her wings. Jojeena, I confirm your love with my perresent of Gedo. He is young, but he will gorrow. He bears you many-colourred cloths, loosening the bales of brilliance piling swathes of material on each outstretched arm.

Gedo, leaning towards the camel. I like him Hussein. Thank you. Where is he going to live?

With us.

I don't think he'll walk up the stairs to the third floor but on the other hand—eyes widening at growing numbers of gawping people police paparazzi—the warehouse across the road is empty. Let's put Gedo there for the moment. What does a camel eat?

Saltbush. But with the salt, he must dirrink much water. If he eats the leaves of the damag tree and the olive and the acacia, his thirst will be less.

Heaving the silks on one arm, I have some apples upstairs.

He will dirrink only again after the moon has waxed and waned. The ship waterred him. His hump is full.

Wait for me, disappearing behind the front door returning dressed in jeans blouse low-heeled boots, come on, let's put Gedo in his new home, to the scrutiny of an everchanging crowd pictures uploading story tagging blog commenting *The Camel and the Damsel* and *Dromedary in the Docks* and *Pets of the Rich and Famous*. Signing finally the last of the lately arrived DEFRA veterineaucratic documents. Rescued by the appearance of naked apes from PETA protesting fake not fur. With no ado about very much leaving Gedo stall-haltered in the warehouse leading Hussein up the stairs to the zone of 禅

15

I LIKED you from the moment I first met you Julia, and I'm absolutely delighted you were successful, Marion relaxing in the lone armchair stirring tea observing room, Hrothgar and Wiglaf busy with dress-up games under the table raiding in Old Norse fashion the wardrobe of the successful supplicant.

Wiglaf waving the poker, emerging in a green poplin skirt, I'm Merlin.

Yes and that's not Excalibur, smiling, we're visiting Julia to congratulate her, not subjugate her.

Have a piece of cake, Marion. It's lovely of you to drop by, and thank you for such a kind note. I'd almost given up on the job . . . so much water under the bridge since the interview, what with—

—*The Dowry of the Dromedary*, wasn't it? A nine-day 'net wonder?

Not only.

Raising an eyebrow declining to decipher, how did you become involved? You almost made celebrity status too.

Tell me about it, drawing a deep breath, those idiot reporters snooping after Hussein and inferring all kinds of garbage. I guess they tracked him down via the Afro-Asian Department and bothered Paul.

Paul?

Paul Brodrick. Hussein worked with him during semester. Paul and I . . . were engaged at one time, fingers knotting strands of hair. He asked me to help him find Hussein before the whole affair happened.

Ah.

GRRR. I'm a wyvern. *Wooosh*, Hrothgar spotted in leopard skin tights crawling from under the table head draped in red tassels dancing as flames, and I'm roasting you alive.

Don't dragons eat cream-cakes?

Tassels like the beards of old men drooping, only if there're no kings' younger sons around. Wiglaf! Cake! Mouths opening closing around sponged layers of jam cream icing.

The reporters were impossible, soooo annoying. Wasn't I Dr Brodrick's fiancée? Was it true I'd broken the engagement? Wasn't it because of Hussein?

It wasn't . . ?

TSK! Of course not. Hussein had nothing to do with Paul and I, swallowing rapidly looking out the window, I only hope the University doesn't kick up a fuss about this.

Stirring sugar in tea, over a few journos chasing after a camel? Hardly.

You don't know Professor Kriß! She's Head of School and was furious at Paul for being *persona interrogata*.

I doubt if there'll be one live link to the story by tomorrow, tea cup settled on saucer. Not like you raked any dirt, so nothing to interest anybody.

I never thought I'd say no comment and think bugger off at journalists, pouring more tea twitching fingers through curls. It isn't . . . well . . . that's not really the end of the saga.

Sipping tea, no? Eye contact avoided.

Well it's just—you know your children are amazingly well-behaved. Would you like some more cake kids?

Heads nodding lips sandwiching cake.

Julia lighting a cigarette, tilting open a window, oh sorry I shouldn't smoke with them here, flicking the cigarette away fidgeting with the lighter. Desmond Sykes requested comment for *The Platform*'s Gadabout's Gossip page on minority groups and inter-religious marriages. He could hardly ask Georgina.

Oh that dear man. How are you getting along with him?

Not too bad, he's asked for reviews here and there.

I know that Julia, beaming, I told him to. No it's nothing, don't make a fuss. So did you write the commentary?

I did . . . and then I realised that a few months ago, had he asked me, I'd have . . . I'd have just said no. I'd have made an excuse—I'd never have even considered it. I mean, ratting on friends' personal details for money, even if it's supposed to be for a good political cause.

Ah.

Mum when are we going home?

Fold up Julia's clothes and think up a new game. Shortly as I have to cook your father's dinner, sweeping cake crumbs from the table cloth dusting hands above the tea cup.

Have you more dress-up clothes Julia?

You can use the sheet to make a tent and play mountaineers if you like?

Boring, nose wrinkling. Wiglaf let's play The Wrath of Achilles. You be Hector, dragging the Trojan brother by the heels from the bed.

NO WAY! I'm MERLIN! Whacking Achilles.

OUCH! NO! YOU'RE HECTOR!

Kids! Before anything, the clothes. Folded please, pointing at the jumbled pile on the floor. Sorry Julia, we can't stay much longer but . . . this is rather a minor incident.

I suppose so. It's just . . . well, it's not really. It's the tip of the iceberg, sighing, I've just let myself go ever since I left academia. Everything I thought, ethics, values, principles have all . . . dissolved and it wasn't until I was staring at what I'd written that I realised.

But Julia, comforting hand covering table-tapping fingers, that's life. We all change what we think.

No. You don't. Georgina doesn't. Paul doesn't. It's a question of integrity in oneself, standing by one's own character and beliefs, irrespective of what others think. I agreed to find Hussein, and honestly Marion, I don't believe that was the right thing to do. But I . . . went along with it anyway.

Hrothgar dressed in red bearing a large frying pan and the poker standing to battle attention, you're the horse Wiglaf.

Marion pinching lower lip between forefinger and thumb, Julia are you a Catholic?

I'm A CATHOLIC AND I'm GOING TO MASSACRE THE PROTESTANTS. I'm SAINT BARTHOLOMEW.

Oh Hrothgar! Pipe down.

Laughing, I'm on Christmas carol acquaintance with God.

Blinking, oh.

Well I almost—but that's what I'm trying to say. Compromising over one big thing leads to another. And you know, the little white lies, somehow that leads to great big fat ones. Or starting to compete with whoever you're with, playing with words, playing language games, suddenly the games aren't just with words.

You don't think that happens everywhere? And especially in the literary world. Words are what make it go round, so long as the words translate to money.

Yes, of course. I must sound completely and naively idealistic. But somehow . . . I don't think I should take this job. I'm not . . . objectively suited to an academic path. I don't even know if I want it.

Stuff and nonsense. Utter garbage, beaming tugging trousers over ample thighs, you've a totally unrealistic view of academia. As full of petty jealousies and shifting integrities as any other pseudo-sanctuary of ethics, and worse, since it's better at cloistering all that behind the facade of intellectual brilliance and dispassionate analysis. Of course values change. I watched a play last week in which the word daddy was virile with sexual bigotry. Recently I read a novel in which the word mother became more and more ominous and freudly monstrous. Is nothing left meaning anything? The reality remains behind shifting values of words. And of feelings, cutting another slice of cake.

You mean a friendly monster, don't you Mum?

Ah jung doubts. No Hrothgar, I mean one's self.

Look, laughing nervously opening the new issue of *Astroloquacious*, it's in my stars. *An underlying crisis in occupational issues.* I don't like the new astrologer.

A wanna-be seer they've recovered?

I'm a SEE-ER, Wiglaf rushing under the table to reef out the green skirt.

You are advised to avoid change and maintain or increase income generating activities. A lot of help, that is.

Well there you are.

NOW I'm MERLIN AGAIN and YOU'RE GOING to be deVOURED by a PURPLE DRAGon. In his tummy there's a prince of fire and stone. But Uther Pendragon marries you at the bottom of the ocean. See.

I'm UTHER PENDRAGON and I'm marrying NO ONE.

No one's lucky then. But Merlin's a bit mournful. I'm not sure I like that prophecy.

Merlin's always mournful Julia, Wiglaf pulling off the skirt sitting cross-legged on the floor.

Marion wrist-tapping Julia, I suppose I've not understood the half of what you've said, but clearly you're going through a bad patch. Let it be, as someone famously sang. Leave any decisions for now about a job you aren't starting till October. You've the summer to think it over. It's six o'clock and we have to make a move. Can I help you cleaning up while the boys pick up the clothes?

That's very kind of you Marion, and thank you so much for visiting. But no, rising gathering crockery, this will only take me a few minutes. And I'm dying for a cigarette, smiling closing the door at the departure of Nordic equanimity.

Dusting the table, WHAT a fool I am! Damn Paul. As if I should just come running whenever he snaps his fingers. And damn Bernard for not making more effort, turning on the hot water tap flinging the dishcloth in the sink, water spraying. Ouch! That's hot. Ha. Like me. Maybe I should call Bernard. Oh god, except I love Paul, wiping wet hands over hips. Georgina. I'll go and see how she and Hussein are doing. They're just so . . . so bloody organised, Hussein teaching English and Georgina critting all and sundry. No wonder Desmond's mad about her, touching rouge to lips fluffing out hair a pouting reflection. But then again, he's mad about anyone, stepping neatly down the stairs outside to sultry twilight air.

Hussein! What are you doing here? Why aren't you at Georgina's?

She says she will not marry me. I walk the streets for meaning, Juli-a, is it wrong or is it right? She accepted Gedo and the silk.

Smiling clasping an arm, let it be, as a beetle once said, let it be.

B. Beat-all. This is an exercise of pronunci-ation for students? You are kind, Juli-a, but I am not thinking of my new job now.

No it's a saying Hussein.

This is of interest to me, white teeth gleaming again. You will explain?

Erm, twirling hair, when you're in a difficult situation and nothing you can do will affect it, leave the situation alone without trying to control it. Eventually enough time passes that the situation has changed without you realising it or having done anything.

That is philosophy or religi-on, perhaps.

Excuse me, balding stocky ill-fitting suit standing invading personal space, are you Mr Abu Dhabi, by any chance?

Blinking, voice hard, no he isn't.

I'm from the Wakefield Gazetteer. I'd like to ask you a few questions, Mr Abu Dhabi. Is this your new girlfriend?

No comment, pulling Hussein sideways down a short flight of steps, we've an appointment with the Father, shutting the door blocking the journapest from entering.

Juli-a! I may not pass here.

Of course you can Hussein, smiling walking forwards breathing in tranquilly incensed air, let me tell you about this church. It once belonged to the Portuguese Embassy, then to the Bavarian. It was destroyed in the Gordon Riots and rebuilt. Look at its simple white walls, square like the ceiling, although, here, you see the altar? Made of grey marble, not so austere. And the mosaic is beautiful, isn't it, all that gold. Eight columns for each golden letter, and look, here she is, Our Lady of Piccadilly, with her own altar, wearing a proper veil like the Madonnas in the Mediterranean countries. We'll have to be quiet Hussein, whispering at the sight of occupied pews, many people come even if they don't believe in her because it's so peaceful. Here, dipping a hand in the font, crucifying a crucifix-less chest, you can too. Kneeling. Hussein sitting gazing bedazzled at the stone shaped as a benefacta.

Mariam the mother of the porrophet Jesus, murmuring, she appears in our pagan poems too, known as Atete.

Atete?

A goddess. For fertility.

Light a candle with me Hussein, taking two of the tallest waxsticks, dropping coins in the box, Hussein lighting wicks, one for me and—

—one for me and Jojeena.

16

HEATWAVE elapsed, London sky cotton wool grey cloaking the herringbone twill of streets squares cul de sacs terraces, dissolving memories of exotic animals fabrics ménages à troisemblances in favour of sweltering temperatures at Brighton the annual exhibit of the Ascot fashion follies equestrian extravaganzas.

Except the litter-airy ouroborus swallowing Georgina and Hussein newly exotic couple the one a purveyor of instant status at any party the other an overnight poet featured in many magazines. Desmond Sykes, scooping the pool, persuading Hussein to read aloud poetry in translation original version for the Neo-Surrealists, by-word for Bayswater, protecting free verse against the rhymsters of the Neo-Augustan School. Matronescent dames plainly earnest Janes peacock-plumaged gays bohemian bandanaed blades congregating monthly for enraptured readings of "A", *Paterson, Among The Beasts, What The Grass Says, This Rock Ruminates*, or laterally literal derivations from Perec Kaplan Brossa Mathews Peterkiewicz, in faux-modestly flaunted apartments decorated with posters of Tate artists bearing no relevance to the recited verse but proclaimed avant the garde by the perpetutraitors of contemporary taste high culture, frissoning pleasure for the lack of recognition.

The last soirée of the season attracting more than the usual conspirators from rival factions no fractions at all to hear Hussein. Desmond gloomily ecstatic at the rise in pimping roadworthiness.

Literary cliques were invented after the disappearance of bear-baiting, smiling at the crowd rubbing hands slapping backs when not stabbing cracks, where's the assistant secretary? We need some more wine. Move those poetry exemplars over to the window sill, the table makes a good enough bar. Let me discourse briefly on the benefits of free verse, free speech, free love, and free intercourse between all nations before introducing our poets for this evening, including a very special gusset. Are we all settled? Good. Over to you, cherub.

My poem'th about the inthethtuouth moon, menthrually thphinxthing her therility:

Pale prothtitute of poetth, thleeping in thecret with your thibling Apollo . . .

Scattered applause, yes very good thank you. . . er . . . next. . . Ms Mouse, is it? Just stand over there dear no the microphone isn't a snake . . . no and it's not for practising fellacious diction either. Ready?

Legs spread
breasts bared
lips rouged
chest haired
knife plunged
pain shared
Freud plumbed . . .

Enthusiastic hand-clapping preceding tales from an inverted world the dialogue of two merry spinsters lamenting fertility the sojourn of a goat played by Nietzsche or a homeless literature professor or an investment banker in the wilds of suburbia. Hussein listening fascinated.

And we come to our presenter, not just our hero for his stunning looks, but the way he will chant his translations, on the fly hey hey, and because his poetry has a pheromenal power and magic. Let it descend upon you, open your soul like a flower, whether you be one of our most urbane, baneful, or fulsome listeners. I give you . . . Hussein Abdillahi!

Standing rhyming mesmerising, none noticing the arrival of a late attendee. Riotous applause.

My my Hussein, what an ovation, thank you thank you I'm filled with the most sepulchral of emotions, shall we adjourn, yes I think we can put away some of the folded chairs, drinks here on the table, nibbles on whomever you can provenance them.

Hussein towering beside Georgina and Julia, bowing to congratulations politely answering questions. Julia tranced by well-known faeces well-to-do traces booksoillers calumnists PR agents publicysts all acquiring pedestalled status.

What do you do?

Oh I'm writing a book commissioned by Tweedie and Tweedie, on mediaeval poetry.

Really. Faaaaascinating, eyes drifting over the crowd, who's your agent?

Agent? Oh I—Bernard?!

Julia.

Agent/publisher/poet forgotten. Staring twirling curls, what are you doing . . . you don't even . . . I'm really pleased to see you, missing cheek kissing mouth, heart beating faster.

I was trying to catch your eye, but I arrived late and you seemed . . . busy.

You're looking a bit stressed, hand-catching, what's wrong?

Nicolette decided to go to the college do, so I called at your place to see if you were home. I was . . . missing you, smiling thumb massaging soft wrist pulse fluttering, and I found this on your door.

This a crude drawing of rectangle surrounding skeleton and leafy branch white against black background undersigned unrecognisably in red.

Frowning, these are Sanuri characters. It looks ghastly.

It does rather. I . . . is it some sort of threat?

Threat? How could it be? And why me?

You tell me, mouth twisting.

Oh Bernard don't be an idiot. We'd better ask Hussein. Come on, weaving around puddles of people approaching the coterie cloistering the Sanurian songster.

Georgina I need to talk to you, whispering, can you ask Hussein to look at something for me please. But not here, nodding at the hubbub-filled room, let's go to the kitchen.

Looking at the drawing rigid as a statue eyes wide dark skin blanching deeply indrawn breath exhaled, Ali. My father sent him. He brings a curse.

Show me, Hussein.

No Jojeena you may not touch it.

Why is it on my door Hussein? What does it say?

It is تفريق, to separrate loverrs in how do you say . . . in, voice choking eyes closing, adulterry, eyes opening unfocused. Two verrses from the holy book القرآن.

Hussein you must tell me what this says—it's meant for me not Julia.

No, head shaking violently, it must not be said aloud!

Julia touching a shoulder, translate it Hussein, and its power is lost.

Sighing, evil on that day—to those who—terreated—our signs as lies, who terreated the day of judgement as a lie. This day will we forget you, as you forgot—the meeting with—this your day and—your—er—dwelling—no, abode—shall be the fire and no one shall be there to succour you. Seizing the arm of the spiritually attacked, Jojeena we must go! Crushing cardboard square shoving threat inside a trouser pocket.

We can't all leave together, unclasping hand seizing arm, and we can't leave officially yet without Desmond making a fuss. We have to keep this quiet Hussein. No press.

In a room full of gossip méchants, Bernard grimacing, good luck.

Julia come with me. If anyone asks we're going outside to smoke. We'll catch a cab and you follow, alright Hussein? Just say you're looking for me. Don't get caught up with anyone, even in the lift.

Jojeena no. I cannot stay here without you. Nor let you leave without me.

Oh Hussein, helplessly.

Quietly growing in stature shrinking in paunch, I'll stay with Hussein and leave with him.

Blue eyes wide staring, just who are you, anyway?

Sorry Georgina, I forgot to introduce you. This is . . . Bernard Reeves, my . . . thesis examiner. He—er—found that thing on—er—my door and brought it here, watching Bernard, you can trust him.

Ah . . . I see. On *your* door. Right. Well. Thank you Bernard, and pleased to meet you. If you wouldn't mind just deflecting attention. Leave us about ten minutes, kissing Hussein, and we'll meet you downstairs at the corner with a cab.

The journey to Warwick street silent. Bernard paying the taxi driver the threatened goggling at a replica of the first missile nailed to the front door.

Gedo is killed, Sanuri head bowing body slumping. Georgina and Julia running across to the warehouse Bernard following. The door gaping open like the wound in the hollow of the innocent throat. Blood staining the hay.

17

WET July rain pricking the windows of a London double-decker bus cityscape invisible from the upper deck front seat except as tearful exclamation marks. Flying blind sitting in silence feeling cold in wet sandals squashed sideways by the bulk of Bernard not pressing salaciously against a leather jacket astride the abandoned-in-the-rain Lambretta after emerging already moistly amorous following an afternoon delight in the back rows of the cinema ahead of progressing to dinner discussions on mediaeval adultery in the company of Nicolette.

Snuggling claustrophobically closer, still like me Julia?

Um-hm, gazing blankly out a misty window at traffic-shafted Shaftesbury Avenue.

Oh Julia, hand creeping under the labium of the summer jacket, I adore you.

I suppose if you must.

Our minds fit like hand and glove, our bodies . . .

Our bodies . . .

Don't do so badly either, squeezing a thigh.

I'm doing badly Bernard.

My sweet give it time. I don't like snatched half-hours and making out in the cinema any more than you, smirking, so UN-FULL-feeling, fingers sliding further along the pliant thigh.

Desire spasming, Bernard I have no objection to the prelude.

Of course not, but naturally we want the Logανde finale. Oh if we could just get away to Ibiza. Imagine: days and days in the hot sun, lying beside each other.

Frowning, you know Bernard, you've become so much more positive, much less cautious. You used to ask me if I love you, now it sounds like a placebo among friends.

Do you love me? Tell me you love me, if only at this moment.

Yes at this moment. But you talk in terms of setting up a *pied à terre*, of Ibiza this summer and Mallorca the next. You're just day-dreaming.

Day-dreaming! Wouldn't you marry me if I were free? I can't be, but would you? Don't you love me like that?

No. I don't.

I don't believe you Julia, not when you respond like this, fingers parting labia electrocuting flesh eliciting a gasp dying sigh Bernaaa . . .

Feel how much I want you, the bulge beneath a hand proof of the tart. Imagine all those nights we could have, hours and hours of nights.

Hours and hours. That's why you married Nicolette.

My god, you don't think we still . . . I couldn't count on one hand the number of brooms I'd need to clear the cobwebs.

Snorting, a vacuum cleaner would save you some effort.

Look. I was in love with her once, I'd be lying if I said otherwise. But she . . . she's French, for heaven's sake. How was I supposed to measure up to that? She just . . . never let me forget it, either.

There you are then, you'd end up blaming me sooner or later if I weren't English. And if she were truly Gallic, she'd have brought out your beast.

Exactly, thumbing the stud of a nipple, like you do. Don't fret pet, we'll temporally locate ourselves.

That won't change the state of affairs, Bernard.

Nothing to change, Julia. We're comfortably having one.

You can pun anything, can't you?

Sweetheart you're puncturing me.

I was talking, actually, about Nicolette.

Do stop punctuating the dialogue.

Gazing out the window discoursing with the self, but only your feelings matter Bernard. You don't give two hoots about mine, dismissed with your pithy *bon mots* and your assertion that comedy should impregnate life universally. You're merely flippant, as if this excuses you from the accusation of being too serious, but you claim I'm without humour. Real humour should illuminate the essential melancholy and macabre elements of life, as well as celebrate the unbelievable elation.

Punny for them, sweetness?

I'm just remembering my horoscope.

Scope for horror? Hot breath invading an ear, tell me all. I know an excellent charm against that.

It's that African curse. Why should it be on my door, playing with the crucifix, and why you, of all people, to be the one to find it?

Good grief, Julia. In this day and age, stilling fingers on the crucifix stroking skin beneath, you're not going to insist on believing it.

Yes I do.

Evidently without evidence.

Oh Bernard, swatting fingers turning to the window blowing hot air against the steaming pane. Hussein said it was to separate adulterous lovers!

And it was meant for Georgina, forehead smacked, proving how primitive all this voodoo is.

Over the droning of the bus nearing the crux of Knight's Bridge, all religions share basic truths Bernard. The devil is in the divine: Christ recognised magical poles—

—and sorcerous Huns?

Eyes rolling, Hussein told me that in the pagan Isharood tribes, the shaman blesses the earth with spit.

Eyes rolling, how obvious. Ejaculation of course.

Christ spat on the blind man's eyes.

Inverting Frazer to prove Christianity? Come on Julia. You're not that naive.

Why not? You admit it's a Modernist perspective, but the same revelation is universal, unilateral. The symbolism of the lamb Bernard. Think. All mediatory gods are lunar gods, with some symbol of horns, or lyres, or bows. Look at Plato's crucified soul of the world: its point of intersection is the equinox, the constellation of the Ram. And, tossing head fists clenching, Christ died in the constellation of the Ram.

:D :D :D slapping a thigh, Julia! What on earth have you been reading? Sacred text analysis on Joe Bellow's Blog?

Sighing looking out the window.

Sweetheart don't be like that, ankle slithering around ankle chin smooching chin, all I'm trying to say is that this is a real elephant between us. Pinkly irrelevant. You, stroking the column of throat, me, we're in love dammit. Nicolette isn't missing anything she hasn't thrown away already.

Yes but the deception is—

—you're sounding like a Harlequin heroin. Again.

And you aren't? Constantly telling me not to worry makes my worries bigger. A little *his-terrier*, even if barking up the wrong tree, would make me feel better.

Darling forgive me. You're tired and cold and still wet, fingers brushing a breast, and frustrated. With everything, I mean.

Moaning softly, head resting on accommodating shoulder, wriggling on the seat failing to dispel the horned hollow, Bernard I'm just so physically wound up.

I just adore you like this Julia, lips whispering in wisps of hair, I could eat you.

Yes but that would spoil your appetite for Nicolette's dinner.

But her dinner would never spoil my appetite for you.

The bus finally arriving in Fulham Road.

Ah Berr-narr. Hello Juli-ah, lips puckering bubble kissing, but you are wet. Come, ze *chauffage central* eez on. Zis Eenglish climate eez 'orrible. I'll breeng you an 'ot water bottle to warm your feet. Eet eez un'ealthy to stay wet.

Bernard winking behind the retreating back, not that unhealthy. Have a whiskey darling.

Head shaking wildly, mouthing are you mad? Gulping whiskey sitting haphazardly on the couch, Bernard benign relaxed in the armchair opposite.

'ere eez ze bottle. Uff, flopping on the couch, legs propped on the pouf, I am zoooo longing for our 'oliday.

When are you going?

Where are we going? To Italy. Ostia first, zen 'erculaneum and Pompeii. I will be eenspecting ze *graffiti* for my book.

Oh. Not Spain?

No not Spain, Bernard smiling fingers tapping the armrest, next year though.

I'd love to see Pompeii Nicolette. How lucky you are. I had no idea you were interested in urban art. Is there much street decoration around Naples? I suppose with it being the south of Italy—

—I'm not, arching a Gallic eyebrow, eenterested in urban art. I'm an epeegrapheest. *Graffiti anciens.* Eenscreeptions on walls, sniffing. 'ow are your feet?

Blushing, much warmer thank you. The whiskey helped.

Eet usually does.

So your book is about . . .

Not Pompeii, voice enthusiastic, but an analeezees of ze social eempleecations of zose eenscreeptions.

Rude ones, patting the wifely knee.

Shrugging one shoulder flicking away patronisation, a great deal eez still to be excavated. Ze *graffiti* give us eveedence of elections, trade, scandal, gladeeatoreeal shows, *etceterá.* Zey also 'elp scholars identeefy ze streets and ze buildeengs, ze private 'ouzes, ze temples—

Ze *lupanar*, grinning.

Zat needs no eenscreeptions Berr-narr. Why eez eet ze only zing ze Eenglish know of Pompeii?

Coughing slightly, Nicolette what about the specimens they've found preserved in the lava?

Oh zose? In ze Museum since a long time. Zey died in agony, face down, 'iding ze eyes. Like ze Palesteenians een an Eesraeli bleetz on Gaza.

Oh, pressing eyes shut gasping for breath.

Bernard leaning forwards, da-don't you feel well?

Chest heaving air gulping, it's nothing. Just . . . that's how they found my mother. Under a rubble heap in Afghanistan.

Ma pauv' petite! 'ave some more to drink. Berr-narr, angling an accusing finger, she eez very tired and wet. Did you come wiz 'er on zat 'orrible *motocyclette*?

No Nicolette, pouring more whiskey, we—er—came on the bus. But we were already wet.

Throat burning eyes watering, while we were walking. I—er—my shoes . . . that's when . . .

What 'ave you done to 'er? You are a—

—God! Nicolette it was raining and—the kitchen door swinging closed behind the warring wedlocked leaving Julia alone morbidly self-mocking on the couch.

Dinner a stoically witty pastime: Nicolette laconically authoritarian classical scholar scholarly classicist Bernard masking concern elevating tone legs brushing under the table elevating trunk. Over cognac coffee chocolates discussing books long forgotten Nicolette manning the piano efficiently Bernard manning the microphone erratically mutilating a repertoire of contemporary *Liebeslieder* replete with crude innuendo Teutonic Lyst least favourite linguam of a file-log scientist.

Pleading tiredness, departing on a wishful note, have a lovely holiday. I could do with one myself.

You need arrest Juli-ah.

You're right. I'll book a cheap flight. Thank you so much for a wonderful evening.

Julia you can't wait downstairs alone, let me hail you a cab.

Nonsense, I'll take the bus.

I'll wait with you at the bus stop. Nicolette where's the big umbrella?

Standing under drumming rain, where will you go?

Lucky dip. One of those one pound flights to wherever.

Can't you wait til . . . when I'm back. We can go together.

Oh don't be ridiculous Bernard. Anyway, here's my bus, smooching a shadowed cheek, signalling the driver. Enjoy Italy.

But, frowning jogging beside the back end of the bus—conductor nodding pony-tailed head, one born ev'ry minit ain't there luv—WHY?

Cupping mouth, I'VE SOME THINking to dooo . . . waving no backward glance.

18

THROUGH the summer working ignoring the University vacation, correcting the proofs of *A Grammar of the Sanuri Language* still finding mistakes misprints a never-ending narrative.

Muffled knocking door opening standing silently.

Hussein! I haven't seen you since my farewell party for you.

I am disturbing you?

Come in, I'm very glad to see you.

Eyes downcast, when cows are about to exit the stall, they lick one another. When men are about to die, they love one another.

Nodding slowly, which of us is about to die?

Sitting fingering a large white envelope, I will tell you a storry. It is funny but also verry sad. In the world there are therree misfortunes. The first is wealth because it gorrows, and when it has gorrown, the king wishes to seize it for himself. Therefore wealth is a misfortune. The second is woman. She falls in love with a warri-or who kills you and flies with her to another countorry. Therefore woman is a misfortune. The thirrd is God who has corre-ated us, one white, one red, and one black. Our father in the beginning was Adam, our mother was Eve. We are all borrothers. As God corre-ated us in the beginning, we should love one another, if we all looked alike. But He made us of therree kinds and we kill one another. Therefore God is a misfortune.

Smiling, God created malaria. Justly He also created the tree bark for medicine. He created love. Justly He also created patience.

It is very sad that we have so many porroverbs. One is against the other and a porroverb can be found to porrove anything we want.

Truly, proverbs can be misapplied. We, however, are not killing each other now.

You remember Ali, my borrother-in-law?

Nodding smiling remembering Hussein interpreting for a magistrate asking after twenty minutes, Well what are they saying? and the innocent reply, Nothing sir, they are just talking. Appreciating the unSanuri directness, yes I remember Ali.

Ali came here a few months ago and took a packing job, but it was my father who sent him. Ali talked to me many times telling me to come back. I had written to my father about Jojeena.

And you didn't listen to him?

Eyebrows lifting quickly lowered, yes I listened. For long hours I listened, hours as long as the road to the watering plain. But there was no water at the end and I was thirrsty.

Window opened cigarette lit, settling in the ergo chair, what did Ali do to slake your thirst?

He killed Gedo.

Ah. The incident in the Soho warehouse.

Nodding, on the tenth day of ذُو الحج. عيد الكبي, the Feast of Sacorrifice. It is lawful to kill a camel with a spear above the berreastbone.

Even a wedding present?

Shrugging, he killed, as you would say, two camels with one spear. That is sad but not so sad. Gedo was not well in the warehouse. He had little air and I could take him out to walk only early in the morning. And many times Jojeena had visits from people porrotesting the keeping of a camel.

You know it was Ali?

Look, placing the white envelope on the table, open it. Read those.

Where did you find these?

Juli-a's door. Jojeena's door.

Frowning, why Julia's door?

Ali is clever. He is also stupid. He read about me in the newspapers and saw Juli-a's name, that she was looking for me that day. He thought maybe I wanted two wives here. Or if one refused I take the other.

Perhaps he thought I did not want to return and therefore I marry an English girl. But that is—you told me your porroverb one day—loading the هودج with the camel.

Reading shuddering, he must have written to your father.

Naturrally. The male tarransmits and I have no borrother. Ali is nearrest.

What does this drawing mean? I thought you weren't allowed pictures?

Frowning, it is آلسِّحَر.

Ah. You use the Islamic Arabic for bad magic and thus it is tolerated. But how can your father—

—This is sometimes allowed, especially this one is even recommended. To seperrate lovers in adulterry.

I see. Why the branch?

It is only a message, a report of what my father did. He went to a gorreen terree and wrote on a barranch seven times *Baduh* and cut the barranch, saying he cuts the love of—a named person—from the heart of Hussein, sobbing softly, then he burri-ed the barranch in the tomb of a dead man unknown. He said verrses from القرآن الكريم and commanded let Hussein son of Abdillahi forget Jojeena daughter of England. Let their hearts die like the man who lies in this tomb.

Hussein if you obey your father now, can he undo this?

Perhaps . . . if I obey.

If?

I love Jojeena.

Sighing, and I love Julia.

Chin lifted, the blood of the Englishmen is silent.

Yes well, life is supposed to be so much easier for those who control themselves. But on the other hand, we don't have such terrible punishments. We have only our own willpower to rely on. This should make the decision less difficult for you.

A fatherr's currse is . . . is a terrible thing . . . It may remain . . . even . . . even if he undoes it.

Look Hussein, despite being Catholic, I believe in faith and I respect different types of belief, whether it's walking under a ladder or repeating a mantra. Although, voice bitter, I can't abide Protestants. The Church is stingy with dogmas, in fact we should be asked to believe much more. The whole point of faith is the impossibility of what's believed in. You once said the Pope should make it clear about Mary going bodily to heaven: it's a fact, not just an Assumption. I can't believe you've lost your faith in the power of words to undo as well as do. Remember the Prodigal Son?

Yes, head shaking, but the porrophet Jesus does not say what happened afterwards. The son perhaps was verry unhappy at home.

Oh Hussein, you know there is more to the story than just the ending.

The father perhaps was reminding him always of his forgiveness and the son was thinking again of the days in the big city.

Hmm. What's the effect of this curse on Georgina? The thing was on her door . . . Or even . . . what about Julia?

A currse cannot touch the innocent. Juli-a is beyond it.

And Georgina?

Jojeena, sighing, I will porrotect her.

So you admit that you are not innocent. What you are doing *is* wrong?

For my father, yes. For me it is not wrong.

But Hussein! The curse affects you, because from your father's point of view you are not innocent. So it will affect Georgina too. How will you be able to protect her? You will both be unlucky and perhaps very unhappy.

If I stay, the currse is on us. If I go home, the currse is on us. It is better to be together and fight it.

How?

I shall not believe in the power of it.

Hussein this is Protestant logic! On the one hand, the power of your father's curse cannot be undone since it exists, like the Sacrament, whatever your thoughts or subsequent actions are. On the other hand, you either ignore or accept it, like a sacramental, according to whether you choose to believe or disbelieve in it. And look, pointing at the outstretched right hand, you're even warding off the evil eye as we speak!

In that I believe.

In the Catholic faith, my Church, the words for the undoing of a wrong are as powerful as the wrong. Provided you believe it was wrong.

It is not wrong. I shall not believe.

Look at it this way. Your father's curse is the wrong. It is evil. You go home and show him that you forgive him, by loving him and doing what he asks. He repents and undoes the wrong. The wrong doesn't exist any more, because he's truly sorry. Georgina is safe. Surely that's easier than fighting.

Eyes wide staring, my father. Is. Not. Wrong. For himself he is not wrong. For what should he repent?

Then you *must* be wrong and *you* can repent. Your Recording Angel will rub it out.

Arms crossing chest, touching shoulder-sitting angels, before eight hours. After eight hours it is written.

Ah. You may as well go on, since you have nothing to lose?

For me and Jojeena, it is not wrong. Love cannot be wrong. It will be storronger than the currse of my father, who is also not wrong.

Eyes burning throat tightening memories of Julia blocked by the view from the window, have you thought of Georgina in all this? What sort of life can you give her?

Flinching, she is a modern English girl. She does not expect me to *give* her a life.

And you are an old-fashioned Sanuri boy and that is exactly what you expect to do.

I CAN GIVE HER LOVE, ebony face rouged, love she could never find anywhere except here, clenched fist thumping chest knuckles white.

Yes well, that's rather the problem isn't it? She's made love to you and she's never going to look sideways at anyone else.

Hands gripping table, standing, SHE WILL NEVER LOVE ANYONE ELSE! SHE WILL NEVER NEED ANYONE ELSE!

Not if you stay, calmly, but if you go back to your country, your family, your religion . . .

Crumpling on the chair, forehead falling on palms, I will never go back.

I have currsed my religi-on.

Hmm. Tapping fingers on the table. Shuffling the paper curses. Staring out the window. Hmm. I want to ask you something.

Looking up, yes?

When you said your father's curse had no power over the innocent, did you mean someone innocent of this particular palaver or innocent generally?

I do not understand.

Hussein you say you can choose to disbelieve in the power of this curse. I cannot. Whatever you say about your feelings for Georgina, and hers for you, Julia and I love each other just as much. But because of my Church we couldn't . . . stay together. I've managed to deal with it, I have my . . . religion, fiddling with a box of matches, my work. She has neither and I know she's very unhappy. Was anyway, selecting a match lighting it watching the flame die. She's no longer . . . innocent of sinful actions.

Eyes narrowing breathing slowly. She was not involved in my fatherr's currse. It will not affect her. But she will never be happy except with you.

She may be as it turns out, voice relieved face relaxed. Our situation is rather different. Anyway . . . I've applied to be sent back to Sanuri in October. I had been . . . looking forward to seeing you with your family.

Sighing seeing memories a small white villa verandah two young men resting one pale one dark one stumbling over a new language one laughing at the pronunciation. Walking the plains one pointing at the landscape landsmen muscles rippling landswomen hips swaying eyes sliding away. You will meet my father.

Hussein come back with me.

Despairing, I cannot.

Read this, opening the *Grammar*.

I cannot stay in this land where men have no white cloths over their shields, and no sword with which to gorreet a man. I will go to the Tshugal Valley, where the garrass gorrows high and the men are men, who speak fearlessly with the Genii.

Do you remember we translated this together? It was very difficult.

I will hear the hoofs of my pony Djamar clattering over the gorround like a gorrown girl who has been given a husband and garreat flocks. She has clothed herself in a costly robe and in the midday shadows borrings food to him, slap-slapping in her shoes of cow's hide. Forehead falling on palms shoulders shaking, Jojeena!

The door opening. Angelika Kriß standing still on the threshold waiting. Crossing the room, touching the mourning Muslim. You're among friends. But you must go home.

Staring, skull skin brilliantine black, eyes raging red-rimmed.

Softly, go home Hussein. Go home.

19

SQUALLING cats courting along the backyard walls behind the Drayton Gardens flat: screeches clawing the silence of the night to a striped tiger skin streaked across the twisted chimney top jungle mingling with sultry sundry other screams hisses wails from within beyond the sleeping ocelot eyes of the stretched sepia houses.

Outsize continental furniture crowding the bedroom glimmering with August moon a clutter of Roman monuments profiled in a *piccola piazza*. Bernard lying awake in the senatorial bed the luminescent clock arrows pointing at XII and III. Groping the peacefully sleeping body nearby, a moonlit tableau of arched back bent legs arms askew stretching turning towards murmurs.

Darling there's nothing like waking up to you all night naked, tongue lining lips arousing response, I adore you. I've never felt this way before, Julia.

Hands teeth tongue thighs talking, panting quickly moaning before shrieking, lying quietly fingers interlaced.

We do need hours and hours, don't we my darling? We're hopeless with snatched half-hours.

Smiling, we? Temporally relocated.

Darling heart. I do love you.

Fingers twirling fuzzy-bear hair, still smiling.

Julia. Do you love me? Tell me you really love me, just once, butterfly-kissing lips, hand exploring fleshly hills and valleys, until teetering on the brink—

Yes I love you, yearning.

—hand stopping short, eyes closing, breath slowing, snoring. Not so softly.

How like a male, sitting staring at the shapeless mound. This is becoming too much of a habit, too much of a commitment, too complicated by far. And I'm not becoming any younger, imagining baby Bernards sibling Julias goo-goo gah-gah first steps first days at school the teen years puberty fears, oh stop it Julia.

I tried so diligently to avoid him
to arm-distance him and snub him
but nothing, no nothing
worked out anything like as planned.
First the other library
where I hid myself (in misery)
had no books to help my history
search on medium evil adultery!
Then I hid myself at home
and worked like a plagued drone
No Mrs Moffat I'm alone
and I won't answer the phone.
Except oh drat that Renaud brat
who thinks I'm up for chit and chat
I've no time for tetes and that
post-mortem slicing of affairs.
She looks a pint of Guinness
with her frothy blonde excess
and she sounds just like an epeegrapheest clone.
So in order to escape her
I've taken up again as Reader
the first Reading Room encounter?
no one but that Bernard bounder!
Have you done your thinking? Oh darling it's been nearly a week.
And the thinking came undone
When he unflied his trusty gun.

It's true that from the first
he was help and not a curse
but a man can spot a rebound
like a bitch sniffed by a bloodhound
I only gained the upper hand
since he was initially so bland
forever worrying if I'd strand
him high and dry.
Impatient every day to see me
gallant ardent and so needy
til all at once he realised he
could make me ohhh ahhh yes!
Such confidence engendered
so much coarseness boldly tendered
how past mistresses were fendered
in crude jokes so poorly rendered;
the conversation always hogged
and when I speak so quickly bogged
in aggressive refutation of all I say.
He takes my words and twists them
all my earnestness a fiefdom
maintained or smashed at his sole behest.
Well! Such superior intelligence and learning
how should I avoid a spurning
for all the good he's done he's becoming such a pest.

You expect me to be there for you when it's convenient, Bernard, but somehow forget to let me know if you can't make it. You can't conduct a love affair without paying attention to the small things. It's just good manners. You're not so uxorious you can't ring me. We're through.

Oh Julia you're absolutely right! I promise I'll be better. I do love you. We can go on, you'll see. We're just so good together, we can't stop now.

Head aching distantly beaten drum. Past conversations replaying male declarations protestations uttered in subsequently disavowed moods of obsessive adoration humility humiliating chivalry.

Meditating, *Hail Mary, full of grace, the Lord is with Thee. Blessed art Thou amongst women and blessed is the fruit of thy womb, Jesus. Holy Mary Mother of God pray for us sinners now and at the hour of our death. Amen. Hail Mary, full of grace, the Lord is with Thee. Blessed art Thou amongst women and blessed is the fruit of thy womb, Jesus. Holy Mary Mother of God pray for us sinners now and at the hour of our death. Amen. Hail Mary*—oh hell, this isn't working. And I don't believe it either. One sheep jumping through the hedge, two sheep jumping through the hedge . . . forty-nine sheep jumping through the hedge, dammit my head feels woolly. Imagining water: dissolving fingers liquefying arms flooding torso rivuleting legs gradually becoming a

,,,,,,,,,,,,,,,,,,

,,,

,,,

,,,

,,,

,,,,,,,,,

,,,,   ,,,,

,,,,   ,,,,

,,,,   ,,,,

,,,,,,,,,,

,,,,,,,,,,,

,,,   ,,,,

,,,,,,,,,

,,,   ,,,

,,,   ,,,

,,,,,,,,,,,,

,,,   ,,,,

,,,,,,,,,

,,,   ,,,

,,,   ,,,

,,,,,,,,,,,,

,,,

,,,,,,,,,

,,,

,,,,,,,,,,,

,,,,   ,,,,

,,,,,,   ,,,,

,,,, ,,,, ,,,,

,,,,   ,,,,,,

,,,,   ,,,,

,,,,,,,,,,,,,,,,,

,,,

,,,

,,,

,,,

Après le déluge, wearily, *moi*.

20

BARITONE growling, *Ich grolle nicht . . . Und wenn das Herz auch bricht . . .* Rolling over sleeping.

Tenor wobbling, *Cari amici, buon giorno! Seguitate a stare allegramente.*

Rising dressing, morning ablutions.

Cerca-a-te, cerca-a-te, piping from the kitchen preceding the smell of toast and coffee. Prancing to Julia clasping a hand, *Là ci darem la mano.*

Vorrei e non vorrei, dancing round the breakfast table, *mi tremo un poco il cor,* sitting laughing.

We've got all day in front of us, free as the birds. What would you like to do? I thought of a jaunt to the countryside but it's not all that sunny. There's the Klee exhibition I'd rather like to see, and for lunch what about that new Catalan place? I could try finding some scalped tickets for Brecht, either for the matinée or this evening. And I imagine I'd—

—I'll go to the Reading Room. I've some work to do.

Oh?

Yes. I can't go on wasting time like this.

Double-taking, you're tired. My poor sweet, smirking, I've worn you out.

No. Actually, I'm going to work.

But this is our last chance of being together. Nicolette's coming back tomorrow.

Um-hm.

Haven't you enjoyed these four days?

Yes, too much.

You can't enjoy adultery unless it's too little?

Kitchen wall clock tick . . . tock . . . tick . . . tock . . . tick . . . Bird song erupting outside . . . tick . . . tock.

Have you any cigarettes?

Here.

Thanks for lighting mine Bernard.

Darling I'm so sorry.

Yes I know.

What's *wrong*?

It's over Bernard.

Cigarette-puffing furiously, I see. I suppose I knew it couldn't last. But why now?

I'm fed up.

You're fed up? Of *what*? We haven't been together long enough for you to become fed up. That takes years.

Not always, but I won't argue. Maybe I want to end it before you're fed up with me. But the reality is I've had it with the way you treat me NO, raising open palms, don't interrupt! This situation won't be repeated. Nicolette won't be doing vivas wherever every week. It'll mean going back to snatched half-hours and . . . mucked-up arrangements and I . . . refuse to go through that.

This'll happen again sweetheart. Be patient. Take a long-term view.

No. I'm already panicking about you being away in August, jet-streaming smoke at the ceiling. I haven't fallen madly in love with you and I don't want you to break up your marriage. But you seem to need me less than I you.

Rubbish, grinding out the cigarette, staring at the ashtray.

That's how it feels. You'll say I want it both ways, of course. To revel in your respect and adoration during the chase and expect it to continue when you've sat astride your goal.

I say Julia. You're making a pun.

That's right, be dismissive. Label it, like you always do, as if that makes my feelings less real. This ridiculous sub-Freudian idea that naming a neurosis cures it has infected everyone. The sillier the name the better, because that banishes the emotion.

Nonsense. The silly behaviour caused by that emotion is still silly behaviour. Otherwise you might as well claim that the feelings and convictions of neurotics and mad people are true.

They are true, to them. You can't treat neurotics with clever names. And madmen may be nearer to the truth than all you clever nitwits.

Are you suggesting, my dear, that you're going mad?

Not on your account!

Well?

Bernard, sighing, you *demean* me. Not just intellectually. I have no personality left, fingers twirling curls, you've invaded me. And frankly, I wouldn't choose you as the role model.

Well. If that's how you feel about it, mouth tightening, nostrils flaring. I'm sorry. Standing CLATTERing dishes, STOMPing across to the sink washing up.

Silly me, expecting you to protest. I should have known. It was inevitable you would demean me, since you found me demeaned. You offered yourself as a cushion and I told you the only thing I couldn't take was the way Paul cut himself off completely, just because we couldn't marry. Remember?

GRRRR, yes. Although why dragging up your past lovers is relevant confounds me.

Tea-towelling cups, Bernard all I want is to stop being lovers. At least for a little while. We'll have to when you go to Italy, it may as well be now. I still want to see you.

NGRHNGH! Julia listen to yourself. You just said, flicking out a finger, I demean you, flicking out another finger, I invade you and you weren't implying in bed, flicking out a final finger, and you wouldn't choose me as a role model.

Bernard you're like a drug. The more I have the more I want. You're bad for me. But I can't just go cold turkey. I have to cut you down slowly.

You have to *cut* me down *slowly*. Spare me your idea of fast! Flinging the dishcloth over the rack leaning to one side arms folded. I'm a person,

Julia. Not your pharmaceutical over-the-counter self-help.

Oh ho. *You* came to me as medicine. *You* told me to use *you*, even though *you* were just using ME!

Use? *Use?!* I was in love with you DAMMIT!

Was? Drying a plate very slowly.

Walking to the table lighting a cigarette, smoke rings dough-nutting laterally to the ceiling. Staring out the window, after what you've just said, you're mad expecting me to say I love you. Why should you even want me to? You don't love me, if you ever did. You just want me, need me, use me, lip curling, because I know what you like in bed. Friendship? HUH! You don't even want to spend the day with me.

Standing centimetres measuring galaxies away, only because I knew the day would lead to the night. I need a break Bernard, please understand. I . . . I'm falling in love with you, wanting too much and . . . it frightens me.

Embracing, lips buried in crisp hair, I do understand. Perhaps we shouldn't have had these four days: I was falling in love with you, too.

21

VOICE dry, it is with great pleasure ladies and gentlemen, that I introduce to you this afternoon Dr Bernard Reeves of London University, staring at the front row Paul towering over Bernard seated smiling presenting and presented attired in dark grey suits white collars muted ties. He will, as you know, read a paper entitled Problems of Linguistic Analysis in the Nominalism of William of Occam. Dr Reeves is a well-known mediaevalist and philologist. He has asked me to emphasise that he is not by training or profession a philosopher, nor does he consider himself worthy of belonging to that more modern school of nominalists who call themselves Positivists.

Dr Reeves has long been interested in linguistic analysis and merely begs your charitable attention towards an amateur. As chairman I'm forced to make this disclaimer on his behalf, voice dryer, since he's asked me to do so, but I'm certain that a syntactical analysis such as his title announces can only come from an expert, and that what he calls amateurish in his approach will prove to be a stimulating liveliness often absent from more specialised work. Gesturing, Dr Reeves.

Desultory applause. Paul sitting Bernard rising speaking.

Dismayed surveying Chair and Speaker, unaware when accepting the invitation of the identities gracing the podium. Listening inattentively, the presentation an attack or defence of Nominalism? The lecture commencing with an exposé of the problem in classical and mediaeval philosophy: Plato's exaggerated Realism—reality outside and above the sensible world; Aristotle's Moderate Realism—reality dwelling in the midst of the sensible world universal concepts faithfully representing the realities not universal; the third answer in the Conceptualism of the Stoics sensation being the principle of all knowledge thought only a collective sensation; the development of the Aristotelian doctrine by the early Scholastics the decisive stage marked by Abelard and John of Salisbury; the early beginnings of Nominalism from Porphyry to Roscalin of Compiègne emerging in its extreme form in the Conceptualism of William of Occam. The abstract and universal concept only a sign a label with no real value since the abstract and universal unapparent in nature.

Recognising potted scholarship and facile divisions in the presented paper; oral delivery simplifying, visual presentation finger-pointing academic sources. Listening to the analysis of the Latin used in the famous Porphyrytic question: *sive subsistent, sive in nudis intellectibus posita sint?* The Nominalists having concluded *nuda intellecta* represented by universals purely intellectual. Imagining the body of the orator naked mind irretrievably cloaked, sex failing to satisfy the desire to possess the slippery intellect.

The role of the universal is to serve as a label, quoting William, *to hold the place in the mind—supponere* is the word William uses*—of the multitude of things to which it can be attributed*. Now what precisely does *supponere* here mean? Blue eyes looking from the paper swerving between anonymous faces returning to the text swerving again at each new paragraph, failing to satisfy the desire to possess that interest.

Question time the customary farce. A well-inflated blue suit standing, eyes large behind rimless glasses, coughing a US drawl.

Ah-hahm. Janelmen. S'rr. Ah believe it was Minahvski who said the ethnahgrapher's perspective is the ohnly wahn pahssible for the fohmation of funnamennal lingooistic cahnceptions, where-ass the philahlahgist's poinna view is fictishass and irrahlefant. Would you agree, janelmen, that we now have to ahdapt a nahn-Aristahtelian arritood to languige?

Mahthemahtics is the ohnly nahn-variable languige and nahn-elemennahlistic languige. W'rrds like *true, folse, prahperty, to know, to hate, to lerv*, and an endless prohcesshahn ahv the mohst imporrant t'rms we use, merst be consid'red as merliorrinal, and, janelmen, ambigoo-ass. Their meanin's are depennent ahn diff'rent but ahnspecified orrers ahv abstra'shohn. It's no exagg'rashon to say, s'rr, that most tragedies, private, sohcial, *and* ethnic, are innimately cahnnected with the nahn-realisation ahv the merliorrinahlity ahv the most imporrant t'rms we use. Janelmen, S'rr. Ah thank you. Ah-hahm.

Giggles querulous looks whispers preceding Angelika Kriß rising insisting modern linguistic methods work in full cooperation with ethnography and anthropology. Wandering far from Occam.

Enamoured of the clay-footed: brave bear humble apostle. Meaningless negative mahthemahtical nahtions sprinting across the bracken of the brain crackling with unreal concepts: amore a theorem proposed by silence am or the corollary of absence.

Voice of a gaunt young man cruising on one low uvular note, scepticism is always ultimately a scepticism of the word, throat-clearing, any period of empiricism is inevitably accompanied by some form of Nominalism. The inseparability of the word and the thing, nasally whining, is the first premiss of all positive forms of culture while the loosing of the word from the thing is the beginning of scepticism and relativism. Sophistic scepticism had already left its mark on Plato. I cannot think, vecularly precise, why the modern version of disbelief in the word calls itself positivism when its main assertion is that the word is not the thing.

Ahmerrikahn rising up ah-hahm rising down hmph queered by a nasalisation of pitch from the gaunt young man with a BRIT-ish con-VIC-tion of suPIRri-O-rity. In the beginning was the WORD and the Word was with GOD, startling Julia, TRUST in the word is not only THE KEY to mediaeval CUL-ture, it is the bridge by which a way to NA-ture of the Deity is found. NOM-inalism thus becomes, for this CUL-ture, the most fundamental of ALL heresies, seizing the empty chair enraged duck quacking, the LOW evaluation of LAN-guage in He-GEL-ian phiL-O-sophy produces mere LABELS behind which meanings can be QUIET-ly shifted. The WHOLE mystery of the WORD is that it is MUL-tiple, in many languages, just as the SACRAMENT is MUL-tiple, and yet u-NIQ-uely identifiable with the thing. DEPART from this at PERIL: se-MAN-tic ANARCHY, chaos, WAR occur, finally sitting.

Session closing, redundant clapping.

Like to meet the lecturer? Angelika Kriß nudging an elbow.

Actually I have. At your party last spring. Besides, he was my examiner.

Julia I'd forgotten. So tacky of me to suggest it, patting the elbow awkwardly. Of course you want to avoid Paul.

Swallowing hysterical laughter, I have to go Professor Kriß. I'm sorry, waving uncertainly, walking towards the door bumping against the gaunt young man.

Hello, pulling a black umbrella from the stand, I was hoping to find an opportunity of talking with you. We've met, I don't suppose you'll remember. We had a very brief conversation—a passage of arms one might say—in an espresso bar, *The Groves of Academe*, to be specific.

Saint Thomas Aquinas!

Hardly.

Small moue of politeness, I'm sorry I was rude.

Not at all, I shouldn't have interrupted, although you were talking quite loudly. Nasal tone purring, I'm sorry you were made so unhappy.

Flushing, I was interested in what you said just now, about the meaning of words changing behind the labels.

Yes. That's how it all started. The word became a mere sign. Then, instead of the Bread being the Body, it became a symbol, with purely subjective significance. Symbolism replaced metaphor, nominalism replaced realism. Ha! Nothing *is* any more! Gripping an arm peering manically, who do they think they *are*?

Alarmed, but it's true, it is all relative. We can't communicate.

Aha! You're making a pun! And you're right. There is no communion, with God or man, because we have lost faith in the word. We've all gone mad. Do you know the Spanish for mad? *Incommunicado!*

Feeling isolated, an untranslatable meaning obscured with a label. The door of the lecture room opening, apostle and bear walking straight against a solid object.

Sorry/Oops/Oh pardon/It's you!/Hello/Julia.

I enjoyed your paper, Bernard. Congratulations.

Kind of you. Thanks.

Wanting to introduce the gaunt young man, hoping for a connecting conversation concerning symbols sacraments words labels language anything other than *incommunicado*. Gaunt young man nodding backing away assuming clerically that having seeded the split-between soul the maturity of truth inevitable.

I didn't know you were interested in—er—theology?

I'm not. Your friend is though.

How are you Julia?

Fine thanks Paul. This isn't your usual sphere.

No. Er . . . I was asked.

Paul I—Did you enjoy it?

Yes and no.

Bernard foot-tapping.

Julia we must go, I'm sorry. There's a—erm—do and we'll be late if—

—Oh yes sorry. I didn't mean to . . . keep you.

Bye Julia/Bye Bernard/Bye.

Watching Bernard Paul walk away. They know I know they're completely aggravated with me and each other *et voilà* exit the anti-Julia team. How low falls a woman excluded from fraternity after having haremed two colleagues.

22

THE paradise of a butcher: sausages of humanity lying packed plump on the grass variously cuisined from tartare to grilled. Late August sun scattering leaden clouds revealing pale blue sky drawing skiving-off London crowds to the Serpentine Lido compliments of generosity royally bequeathed by old Charlie.

Pour se distraire de son malheur en philosophie, Mathilde voulut être parfaitement séduisante.

Stendhal-reading sunbathing more *rouge* than *noire* attempting to recover respectability through immersion in the canon: *Pour se distraire de son malheur en séduisance, Mathilde voulut être parfaitement philosophique.*

You still haven't told me, Julia darling, why you left the poetry reading post-haste with Georgina and my guest of honour. *Debasing* in the extreme, patting the red-bikinied rump, so don't complain if I'm ghoulishly attentive.

Easier to deal with you attentive, swatting away the ghoulish hand, than inquisitive. You look less goulash and more like a stick of *gelato tricolore*, anyway.

All the better to have you eat me, my dear, removing the half-spectacles, squinting in the bright light at the double display of desirables.

You missed a trick Desmond, yawning rolling over, you mean lick you.

I do bring out the breast in you Julia. Have you any idea, *any* idea, just how *frustrating* it is to lie beside you, fingers spidering over stomach, in all your glory?

Desmond I do like you, lifting the spy'dher, except when you start pawing me, dumping arachnid invasion on the nearby crotch.

So pulchritudinous and sooooo puritan, sighing.

I'm neither, closing eyes imagining Bernard caressing fleshly senses bringing a body to orgasm, clenching pelvic—

—I say Julia, are you doing tantric sexercises? It's better with two you know.

Opening eyes, elbowing body upright, I'm a fool Desmond. I split up with my boyfriend because of old-fashioned morality.

He invited you to a swinging party? You could've asked me!

Hell you're no use. I'm going for a swim.

Wait. I may as well join in the wetness.

Swimming fast leaving Desmond far, floating in a liquid embrace free of the instruments of communication so denigrating in the failure to convey the non-existent penitent pleadings for repatriation by the forsaken object of misappropriated desire. Agonised at the memory of what had once existed.

I missed you, wrist catching. You know water worship is very Freudian, pulling Julia down to the towel.

Flinging wet hair droplets showering scrawny chest, that makes you an Adlerian. Listen Desmond, lying beside but not close, there isn't by any chance a minor editorial job at your paper?

Dear Julia, if there were, you'd have already joined the pleasantly proliferating young wanna-be prosists and poetistes clamouring against my body. Sighing theatrically. Alas! I'd have wicked my way before having to relinquish you to the disHonourable Mrs Robin Trout, unfortunately the worst of literary snob. She wants names and not nubility.

What, I wonder, did you do to acquire a name? Write obscurely clever books like that Christine Brooke-Rose back in the hippy era last century? Everybody's forgotten her now too. I suppose you were devoured in the jungle of reviewers?

You tell me what happened to Georgina and Her Swain . . . and I'll tell you about my brush with the gory, sliding a finger over the bikini seam.

Fat chance Desmond, flicking away the finger. So these jobs are that coveted?

Literarily squeaking Julia, everything is coveted by everybody, somewhere or other. Just like I covet those bodies over there, pointing to a group of Mediterranean-brown players flinging a volleyball over a net, but what do you want with such a doggy-stiled position? I thought you were all set for an hallowed launch to the echoing towers of ivory?

I'm having second thoughts.

Fecund I hope.

Tsking, no.

Seriously! Most of us would happily claw our eyes out for tenure.

It's a standard three year contract Desmond, don't exaggerate.

It's a leg up the ladder, old girl. Do you know Julia, the only difference between reviewers and meviewers is that the latter are protected by regular monetary manure and the sanctity of the unscalable wall?

Me-viewers either have an abundance of time or money. Most academics I know have neither. Can they not just be clever and actually deserve their job, as reviewer and academic? How do you know they're not good at both?

At least one. You're absolutely right, sighing, I'm speaking as a has-been who's seen 'em coming in a few positions and going as well. Just like me once upon a time. Go look up *And Then There Was No One*.

Never heard of it, rolling over to absorb UV AB&C sunny-side up.

Exactly, scratching an ear. Foolish critics, so sincere in admitting misplaced praise.

Desmond it's never the same lot upgrading and downgrading though, is it, like those credit rating people.

Of course not. They all die off, eventually.

Old judges never die, they just lose their court.

The trials and tribulations of the literary judiciary.

The decline of the metaphor, exhaling heavily. Provençal poetry once abounded with legal imagery.

Death is the mater of metaphor. It all returns, just in a renewed form. Look Julia, twisting upright returning spectacles to nose, you're a bit of a recluse and if you want to be taken seriously and not sillyarsely which I admit with yours you'll have a bit of difficulty but, snatching back a hand in advance of a forceful swipe, you need to meet more people. Be loud, be noticeable, be everywhere. And do it effortlessly as if it's an accident. It's not like one has to be terribly smart about it these days.

Easy for you to say, yawning, you've been there and done that.

I'm *soiréeing* at my flat in Chelsea tonight. A few friends, I'm very selective with my buffet. The Brits will drink in hell for having invented the cocktail party, and Hell will be one continuous dirge with nowhere to sit down and no-one filling the glasses, and everyone dragged off to meet the noisiest bore, hands miming clap-trapping puppets. The party purveyor, the Honourable A Nonimows, will prance round with a viscometer, measuring the success of the do by the numbers of hangers on.

Giggling, who's invited?

The sour pusses of London, naturally—critics, publishers, editors, authors, agents, script-writers, film producers, directors, investors, C-grade celebrities—

—At your *soirée*?

Well, the Honourable Mrs Robin Trout for one. And the editor of *Metamorphosis*. I want her to implement his policy. She won't, but one can always dream.

What's she like?

She knows *everyone*. She'll adopt you with inexplicable and antithetical enthusiasm. Before she forgets your name.

You said there was no room on *The Platform*.

Her temporary enthusiasms don't include access to *The Platform*. But there are other platforms darling. Come on, standing shaking all three legs bending forwards to roll up the towel, we'll be lobsters if we stay much longer. And I need time to arrange the catering.

I'm a radio actor, shuffling lankily around Julia, but I'm playing the narrator at the moment. What do you do?

I'm a mediaevalist, side-stepping clod-hopping feet.

How interesting. I know François Villon, he was just on the BBC and I had to read the translations.

Hngnh, really! Villon is much too modern, the beginning of decadence. Oh sorry, there's Desmond. I must catch him. He wanted to introduce me to someone. Be right back, smiling disappearing behind potted plants no backward glance.

You're not a bad dancer Desmond, surprisingly enough.

It's rather hard to dance badly to African percussion, no matter how uncoordinated you are you always look as though you've chosen one of the syncopated rhythms. Enjoying yourself?

Enough.

I'm SORRY it's . . . an in—tual —-ty AFTER ALL.

THOSE DRUMS ARE LOUD! WHAT DID YOU SAY?

Oh that's better, that *was* a bit of bombastic tribal booming. I said, the *soiree* isn't so intellectual.

No you seem intent on making it intersexual. Relax your grip Desmond. This isn't Latin American, stepping away.

Dear Julia, dancing was invented for the delectable frustration of the contiguity of the limbs.

No it wasn't. It's a fertility rite.

Contiguity with your anatomy would be very fertile.

How like a male, moving insistent hand from insensitive buttocks.

Compare me to a man and I'll think I am one, hips swaying as a futility right.

Laughing, you're reminding me of that gelato. If learned language is supposed to be sophistry-laced, our vernacular is pathetically troglodyte as a means of communication.

Meeting the radio actor in the lift after not meeting the Honourable Mrs Robin Trout, walking along the Embankment suffering the appellation of dear darling dreamboat listening reluctantly to an ethnic analysis of *The House of Bernarda Alba*.

23

THIS is my bus stop, sitting on the orange strip of seat in the shelter, thanks for the chat. Have a lovely evening.

Angelface, where in heaven do you live? No buses go along here at this time of night.

The N39 does. I'll be fine thanks.

What are you doing next Wednesday? I've free tickets to the theatre.

Silently: if they were paid you'd have asked someone else?

Aloud: Sweet of you but I'm flying to Istanbul tomorrow.

Istanbul? You're leaving me so soon! For how long?

Two months, possibly three.

Really? Eyebrow ricocheting up, Ms Constantinople I'm not convinced this is your bus stop.

Touché. No it's not my usual one. But the N39 stops near my door.

You're very beautiful in this streetlight. Like a Botticelli.

Grimacing, actors! No wonder you're always surrounded with giggling groupies.

You're hardly one of those.

No. Look, gesturing back along the path, thanks for walking with me this far. There's no point waiting.

On the contrary. I want to see just where the N39 takes you. That way when you don't answer my calls I can stalk you at your home, imitating composer Erik.

Laughing, le *Fantôme* met an unhappy end in the Bloomsbury *Opéra*.

Ha! You live in Gordon Street.

No. And anyway, you don't have my number and I'm flying out

tomorrow.

Oh yes. To Istanbul. Spinning once sinking to one knee, you know that I adore you, utterly adore you?

Face paling hand clutching throat, my god!

Rising smoothly, well that's not quite the usual reaction. What's wrong?

Nothing. You just reminded me of someone.

Actors tend to do that, grasping hand, we're always being copied. Whoever said art imitates life had no idea.

You don't even know my name, repossessing the hand.

Desmond was more than happy to share it, Ms Grampion. Julia. My empress.

I assure you not.

The least you can do is ask for mine. Marcus Valentine. I'll be yours.

Nice meeting you Marcus. Oh look, pointing, there's the N39.

Julia I'll pester Desmond you know. He can be bribed. I want to talk to you about a zillion things, you with your pouty lips and your perky—

—Stop right there—

—Ideas darling, ideas. I'll bet you're religious. Everyone's on a religious kick these days. Finding themselves. I just know I'll find myself a knave.

Fingering the crucifix, I'd say you've found yourself as a knave already, looking towards the Bridge of Battered Seas, squinting smiling delightedly, HUSSEIN! HUSSEIN!

Swerving trotting from the stone arch crossing the road, long strides towards Julia.

Juli-a I'm so pleased to see you.

Julia I'm so not pleased to see him.

I went to the Birritish Museum/Ah. So *that's* where you hang out./to say goodbye but you weren't there./You're not really going to Istanbul?

You're going home?/He's going home? Where are you going then?

Yes tomorrow. The plane he leaves from the Heatherrow when the red mane of the li-on flows across the plain of the night. Will you walk with me?

No she's catching this bus here./Hussein this is very sad./Well no it's jolly good actually.

I would like to talk Juli-a.

I'm—er—so *awfully* sorry Marcus, neatly smiling extending a hand, my friend is leaving. Looks like I won't be taking the N39 home. But it was lovely of you to wait. Enjoy your evening.

Alla prossima, imperatrice. Enjoy Istanbul, striding away whistling no tune recognisable.

Walking past the All Bright Bridge towers standing dark tall, guardian angels of steel-winged silence Thames flowing diamantine black beneath.

I'm very sorry you've decided to go, Hussein.

I also. I came to say goodbye to your river. It is bea-utiful and sad, your river.

Will you ever return?

I do not think so. In many years, perhaps, when I am verry old. What the wind has blown away is not found again.

It wasn't just the wind.

No. It was the thunder, much thunder, which now is in my heart roarring like a black-maned li-on . . . Look Juli-a. The new moon, pointing, we call Safar. Unlucky.

Why?

We should not tarravel in Safar.

Sitting momentarily watching beauty and sadness.

How is Georgina?

Jojeena. She has gone to her family by your lakes in the North. She says the lakes are like Japanese pictures. She writes very short poems about the lakes. So short they are like our porroverbs. Look.

No light to see words written on unfolded paper. No poetry recited from memory.

Hussein do you miss her?

I have waited to leave these five weeks, each day a knife twisting in my heart. The knife is not yet blunt. Paul has been so kind. He lent me some money for my ticket, because I lost the money with the other flight. I will pay him when he comes to Sanurri.

When he—to Sanuri?

In October. He will work another year. I will take him to my family.

Oh.

He was worri-ed about you. He asked me if my father's curse could make bad luck for you. Or make you bad.

Make me bad? *Hngnh!* Self-righteous prig! What did you tell him Hussein?

You are innocent of my father's curse. It can bring you no bad luck or make you bad. It can have no effect on you. You are not guilty of the sin it curses.

Not guilty . . . well not of that. Other things. A proud heart. A poisonous mind. You're innocent of that Hussein. Your father's curse brought me bad luck.

Were you proud with that man? Or po-isonous?

No. Yes. Well. Only because he's an idiot and I wanted nothing to do with him. He followed me from the party to the bus stop.

But why did Paul . . . you were not innocent?

We broke up. I had a fling. The truth is—

—A fling?

An affair, a new relationship. Something . . . temporary. Temporally dislocated, snorting, I didn't love that person. I'm guilty of that, at least.

Is this what . . . what Jojeena will—

—Perhaps, but I don't think so, head shaking, she loves you Hussein. You're so very good for each other.

But she was not innocent in my father's curse.

And neither are you Hussein, standing clasping arm. Will you have an affair to forget her?

No, rising stepping beside Julia. The women of my country are bea-utiful. One day I will marry. But only after I stop seeing what is lost.

She will do likewise. I don't have that strength.

Pray to your guardi-an angel Juli-a, touching shoulders without angels, pray to your guardi-an angel for me also. Jojeena is back. I saw her light. She thinks I have gone. I walked and walked, like the night when I said goodbye the first time and stayed.

You'll only hurt yourself more if you go to her again.

I have to face the whole night, crossing hands touching shoulders, help me Juli-a.

I'll walk with you. Are your things packed?

Yes, my bag is in the left-luggage at Paddington.

Let's have breakfast at the all night caf in Old Compton Road. We can take a taxi to Paddington from there. My treat.

You are good and kind Juli-a.

Walking talking hours belonging to the moonless summer night criss-crossing the river passing the landmarks of memoribund the Tate Galleery Lambeth Palace Westminstral St James Park Pallbearer Mall Covet Garden the British Mausoleum, aubade mist greeting the sojourners at Paddington Bear Station.

Retrieving luggage, walking to the platform, there's Paul! You didn't tell me he'd be here.

Hussein waving at Paul, no I did not. Dropping bags clasping the believing deliverer tightly, thank you for coming.

Frowning, I didn't know Julia would be seeing you off, eyes narrowing.

I wanted my two best friends to say goodbye together, pearl-white teeth splitting dark lips.

Raising eyebrows, oh. You look tired Julia.

It was a long walk. We visited Hussein's memories.

Ah . . . well . . . I'm . . . I'm glad to see you.

I will parray that your guardi-an angels will meet again and fold their wings together. Perhaps one angel is less severe than two.

Hussein I hate long farewells. We won't stay and wave. Your train is ready.

I understand Paul. A wave tarravels far like a bird who cannot be caught. But it is the dove of peace.

The pigeons will fly with you to Heathrow. As our farewell waves.

Juli-a please tell Jojeena I wave at her from the air. I send her a dove of peace.

Shaking hands kissing crying hugging goodbye last whispers, boarding the train. Turning walking to the exit no backward glance.

You're going to Sanuri too.

Yes. Next month.

Good luck Paul, gazing at the cobblestones, I hope it works out for you.

I hope it works out for you too, holding arms drawing bodies closer.

I haven't been really happy since we . . . split up. It's as though . . . I keep betraying myself. I still love you.

I love you too. Are you going home on the tube? Standing at the bus stop watching the dearly beloved face.

It's better for me to take the bus, legs wobbling tiredness sweeping leaning against the body no longer there. Couldn't we . . .

I'm leaving next month. A year is a long time.

Or not long enough.

Yes. The summer was too long. A nightmare from Dante.

An allegorical dream-vision.

Yes, kissing brow stepping back signalling the bus, with Hussein as the coded oratory.

24

I'M MARRIED.

So'm I. My wife's on tour at the moment. She plays the cello, didn't I tell you? Doing very well, bless her.

Really, staring anywhere.

Tell me about yourself. Obviously your husband's in Istanbul.

Nodding, noting the flamboyant dress sense of other theatre goers.

Darling, voice throbbing, I adore you!

You remind me of someone I used to know.

I know, an old boyfriend. I've heard that line before, smiling, can't you be a little more innovative?

Third bell ringing, joining the trudging bodies clattering towards the stalls. Wonderfully effective first act, don't you think George?/I wasn't *moved*, you know. It didn't make me *emote*./How about you Cecily, did it make you move?

Seated in the first row to the side theatrical illusion destroyed, every stroke of greasepaint wig-line tatty thread-bare patch each puff of stage dust visible. Marcus Valentine commenting *ad nauseum* on the experimental verse-play transposing the Middle Ages with mock-Elizabethan English to the Modern Age. A successful exposition of the depth of directorial misunderstanding.

After the play walking to the restaurant Occitan words whispered:

Sols sui qui sai lo sobrafan quern sortz

Al cor d'amor sofren per sobramar . . .

Marcus it's true you've an actor's ear. But it makes you no less absurd spouting Troubadour poetry at me.

Julia! You've cut me to the quick. No one's too absurd to express falling in love. Love *is* absurd.

You don't say?

Alright I don't, twisting sideways, I do, slobbering not kissing.

Oh stop that, mouth wiped lips pursed. The general absurdity of love is particularly irrelevant to us.

Your logic is absurd. You just called me absurd. Ergo sufficient absurdity, walking resumed.

That doesn't even merit a response, concentrating on stepping on each pavement slab-join.

But Julia I adore you. My adoration is a force, a torrent, unstoppable, a pining unto death!

Romance died with the Catharist heresy.

I'm all for keeping to the Romance Languages, even with food, stopping at a Spanish restaurant.

Groaning, you remind me—

—of someone you know, snatching a hand kissing it. Julia you're a mediaevalist, you fill my life with romance. I'm just sharing it with you.

Snatching hand back, I'm an empty vessel that holds no romance.

I'll make you, arms wrapping waist, women love being chased and men love the chasing.

Thrusting arms aside, you're supposed to wait until after I'm drunk at least. Shall we go inside? I'm starving.

Seated in a darkened corner, knees canoodling, I mean it Julia.

Marcus I'm *happily* married. And a Catholic. I'm just feeling lonely at the moment, lip curling, right time of the month.

Makes you all the more desirable! Didn't the play make you *emote*? That essential conflict of *love* and *duty*? Love conquers all Julia. Having loved utterly one loves always, even after the loved one ceases to exist.

Utterly nonsensical! In which case, placing the napkin back on the table, here's your chance to prove it, standing gulping a large glass of *sangria*. I'm ceasing to exist. Bye Marcus.

But we've ordered dinner! You can't leave now! Sit down and stop being so melodramatic.

Exiting no backward glance.

Catching the first bus at the Charing Cross Road bus stop naturally a number 14 driving away from Gower Street staring out the window unseeing until arriving in Fulham Road. Steps retraced to a flat in Drayton Gardens. The light in the upstairs window beckoning, Nicolette opening the door.

Juli-ah.

Hello Nicolette, swaying slightly, I—I've just been to a party round here a—and I thought I'd call—on my way home to—to see how you were. I saw your light . . . I hope I'm not disturbing you?

I was working, lips non-committal. Een fact I was just going to ze bed.

Oh. Ah, leaning against the door frame, erm. Well, giving minute attention to floor walls ceiling, did you have a nice holiday?

Yes, smile bright voice light, eet was wonderfool.

Oh. Super. Er . . .

Why don't you come een for a minute? Unteel ze next bus arrives. Eet should be 'ere very soon.

Glancing at the bedroom door sitting on the sofa quickly, I'm very sorry —to—intrude like this. I really don't feel very well. I must have—er—had too much to drink.

Zat was stupeed. I will breeng you some beecarbonate. I 'ave already turned off ze coffee machine.

Thank you Nicolette that's appreciated, staring at the floor listening to footsteps receding, rising crossing the room searching for a sign of Bernard in the scattered notes books scribblings on the table peering at the epigrahically neat cursive. Verdict: ruthless.

Are you feeling better? Proffering a glass filled with bubbling white brew.

The room does rather spin when I sit down, swallowing the bubbles face wrinkling, thank you so much. Your books, I was . . . I was just browsing. Did you find all you wanted in Pompeii?

Not now Juli-ah. Eet eez late and I don't want to disturb 'eem. Eef you're feeling better . . .

Oh he's her—asleep? Yes I'd better be going.

You've not seen 'eem . . . would you like to?

But—but—but he's asleep!

'ee sleeps with ze light on. Only voices bozzer 'eem. At zat age zey sleep like zat, clicking fingers.

Whispering, at zat age?

Onze. My son Lucien. 'ee returns to school next week.

Son. Pain drilling from neck to entrails light spinning away crashing headlong to the floor.

Juli-ah, shaking a shoulder, Juli-AH.

Blinking focussing gazing past the shadowed face in magnification to a crack in the ceiling overhead. Sorry, gasping, so sorry.

Pauv' petite. Let me 'elp you to ze sofa. Staggering three metres collapsing THUMP BOING on the couch Nicolette unarming Julia. You 'ave meexed your drinks? Shall I bring you a *tisane*?

No no. I'll be . . . I'm fine thank you, smearing teared mascara. I'm . . . I'm glad Bernard's not here to see me drunk. I'd better go before he comes back, struggling to rise.

Hand on shoulder, 'e eez not 'ere Juli-ah. 'ee eez een *Paris* working on a manuscreept. 'ee won't be 'ere for a few days. Don't worry, I won't mention anyzing to 'eem.

Eel zink—he'll think I'm completely unreliable.

'ee zinks you are completely admirable. 'ee wants you to fineesh ziz book.

Really? I just have so many doubts you know, tongue tripping words rushing cascading waterfall of uncertainty repeating elaborating conversations held elsewhere, I'm not sure I'm cut out for being an academic.

Neutral nodding, *hmm.*

Nicolette I'm keeping you up. It's very late. I'd better go.

You shouldn't let yourself 'ave zo much stress. Did you not take an 'oliday?

No—er—I—researching for the book.

Naturally.

May I see . . . Lucien?

In 'ere, a small room never noticed. Soft light falling on dark straight hair pale skin thin body tangled in sheets. Slight snoring.

Thank you Nicolette, door closing softly. Standing in the hall pulling on coat staring at the mirror, odd I never noticed your *Madonna del Divino Amore* before. Are you Catholic?

Mais oui. What else? Nicolette clasping hands prayerfully.

Ah, sighing deeply, my apologies for imposing.

Eet was nahzzeeng. *Au revoir* Juli-ah.

In the Gower Street garret bruising knees in prayer.

25

MELLOW mid-tempo ambient music piping from hidden speakers black-suited bright young things circulating cold canapes alcohol warm hors d'oeuvres amongst guests katzenjammer a politically correct level.

We never launch our authors Tweedie, nor give parties. But we love the bastards.

Smiling a Scottishly shrewd smile, aye Gottlieb, thaht's a faine point o' view. But we faind it pehys t' make 'em love 'emselves. There's nowt laike 'n ah'th'rr's buisted ego t' produce guid average-selling text.

Shaking a god-loving head, yes and look Tweedie, what happens to the firms who spend vast sums on entertainment and splashy advertising. I buy them up for a song.

Och away wi' ye man. Ye'll n'v'r buy up Tweedie's. And our ah'th'rrs want nowt wi' the laikes o' beast-selling brew'ries, winking.

The public wants best-sellers and beer and we give it to them, snorting, no point chasing after the middle-list. Diversification Tweedie, that's the secret to success. We do our bit with a few elevated brow-bashers, keeps us afloat with the literary journals. And if an author doesn't sell after I've put her in print, well! She can hardly complain, laughing. Should be grateful she was put there in the first place! Remembering of course that she can go from being a nobody to a somebody overnight with these big online book sites.

Ahdv'rtising flatt'rs 'em. Makes 'em feel imp'rtant. Makes 'em wraite m're. And they love p'rties, Gottlieb.

Oh yes. The right sprinkling of other authors, other publishers, pesky agents, naff reviewers, impressionable outsiders to goggle and gush and fawn and buy the books.

Aye. If they s'rvaive thaht lort, they'll s'rvaive me.

But you rarely produce a best-seller Tweedie.

Aye. But all our mid-list sells. And thaht's why Ai've an 'xperim'ntal list and a schol'rly list and you've nowt, grinning. Up yer kilts, lad. 'ere's t' At Court: Love.

Julia talking to Georgina, noting through the checkerboard of coiffures an elegant self-assured Nicolette standing beside a tanned ebullient Bernard.

How were the Lakes?

Drizzly.

When did you arrive back?

Last weekend. No point staying longer. It's already September and the weather will just worsen.

Hussein asked me to say he sent you a dove of peace.

A dove?

Bird wings, waves waving goodbye ... erm, I read your *haiku*. Very fine.

That's sweet of you Julia. Thank you, staring at the martini, I almost went back to Japan, inhaling quickly, the Foreign Office wrote back with an offer from a local company. But Angelika Kriß bullied me to stay and graduate next summer.

I'm biased, but you're better off finishing. She's right.

Of course. There's never any doubt about what's right.

No, the only doubt is how wrong is something wrong.

Girls! Hands sliding over curves on one side promptly removed on the other suffered silently.

At least Julia lets me treat her like a pet, pouting, you're such a prude Georgina.

You're such a pimp Desmond, smiling nicking the long quivering nose. There's a time and a place and a man. The right one for all three. Julia's too generous for her own good. Leave her be.

Gladly, releasing Julia, if you'll satisfy my curiosity. You know it's killing me, fingers clasping throat, not to know what you did with my Sanuri guest. Julia I've a rendezvous with you later, raising an eyebrow beckoning Georgina to a pair of vacant chairs.

Smiling selecting a drink from a passing waiter-borne tray.

Juli-ah. 'ow are you? Not drinking again, I 'ope? Prodding Justin, she came to my flat drunk. And fainted.

Tittle-tattling Nicolette? *C'est tres méchant.* How's the book coming along Julia?

Oh. Erm, blushing, it . . . it could be going better but . . . the summer . . . you know how it is. So hot. Difficult to work and . . . whatnot.

Nodding, the thing is to go somewhere and cool down, winking.

Laughing, I made it as far as the Cockney Riviera. The book just seems so boring now. Bad enough having to re-read the thesis before defending it. But having to extract a book from it. Justin I swear I'll never let you con me into such a thing again.

Perfect, raising whiskey tumbler in salute, you're showing all the appropriate symptoms. Call when you hit the half-way mark. You'll need lunch and a pep-talk as a minimum.

You never gave Berr-narr such encouragement.

Ah Nicolette. Berr-narr and I practically wrote At Court: Love. I had him sitting by my knee while I guided his hand every afternoon.

Turning abruptly aside hiding a snort coughing as camouflage.

Everything alright Julia? Justin proffering a glass of water eyes sparkling.

Yes fine. Just the idea . . . that I'll finish the book I mean, coughing, because of my new job. I start next week and I have my doubts about making progress on time.

Of course you will Juli-ah, sipping champagne, Just-in will make you pay back ze advance eef you don't. Same as when ze poofs 'ave to be changed too often, smiling slightly.

I'll tell you a professional secret, loud stage whisper, all authors with the exception of Bernard are bone-lazy. They hate writing. Need all kinds of stimulation. Whips. Chains. That sort of thing.

Frowning, Just-in! You—

—Sounds delicious Justin, Desmond peering over a beguiling shoulder, are you telling tall stories out of literary school?

Voice icy, Just-in! I—

—My dear Desmond, you *are* going to review our new book, aren't you? Bernard Reeves' At Court: Love.

If you—

—Oh Nicolette so sorry. Desmond, pointing to the plaintiff pointing to the bailiff, Mrs Reeves etc.

That's not what—

—How do you do dear? Shaking hands, the pleasure's all mine. Review Bernard's book? Justin there's only one person, twining an arm around an hourglass waist, to do that. This sexy young mediaevalist about whom I'm draping myself. Now if you've the whip, I can furnish the chain.

Tsking, Desmond that's enough, sliding from the embrace.

Just-in I want to talk wiz Juli-ah. Take zis lounge leezard away.

Oh ho yes please do, ;) at Justin :D sashaying through the crowd.

Eet eez all wrong, head shaking vigorously, books are not reviewed by ze auzzor's friends.

Better a friend of the author than a rival writer with an axe to grind.

Ze value of ze review eez null.

A qualified friend with a close working relationship will be more than stringent.

Exactement!

Oh this is going nowhere, round-the-room casting for a rescue. Justin watching the head-to-head sauntering across with Georgina.

Where ees ze publisher Tweedie, I will speak wiz 'eem myself. And Bernard. Eet eez rideeculous.

Julia so sorry to interrupt! Smiling offering a champagne glass taking a hesitating arm, but Georgina wants to talk to you, pushing the two towards the balcony. Now Nicolette . . .

What's all that about? I never said anything to Justin about wanting to talk to you.

Justin manoeuvring Nicolette. She's on the warpath about Bernard's book.

Nicolette?

His wife.

Ah.

She's a battle-axe, in a good way. But erm . . . isn't very taken with the idea of me reviewing his book.

No well I can imagine, voice gentle. Can't be an ideal situation, sighing staring at moonlit rooftops street below filled with the roar of traffic.

Missing Hussein?

Yes. No. More missing . . . part of him.

The poetry part?

Hnh, lighting a cigarette watching smoke rings unravel, nothing quite like writing poetry and reciting together. But that wasn't what I meant.

Oh? Erm . . . well the only thing I can suggest would sound rather vulgar.

That of course. But no . . . I went to the Lakes to be by myself and do some thinking. Julia . . . I missed my period. Before Hussein left, gazing at the moon.

Oh no. But . . . you were on the Pill?

Yes, grimacing, and like every other idiot who's taken it late never thought anything more of it.

What are you going to do?

He'd already decided he was leaving and I wasn't about to complicate matters. Bringing up a child alone is not an option. Nor was having him stay because of that.

Staring white-faced, it's what you've already done. But Georgina! How could you not tell him?

Julia stop being so melodramatic, spinning round leaning against the balustrade blue eyes narrowing. Women have been conceiving and not telling men for centuries, surely you of all people know that. The difference is that most of them died in the process of cutting out a gob of cells. Or were killed because they didn't. And the infants were exposed anyway, stamping out the cigarette.

Gulping champagne, quietly, there's always adoption.

Don't think I didn't consider it, finger rubbing elegant length of nose, degree notwithstanding. But Hussein would have found out, sooner or later. If not before the birth, then after. Imagine how he would have felt, head shaking slowly. No. I couldn't do that. It's over Julia.

His father's curse did bring you bad luck, after all.

Hnh! Perhaps. But the point, gesturing back to the street sky moon, is what we do with the luck that arrives. You promise not tell him, eyebrows lifted gaze intent, or anyone? Only you and Angelika Kriß know.

I promise. Lifting a hand dropping it, will you be alright?

Let's go back inside, it's chilly out here, stepping across the threshold draining the glass, and I have an idea I want to discuss with Justin. Oh hello Bernard, smiling politely, you're looking like you're looking for someone.

Nodding, yes. I hear you're going to review my book Julia?

Nicolette isn't exactly enthusiastic, staring at the ribbing of a pair of lace sandals.

Leave that to me, Georgina touching lips briefly to cheek, I'll chase up Desmond about it. Bye Bernard. Hands lifting limpid waves freeing doves of peace.

I've missed you. My god how I've missed you.

How like a male.

The short-shrift answer, signalling a waiter, taking two glasses giving one to Julia, but you can't generalise like that. Superficial love characterises both sexes. You knew I needed to absent myself. I'm no stronger than you are. But now . . .

You're proposing now what I suggested before, twirling curls, and you know neither of us will stick to the new rules.

We did lose the plot, hand seeking hand not withdrawn, but there's no reason why we can't keep it casual. Best friends with benefits? Let's sit down there, pointing to chairs half-hidden behind a bamboo screen.

Sitting swirling the liquid in the glass, Bernard we're too selfish. You're too self-absorbed, I'm too self-effacing. Either way we're a bit too self-obsessed.

That's generally enough Julia. What were you expecting?

Smiling sadly, not obsession. Paul and I . . . I still love him Bernard.

Ah, swallowing a gulp of wine, are you seeing each other?

No, head shaking, he's off to Sanuri. It's for the best. The luck of that curse, maybe.

Oh Julia I'm sorry, leaning close, breath warming cheek. Look darling, I know I'm selfish—

—Bernard so'm I. We're too similar.

And we're collaborating on a book—

—on Adultery—

—on paper, laughing eyes tearing, darling what's the matter?

Why didn't you tell me you had a son?

Frowning, it would have made a difference?

I want . . . wanted children Bernard, wiping eyes, and you couldn't divorce Nicolette?

No, fingers spinning wine glass. I have a son and he barely knows me. Nicolette has him enrolled in that school in France and her parents look after him throughout the year. So no particular impetus for me to . . . discuss children.

The perfect solution then, pouring the last of the wine in the neighbouring potted palm, is to marry Paul and claim maternity of your future kids. Keep Church and State happy.

Snorting wine, cynicism becomes you Julia.

Except I was serious.

Whoever's THAT? Stage whisper to the right, LOOK at that moustache. It's not even Christmas yet.

Black boots and red suit missing, lugubrious tones to the left, *that*, Justin, is the mother of all father-complexes. The husband of Marion Farquharson.

Professor Jarvis-Anderson! Bernard rising at the professorial approach hand extended, good evening. Oh, gesturing, and our candidate Ms

Grampion. Do you remember her? Already with a book contract for that thesis of hers.

O-of course I remember her, shoulder forward-twitching, Jul-lia works in my Department.

Face-palming, how could I forget.

Hello Marion, standing smoothing palms over dress, what are you doing at a Tweedie party?

I used to be a Tweedie turkey laying golden eggs, grinning kissing each cheek, now I'm a Gottlieb grouse popping out lead balloons. Let me introduce you to a few old-timers besides Desmond.

No longer a language-listening learner missing the keys to decipher meaning. Slipping from one conversation can you believe I had to stage a massive reconciliation with him to get another ten thousand words of copy to another there's clearly no future in print books to the intercontinental *les sheunes filles anklaises sont si faciles à sétuire, après tout.*

Par les étrangers, oui. Ce qui ne m'étonn du reste pas. Leurs hommes les traitent comme des animaux. Un moment c'est sentimentalité absurde et le romanticisme extravagant, un autre c'est l'indifference et l'égoisme complet. Ça prend trop de temps, l'amour, trop d'effort. N'est-ce pas, Mademoiselle?"

Smiling inclining the head very Englishly to the right.

Pourtant, leur attitute est bien tifférente avec les femme étranshères. La passion, les émotions, le grang sérieux, tout est permis parce que c'est eksotique. N'est-ce pas, Matemoiselle?

Smiling inclining the head very Englishly to the left, *oui. C'est vray. C'est sollemeng quand nous avons l'owdace d'aytre féminines aussi qu'il nous traytent* —like doormats, laughing nodding to Georgina chatting with the Mrs Honourable Robin Trout confirming to Justin the review of *At Court: Love.* The zodiac promising *in September the tone changes suddenly.* Before the fall of the curtain: Bernard.

The capacity to desecrate self-love and create a greater passion . . . that's what Paul Hussein Georgina share. Maybe not in any way visible to the outside world, it's within them.

Nodding, yes Julia. The perfect solution is to find someone equally self-full and self-less. You might.

I might, offering a cigarette no lighter, or maybe I *will* become a Catholic. Or a Muslim. Or a Wiccan.

Or fall in love.

Been there done that Bernard, gazing at blue eyes *sans* he(-)sit(u)ation, I expect no man to give me all I want—

—you might find a woman who can? Or follow in Desmond's footsteps?

Laughing, never say not at all. Relationships need imagination and self-absorption excludes it—you can never feel what your partner feels, tapping the unfelt knee—haven't you noticed, truly selfish people are truly not creative, but rather interpreters of living, imitators of art? You and I are pasticheurs.

Ah Ms Grampion, Thulish bass rumbling, would you pass by my office next week pll-lease? I'd like to final-lise the year's programme.

I'd be delighted Professor.

Stroking the handlebar, I'd like you to take the three undergrad majors doing the L-language Paper next term.

Really? Refusing to twirl curls.

Yes. Precisely your area o-of expertise. The bare bones of language: Dan Michel's *The Prick of Conscience.* The problem of pal-latal diphthongisation in fourteenth century Kentish.

ABOUT THE CONTRIBUTORS

David Bellos is Meredith Howland Pyne Professor of French Literature at Princeton. The translator of Perec's *Life A User's Manual* and the author of the authoritative biography of the writer, Bellos has also published an irreverent introduction to translation studies, *Is That a Fish in Your Ear?* and, most recently, *The Novel of the Century, The Extraordinary Adventure of Les Misérables.*

Chretine Broke-Prose is, inter alios, a plagiarist, parrotiste, and peddler of pastiche.

Jeff Bursey is an exploratory Canadian novelist, short-story writer, playwright, and literary critic. His books include the novels *Verbatim: A Novel* (2010) and *Mirrors on which dust has fallen* (2015), and *Centring the Margins: Essays and Reviews* (2016). Verbivoracious Press will issue the paperback version of *Verbatim: A Novel* in the fall of 2017. The segments presented here are from a work-in-progress titled *Ennead.*

Louis Bury is the author of *Exercises in Criticism: The Theory and Practice of Literary Constraint* (Dalkey Archive Press) and Assistant Professor of English at Hostos Community College, CUNY. He writes about visual art for *Hyperallergic* and his other creative and critical work has appeared in *Bookforum, The Brooklyn Rail, The Los Angeles Review of Books, Boston Review,* and *The Believer.*

Peter Consenstein has been writing on contemporary French poetry, experimental literature, and the group Oulipo since the mid-1980's and is now also translating. He published translations of Dominique Fourcade's *IL (IT)* (Albany: Fence Books La Presse, 2009) and *en laisse (on a leash)*. Consenstein will publish his translation of *Petit traité invitant à la découverte du jeu subtil de GO* by Pierre Lusson, Jacques Roubaud and Georges Perec in 2018 and is completing his translation of *Son blanc du un* by Dominique Fourcade. He is a member of the French Voices Award jury, which supports the translation of contemporary French literature. His latest published chapter, "L"identité juive de Georges Perec," was included in the book *Relire Perec* (Université de Poitiers: La Licorne, 2017). He serves on the ANR (Agence nationale de la recherche) Difdepo ("Différences de potentiel") project, which is dedicated to analyzing and presenting the work of the Oulipo. Consenstein is a professor of French at the Borough of Manhattan Community College since 1993 and he was appointed to the faculty of the Ph.D. program in French at the Graduate Center of the City University of New York, January 2005.

Jenelle D'Alessandro is an emerging writer living in Los Angeles, and a graduate of Fuller Theological Seminary ans UBC. Her work has been featured in various online magazines such as *Lines + Stars*, *Pigeonholes*, and *Bitterzoet*. She has a special interest in theology, translation, virtual reality, and neuropsychology. She is working on her first chapbook, a collection of homophonic reimaginations of far-flung Whitman translations.

Steph Driver has worked in the education, electricity, health and community sectors, debated in ecumenical, secular and interfaith groups, camped and hiked, cycled, bungee jumped, and (briefly) flown an aeroplane. She calculates, imagines, writes, draws, programs and knits. She talks a lot, and endeavours to listen. Sometimes she succeeds. She is currently at the University of Essex experimenting with computer aided constrained writing and text in unprintable media.

Dennis Duncan teaches English at Jesus College, Oxford and is a research fellow at the Bodleian Centre for the Study of the Book. He is writing a history of the book index, from the middle ages to the present, while recent academic articles have looked at Italo Calvino and writing machines, Mallarmé and jugs, and James Joyce's influence on mid-century French pornography. A monograph which sets the early Oulipo in their intellectual context is forthcoming.

Stephen Saperstein Frug is an independent writer and comics artist living in Ithaca, New York. His photographic novel HAPPENSTANCE is being serialized at http://happenstance.thecomicseries.com/.

Paul Griffiths is the author of *let me tell you* (2008), a novel in the vocabulary of Ophelia. His contribution to this volume is a sestina each of whose lines is a *beau présent* for a member of the Oulipo, the remaining member being similarly honoured acrostically.

Christiana Hills is a literary translator from the French, notably of Oulipienne Michèle Audin's *One Hundred Twenty-One Days* (Deep Vellum, 2016). She is currently a PhD candidate in Translation Studies from Binghamton University (NY) and lives in Raleigh, North Carolina.

Tom Jenks' works include *On Liberty, Repressed,* a database treatment of John Stuart Mill (Knives Forks and Spoons Press), *An Anatomy of Melancholy,* a Twitter re-write of Robert Burton's *The Anatomy of Melancholy* (Sad Press) and *Items,* a one-thousand fragment verbivocovisual sequence. He co-organises The Other Room reading series in Manchester and edits the avant-objects imprint zimZalla.

Peter Landau is a writer, editor, doodler, drummer, husband and father, among other things. Follow his one-liners on Twitter (@PeterLandau) and his daily drawings, currently inspired by obituaries, on Instagram (https://www.instagram.com/peterlandau/).

Marc Lapprand is a Professor of French Studies at the University of Victoria (Canada). A modernist, he is a specialist of Boris Vian, whose edition of the *Œuvres romanesques complètes* he directed with the prestigious Bibliothèque de la Pléiade (2 vol. Gallimard, 2010) and also a specialist of Oulipo (two books and numerous articles). His more recent research is on Literary Darwinism (Dossier published with *@nalyses* in 2014).

Michael Leong is Assistant Professor of English at the University at Albany, State University of New York. His most recent book of poetry is *Cutting Time with a Knife* (Black Square Editions, 2012).

Andriana Minou is a musician/writer living in London for the past 13 years. Her work as a writer and poet has been published in several journals and anthologies by Strange Days Books, The Paper Nautilus, Rattle Journal, FIVE:2:ONE, poetix, Story Brewhouse, codepoetry, chimeres and more. Her short story collection, *Underage Noirs* was published by Strange Days Books in 2013, while her fragmental novel, *Dream-mine*, will be published by the same publisher this autumn. *Hypnotic Labyrinth* is one of the fragments of this novel. She is a co-organiser of Sand Festival (a DIY literature festival in Greece), and a founding member of the Vladimir&Estragon Piano Duo, the Oiseaux Bizarres Ensemble and Coocoolili. Her work as a pianist, performer, composer, songwriter and librettist has been presented in various venues around the world. www.andrianaminou.com

Warren Motte is College Professor of Distinction at the University of Colorado. He specializes in contemporary French literature, with particular focus upon experimentalist works that put accepted notions of literary form into question. His most recent books include *Fables of the Novel: French Fiction Since 1990* (2003), *Fiction Now: The French Novel in the*

Twenty-First Century (2008), *Mirror Gazing* (2014), and *French Fiction Today* (2017).

Doug Nufer is the author of four books of poetry, including *We Were Werewolves* and *Lounge Acts*, and seven novels, including *Never Again, Negativeland, By Kelman Out of Pessoa,* and *Lifeline Rule,* which all follow various formal constraints. *The Me Theme* is his most recent book.

John K. Peck is a writer and printer currently living in Berlin. He has written for *Salon, McSweeney's, Jubilat, Nerve.com, Last Exit, VOLT,* and other publications, and has been anthologized in *The Best of McSweeney's Internet Tendency* and *Stories From the City: A Slow Travel Berlin Anthology.* He is the editor of Degraded Orbit, a travel, art, and gaming site, and along with his wife is co-founder of the letterpress and book arts studio Volta Press. (johnkpeck.com)

Pablo M. Ruiz is from Argentina, where he studied literature and linguistics at the University of Buenos Aires. He completed his PhD in comparative literature at Princeton University and now teaches Latin American literature at Tufts University. In addition to academic articles, he has published travel pieces, translations, and palindromes. He wrote a book of literary criticism called *Four Cold Chapters on the Possibility of Literature Leading Mostly to Borges and Oulipo,* published by Dalkey Archive in 2014. He is founding member of the Outranspo.

Philip Terry is Philip Terry is the author of *Oulipoems, Oulipoems 2, Shakespeare's Sonnets, Quennets,* and translator of Raymond Queneau's *Elementary Morality* and Georges Perec's *I Remember.* His novel *tapestry,* which combines magic realism and Oulipian techniques, was shortlisted for the 2013 Goldsmith's Prize.

Katja Waschneck is a PhD student at the University of Essex with the Department of Literature, Film and Theatre Studies. As her PhD contains both theoretical and practical elements, her research interests cover a broad range of topics, but they all have one aspect in common: constraints. Katja is especially interested in the connection between literature and film, and her research interests include experimental film, avant-garde cinema and independent film making.